ONE DAY AFTER NEVER

WHITNEY WALKER

*Sherri —
Hope you enjoy Peyton & JT's journey! Fight for ♡ —
xoxo
W.W.*

One Day After Never

Book One of the Second Time's the Charm Series

Copyright © 2019 by Whitney Walker

First Edition

All rights reserved. This book or any portion thereof may not be reproduced or used in any manner whatsoever without the express written permission of the publisher except for the use of brief quotations in a book review. If you would like to use material from this book, prior written permission must be obtained by contacting the publisher at whitney@whitneywalkerwriting.com. Thank you for the support of the author's rights.

Published by Serendipity Stories

Whitney Walker
www.whitneywalkerwriting.com

Cover design by IF DESIGN | Ida Fia Sveningsson
Edited by Ella Medler | ellamedlerediting.yolasite.com/

One Day After Never is a work of fiction. Names, characters, places and incidents are the products of the author's imagination or are used factiously. The author's use of the names of real places, events, or public figures are not intended to change the entirely fictional character of the work. In all other respects any resemblance to actual events, locales, or persons, living or dead, is entirely coincidental.

ISBN: 978-1-7341895-0-6
eBook ISBN: 978-1-7341895-1-3

Dear Reader –

Thank you for sharing in the journey of Peyton and J.T. gracing these pages! I've known the twenty-four characters in the Second Time's the Charm series for five years as they came to life in my head, and I can't wait for you to meet them! I wrote in five different countries, countless coffee shops, the hair salon, and several doctors' offices. Mostly, my writing was squeezed into fifteen-minute increments of time from which I could barely tear myself away to do real-life. None of my female characters are morning people, because how I could write something I don't understand in the least? Nonetheless, because of you I've been writing at 4:30 or 5:00 a.m. as long as I can remember! You are worth skipping the snooze!

I owe this to all of my tribe who have lifted me up, cheered me on, listened, and shared my life. I'm all of the characters and so are those who have made me who I am. It's my give-back to anyone who might need to get lost for a while in a story, a change in perspective, the guts to take a risk, or to realize they are exactly where they belong.

Why did I write this book? I had no choice. One story became two. Two became four as my own story has unfolded.

I was trying to stay sane (relatively speaking, of course, since I am still an aspiring unicorn). One day, people began talking in my head and movie scenes were playing. I literally couldn't focus on anything else, like people. My job. Everyday responsibilities. Sleep. Driving (think 2014 before your phone and car understood your voice!) I typed on my phone at every red light. No crashes. Plenty of honks while I finished a sentence. Or three. I literally ran from a couple of yoga classes to grab paper and start writing down the words.

This book is for you if...

You've ever dreamed of a second chance or a do-over. If you have ever learned a hard lesson and wished you could share what you learned so just one other person wouldn't feel alone. And, of course, this book is for you if you are an unapologetic, hopeless romantic and believe that true love always deserves a fighting chance!

If you love the book…I'd be forever grateful for a positive review! And I'd love you to join the amazing women in our tribe!

Subscribe at https://www.whitneywalkerwriting.com/ and you will be invited to join our Facebook group. You will also be in the know for new release details, receive exclusive content and have the chance to win merch! I am happy to sign books or do a video chat with your book club. Contact me at whitney@whitneywalkerwriting.com.

If you didn't…tell me why at:
info@whitneywalkerwriting.com. I'd love to know how to keep making better books. And I'd greatly appreciate if you remember Mom's rule if you have nothing nice to say when it comes to a review.

Until next time –

Fight for Love!
XO Whitney

With gratitude to my beautiful, inspirational co-conspirators who've taught me everything I know.

And to...

Liz G. – for helping me realize I was in good company on the bathroom floor, what life could be after I picked myself up, and the community service project that followed.

Gabby B - for the gift of knowing there is no more valiant pursuit than fighting for love over fear.

Joe – for a years' worth of asking for a chapter that had yet to be written.

Anya & Laura – for believing in the dream written on the napkin.

Amy M. – for little hearts in the margins from the very first chapter.

Amy D. – for the gifts of just the right books at just the right time.

Tina – for your "quotables" and being the cheeriest cheerleader a girl could ever ask for.

George – for defining true love, letting it unfold, and giving me the safest place I've ever known in your arms.

...and of course, my dad. Your belief in me has kept me going as long as I can remember. And to the woman who started it all, because she said I could be anything I wanted to be when I grew up and she was always right. Thanks, Mom.

...and to my two beautiful babies, everything I do, I do for you.

NOVEMBER 6th
CHAPTER 1 | Peyton

Sunshine and snow, 90210 glitz and glamour, and a new dream to chase were all good reasons to leave my hometown 313 for the 405 of Los Angeles. I was sure I was trading up and Detroit couldn't compete. Everything I had known to age twenty-one had ended when I boarded that plane. I never planned to return. Even though the captain of our airplane had just welcomed us to Detroit, I don't feel welcome here. The only thing that could bring me back is another ending. With it, I'm forced to endure another beginning. As an orphan. I suppose this is a little overdramatic, since I am an adult after all, but blame the three years and four months I've spent in L.A. where having a flair for over the top reigns supreme.

The frosted glass doors to baggage claim slide quietly, curtains opening to reveal characters in a first act. The scene features the crowd of people waiting to greet incoming passengers, my mind comprising their backstories. There is, of course, a man with a plastic-sleeved single rose, looking anxious. He is probably hoping the real version of the digital woman he has gotten to know matches the image conjured up in his head. Could she be the one?

Then, a formerly good-looking, now unshaven and dark-circle-eyed dad is smoothing the hair of two toddler girls, a mostly matched set of twins. The blond curls of each girl are fastened with a little pink bow on the right side, an impressive accouterment. I guess he hopes to impress their mother, returning home from her first weekend away without them. They each have a red balloon tied to their wrist with white ribbon, but they are a bit deflated. It's likely that is how he feels since he didn't quite get to shaving, but the brownie points for the barrettes and balloons should outweigh. I bet he can't wait to tag out! Maybe her life will change with his newfound appreciation for all she does.

A middle-aged woman, left hand locked in solidarity with the man next to her, holds a sign in her right hand featuring a picture of a young man in camouflage. The poster headline reads 'God Bless the U.S.A. & God Bless Sam.' I wonder if his name predicted his destiny. His life is on that sign. He looks strong and handsome, as expected, has a dog and a motorcycle from the pictures that are there to greet him. He also has a new baby. Next to the couple stands a young woman with an infant in her arms. I guess it's a boy but it's hard to tell in the red, white, and blue starred and striped one-piece outfit. Hopefully, Sam doesn't need to be reminded of what is here for him. Silently, I say a little prayer that the Sam they know is coming back, beginning his life as a father. New babies and new mothers shouldn't have to contend with new wounds. Old wounds are enough for any couple.

An elderly woman with a cane squeezes between me and the woman next to me, who has also stopped to observe the crowd. She hobbles with a hurried step toward a dingy blue jean overall-clad, gray-haired man as he moves forward toward her. Her cane clatters to the floor and he swoops her up in an embrace of young, new love. They are lost in an infinitude of moments, he cradling her as his most prized possession, gently but firmly, burying his head into her neck, taking her in. They hold each other close while the world goes on around them, claiming space in their own little one.

I contemplate all the love in this tiny area of reunion and introduction. Whether old love or new, romantic or familial, just waiting for reciprocation. This scene depicts what each one of us wants and needs. Someone waiting for you, as if you are the most important person in their world and they are grateful for your arrival.

I fear that love may never show up for me with a sign, a hug, or a kiss.

I make my way to the luggage carousel just as the black rubber jerks to life with a protesting groan. The first generic black suitcase drops down the ramp with a resounding thud. Each bag crests over the top and makes its way around the belt until greedy hands sweep it away. I am thankful mine is among the last to make its way out—more time to avoid facing my new beginning.

Crossing the threshold of the funeral home, I am greeted by a signboard in the center of the walkway. It's rather undignified. All the days of one's life are summed up in white plastic letters pushed into the lines of the black signboard, cocked slightly left on a tarnished metal stand. I feel the need to straighten it as I walk past. My fingers trace the letters forming her name, Caroline Rhodes Jennings. I pull my hand away before I get to Parlor 1, with the arrow pointing right. My mother doesn't even have her own sign. Gertrude Ross, Parlor 2, is listed below. Gertrude is the name of someone who has lived fully, not the name of a young woman.

The sign might as well say WELCOME, ORPHAN, because that's what the letters spell for me. My eyes follow the arrow to the right, and I summon all the courage I can to step through the doors of Parlor 1. My senses are overloaded. The smell of death, or more like the attempted cover-up, is indescribable and overbearing. Eyes assessing, moving from left to right, I take in the mismatched and antiquated furniture, sad that this pathetic space will be intermingled with so many last memories of family members. Music playing in the background reminds me of the haunted mansion ride at Disney World. Creepy is the only adjective I can put my finger on. There is no choice but to urge myself forward.

Move one foot, Peyton.
Right.
You've got this. Now the other.
Left.

Been doing it since you were one. Twenty-three years.

I am not practiced at this, having been to only one funeral prior, and it was held for a neighbor, who was very old, and not someone I was close to. However, I don't believe one hundred funerals prepare you to walk through doors where your mother awaits you.

In a coffin.

Whom you hadn't bothered to see in years.

And you didn't even know was ill.

I steady myself on the first chair I can, hand sliding over the wood across the top while my fingertips caress the smooth velvet seat back. I gaze the length of the room toward her coffin, my breath shallow. It's taking everything I have to hold back tears and concentrate on breathing.

Oh, God. I want to turn around and run in the other direction but's too late. One foot over the threshold, I've made eye contact with my grandmother, with no time to prepare.

She is barreling toward me with open arms. One hand on each of my shoulders, she pulls me into an awkward hug. Affection is delivered at arm's length. Pushing herself back away from me, head tilted in pity, she simpers, "Oh, Peyyyyy-tonnnn." Even if this is a genuine attempt to comfort me, she is the last person I would allow to do so. My grandfather stands behind her. Nothing new there, just like his stoicism. "Aren't you so pleased with the arrangements?"

I am not an awful person, grateful they had handled the details, but I know what she wants to hear, and I am an actress. "Oh yes, Grandmother, thank you so much. It's exactly what I would have done." Hardly.

"It's been so long since we've spoken, but I guess that will change soon enough."

I don't see how my mother passing away will change the fact that I want nothing to do with them.

"You are almost twenty-five now, aren't you?"

We are flanked by a wall of bodies marching toward me shoulder to shoulder, soldiers coming to battle. My relatives have made an obligatory appearance at this visitation. As I search face to face, features I recognize as my own cause a small bit of bile to splash the back of my throat. Genetics or otherwise, I don't want to share anything with these people.

My "aunt", also known as my mother's spoiled little sister, emulates her mother, fingers curling into my upper arms. "Oh, Peyton, we've been so worried about you and your mother!" Hardly, take two. If they had been worried, things would have been different.

The equally spoiled little brother turns to me, then his sister. "How long has it been? I think Christmas… gosh, what, five years ago? Or was it six? It was a wonderful Christmas if I recall."

"Oh yes, aren't they all, Will?" They laugh as if it's a private joke and they have forgotten me. No sugar-plum memories of Christmas bliss for me.

"Why, you are all grown up now, Peyton," Will continues. "I don't believe I've seen you on television or in a movie yet, have I? You aren't another one of those starving actresses, are you? Or, wait, are you a waitress so you get free meals? You don't look like you are starving."

A memory of my mother surfaces. I hear her voice in my head, "If you don't have anything nice to say—" I should keep my mouth shut. He answered his own question anyway. "I should go," I say instead. It's time for the inevitable. "I haven't been inside to see my mother yet."

If only she were alive to protect me.

NOVEMBER 7th
CHAPTER 2 | Peyton

Sometime in the middle of the night, I wake in my bed of sixteen years, a double bed pressed against the cold, drafty wall. It is nothing less than startling and I sit up straight, the unfamiliar surroundings teasing and haunting. Slowly, I lie back into the pillow, eyes darting around the small room.

Against the wall, hand puppet shadows dance in the glow of moonlight and eerie creaking has my head whirling towards each sound. It scares the shit out of me. I talk myself off the ledge, out loud, though no one else is present to hear. "Scared of trees, Peyton? Seriously?" Returning to L.A. can't come soon enough. No trees to see from the third floor. Pulling the bedspread up to my chin, as if it will somehow protect me, I sigh deeply. Sleep is going to evade me now. The only reason I fell asleep in the first place was that my body couldn't take another minute of crying. Luckily, at least for the moment, tears are evading me. Maybe I have hit the quota on tear production for the day. Or possibly for a lifetime.

Pulling as much oxygen into my lungs as I can, I work to quiet thoughts jumping feverishly in my head. More tears spring from the corners of my eyes, running down the side of my face into the pillow. No quota reached. I squeeze my eyes tightly, a dam to the impending flood, and feel my eyelids sore and swollen. Tomorrow will be a ban-the-mirror day. Moving my jaw side to side I notice it is sore, surely from all of the clenching I've been doing.

I replay the events of yesterday. My best solo act yet. Today will offer no reprieve. Today I will brave the unbearable. I shudder, thinking of the hours that spread before me. But then, I think of the other people who had come to pay their respects. Hundreds maybe? I relive the receiving line, speaking the words "Thank you for coming" again and again for hours. Who were all those people? My mother touched so many and I didn't know. Countless former students and colleagues from throughout her thirty years of teaching spoke endearingly.

"Mrs. Jennings was my very favorite teacher, ever."

"Mrs. Jennings changed my life."

"Mrs. Jennings was the most wonderful human being I ever had the pleasure of knowing."

"Caroline was the most caring person."

"Your mother was one of the best teachers we ever had."

"You have no idea what this loss means to me and my family."

"We will miss Caroline more than you can ever know."

So many people seemed to know my mother in a way I never had. She had reached the hearts of many, just not her own daughter.

I am the lone guest at this pity-party. Do I dare check the time? Flipping the phone on my nightstand over, I see the time is 6:04 a.m. My body on Pacific Time, I know that a 3:00 a.m. wake-up won't bode well for my making it through the events of the day. I have to try to force myself back to sleep. Sheep? Stars? Something? Anything? Fail. Fail. Fail. I toss and turn until dragging myself to the shower seems the best option. The sky is just waking up, and I have forgotten how bleakly gray the winter in Michigan can be. I am going to need reinforcements against my lack of sleep and the bitter cold I feel in my bones. Starbucks is essential.

Moving robotically through the motions of hair drying and makeup application, I can barely apply liner to the puffy-from-crying eyelids. Usually, my eyes are my best feature, bright blue, prompting many to ask if I am wearing contacts with the fake ocean-like color imprinted. Today though, they are a hazy cloudy sky-gray with just a tease of blue, and certainly, the red rims detract from their beauty.

Standing in front of my closet, prolonging the inevitable, I take in the timeline of my past. Pushing my high school varsity jacket to the left reveals the last prom dress that I wore six years ago. The year of the fluffy netting skirts. All my friends had the same dress, but the color and adornments were unique to their personalities. I am a simple, no-frills girl. Then, and now. The royal blue I chose to highlight my eyes. A satin strapless bodice cinched at the waist with a wide black velvet sash that wrapped into a sleek, oversized bow in the back. It accentuated my breasts, a bit too big for my petite five foot two and three-quarters frame. I have my mother to thank for the oversized feature, one of our few shared genetic imprints. People often said we had similar facial features, but I never saw it. I always assumed I took after my father's side.

My mother was slender and without curves but mine is more feminine. My skin is on the fair side, and unlike my mother's dark, straight, never-out-of-place hair, I have waves of blond that always seem to contradict my mood. Sometimes I want it straight and it is determined to keep its natural, soft curls. Other days I try to scrunch it for the sexy, beachy look and it wants to stretch out straight down to my breasts. I've learned surrendering to its schizophrenia is easier than the time spent willing it to comply.

I remove my funeral dress from the hanger next to the prom dress. The prom dress was so much more fun to buy. I'd had to procure a black dress the night before I boarded the plane. When packing, the realization hit me that my wardrobe is full of skirts that barely, if I am being generous, cover my ass. I do live in L.A. after all.

The four hundred-dollar price tag is still attached and hanging down the front, a flagrant reminder of the running tab I have with Kyle. I sigh heavily, knowing the item will come at a cost much greater. I slide into the dress feeling nothing like myself. Standing over my suitcase, I realize my black heels are more stiletto than sensible, especially for November. They could be construed as hooker heels. I contemplate checking my mother's closet for a more conservative pair, but I need something to feel familiar. I slide my feet into one then the next. My feet will hurt like hell today, but the pain will be masked by the hurt I feel in my heart.

I am losing my patience in the much-too-long-for-an-overpriced-coffee line. Don't people sleep in Michigan? I overhear a ridiculous order, that being a venti, soy, extra hot, dry foam, with a splash of sugar-free vanilla. Seriously? There should be a rule against more than three adjectives paired with espresso. The woman in front of me turns backward, rolling her eyes in exasperation. I lean toward her and whisper, "How does one even know they like a drink with that many adjectives?" Clapping a hand over her mouth, she tries to contain a laugh, but it spills out. I react with an unexpected smile but try to duck my head, not wanting her to notice my disfigured lips and eyes. I'm caught.

"It's early to be having a bad day already."

She lays her hand on my forearm and I feel I may drown in her wave of compassion.

"More like a bad lifetime." I will the corners of my mouth up into a smile, but they don't cooperate and get stuck just above flat. That was probably a bit overdramatic to drop on an unsuspecting stranger.

Undeterred, the woman offers consolation, "I'm sorry to hear that. I hope it gets better for you."

"Me too." I have to choke back a fresh set of tears. It is utterly exhausting to live on the verge of tears, trying to keep the next set held back for fear of losing control completely.

As I lose the battle to wipe my tears away as fast and furious as the back of my hands allow, dam compromised, the woman offers, "I have a suggestion if you are interested."

Swallowing hard, hoping emotion won't get the best of me and words will still come, I answer, "At this point, I'd be crazy not to be." My voice is still available, though quiet and lilting, as I force the words out around the tears.

She points through the window to our right with her index finger and my eyes move to follow. "See that yoga studio right there? It might help."

"That's funny, a few people have told me that lately. I've never done it, and I'd like to try." I hesitate. "But is it expensive?" Though I have some financial options I can leverage if necessary, it will only add to the indebtedness, and the tab isn't one that I want to continue to run up.

"I bet they can work something out for you. They like to make sure everyone who needs yoga can do yoga. Just tell them Liz sent you. I'll tell them to look for you, and sorry, how rude of me." She offers her hand. "I'm Liz."

I have forgotten what it's like to be in the Midwest. People are kinder and gentler here. Help with no strings attached, from a complete stranger, seems foreign. "Okay, thank you so much. My name is Peyton." I sniff, then shake Liz's hand. "It's nice to meet you, Liz, and I'm going to do that. I'm going to go to yoga," I say determinedly. I can do this. I should do this. "Thank you. It's nice to have something to look forward to again."

As I enter the funeral home to endure another day of my mother's death, I feel so alone. Really alone, not the lonely from earlier occasions, when I chose it. It has chosen me now. If I get married, there is no one to walk me down the aisle. I won't have my mother by my side if and when I give birth. I never thought about having my mother there for the big moments until now when I can't any longer. Girl doesn't appreciate her mother until it's too late. I am living the cliché.

Here we go again. Another fake hug at the door by another "aunt" with her plastered smile. Neither the smile nor the hug is comforting. Catherine sizes me up from head to toe, where she pauses at the shoes. Her eyes slowly track back up my slender frame. "You have grown into a beautiful woman, Peyton." The compliment is fine enough, delivered with sincerity, but I will dismiss anything that rolls off Catherine's lips as only some semblance of truth.

Hovering over my mother's casket, I find the tears to be off duty this morning, a strong will from deep within keeping my guard up. I stand alone looking at the closed eyes and folded hands of my mother's cold, lifeless body. The little interaction we've had in the past four years makes this woman feel more a stranger than she should be. She tried so hard. I ignored so much harder.

I am distracted by a man's laugh. A laugh that captivates me. It sounds innocent and filled with life, so contrarian to the moment I can barely restrain myself from spinning toward the sound. Not intentionally eavesdropping, I catch that his laugh is in response to a woman's inquiry of whether he is still off trying to change the world and fix the broken.

"There is a lot to fix, but I'm trying," he answers after the laugh.

"Well, Caroline was awfully proud of your work."

"Well, thank you, but I'm no saint. Some days I want to give up the fight and run away to Australia."

He had me at the laugh, but specializing in broken? Running away to Australia? He has captured my heart before hello! I need to meet him, know who he is, and how he knows my mother.

I close my eyes and slowly turn in place. I make a quick promise to myself that if he is hot, I will be a good girl forevermore.

A very good girl. I promise. Holy hell.

Messy, naturally highlighted hair the color of honey frames a handsome-like-I-have-rarely-seen face. He is tallish, probably five foot eleven, but still tall compared to me even in my too-high heels. His dark jacket hides his frame, though he seems thin, and my imagination fills in the blanks. His gray shirt and black and blue chevron tie are crisp and modern.

Giving all his attention to the conversation, I only see his profile and the curve of his strong, square jaw. His nose turns up slightly on the end, his cheekbones are high, and long eyelashes make his blinks appear to be happening in slow motion. Tan skin, unnaturally so for November in Detroit has me ridden with curiosity. My mind conjures up an image of the exotic sun and sand he may have just returned from visiting. He must sense my intense stare because his head begins to turn in my direction. My eyes quickly dart toward the floor, and my chin dips, but I believe I have been busted.

When my gaze lifts, he is facing me with a sympathetic smile, and I know that he knows who I am. He has the upper hand since I do not have the same luxury. I force my lips closed into a shy smile as he turns back toward the woman and I hear him excuse himself from the conversation. When his whole body is facing me, and it's clear that he is going to close the short distance between the two of us, my heartbeat stutters. This man is full-on beautiful. Capital B. My type is usually tall, dark and handsome, but for this man, I can make an exception. His smile weakens me in the knees, and I realize this is a completely inappropriate reaction for this situation. Am I at my mother's funeral pining for a man?

As if he comes to the same realization that his reaction is incongruous to the circumstances under which we are meeting, he appears to force the corners of his mouth back into the original sympathetic smile. However, he is unable to hide the remains of my impact in his eyes. Bright blue that rival my own, they look as if they hold a million secrets in the light and dark shades that mingle together. His eyes draw me in, involuntarily causing mine to narrow into slits, squinting from their brightness, like walking from a darkened place into the sunshine.

"You must be Peyton," rolls off his tongue as his hand reaches toward me. I can't help losing myself in those eyes that seem to peer into mine in a way that says he knows everything about me already. I am exposed. Internally commanding my hand to rise to meet his, my brain and limbs no longer seem to be connected to one another, or perhaps they are just ignoring me, also taken aback by the devastatingly handsome stranger.

Still mesmerized by those eyes and lips and the rest of him, I should have known my hand held in his would do nothing to calm my senses. His hand is soft, warm, and immediately comforting. We hang on just a second too long for a regular nice-to-meet-you exchange.

My heart catches, takes pause, then subsequently beats anew, different, and irrevocably changed somehow. His fingers close around mine as his left hand moves up to cup my elbow. Unable to speak, I stand motionless, eyes still locked in place.

He is undaunted by my stupor. "You look just like her. Mrs. Jennings. So you're Peyton, right?"

Still not finding my outside voice, I manage to lift my head up and down, some semblance of a nod.

"I'm very sorry for your loss, Peyton. Mrs. Jennings, your mom, was a great woman."

So I've heard.

Swallowing hard, I manage to squeak out, "Thank you." Then I realize that I still don't know his name, but must. Right now. I find my voice and more confidently ask, "And you are?"

"J.T. Walker. Your mom was my teacher and counselor."

"Thank you for coming, J.T." I have to try out his name and see how it works for me. It does. This seems wrong but feels so right.

My attention is diverted to another hand on my arm as Catherine appears out of nowhere and interrupts, "Peyton, I need to introduce you to someone." Her fingers curl around my arm as she pulls me forcefully toward a group of people gathered nearby. I look back over my shoulder to where J.T. was standing the moment before. His back is already turned as he converses with another man who looks to be about our age. Somehow, in an instant, everything seems different. I can do this. Fake smiles hurt less than the day before, and forced conversation is more tolerable as I introduce myself to all of the people gathering here in celebration of my mother's life.

I listen more carefully to the compliments paid today. Have I underestimated my mother? Maybe there is a lot more to the woman than I had taken the time to understand. What if I will never know? Overwhelmed with this thought, and for the first time today, I cover my mouth to catch a sob that rises in my throat and forcefully seeks an exit. Blinking hard to hold back the tears I know are a moment behind, I look around for the nearest breakdown-appropriate escape. I see a perfect corner to hide away from the crowd and hurry in its direction. Rounding the corner, I come to an abrupt halt as I bump into a man amid his own full-on cry. It is a toss-up who is more startled. His head lowers to make his face indistinguishable, and he brushes past me quickly toward the building exit. I start to chase after him, to find out who he is, as he appears more distraught than any of the others here, including my blood relatives.

No! My path toward the door is compromised. A large man cuts me off. I try to look beyond the formidable frame but can't pass. Imposing hands reach for both of my shoulders as he canvasses me. Face. Breasts. Hips. Breasts. Gross. He pulls me in for a hug but I keep my arms straight and limp at my sides, not returning the embrace. "Peyton, say hello to your Uncle Gus. I can't believe that this is the first chance I've had to say hello." His voice makes me want to spit in his face. I know his suit is expensive, but he can't help but cheapen it. His slicked-back hair, the red face that screams I drink too much, and politician-esque charm are revolting. Hell isn't a horrific enough place for Gus Rhodes to rot and burn.

I sidestep Gus, mumbling, "Excuse me, please." I can feel his persecuting eyes on my backside as I push past him through the crowd. I know he is looking at my ass. He even gives a little cat-call whistle. Barely subtle. Bountifully disgusting. After today, I shouldn't have to deal with these relatives ever, ever again, and this fact causes glee to do a little dance up and down my spine.

Finding the stranger now is a lost cause. He has disappeared through the front door, leaving me perplexed. Why on earth would someone hastily exit as he did? Was he embarrassed by his emotional tears? Avoiding someone seeing him? I don't have time to continue the conversation in my head as a female voice speaks to me from behind. A woman with a sliver rectangular nametag, in a dress that should have stayed in 1972 when it appears to have been made, stands before me. "Peyton? We're ready to get started. Are you ready?" Is that a rhetorical question? Is anyone ever ready for this?

NOVEMBER 8
CHAPTER 3 | Peyton

Upon waking, I know it's late, sunbeams cascading through my window from high in the sky. I roll over. It feels like I have a hangover, only with no fun involved. Reaching for my phone on the bedside table, and finding that it is ten minutes after nine o'clock, makes me grateful. I have fewer hours to get through in this day than expected. I've been in bed for nearly fifteen hours, and much preferred these last fifteen to those prior that included a funeral, luncheon, and cemetery. A feeling of finality sweeps over me. I am alone in this world now. Truly alone. Now, I am only accountable to myself, and can only disappoint myself. This fact terrifies me and feels empowering at the same time.

Too much thinking is going to make me crazy, so I make the choice to take this whole thing one moment at a time. And in this next moment, I am going to distract myself by trying to get a glimpse of one J.T. Walker. Throughout the funeral and luncheon, I had tried to sneak glances in his direction. I could feel his presence and kept working the crowd to get closer to him just to try and take him in. We hadn't said another word to each other, and I wasn't sure I wasn't making up the attraction.

Swiping my finger across the smooth screen of my phone, bringing it to life, I quickly type in my passcode and bring up the search bar. I type in his name and scroll through the thumbnail images that appear. Not one contains a glimpse of the man I'd met. I try various searches on Twitter and Instagram but to no avail. Damn it. You just never know how someone might name themselves on social media. There is also the small fact that I have no idea what the J and the T letters that comprise his name stand for.

My cyberstalking is interrupted by an incoming text across the top of the screen.

morning, babe – hanging in there?

Kyle. It is the first thought I've had of him in much longer than I should admit. Even to myself. Shit.

hey – still in bed. guess u could call it hanging…

A second later his face is covering my screen with an incoming call. Thankfully, he isn't adding video as I surely look like hell. It's likely that yesterday's makeup, post crying and sleeping, has made its way to parts not warranting its presence. Hesitating before answering, to mentally prepare myself, I finally press the green button and move the phone to my ear.

"Pey, how's it going?"

"Hey there."

"You missed a wicked party last night. Well, and this morning."

Really? This is where he goes? Thank you for the news, Mr. Sensitive. I was a little busy burying my dead mother. Deeming it not worthy of the effort to call him out, I reply soberly, probably the opposite of what he is right now, considering he is calling at 6:10 a.m., "It was Friday so of course I did."

"When are you coming home? You know I hate sleeping alone. And waking up with a raging boner and no one to knock it down is even worse."

I take in his selfish words and the disrespect he has just displayed. This is nothing new. But what is new is the realization that I've grown well equipped to deflecting, and sometimes even defending, his heartless actions and bad behavior. We always have fun as a couple, don't we? At least as long as we are partying together. For real life, however, I'd seen another side when the call came informing me that my mother had been in the hospital with pneumonia and hadn't made it out. I'd stood motionless in the middle of the room, my mobile phone falling to the floor as if it could take the news with it. Away from me. When he'd asked me what was wrong, and I had told him, he'd barely stopped playing his guitar to reply, "Bummer, baby. Well, you haven't seen her in forever anyway, so it's not like much has changed. Right? Maybe you will get some dough out of it."

All that I had wanted was big arms to hold me and tell me it would be okay. That I didn't have to go back to Detroit by myself and handle everything alone. He hadn't offered to come with me or held me, or anything else that would have resembled emotional support. Being that he is already nearly a decade older than me, it isn't as if he is going to grow up quickly and get it, is it?

At that moment, I had known it was the beginning of the end. Extracting myself from his life—our life—will be no small feat. He's said on more than one occasion that the secrets I have locked away could lock him away, and if I don't marry him I'll have to take them to my grave. I am not sure that he didn't mean it quite literally.

"I'll be back next Thursday." I don't say I'll be home. I am not sure where home is for me any longer.

"Okay, babe. Try not to miss me too much."

With all that I have to do to sort through this house and my mother's finances, I am pretty sure that I am going to be a little too distracted to spend my time pining over the fact that I am two thousand miles away from him.

"You could come here and help me," I say, voice unsteady.

"No way, Peyton. I don't do death. Too real."

Well, he is right about that. And I am right about him. I could be setting myself up to spend the rest of my life with a man that admittedly couldn't handle the inevitable, such as death. I wonder, however, can he even handle life?

"Besides, Pey, you know I hate planes."

The more he talks the more I wish he wouldn't. Don't people do things for the people they care about even though they are scared?

"Okay then." I try to tame the bitterness I feel, but my voice is still more harsh than soft. "I'd better get moving. I'm still in bed and have a million thank you notes to write for everyone that came to the funeral. It was pretty incredible actually."

"Good luck with that. Talk to you tonight, okay? I'll call before we go out. We're hitting that new club Luke was telling us about last week. It's supposed to be the place to be these days."

"Okay, sounds good. Have fun." Then I think to add, "But not too much fun." I am usually by his side for the mayhem he finds, and he did just confess to not liking to sleep alone. He hasn't been out without me in, what is it, probably close to a year now? Has our one year together come and gone? Is it coming up soon? The date is on the tip of my tongue, but why don't I remember? Surely it should be significant enough to remember. Maybe I have killed too many brain cells this past year. Maybe it is early onset Alzheimer's. At least that wouldn't be self-induced. I could justify not knowing. I realize there has been a long, awkward pause.

"I'll behave, Peyton. I love you."

Wait, what? Did that just happen? Maybe I should have taken a trip away from him sooner. I am caught off guard, and not completely sure how I want to reply, but before I know it my response is spilling forward, "You too, Kyle." I feel weak, and a bit bewildered. Perhaps by this point in our relationship, this declaration of love should have already happened, but it hasn't. And sadly, I can't help but think it was better that way.

Swinging my legs to the side, over the edge of the bed, I let my feet hit the wool rug covering the old oak floor. I arch my back and stretch my arms, clasping my hands over my head. I sigh out a big breath as I peer through the open door, across the hall, at the door of the master bedroom. My mother's bedroom. I've walked past the room at least a dozen times now, not daring to cross its threshold. Too painful. Too raw. The door is open just a crack, but in the wrong direction for me to see into the room at all. The white painted wood door beckons me, teasing and taunting.

Pushing myself up off the bed, I stand in place waiting for my legs to stop trembling. Every cell in my body is tense and on high alert, adrenaline coursing. I am wide awake now. Something is pulling me forward, like in a horror movie where the characters are powerless to resist some unseen force that the audience is sure will cause their demise. No, no, no screams inside my head, urgent and demanding, but courage drowns out the voice. "You can do this," I say aloud as my fingers curl around the cool metal door handle.

With purpose, I push the door and my body into the room in one motion so there is no turning back. Finding myself staring into my mother's mirror affixed to the dresser, I see for the first time the resemblance to her that others always insist I bear. It is remarkable!

As if placed there purposefully to call me closer, a picture of me and my mother sits atop the dresser, in front of the mirror. I squint at the frame, trying to recall it being taken, which I can not. I pick up the frame and run the pad of my thumb across my face. Am I twelve? Thirteen? Anyone who looked at this picture would have thought the women sisters, not mother and daughter. She had always looked young, but I hadn't realized how young. She was a young mother, having birthed me at twenty-four. This is the age I am now, and I can't imagine having a child of my own. Maybe I wasn't intended to be part of her plan.

I slowly survey the room, each object evoking a little stabbing sensation on my insides as it registers. First, a ceramic heart-shaped trinket box with a painted pink rose on top. I lift the top. Inside are little teeth. My baby teeth? How disgusting! Why has my mother kept these? Several books adorn the nightstand. There is a book about love languages. My mother was reading a relationship book? I lift the book to reveal the title of the book below, The Agenda of Love. I think back to Kyle saying that he loved me. Why has he said it now when I am gone? And over the phone? Absence makes the heart grow fonder? Does he miss me? Or is it, perhaps, that he has his own agenda? I will let my guard down and assume nothing will happen while I am gone. I am burying my mother and that would be cruel. But then again, maybe he was hedging in case he brought home another woman tonight. Or worse yet, already has. Why does my brain go there? Maybe he does love me and finally chose to say so?

My eyes canvass the double bed. It is neatly made, a navy and white flower-patterned comforter pulled taut. White eyelet lace pillows look so pure and innocent in their places, all prim and proper. My mother probably made the bed every day of her life and spent an extra ten seconds on each pillow making sure they were in their right place. Though she tried to pass on the habit by explaining that making the bed tells your brain you have already accomplished something so early to waking, it never stuck.

When my eyes land on the nightstand on the other side of the bed, one eyebrow shoots up as my head involuntarily cocks for a closer look, curious about what I see. A three-inch, leather-bound, masculine looking book lays on the table. Gold imprinted letters catch the sunlight just right and send a small gleam of reflection. I walk around the bed to the other side and pick up the book, index finger tracing the letters of THE BIBLE. My finger then trails the three or so inches to letters at the bottom of the cover. Those which read JACK MANNINGTON. I look around the room more quickly now, for a glimpse of anything else that could be remnants of… what? A lover? Boyfriend? My mother had never spoken a word about a man. Had I asked? Had I just assumed that my mother never had a man around? The yard was immaculate. Why hasn't it crossed my mind that perhaps she had help keeping it so?

I see nothing glaring, but carry my shaky self back to the dresser, avoiding eye contact with myself, and open the top drawer on the right. My mother's bras. Middle drawer. Underwear folded perfectly and arranged by color, of course. As I reach for the handle of the drawer on the top left, I take in a sharp breath, peeking into the drawer with just one eye as the other tries to avoid seeing anything unthinkable. Socks. Female ones. I blow out my breath then look over my shoulder at the closet. Opening the double doors that I remember my mother installing to replace the traditional bi-fold ones, I close both eyes this time. When I open them, I am smacked in the face with the reality that the contents reveal, plain as day, that there is a him to the her. The his and hers closet can't be more obvious, the line of demarcation a black suit jacket of his and a long pink and orange floral dress of hers.

My breath whisks away from me as my eyes fill with tears. I am surprised to find they aren't tears of sadness, however, but relief. My mother hadn't been lonely. Relief is quickly replaced by distress and guilt when I realize I'd never—until right now—given a shit if she was. What kind of a monster am I to know so little about her?

I stand in the room wishing that I could know more, but payback or karma or coming full circle really is a bitch.

Lost in self-loathing, my thoughts drift to the man that I'd stumbled on crying before he ran, Cinderella-like, out of the funeral home. I wonder, could that have been him? Jack Mannington? The man who had shared my mother's bedroom and probably her heart? The thought sends me scrambling down the stairs, the sound of fast footsteps echoing on the hardwood, to the kitchen counter. I had laid the book of visitors and thank you notes across the small island when I returned home last evening. I start at page one of the guest-filled book looking for the name I've seen on the Bible upstairs. Not finding it at first glance, I return the book to the counter and decide to make coffee before going through the book page by page.

I hit brew on the coffee pot and can't resist picking up the book again. Opening the cover, tears brim, then streak my cheeks. I don't bother trying to wipe them away, just keep blinking so the letters remain in focus. Caroline Grace Jennings is written in the cursive writing of a stranger. Then in print: October 24, 1965 – November 3, 2014. I think of her birthday just past. All I did was send a text. I didn't even call. I didn't ask if she had plans. I didn't post anything on social media about her. I suck. And I can't apologize any longer.

I turn the first crisp page to escape the date mocking me. Balancing the steaming mug on my knee, I open a small drawer in the table next to the worn brown leather living room chair where I sit. As I'd hoped, it holds a set of coasters. Tricolored wood with Naples, FL scrawled in a fancy font in the bottom right corner. I wonder if my mother had been there to buy these or if they were a gift, but, of course, it is just another question for which I have no answer.

Picking up on page sixteen, where I'd left off in the kitchen, I find no listing for a Jack but do find an unexpected surprise. An entry for J.T., with a Chicago address listed beside his name. My brain conjures up a truly ridiculous scenario with J.T. receiving the thank you with my return address, showing up on my doorstep, then sweeping me off my feet, overtaking me with kisses. Where the hell does this come from? Maybe the stress is tearing my rational thinking to shreds. Here I am, paper-stalking a mystery man of my mother's while dreaming up fantasies for myself with another funeral guest. All the while, I remind myself, I have a boyfriend who, um, apparently loves me.

I use a hot sip of liquid down my throat to clear my mind, and then finish reading through the stack of pages in the book. Nearly forty pages with eight names to a page. Over three hundred people, but none named Jack. Frustrated, I return to the kitchen, pour another steaming mug of coffee, grab a black ballpoint pen, the thank you notes, my laptop, and return to the chair. Not having a clue what to write in thanks for attending a funeral, I bring up my search engine and start to type. Instead of searching for how to write funeral thank you notes, as I'd intended, my fingers, seemingly of their own accord, have the letters Jack Mannington scrolling across the search bar. No returned results are worthy of my cyberstalking. Not a damn thing. Two strikeouts for the day. Who are these men who manage to hide in the digital age?

Finishing my original search, I grab the pen and a thank you note in a huff and open the book again. I write like a mad woman until my eyes are blurring and hand cramping. Nowhere else to go, I lean back into the chair to stretch my back and ailing fingers. I make a fist and open my hand, again and again.

I make my way back to the kitchen and look through the cupboards, pantry, and refrigerator. All are full. I guess that is usually the case when one dies unexpectedly. But what if you know you are going to die? Do you eat everything and not go shopping? Not refill the cabinets? Restock the milk? At least there would be the chance to say goodbye. This thought makes my body cover in goosebumps. There is no chill, but I shake like there is one blowing directly across my skin. I am terrible at goodbyes, always stretching out the text string or hanging on the phone awkwardly. But this one I would have welcomed over the alternative.

Sighing heavily, I realize that even with plenty of food in the house, nothing sounds appealing. I don't have any appetite. What should I do next? Putting my coffee mug in the dishwasher gives me an idea. The nice woman I had met, Liz, had told me to try yoga. I laugh to myself as I think, "No time like the present." The L.A. yogis brag about the peace they have living in the present thanks to the practice, and peace is something I could use right about now.

Finding that there is a yoga class beginning in forty-five minutes at Exhale, the studio Liz had pointed out, I walk through the doors fifteen minutes before class begins.

To the right, three brown leather chairs cozily encircle a round black ottoman, a pupil in the middle of a caramel colored eye. The semi-circle sits in front of a faux-stone fireplace of gray and light brown which climbs the wall to the ceiling. The fireplace is lit and has the lobby warm and welcoming.

I observe other students sitting on six tan leather benches for two, removing their shoes. Each pair claims one of the black Ikea cubes, stacked five high and eight long, covering the wall to the left. I slide into one of the butt imprints worn into the bench closest to the cubbies.

Straight ahead is a sleek and modern black wood desk with two iPads perched atop. I almost chicken out mentioning that Liz has sent me. I fear I will sound like a fool asking for the Liz special, but I really don't want to add to the list of items that are accumulating on Kyle's credit card. I know yoga is expensive and Kyle is already helping me bankroll a life I pretend I can afford. She'd seemed so sincere in her offer, I somehow feel it isn't an imposition.

When the woman in front of me has finished checking in, I step forward and swallow my pride. "Hi. This is my first class. Liz said to mention she sent me?" My voice rises at the end to make the statement sound like a question.

"Oh, of course!" She presses her lips into a line and looks upward in thought. A moment later she snaps her fingers as if something comes to her. "Peyton?" I nod enthusiastically. "Hi, I am Kristina. Liz was hoping you'd make it! Just need a couple of signatures from you. Welcome!"

And with that, a clipboard is in front of me. That was easy, I think, taking the papers from the woman with the broad smile radiating calm. Maybe someday I can come across like that as well. Or not. At least I have made it here. Gotta start somewhere!

I look up from my clipboard at a tall and slender woman who has approached me. Her sculpted body and sparsely wrinkled face contradict her shoulder-length gray-silver bob. She had been talking to other students when I entered. She has kind eyes that smile even when she is not. Her hand reaches for mine, "Hi, Peyton. I am Alexandra, a teacher here. I'll be teaching class today. We are so glad that you could join us."

"Well, I have Liz—" I stop mid-sentence. "Sorry, I don't know her last name—to thank."

"I'm guessing I know that Liz."

"Well, if you see her, can you please thank her for me?"

"I'd be happy to. By the way, nice sneakers. Chanel Couture? Did you get them in Paris?"

"They were a gift from my boyfriend but thank you." I wonder how a yoga teacher knows about Paris fashion and want to ask but another student has commandeered Alexandra.

I pass the paperwork to Kristina, who smiles up at me and stands quickly, coming around the front of the desk. She waves at one of the iPads Vanna White-style. "Next time you come, just check in here." She types PEY in the search field and my name pops up. She clicks on it and to the right appears a square box to check in. Just click here. "We have over fifty classes a week, and you have an unlimited membership so you can come anytime."

I'm overwhelmed with Liz's generosity.

"Follow me and I will show you the studio," Kristina says bubbling with pride and starts down the long hallway behind the desk. On each side of the perfect-day lightest blue-sky painted hallway are quotes facing one another, stenciled in black feminine, swirly fonts. The first reads:

"Yoga is the journey of the self, through the self, to the self." – Bhagavad Gita.

Yikes, this is going to take some yoga dictionary to understand. How the hell do you pronounce Bhagavad anyway? Hopefully, there is no test prior to becoming a student here. I think that is definitely 300 level.

"The mind is everything. What you think you become." – Buddha.

I know Buddha was smart so figure I'd better pay attention to this one. At least I can pronounce Buddha. I envy the person that reads it and thinks, rock on! Certainly, if that is the truth, then I am on my way to becoming, well, I can't really go there. I make a mental note on that one. I have a lot of work to do.

When I read "The future depends on what we do in the present." – Gandhi, panic sets in. Before this week, my present was filled with, well again, I am here now, right? I should definitely roll with this present. And also the present given to me by Liz.

"Peyton?"

Kristina is pushing a rolled-up purple mat into my hands. I'm busted for being in my own little world. I'm present now, in front of the studio door, shaking like a leaf. "Thanks."

She pushes open the heavy wooden arch-shaped door to reveal the narrow, dark wood-floored room with dimly lit ornate lanterns hanging along both sides. She motions for me to enter. "Have a great class!" And with that, I am on my own.

I unroll the mat and realize my older legs don't prefer a cross-legged position any longer. I don't consider myself athletic or flexible, and I am pretty sure I am going to make a fool of myself. As if she can sense my hesitancy, Alexandra gracefully swoops in, bending over and whispering into my ear, "You've got this."

She starts class by welcoming all the new students. I am glad I am not alone on this new journey!

"All that is required for the next sixty minutes is the ability to breathe."

I relax. I can handle breathing. And, since it's basically dark, no one will really know if I screw up a pose or twelve, right?

Relaxing into what she calls child's pose as we lean our hips back on our feet and outstretch our arms in front of us, I let the stress of the last few days release from my muscles. Making my way through the first sun salutations and a warrior series, I love the teacher telling us to find softness and strength together. It speaks to me! I have always wanted to be the tough girl, but underneath, beneath the show that I work so hard to put on, I know I am not like my other friends. They are happily living the L.A. life with ne'er a mention of aspiring to more. I know there is something deeper to life, I just don't know what.

Before I know it, Alexandra is instructing us to slowly lie back onto our mats for the final pose. I am not sure how it's considered a pose to be lying still on one's back, but I am new to this so who am I to argue? It feels damn good. I am warm, and sweaty, and calm. I start to remember what it was like, what seems a long time ago, to feel happy and at peace. It has been too long. Next, we roll onto our sides into what Alexandra calls the fetal position. She tells us to leave anything behind that we don't want to carry with us. I've got a Louis Vuitton set of luggage to unpack if that is the case.

I roll up my mat, feeling ready to take on the big, bad world again. Stepping out of the studio with renewed purpose, I know exactly what to do. A minute later, the phone is ringing on the other end of the line I have dialed.

"Pey, how's it going in the D?"

"Hey, Brad. It's okay." I pause, knowing he is probably well aware of what Kyle is up to. Brad is nearly omnipotent. "How about there?"

I sense he suspects what I am up to when he laughs. "Oh, nothing much. Couple parties. You know. The usual."

Damn him for insinuating without dishing. Well, hopefully, when I ask for the next favor, he will be just as discrete. It comes along with the territory. Stars, celebrities, those of privilege. Call them what you like. He knows where and how to find them. Brad always gets the scoop. To call him paparazzo doesn't do him justice, however, because he is not paid for gossip, but for crime and punishment. When someone suspects trouble, it is Brad who discretely, and expensively, delivers the news, good, bad or ugly, depending on which side you are on.

"So, to what do I owe the pleasure of Peyton Jennings calling? No one calls me just to chat."

Shoot. I hope I haven't offended him, and sadly it is the truth in my case as well. "I'm sorry. That sucks. And I am just as guilty, because," I bite my bottom lip hard, knowing how the words are going to sound, "I need a favor."

"For you, darling? Anything."

I know he means it. If Kyle hadn't gotten to me first, we may have ended up together. I'd avoided finding out too much, as saying Kyle falls into the jealous type category is an understatement. I can sense that he is attracted to me, and I think maybe the rough exterior he presents is more for show than he lets on. It's surprising he is friends with Kyle, considering.

"I need a number for an address, please." I exhale, realizing how nervous I am. I pull up the photo on my phone that I took of page 16, just in case, and rattle off the Chicago address. Realizing I may as well capitalize on him being on the line, I add, "And I need some dirt on a Jack Mannington from somewhere in Detroit."

"Uh, geez, Peyton, want to be a little more random? What the hell is going on there? Not one but two conquests? In such short order? At a funeral, no doubt?"

Shit. While it is half the truth, by his tone, I can tell that he is now the one fishing for dirt on me, probably to protect his friend. I backtrack. "Ha, that's very funny, Bradley. Don't get carried away. I'm in Detroit, not Hollywood. Don't be making up any crazy stories in your head." Making up stories in the head is my job today.

"Okay, Peyton, I am on it. I'll text you what I find out. See you when you get back."

"Thank you. Thanks so much, Brad." Then I feel I should add, just to alleviate any last-minute doubts, "It's about my mom." He'd be an ass to argue with that card being played.

"Gotcha. Okay, I'll do my best."

"Like always."

"Always. See ya, Pey."

I hang up and turn the key in the ignition of my mother's car, realizing, once again, that I have nowhere to go. I turn the key backward and look around at the quaint surroundings.

The hissing November wind bites at my cheeks the moment I step out of the car onto the charming street. The gray of the season needs extra light, and small white ones wrap each tree branch and trunk. They twinkle despite the early afternoon time. The studio is nestled between cute shops with old-fashioned black and white striped awnings featuring home décor and boutique clothing. The little girl in me window-shops at the toy store I pass, marveling at the fact that the indulgent Barbie dream house I always wanted is still coveted.

It's cold, so I choose the closest restaurant, advertising 'Best Sushi in Town' atop a mound of fake snow on the glass of the front window. It's crowded with lunch patrons, and I slide onto a stool, joining plenty of company at the bar.

I stay through the Happy Hour sitting at the bar, making more

Midwestern small talk with other friendly singles and couples. As I am digging into my purse for my credit card, not Kyle's, the vibration of my phone brushes against my hand. Hoping it is Brad, I flip it over in my palm to see that indeed it is. Two new messages. The first contains a phone number with an 847 area code. Chicago! My stomach does an arbitrary little flip-flop. Then it drops as I read the second message containing an address and phone number I know from memory.

They are my own.

Shit! Have I kicked Jack out of his home? Why wouldn't he show himself at the funeral or meet me? How will I find him now that the only information I have on him is also mine?

This bit of knowledge keeps me, albeit briefly, from thinking that I now may be able to track down J.T. Walker. I shake my head in disbelief while I walk back to the car, position myself into the seat and open Brad's message again. Fingers trembling as I dial, I hold the phone close to my ear as it rings three, four, then five times. The recorded greeting starts to play. "Hey, you've reached us. Well, not really, since Zach," the voice changes, "J.T." (His voice!) Another change, "And Owen… can't take your call. Please leave us a message on our vintage answering machine and make it good so we can laugh. And don't forget to say which one of us you are calling for," J.T.'s voice chimes in again. "Or don't." Laughter ensues, then the beep. Who has a home phone these days? And does anyone actually check messages? And all of them will hear my message? I clear my throat and summon some bravery. "Hey, this is Peyton Jennings. I'm calling for J.T. Can you tell him that there are some people in Detroit that want to hang out?" I sound confident and cool. I am truthful with the message, as several of the other students did say they wanted to get together in Detroit, and after all, there is at least one for sure. Even though I shouldn't.

I am about to hang up when I hear rustling on the other end of the line. "Hello? Hello?"

I press the phone back to my ear. "Oh hey, I didn't think anyone was—"

The voice interrupts, "Sorry, was outside grilling. Don't ask me why. It's like twenty below. I heard your message but had a plate of steak in my hands. Glad I caught you, because J.T. is still in Detroit. I'll give you his cell. Gotta pen?"

I look around the car quickly, and like the good Girl Scout my mother was, find one in the console. I write the number on my hand, above my thumb. I may never wash this hand again. I quickly thank the man I assume is Zach or Owen and try to think what the hell I can text J.T. that won't make me sound like the stalker I am.

The backspace my new best friend, fourteen minutes later, I'm still sitting in the same parking spot guiltily contributing to global warming with a running engine for heat. I struggle to find anything that works. I start with the same line I had used on the answering machine but can't use the words 'get together' in a text. No way could a guy miss the sexual connotation. I try asking if he wants to hang out but that seems too childish. I mistakenly type 'hook up while you are still here?' Oops. Subconscious speaking? This is ridiculous. I should just call. Nothing can be left to interpretation then. But then again, doesn't a little piece of me want him to interpret, or misinterpret, my double entendre and sexual innuendo? Besides, no one calls when facing potential rejection. Thus the beauty of text! Much less scary and painful if it happens.

heard u r still in town…me too. bored. just in case…thought I would see if you want to grab a drink?

My finger hovers over send as my stomach fills with a full kaleidoscope of monarchs migrating south. Hit the button, Peyton! I think of the time Hayden was sending a message to someone she was stalking on Facebook. She wouldn't hit send so I ran across the room and, before she could protest, hit send myself. We had fallen into a fit of giggles. As I smile remembering, my phone still cradled in my now sweaty-palmed hand, buzzes.

hey u! thx for text! curious how u got #??? hanging with mom 2 nite - raincheck?

A grin overtakes my face. Not a yes, but not a no either. I can work with that. Typing back, then rereading just to make sure it is acceptable, but not overthinking, I hurry to hit send on a message that says:

I'll take a raincheck

His response is just as quickly received. Men never think too much. Well, maybe sometimes they don't think enough either. And here I am, overthinking again. His message says:

tomorrow? dinner?

Whoa! Has this just gone to a full-fledged date? Only I can overanalyze two words! It is dinner. How can I not think it is a date? I am pretty thrilled he didn't ditch hanging with his mother on Saturday night for me when he is clearly interested. And I will see J.T. Walker again tomorrow! Two happy moments are even better than one.

My phone buzzes again in my hand. He is calling! I look down at the phone to answer but see Kyle's picture smiling up at me. Shit! What have I just done? A drink is one thing, but a date? My voice isn't steady as I answer the call. I probably shouldn't be answering at all, "Hey you."

"Hey, babe, everything okay? Brad said you were digging up some dirt on your mom."

Two thousand miles, less than thirty minutes. Thanks, Brad. Thanks a whole helluva lot.

"Everything's fine," I say, then unwavering add, "Totally fine." Kyle isn't a details guy, so I expect him to drop it. He does, changing the subject to his favorite topic. Himself, of course.

"Great day today. I got callbacks. Wait for it," he says, clearly amused. "Not for one, but three roles. Signing Shannon as my agent was the best thing I've ever done."

Ever? "That's great, Kyle. Really great." I don't want to tell him that Shannon had told me that if he fucked up any of the auditions because his "party boy" reputation was true, he was done. Kyle could be considered quite successful for all intents and purposes. He works consistently in B movies and has been on several television shows, just none that had made it past a couple of episodes. Like most everyone in Hollywood, minus the one percent that has already made it, he is waiting for his 'big break' His success has afforded us plenty of lifestyle luxuries, but also more than our fair share of trouble.

I really do have everything I thought I had ever wanted. I have friends, maybe of the shallow and materialistic variety, but still. They were Kyle's friends, but they have adopted me. They even gave me a place to live when I needed one. My last relationship, defined by the loosest sense of the word, as in it existed because I was loose, ended and I had nowhere to go. I've only been able to stay because Kyle subsidizes my rent. I'm ashamed to admit I work, stereotypically and pathetically, a waitressing job while auditioning for roles of my own. I'd been so happy just minutes before. Now, I think about the real reason I haven't been home in so long.

The ashamed girl inside me didn't want to hear "I told you so" from everyone who had warned me. The Michigan governor had a grand scheme to build the 'Hollywood of the East' in an attempt to revitalize the flailing manufacturing-bound economy. Forty-six movies were shot in 2010 in Michigan, along with countless television productions. This had given plenty of us young actor wannabes false hope and lucky breaks. It had been easy to get small roles. I look the classic all-American girl-next-door part. Landing callbacks and spending late nights on set sneaking exciting glances at Josh Duhamel and Hugh Jackman in Transformers and Real Steel. I even got to meet my idol Courteney Cox. Me! Meeting Monica! It had me believing in the dream that I could be the next Friend or the leading lady to one of Hollywood's hottest heroes. It had me believing in the dream of running away, making it big, and never looking back on my meager and painful upbringing. I would show them all. I dropped the few college classes I had been taking at a local college while living near campus in a grungy apartment, took my last movie paycheck and landed in L. A. with barely a penny to my name and no plan to speak of.

I was young and hopeful. I was innocent, optimistic and naive. Or just dumb. I hadn't earned my lifestyle in a respectable manner. Rather, I'd ridden the coattails of one man after another, with complete disregard for my body. In other words, I'd sold my soul to devil after devil. And not believing myself worthy of more, I let each one treat me as less.

Tears stream down my cheeks as I realize I haven't been listening to anything Kyle has said the last few minutes. He won't notice I am crying. At least I had that going for me.

"Sounds great, right?"

"Yeah, great, Kyle. Just great. Hey, I gotta run. Can we talk in the morning?"

"Really, baby? You are too busy for me? What are you up to?"

"My carry-out is ready. I'm starving."

"Okay, well, miss me."

"I do, Kyle." I hang up the phone. I sit with my shame a few more moments until I close my eyes and see an image from the yoga studio wall. Letters dance to life as I breathe, long and deep. The future depends on what you do in the present.

And with that, I return the text to J.T.

sounds great – just say when and where!!!

My phone buzzes again.

Phew – you took long enough to answer! ☺ Text u tomorrow

He has just won my heart a bit more by sharing his insecurity. I'm probably not worthy of him, yet he is the one worried I might say no. Surprised, but pleased with his being real, I slide my phone back into my purse and say out loud to myself, "I can't wait!"

Now, what to wear?

NOVEMBER 9th
CHAPTER 4 | Peyton

I may have topped one million looks at my phone by the time I make my way to the yoga studio on Sunday morning. I had woken up early, still not having slept well, but better than the prior nights. It is much easier to wake up with something like a date to look forward to, instead of, say, a funeral. I know better than to keep looking, 'a watched pot never boils' annoyingly ringing in my ears, but still. One more glance at the screen, just one last time—it's only 9:49 a.m. for goodness' sake!

As my body moves through the motions, my brain is swirling ribbons of crazy. Still wondering what I will wear with my non-Midwest-appropriate wardrobe. Where will we go? Should I drink beer or wine? Does he want sophisticated or sassy? Sporty or classy? Are the two mutually exclusive or the best combination? Holy hell!

I hear the teacher say, "Step your right leg back to a lunge. Your right leg steps back. Your right leg."

She's talking to me. Quickly, I switch my legs, and not very gracefully. Once again, I am so grateful it is dark in the studio. In the quick scan of the room I had done after the teacher corrected me, it hadn't appeared that anyone was glowering at me in annoyance. On the contrary, everyone seems to be lost in her or his own little world, eyes softly gazing forward and faces full of concentration and determination. Some even have their eyes closed.

I hear the teacher suggest that we each stay focused in between the four corners of our own mat. Oops! Busted again!

"Close your eyes, focus on your breath."

I can do this. I close my eyes and topple left the moment I am balancing on one arm and two legs. My eyes fly open as I catch myself. Maybe I will save trying that for the third class. I can focus on my breath though. Just one at a time. I make it through four whole breaths before another image of J.T. fills my head and the questions start again. Does he work? Why does he want to run away to Australia instead of, say, Paris? Paris could be nice for romance. Oh, dear God! Focus much, Peyton? I scold myself and get back to my breath. An improvement. The next time I make it through five whole breaths before I chase after my runaway brain in the middle of imagining what our first kiss will taste like.

By the time I am moving to lie on my back for the ending pose of Savasana, or corpse pose, I don't want the class to be over. I haven't stopped thinking at all. I don't feel calm or peaceful like I had the day before. Then the teacher's voice oozes soothingly, "And push yourself up from fetal pose leaving behind your burdens and cares." I've just missed all of Savasana. Then she says to find some gratitude. This one I've got. I've burned enough calories to have a fru-fru drink at Starbucks.

But first, I must check my phone! Right on command, my stomach flip-flops first, then the rest of my body chimes in. Clammy palms. Heartbeat capitulating wildly. Head dizzy in delight. All for one single text message. Pathetic much?

morning! still on? any Detroit faves?

I love how he capitalizes Detroit to give his hometown the respect it deserves. Just one of the annoyingly pervasive questions in my head during class, I have an answer prepared. I have no idea if the restaurants I am considering are still as I remember them, but at least I will make suggestions. My favorite pizza place for the low end, favorite sushi place for the middle, and steak place for the high end. I'd tried to become a vegetarian when I had first moved to California, but the steak-and-potatoes piece of my roots was too hard to deny. If he picks sushi I'll be eating it two days in a row, so that nearly qualifies me as vegetarian, doesn't it?

not fussy… but Gabe's, Sake's and Modern are the faves, since you asked!

I secretly hope he will choose pizza or sushi, as my last option is definitely more date-like than the other two. Guilt has been alternating with excitement all morning, but excitement is winning out, at least at this moment. He answers:

sushi for my CA girl – but of course – sounds great

His California girl? His girl? Am I reading more into it than he means? Probably. Definitely. I swing back to guilt over excitement. Before I have time to torture myself further, my phone buzzes again:

text ur address and I'll pick u up @ 7

This has officially crossed the line with a not just dinner but a pickup and drop-off from dinner, yet I hesitate none in replying. Let chivalry reign!

thank you – see you @ 7!

I add my address and hit send before my head can overtake my heart.

Seven hours and twelve minutes later, I am wearing new jeans and a long sweater that flatters my top, but covers everything below. I have admonished myself for spending money I don't have over the last two hours. Applying yet another coat of lip gloss in front of the mirror, I seal in the color with a loud smack. A little more sleep has done me well. The dark bags and red-rimmed eyes are not exactly a distant memory, but at least I look presentable.

I begin to pace, nerves getting the best of me, back and forth in front of the window, as if catching him in the act of pulling up will somehow make this all a little easier. A bundle of energy and anxiety, I want to impress, but am also concerned I haven't spoken to Kyle since the night prior. I've texted several times with no response and know that there is probably only one explanation. He'd been high as a kite on something and then crashed, and is probably passed out and not remembering that he has a girlfriend since I am not right there next to him. I only hope that he doesn't call while I am out with J.T. We should be wrapped up with dinner by the time Kyle would be dragging himself out of bed and knocking back several red bulls, or using another substance I don't want to consider, to get himself ready for another night of, what was his phrase? "Sheer bliss, baby."

The sound of a car pulling into the driveway startles me from contemplation, and I smile to myself. Despite my careful watch, he's surprised me. Maybe it is just the start of sweet surprises. By the time my hand is on the wrought iron door handle, he is knocking. I pull the door open and he looks as disconcerted as I felt a moment ago.

"Hey," he says shyly, like he needs a minute to compose himself. He stuffs both hands into his pockets, and looks away, but wears a big smile. His blond bangs fall so perfectly across his forehead they look fake, hair on a mannequin, perfectly painted into place. "I was hoping for just one more minute there." He pauses then, and if it is possible, his smile broadens. "Beautiful girls have a way of unnerving men, you know."

It is adorable, emotions right out there in the open for the world to see. He is so real! And hot! And has just called me beautiful.

I mirror his endearing grin. As we turn to descend the porch stairs his hand finds the small of my back in the perfect sexy-not-creepy-at-all spot, guiding me gently down the stairs. My whole-body tingles with his touch, feet barely feeling the pavement. He reaches for the car door with a sideways 'don't you even think about it' look, and, pulling it open, waits for me to sit down before closing it softly behind me.

NOVEMBER 10th
CHAPTER 5 | J.T.

With a loud crack of thunder that makes the panes of glass tremble in the window frame, I am jolted awake. Damn. The weather is as strange as what is going on in my life at the moment. Damn. What a night last night had been. When I pulled up to Peyton's house, I'd been second-guessing my decision to suggest the date. After bounding up the porch steps confidently, I needed an extra breath to calm my rapidly beating heart. The rapid heartbeat wasn't from the steps. She'd surprised me by pulling open the door. It takes a lot to surprise me, life having taught me it's advantageous to always be on guard, but Peyton had literally taken my breath away! She is beautiful. Angelic beautiful, classic beautiful, devastatingly beautiful. There aren't enough adjectives to put before the word beautiful to describe how I see her.

She captivated me the moment we shared our first intense gaze and I'd known exactly who she was. The daughter of a woman for whom I held the utmost regard. The difference last night, however, was that her tired and distraught features from the funeral had softened and were even more beautiful.

The porch light had illuminated her blond waves and face, and though I tried not to let my eyes drift from hers, I couldn't resist taking in the way her sweater beneath her unzipped jacket had accentuated what I could only imagine as perfect breasts. Her high cheekbones, highlighted with soft pink, stole my attention, and those full lips seemed to be poised in a pout that was just for me, ready for me to steal. Her curious eyes sparkle blue as the cloudless sky but with just enough gray to reveal pending storms. I tried to steady myself before I was caught, but I'd seen in her eyes that I was busted. No better way to dig myself from the hole, I'd had to stuff my hands in my pockets to avoid the potential of her noticing how they were shaking with nerves. I felt like a middle schooler again, in the back of the classroom, trying to duck my hips back to avoid the dead giveaway that I'd lost control of my emotions.

Knowing that with a well-placed compliment I could basically weasel my way out of the most tenuous situations, I was sincere when I confessed she had unnerved me. The way her eyes had smiled in return as her lips curled up in gratefulness, and she thanked me, uncoiled the knot in my stomach. Then, we had turned to descend the porch steps and my hand had reached for her in a protective reflex. When I'd made contact with the small of her back the intense ripple of pleasure, yet again, had me questioning whether the date was a good idea.

I knew to keep the conversation high level, answer questions with questions. Both of us were like young children with injuries that could be coddled by deflection and distraction when anything real bubbled too close to the surface. She seemed to want to reveal less than I did, if that was possible, so she appeared perfectly happy to let my games and light content suffice, laughing playfully all the while. My last area of anguish was easily extinguished with a truthful, easy-to-deliver answer. When the waitress had asked for our drink order, I'd only had to answer that I was driving. None of this is a long-term strategy, but hell, I am taking this all one minute at a time.

I had expected that sushi would be safe. Who knew that she would look so incredibly cute and sexy, an unlikely combination to achieve at the same damn time while clumsily trying to use chopsticks. I was a sucker for her nose crinkling up in thought as I asked her questions like what historical figure she'd most want to have over for dinner. Her answer had been Jesus. "Who else could possibly compare? Though, Audrey Hepburn would be a close second choice." What would she feed Jesus? That had stressed her out, as she'd bowed her head shamefully but tilted puppy dog eyes to mine. "Frozen pizza? Hot dogs? Macaroni and cheese? Maybe all three, buffet-style? Oh, and wine, of course. Wine classes up all of those dishes!" I recalled the expression on her face when I'd stoically folded my napkin while shaking my head, telling her, "I'm afraid I'm going to need to end this evening earlier than expected." Then clearing my throat authoritatively I'd added, "I'm sorry, but not cooking is a deal breaker for me," all the while pressing my lips into a tight, thin line so as not to burst into laughter.

I'd only intended to leave her hanging wide-eyed for a moment, but then I saw the pink blush across those damn fine cheekbones. In an effort to correct my bad behavior, I placed my hand over hers and felt something inside of me shift.

No. Shift isn't a strong enough word.

Ignite seems more appropriate.

Something long pushed away, buried, shelved for never. The spark exploded some familiar, yet forgotten, feeling back into my being. If I thought I was going to get away with not falling for her, that was the moment I officially crashed and burned.

Whispering sadly, she'd said, "Oh. Okay. I guess just take me home then?" She phrased it as a question, one she was obviously hoping I wouldn't answer, and I'd squeezed her hand and smiled broadly. "I was totally kidding. I love to cook. Don't care at all if that is all you can make. My roommates and I put Jamie and Guy to shame!"

Her response had been priceless, her own smile extending from ear to ear, perfect white teeth glistening. "Well, so was I. Just so happens I might be a little gourmet myself!"

Crash and burn take two.

"You so got me," I'd retorted, then followed her eyes down to the table where our fingers were threaded together. She had more than just gotten me in a joke. She had my head and heart.

Peyton filled in the details on how she'd gotten my number,

minus the details of who actually wanted to get together in Detroit. I suppose she was making excuses to stalk me, which is just fine, as she saved me the trouble of having to concoct my own little reconnaissance mission.

We covered facts about ourselves, literally, from A to Z with my favorites about her being C for her chocolate addiction, and G for giraffes being her favorite animal because they symbolize good luck. I hadn't had the heart to tell her it is actually the elephant, not the giraffe, known for its luck-bringing potential. Hell, who was I to argue if giraffes work for her? I loved her R, as well, where she had said running shoes were her "best frenemies", and then Y for yoga as her new favorite way to spend her time. It wasn't as if I should have found that surprising, as I'd certainly heard more than an earful about the benefits, but when she spoke about yoga she was so impassioned I was convinced even the biggest doubters would flock to try it immediately. This nearly ensures my mother will soon become her biggest fan.

My favorite part of all, however, was how I'd made her laugh at my answers. Happiness echoing through the restaurant, a sound I believe I will never tire of hearing. I am not even sure that I am funny, but it made me feel like a million bucks, nonetheless.

As we'd slid from our respective sides of the booth, I found a way, once again, to make physical contact with Peyton. My leg under the table gently brushing hers had nearly rendered me incapable of standing to exit. I shook my head at myself as I paused a moment, appearing to let her out, but in actuality trying to tame the weakness in my thigh muscles that on any other day are strong and powerful. Karma is a bitch. I've given plenty of ribbings to friends unwise enough to admit a girl had brought them to their knees. But now, I know what they mean. Even if I am not sure that I want to.

By the time we'd reached her house I was hoping for more, perhaps inside the confines of the four walls, or more specifically, one particular room. When we arrived, and I'd walked her to the door, things took a turn I wasn't expecting.

Now I lie here apprehensive and anxious about where we left things. One thing is certain, however, and that's how much rejection sucks.

Grabbing my phone from the nightstand, I check the time and see two things. One, the absence of a message from Peyton, and two, that I have no more time to lie in bed pitying my sorry ass. As if on cue, the voice of my mom drifts up from the lower level, "Joe, honey, let's go! I have to teach."

CHAPTER 6 | Peyton

I am pacing.
No, not pacing. Stomping, pouting, restlessly traipsing around my house. I. Am. Such. An. Idiot! Why hadn't I just told J.T. the truth last night? Surely, he'd felt the rug was pulled out from under him when our too-good-to-be-true evening came to a screeching halt on my fricking front porch. I'd fled like a child, with no explanation, leaving my name with a question mark punctuating the cold, dark night.

Had I crossed even the slightest line, it wouldn't have ended until the finish line.

Stupid stalking, stupid agreeing to a date. Sushi was safe? Like hell! Nothing was safe. I wasn't safe in his presence to control myself! But what I had felt was real safety, the kind where I knew to my core that he would protect me always.

The November rain falling sideways is pelting the windowpane, mocking me as the branches of the trees beat against the glass of my bedroom. I am jumping out of my skin every five seconds because of its horror-movie sound effect likeness. If J.T. was here, by my side now, or in my life, I know I would feel comfortable in my own skin. The way I felt throughout our entire evening together. His gentle nature was evident in the few touches that had barely whispered across my skin. And his easygoing and polite demeanor was impossible to miss with every person we had encountered, from the valet to the waitress, to the elderly woman he helped ease into her seat before her husband made it to the table. He was a true gentleman who appeared, contraindicative to all things me, to be the least selfish being I've ever encountered.

I know in my gut this makes me unworthy, but there is a part of me that is hopeful I could be. Though I'd avoided eye contact at all costs, it still seemed he saw all of me. Maybe everything I think I know about who I am is wrong.

Grabbing a black pair of yoga pants that slump in a pile on the floor next to my bed, I push each leg into them. Annoyingly they're inside out. I pull them off and quickly reverse them, hopping on one leg closer to the suitcase. I grab a sweatshirt off the top of the stack of clothes and pull it over my head, trying to smooth the wrinkles and vowing to put my clothes into the dresser when I return.

A quick look into the bathroom mirror reveals a lost cause, and forgoing even a brush to my hair, I sweep my blond locks up into a messy bun with one twist of my wrist and adept fingers that seem to be trembling slightly. Descending the wooden stairs, bare feet echoing off the walls, I slip my toes into my tennis shoes, not taking the time to put them all the way on. I opt to take the seconds to pour another cup of coffee before sliding the keys into my pocket and retrieving my clutch from the counter. A quick glance to the clock on the microwave says I only have a slim chance of catching him.

Slim is good enough. It has to be.

I need, not just want, to see him again. He deserves an explanation, and consolation, and whatever else will constitute an appropriate apology. It needs to happen before he steps onto an airplane and potentially never sees me ever again.

I am pulling to the curb of the departures area, thankful we had spoken about his early flight back to Chicago. During our favorites alphabet game, at the letter "U" he'd said, "United Airlines. My second home." He hadn't gone into details as I'd been distracted by the fact that he'd flown to Detroit just for my mother's funeral, as had several other students. My mother was worthy of people flying to celebrate her life. I'd made a mental note to ask later why he spent so much time flying but it hadn't come up.

I shift into park and grab my phone, texting one-handed:

where do u happen to be at this moment?

It immediately buzzes:

in line hoping to avoid a Monday morning tsa strip search ;)

I breathe a huge sigh of relief at the realization that I am not too late. I haven't missed him and let the best thing I've had going in a long while fly off into the sunrise. I text again:

do u have time to come outside???

With the next buzz, *um sure???* flashes across my phone. I open the car door, a bundle of nerves, the pit of my stomach rumbling, perspiration pooling in undesirable areas despite the temperature outside. I walk around the car, peering into the glass of the passenger side window for one last useless look at myself. I lean my hip against the door to look casual, though the real reason is to steady myself. I wish I could blame the cold, but know my teeth are chattering with nerves instead.

The glass door to my left slides open and J.T. steps through with a small shiver as the cold air hits him. He is unshaven, jean-clad, wearing Timberland boots and a black jacket too thin for the weather. My heart is motionless in my chest, stopping upon the sight of him. I loved him in his suit at the funeral and jeans and sweater last night, but this casual, rugged look ups my attraction to him more than a notch. His hair is unkempt, looking as if he'd run his hands through it before walking out the door. Messy, yet put together, a look that could grace the cover of a men's magazine.

J.T. looks away from me to his right, giving me one more second to attempt to compose myself, before his head slowly swivels left toward me. When our eyes meet, he squints a bit, as if questioning what he is seeing, but I don't miss the way the corners of his mouth tilt up slightly when he catches my gaze. I lift my arm in a shy, awkward wave. He repositions his backpack slung over one shoulder and turns toward me with his suitcase rolling behind. The way he moves is strong and powerful, yet his demeanor is so calm and demure I can't reconcile the two in my head. Two opposing sides of him, and I am waiting for the real J.T. Walker to please stand up.

He stops in front of me, lets go of his suitcase and shoves both hands into his pockets. The cold exposes my deep exhale as the cloud of my breath hangs between us. My mind, still processing how beautiful he looks, is too busy to compile the words I have come here to say. Luckily for me, he fills the awkward silence that resembles the exact moment I had left him in the night before. He still wears an inquisitive expression when he finally speaks, softly, with a kindness I don't deserve, "Why in the world are you standing out here in this freezing cold?"

I'm really being held up by a hunk of metal, but I am grateful to still be upright. "I owe you an exclamation." Then, rolling my eyes and shaking my head, I correct myself, "I mean explanation!"

I have to look away from his intense gaze that peers too deep. I get to hear his amazing laugh. "Exclaim away."

"I'd like to blame the cold for freezing up my lips or tongue or something, but you probably already know it is you that is making me forget how to speak. Oh, and breathe. And then there is the little matter of my heart that apparently has forgotten how to beat normally after twenty-four years. So, there's that." I turn my head back to face him. A captivating smile rewards my honesty.

"So, you're saying there's a chance?" His voice is barely above a whisper, as if he is afraid to put that question into the universe.

"More than a chance, J.T. I owe you an apology. I know it sounds ridiculously cliché to say it was me not you, but…" My words trail off because my breath won't come to push more out of my mouth. He is standing so close now I can smell his absurdly divine smell of masculinity. I want to put my hand behind his neck and thread my fingers into that hair and pull him close enough to feel the roughness of his stubble against my face.

"What, Peyton? It's okay to tell me. Really."

His tone is so comforting I could have spilled every fear, want and need I've ever had, including wanting and needing his mouth against mine right this moment. Still, I bite my lip, hesitant to speak, as I can predict what this good guy is going to say. I make fists with my hands and hug myself against the cold and shiver.

"Okay, you're killing me, Peyton," J.T. says moving forward, pulling his hands from his pockets and placing them on my upper arms, rubbing slowly up and down to warm me. Moments later, he unzips his coat, his warm hands unclasp mine and pull them unto his chest, laying them flat and covering mine with his much larger ones. The warmth I feel with his touch radiates throughout my body and I feel my cheeks flush pink. I barely hear my voice as my two favorite letters breathlessly gasp from my lips as he steps even closer, "J.T., I'm so sorry. I didn't mean to leave you like that last night." My cheeks flush warm with a crimson blush, eyes drifting to the pavement. "I really wanted you to kiss me." I cringe, recalling how I had pulled back from his pursed lips and closed eyes, knowing how the rejection must have hurt his pride. "It's just that I—" Why is this so hard to just spit out? "I have a boyfriend. In L.A."

Immediately, his chest is moving away from mine while he releases my hands, zips his coat and returns his hands to his pockets. I knew he would react this way. He looks at me sideways, as if maybe, like last night, I am going to say, "Gotcha!" as the punchline to a not-so-funny joke.

Ascertaining I am serious, he speaks hesitantly, "Okay then. I am really glad that nothing happened last night." He glances back toward the door, looking as if he'd like to escape through it about now. Turning back toward me with the same curiosity as when he'd first seen me standing here, he asks, "But you just said there was more than a chance."

I lean toward him, his magnetism impossible to resist. "There is, J.T. I don't know how much time I will need, but before I met you, I'd already concluded the relationship needed to end. There are just some…" Hesitating, I search for the right word, "Complications."

He smiles, looking genuinely relieved. "Well, you've got nearly three weeks. I mean, you can have more than three weeks, but I'll be way out of pocket for about three weeks, so I won't be around to bug you. Though I'd be lying if I didn't say I am not going to spend more than a little time thinking about you, Peyton."

It is my turn to look back questioningly at him now. "What do you mean three weeks?"

"Tomorrow I'm leaving for Africa. I work for an NGO."

WTF? I'd had a whole date and hadn't asked what he did. I realize that he asked most of the questions last night and I rudely hadn't even asked him about his work. Self-absorbed should be my middle name. I quickly try to process what I know about him. United is his second home, and the comment at the funeral about his saving the world and fixing the broken. Fixing the broken. Like me.

I know a dictionary of movie-set terms and acronyms like PA and AP but I have no idea what an NGO is, let alone what it means he would be doing in Africa.

Probably because of my incredulous expression, he bails me out of my cluelessness. "NGO is a non-governmental organization. A non-profit not run by the government. I've got chickens to corral, wells to build, and businesses to start. Well, me and the team of people I am taking. And we're delivering t-shirts. My roommate Zach started a shirt-for-shirt business, copying off those famous shoe people, so my roommate Owen and I decided to incorporate delivering those into our trips. It's incredible."

The way his face lights up with passion for his work makes me fall just a little bit harder. "Wow, that's really cool, J.T."

"Speaking of cool, it's freezing out here and you need to get warm. And unfortunately, I have to go. I really appreciate the fact that you showed up here today. It was a great surprise, and I'd be full of shit if I didn't say that I wasn't a little bit devastated at the end of what I thought was a fantastic date last night."

It is inevitable that a smile overtakes my whole face. I lean forward and throw my arms around his neck. I feel the warmth of his whole body surround me and strong hands on my back. Oh, to be held like this. He whispers into my hair, "I hope your complications aren't too complicated." Shivers cover me from head to toe. And they are not from the cold.

Our lips meet in the briefest encounter, soft and tender, the exclamation point on the best embrace I've ever collapsed into. Cupping my face with both hands, he quietly says, "I hope to see you soon, Peyton Jennings," and my heart melts. I hope so too, J.T. Walker.

NOVEMBER 11
CHAPTER 7 | Peyton

Yoga on Tuesday has my limbs in new poses and my head in new places. For the first time, I keep my eyes closed for the majority of the practice and actually manage to spend more time focused on my breath than on my crazy. My only point of yoga contention had been my brain arguing with the teacher stating that everything is temporary. I don't want what I am feeling about J.T. to be temporary. On the contrary, I want to hold on to the flutter in my belly and skip of each heartbeat every time my phone buzzes. J.T. texted last night, saying:

very much hoping three weeks is enough…if not, save my number ☺

I returned his text:

will be counting down the days…!

I am counting down the days to see him again, but I am also on borrowed time to dissolve my relationship with Kyle. It isn't going to be easy, and the days left may not be enough.

Because I rock yoga class, I feel brave enough to visit my mother's grave. I navigate the long and winding road through the cemetery slowly and carefully, taking in the variety of headstones and grave markers.

Just when I round the last corner before my mother's grave, the tears well. The mound of dirt rising above the ground still shows the slightest bit of brown through the snow. Approaching the grave, I brake, stopping the car to catch the tears that are falling. It takes both of my hands. My chest aches. I close my eyes and lean back into the headrest, thinking of yoga and pulling in a long, deep breath just like they tell us to do every class. Breathing makes it possible to get through anything.

Opening my eyes again, I see movement. My head instinctively jerks toward a man entering his car and pulling the door closed. My view of him is obstructed by a tree, but he appears to be leaning forward into the steering wheel, matching my pose of a minute ago. I look back toward my mother's grave and see a wreath of the seasonal evergreen I'd been admiring on others' graves. Pulling forward, I see the crested mound and dirt footprints glaring against the white. My eyes follow each step as they lead, as I suspect, to the car where the man sits.

I jog towards the car. The man still crouches over the steering wheel, and fearing I'll give him a heart attack upon approach, I stomp my feet as I get closer. He turns toward the noise and his eyes widen. He recognizes me.

He opens the door and stands before me, tall with a slender frame for a male. I take in the square shape of his head and angled, rugged jaw. His lips stretch wide and flat, and he has a deep cleft in his chin. A hint of gray tinges the hair just above his temples and the ends of his high arched brows. His eyes are a rare hazel with just a fleck of brown, and kind. They match my own, looking tired and weary.

I am sure it is the man from the funeral home.

He wraps his arms around me. I feel safe in his embrace, as I do in J.T.'s. How do strangers keep rocking my world like this? Shocked and surprised at how my body reacts, my arms lift and I find myself in the unlikely position of hugging back.

We hold on to one another, connected by the unexpected bond of sorrow, until I step back, unable to wait another second to find out if indeed this stranger is who I think he is. "Jack?" I ask without hesitation.

He looks down as if embarrassed I've had to come to the conclusion on my own, and outstretches his hand to shake mine.

"Yes, Peyton."

It seems odd to shake hands after the hug we've just shared but I take his hand anyway. "Nice to officially meet you, Jack Mannington. Though I know your name, I find myself at a distinct disadvantage. I believe you may know me much more than I know you."

Again, all he can muster in response seems to be, "Yes, Peyton." Awe fills his eyes as he peers intently into mine. It appears he is as ill-equipped for this meeting as I am, regardless of his one-up in knowledge. Finally, he asks, "How do you know my name?"

"The Bible. In my mother's bedroom." Realizing I've placed too much emphasis on the word mother, I look directly at him and ask, "Your bedroom?"

He lets out a soft laugh. A kind and gentle laugh that reminds me of J.T. "Yes, it was mostly our bedroom. I inherited my parents' house as well, so I spent some time there, but I preferred to spend my nights with your mother. With Caroline."

His eyes well with tears and his voice breaks as if on cue when her name crosses his lips. He blinks hard and I see his Adam's apple bulge and rescind as he swallows. "I hope you are not angry. I would have loved for her to move in with me, but she wouldn't give up her house. She said she wanted a place for you to come home if you ever chose to."

I've just learned more about my mother in this ten-second exchange than in the past year of my life. The grief is overwhelming. I cover my mouth with my hand to hold back the tears. He cups my shoulder with his hand. "It's cold out here and we've got plenty of time, and better places, where we can—" He pauses as if to search for the right words. "Get to know one another."

He turns toward his car, the door still open, and leans into the driver's seat. Rummaging around, he stands back up having produced a pen and piece of paper and is writing his phone number using his other hand against his bent knee as something solid to brace himself. "Here is my number. I hope you'll call," he says pleadingly. "If nothing else, would it be okay if I came to get my things before you go back to California?" He stops for a moment before finishing with, "I assume you are going back to California?"

I am not sure if he wants me to stay or hopes I am getting the hell out of here pronto, but I am too cold to stick around and read between the lines. "Of, of course. I'll call you." I stutter a bit, maybe from the cold, or maybe from trying to process what has just taken place.

Sliding into his seat, he closes his door, gives a friendly wave in my direction and slowly pulls away leaving me standing there alone, shivering in the cold.

I spend the next few hours contemplating what has happened today with J.T. and Jack. How it felt to let my heart open, if only in the slightest, to virtual strangers. I feel vulnerable. Is this a good idea or am I playing emotional roulette, with regret sure to land after the winning spin. I'd like to skip the potential heap of devastation but the scrap of paper calls to me from the counter. Only ten numbers in Jack's handwriting are written on the paper yet it seems to hold so much more.

I circle around the paper over and over again as I clean the pantry and cupboards of the kitchen, boxing up food that I can donate to a local food pantry before I leave. What secrets might Jack hold about my mother? Had she taken her secrets to the grave? I know I won't hold out long with these questions lingering.

I put an unopened box of cereal into the eleventh brown box and glance over the organized chaos. It hits me. What if Jack might actually want—or worse yet, need—this food? What if I am giving away something that is actually his? I pick up my phone and dial the number on the paper, swiftly hitting the call button before I can reconsider.

"Hello," Jack answers smoothly, putting me at ease.

"Hi, Jack. It's Peyton. Peyton Jennings."

"Peyton," he exhales audibly, like the weight of the world has just been lifted from his shoulders. "I was hoping you'd call."

"Would you like to come over for dinner, Jack?" I surprise myself extending the invitation.

"I'd really like that."

"I know you don't need directions," I say lightheartedly, with a small laugh to break up the tension. "How does 6:30 sound?"

"It sounds great, Peyton. Do you drink wine?"

"Only red or white."

It is his turn to laugh. "You sound like your mother. She wasn't fussy about her wine either."

Another fact I didn't know. How many more similarities that I've not taken the time to appreciate do we share? How much more can Jack teach me about the woman I barely knew? I might even come to understand myself.

I start watching for Jack's arrival ten minutes before I am expecting him. He isn't used to knocking on his own front door. It would be awful to make him feel a stranger in the house he probably knows as well as I do. I open the door as soon as I hear his car door close. He takes the porch step in a comfortable, easy manner, like he's probably done many times before, but then straightens and hesitates.

Am I the cause of his trepidation? Or is it coming back to a house without Caroline? I can control one of the variables in that equation. "Pretty sure this is more your house than mine, so I'd feel pretty silly saying make yourself at home, Jack." My outstretched arm tells him to lead the way past the door into the foyer.

He steps forward and to my left, stopping in front of the coat closet. Opening the door, he reaches for a hanger. A tear slips from the corner of his eye when he stretches forward and brushes his fingertips down the sleeve of a woman's black wool dress coat. He doesn't bother to wipe the tear away. I turn and walk toward the kitchen, giving Jack some space to grieve in the house that is no longer inhabited by the woman he clearly loved.

When he silently enters the kitchen, I am peering into the refrigerator, assessing its contents for what I can make for us. Not one, but two bottles clink onto the counter. I look over my left shoulder toward the sound, and Jack, wrapping each hand around a bottle's neck, says, "Red and white. I think I am going to need both of them. The question is which first?"

I tuck a bag of frozen veggies under my arm while pulling a bag of shrimp from the freezer. Holding both toward Jack I ask, "Okay?"

"Sure thing. I'll go with white for the seafood."

I retrieve a box of rice from one of the boxes I packed earlier and get to work. Everything in the kitchen is where I remember, or in its logical place, of course.

Jack stands before me with two glasses of wine. I take one and bring it to my lips, breathing in the fragrance and taking a long, slow sip. It is good wine. My L.A. consortium has taught me to appreciate the differences between the cheap stuff I buy and what my friends and Kyle buy.

I scoop stir-fry onto two plates and move to set them on the table in the kitchen. Though muscle memory tells me to sit in the chair closest to me, my designated seat at the table, I stand back to let him choose, not knowing which place was his. He is motionless, staring at the plates, hands still affixed to his sides. I panic a moment. Does he find it unappetizing? Then I realize his eyes are closed to hold back welling tears.

"Would you mind if we ate in the living room?" he asks, voice strained, pushing the words around an obvious lump.

"Of course not." It isn't the food. It's the memories.

We make our way to the living room, he with the wine glasses and I with the plates, while he composes himself. "She would have never let us eat in the living room."

I smile in remembrance of hating the simple fact. I thought all of my friends got to eat in front of the television, but no, my mother insisted on "family dinner" in the kitchen until I was old enough to escape home for as many hours as possible. "Oh, don't I know that one, Jack!"

He returns my smile. "I bet you do."

I tuck my leg under me on the couch, and set our plates on the coffee table, as Jack sets his wine glass on the floor next to the beige patterned chair. He nestles in, and uses the ottoman for a makeshift table.

When he looks comfortable, I ask my first burning question. I might as well start at the beginning. "So, how did you and my mom meet?"

"At school. I taught at Hillman too. Actually, I teach at Hillman. We met when you were pretty young. Right after you started ninth grade."

A whole decade. How has an entire decade gone by and I don't know this?

"She wasn't interested at first. She said it was complicated. I kept pursuing her because she had one of the kindest souls I'd ever met. I couldn't walk away. Good thing I am tenacious because she was definitely more than a bit stubborn."

He takes a sip of wine, probably to give me time to confess to sharing her character flaw. I flatten my lips into a thin line and smile sweetly, not taking the bait.

"It took me nearly a year to get her to agree to a first date. It was in August, an obscenely hot night, when we finally went to dinner for the first time. We went to Monty's. You know it?"

I nod quickly, wanting him to continue.

"We sat outside until we nearly melted and then laughed like crazy when each of us said we were being polite and had wanted to go inside an hour before. Both of us were too old to do anything but get to the point on what we wanted for the rest of our lives, and that sparked a fierce dialogue. It just so happened our plans coincided quite nicely."

I am all in for the storytelling. "How so?" I ask.

"Well, for one thing, we both wanted to run away to Australia."

My eyes widen as I question the origin of my own escape plan, and J.T.'s reference to the same. Jack is into his story and carries on without noticing my reaction, "But then, she shared why she wasn't going anywhere." Sadness washes over his face. "Nor was I. My mother was also sick."

I hear also sick but don't want to interrupt. Was my mother sick for ten years and kept it hidden?

"We decided our paradise at home would be building an amazing garden where we could read, and hitting as many of the states as possible. We made it to thirty-six. Unfortunately, California was our next stop. We were planning to come next June." He looks away, likely needing a break from the intensity.

I am confounded by the mysteries being revealed with each passing minute and can't decide if I'm delighted or fearful to have Jack uncover the rest of my mother's secrets. Does he know about my childhood too? Can he shed some light on the father I've never known or had every detail I'd never managed to garner from my mother died along with her?

Before Jack can continue, my phone rings in the kitchen. My wine glass is nearly empty so I grab it and head to the kitchen for more. "I'm sorry, I need to grab that." The ring is a tone Kyle had chosen for himself. I picture him laughing as he scrolled through the list of potential options, choosing the one called 'chaos'.

I swipe the phone to answer, pushing it to my ear with my shoulder while I pour. Carrying the bottle back to the living room, I raise my eyebrows, questioning Jack. He lifts his glass to be filled. I mouth, "Be right back," then climb the stairs to my room for privacy as I try to make sense of what I'm hearing on the other end of the line.

It sounds like fireworks exploding in the background, and I wonder where Kyle might be viewing fireworks and why he would call in the middle of them. Clearly not the ideal time for a conversation. I also hear women laughing. Multiple women, more specifically. Bedroom door closed behind me, I lie back on my bed in the dark wishing I was still on the couch, enraptured in what I was learning about my mother. In my answering Kyle's call, guilt had won out. I knew if I didn't talk to Kyle when he called, he might suspect something was up. The tables have turned, however, as now I am the one wondering what the hell is going on. Not saying a word, I just wait until a woman says, "Hello? Hell-ooo?" Slurring, high-pitched words pierce my ear. The voice grows more distant. "Kyle, I think somcone wants you." Laughter. Kyle's muffled voice. "Who doesn't want me?" Boisterous laughter. "Hello?"

"Kyle, it's Peyton. You, or somebody, called me."

"Pey, baby. Where are you?"

"Detroit, Kyle. Where I've been for days. Where are you?"

"I'm on a boat," he sing-songs.

Screw a mermaid, Kyle, not another woman.

"Somewhere. I'm not sure where. Remember Smitty? Remember his yacht? He's got a new one. Even bigger than the one I brought you on. It's motherfucking incredible."

I close my eyes, trying to block out the memory. Now I am keenly aware of what is in the background. My muscles clench. It isn't fireworks, but gunshots, echoing off the water. The last time we had ventured out sailing with Smitty there was plenty of booze, and more cocaine and guns than in any movie I'd seen. Only it wasn't a movie scene, it was real life, and I had feared for my own.

At first it was fun to pretend I was rich and famous, hanging with the A-listers that were also on board, but like they say, "It's all fun and games, until—" Someone blows their head off. Each drink and line transformed testosterone to larger-than-life caricatures of their sober selves. I felt the need to ante up my own personality to conform, not wanting to reveal that I was much more sober than the rest of those in attendance. Kyle had become an entirely different man, his alter ego not a desirable one, with his voice and aggression rising in unison. When I'd watched his fingertips running over small guns, big guns, and guns of all sizes in between, my stomach churned. Some men touched babies or puppies in the wistful manner he had admired the destructive metal. I had wished I could see it as sexy and powerful, but villainous and evil won out.

The others, stoned out of their mind, retreated to the back of the boat, boasting of their shooting ability, and round after round ricocheted into the black night. I escaped to the opposite front corner of the boat, as far from the danger as I could get, even if choosing lonely among many sucked. Thank God I did. One of the vow-you-will-never-say-who, no names mentioned celebrities on board decided to emulate Leonardo's famous Titanic "I'm flying" scene. Drunk off her ass, there was a good probability that if I hadn't dragged her from the metal rail she would have fallen to an untimely demise. The woman had swatted at me and nearly knocked me to the ground in protest—no good deed goes unpunished—and then I had decided if I couldn't beat them I had better join them.

With no way off the boat for hours, I proceeded to lead the consumption of several rounds of toasts culminating in shot after shot of liquor, until the night blurred into sunrise. I could never recall what took place after the third (or maybe fourth or fifth) shot downed. What I will never forget is the bruise that encircled my left wrist, and its counterpart around my right bicep, severe enough to color the purple, green, and yellow spectrum over the next few weeks. While I was sure the shape of both bruises resembled four fingers each, I was unsure how either got there.

I cringe. And not even because of the memory. After a loud thud it grows quiet on the other end of the line. "Kyle, are you okay?" I hear nothing for several seconds, then indiscernible noise.

"Okay, baby, sorry about that. I just shut myself in the bathroom. Wow, this ship is really rocking."

Or maybe you are wasted, Kyle. My inside voice. "Please be careful, Kyle." I wonder what percentage of people grow out of their partying phase. What if it isn't a phase? Where does the line cross from fun to addiction?

"I miss you, Peyton. So much. More than I've ever missed anyone. When are you coming back again?"

He declares he misses me but doesn't remember when I will be home? "Thursday."

Pounding pulses through the phone line such that I am forced to pull it away from my ear. Muffled screams follow. I'm done with this conversation.

"Oh yeah, okay. I'll see you Thursday then, Pey. I gotta go as these animals are going to rip the door to the john down if I don't get out of here. I love you. I mean it. I love you."

"Yeah, you too." I know it's a lackluster response, but he probably can't hear or comprehend anyway.

I hurry back downstairs, freezing in place on the bottom step. Peering across the room to where Jack is kneeling on the living room floor, pictures and paraphernalia that tell my life story scattered around him. My hand lands across my heart as my breath catches. I had no idea my mother had saved all of this. I'd felt so disconnected from her, and though she would ask repeatedly for information on my friends and activities, all the rage and blame I placed upon her had prevented me from giving her the satisfaction.

Sensing my reaction, Jack stands, motioning me toward the items on the floor with his left arm. "Holy shit." I look at him incredulously. "What is all of this?" I kneel, and he kneels beside me. I pick up a yellow third-place ribbon from fifth grade field day. *Sack Race* is scrawled across the back in black marker. Smooth satin slides between my fingers and the matching smoothness of my cheek as I wipe away a tear that falls. A little piece of rectangular, worn cardboard indicates my first swimming lesson at the age of five proclaimed me a guppy. Playbills from each high school production predicted my future, and every report card from kindergarten to senior year was neatly piled and bound with a rubber band. I pick up the cap I wore for graduation, peacock blue with a white tassel. The strands slide over the top of my hand, tickling my skin. I'd been so bitter that some kids had a crowd there to celebrate, or at least their mother and father, when I only had one single solitary person. One picture of the two of us from that day is near the cap. We are both stiff and straight, uncomfortable, with too much space between us. Jack looks at my hand as I reach to pick it up, then into my eyes.

"You were beautiful that day."

My eyebrows rise. "How do you know?"

"I took the picture. I wasn't a helpful stranger," he chuckles, releasing some of the tension, "I was there for all of it. Your plays," he says picking up one of the folded papers with Annie scrawled across the front. "Never missed one. And your graduation? I wouldn't have missed it for the world. You have no idea how much I had to hear about how proud Caroline was of you."

"But—" I can't finish the sentence, unsure of what can possibly come from my lips to make sense of this. Out of the corner of my eye, to the right, I notice several tubes of rolled-up cardboard. I lean over and pull one from the pile, rolling the rubber band from the middle down the length of it and unrolling the scroll to reveal the *Scream 4* movie poster. I open the next, and the next, until the curling-edged rectangles cover the floor. Every movie I'd been in, even if only half of my head was visible on the big screen, is accounted for.

"I've got one more thing for you," Jack says scrambling to his feet. He heads toward the stairs. I hear his footsteps stop overhead at the top of the stairs, knowing he's entering their bedroom. He might need a minute. I lift a stack of pictures tied with a ribbon and untie the bow. It is arranged from the beginning. Me as a newborn in a small tub in the kitchen. Me on a tiny two-wheeler. A picture of me pointing to the gap where a bottom tooth had been. I flip this one. On the back in her writing is *My first tooth lost* and the date. All my first are here. My first dance. My first car. Friends throughout my life. Pictures I don't remember being taken and didn't know existed. I lose track of time but realize Jack has been gone quite a while.

"Jack?" I call out but remain captivated by what lies before me. Hearing no reply, I ascend the stairs and round the corner to see Jack sitting on the bed. He clutches a pillow to his chest, tears streaming silently down his face. I sit beside him.

"It still smells like her."

I thank God he has had the chance to return home before her

smell has vanished.

"I'm so sorry, Peyton."

Why is he apologizing to me? I am the one who has been awful to my mother. "You don't owe me any apology, Jack."

"Yes, I do, Peyton. We should have told you that she was sick."

We. My mother had been part of a 'we' and I never knew.

"What she had was called bronchiectasis."

"What is that? How did she get it?"

"A lung disease. And bad luck. They don't know what caused it. Half the people who get it, they just don't know why. She was taking antibiotics, and everything seemed to be under control. I can't believe she's gone. I miss her so much."

"Me too, Jack." I know his missing her one-ups mine. It's different to lose someone you have every day. My handful of days from the last few years isn't the same. But we've both lost the chance to have more days. "Why didn't you tell me?"

"She insisted. She wanted you to follow your dream. She didn't want to be a burden. She was fiercely independent. We were both in denial about how sick she was. Pick your day, pick your excuse. I've spent a year convincing myself she was right, but she wasn't. If it's any consolation, it doesn't make it any easier having known, because I didn't get to say goodbye either, and I've spent an awful lot of the last year scared and sad."

Dark shadows dot the legs of the gray pants that he is wearing, remnants of the fresh tears sliding down his cheeks. I reach for the tissue box on my mother's nightstand. He blows his nose then takes a deep breath. "It was weird. She didn't seem that sick. We even thought maybe it was fall allergies aggravating her condition, because we'd had a late stretch of Indian Summer. We went to bed one night, and I reached over and could tell she had a fever because she was burning up. She couldn't breathe, but that was nothing new, so we waited it out for the day. Her coughing got worse through the night. I didn't like the lack of color in her face in the morning. She refused to let me call the doctor, so I literally carried her to the car and took her to the ER. By the time they had her in a bed and were admitting her for pneumonia it was too late. They filled her with antibiotics, but I watched her go from vibrant to—" He couldn't continue to push out the words through the tears. Dead. The word escaping his lips would make it permanent. He doesn't finish the sentence. "It was so fast. I should have called you right away. You might have made it. I was so hopeful I wasn't even thinking about saying goodbye. I didn't call you and I didn't say goodbye. They said her lungs were just too damaged from years of disease. I just didn't know. I'm trying not to be pissed at her too! Lot of good that would do me, huh? But if she had taken it more seriously, she might be here, and I am mad at her for leaving me way too early. Can you forgive me for not calling you in time?"

I look toward him reassuringly. "I think I am the one who needs to be asking for forgiveness. I left her long before she left me, Jack."

He turns toward me with understanding eyes. "We'll get through this together?"

It's a question, not a fact, but I feel a great sense of peace in his offer. I fear being alone in the world more than I fear the risk of letting Jack in. "I'd like nothing better."

Relief washes over Jack, visible in the way his face softens, the deep crease between his eyes smoothing. The wrinkles that had formed from smiles through the years became more prominent as his lips turned up at the corners. His eyes surveyed the room longingly, and then he breathed into the pillow he was still clutching. I knew that he was stealing every last memory, trying to feel her presence in her smell and her things.

We stood up and he instinctively reached to smooth the comforter until no evidence of our presence remained. "I should go," he barely whispers into the air.

It felt a little crazy but seemed the right thing to do as I offered, "Do you want to stay here tonight?"

His eyes meet mine. "Are you sure?"

"Yes, Jack, you are more than welcome."

By his look of gratitude, I am sure I have made the right decision. It is about time.

NOVEMBER 12
CHAPTER 8 | Peyton

I wake to the smell of coffee. Coffee I haven't had to make. It's a nice benefit to having Jack in the house. I grab my one and only sweatshirt from my suitcase and pull on my leggings. The bed is freshly made across the hall.

"Good morning, Jack! It sure is great waking up to this smell!" I say cheerily while reaching for a mug and filling it to the top. Jack's stare is piercing and I look up to meet it. One eyebrow is cocked in my direction. He looks ready to proceed with caution.

"You're a morning person?"

I take a large gulp from the cup and let the hot liquid scorch my tongue and throat. I could be. Maybe someday.

In my hesitation, he answers for me, shaking his head and chuckling, "You are your mother's daughter, Peyton Jennings. Right down to the denial part. It's okay, I am used to it. The only difference being that your mother just used coffee as a vehicle for cream, and you seem to have nearly finished that cup without a thing in it."

I am glad that he called me out, and that I share another trait of my mother's. He loved my mother, flaws and all, so maybe he can let my transgressions slide too.

"I'll be heading out shortly, but I want you to know I have enjoyed our time together. I have plans tonight, and you leave tomorrow, yes?

"Yes."

"Can I drive you to the airport?"

"That would be great, but I need to leave at seven o'clock. In the morning."

"Okay, no problem, Peyton. Good thing I am a morning person. Could you do me a favor today?"

"Sure, Jack. What is it?"

"Two things actually. Will you think about coming back for Thanksgiving? It will be awfully hard without Caroline, and I have a family I'd love you to meet. And…" He hesitates, looking nervous. "This is your house now, Peyton. I'll get with a lawyer about the paperwork. I understand if you want to sell it for the money. But in the meantime, would it be okay if I stayed here a few nights a week?"

Two questions. That's all he asked. But they are loaded questions for me. A family I've never had? Could his kids become the siblings I've always wanted? And, I have a house? That I can sell and finally stop just getting by and having to take money from Kyle to keep up the expensive California lifestyle?

He has only asked me to think about it, thankfully, so I answer, "Sure, Jack."

Thinking is not something I am particularly fond of, but Jack has raised a tsunami of thoughts. Should I sell this house for the money? Would I be selling Jack's home? How does Jack know it is my house? Is there a will I don't know about? Could there be an inheritance? Not so practical questions rage a war as well. Why did my mother keep Jack hidden from me? Does my family know something I don't and that is why he had avoided being caught at the funeral home?

I need yoga. It will give me an hour to evade being swallowed alive and drowned.

"Hey, Peyton!" Lynn calls out as soon as I walk through the door. I almost feel like a regular.

"Hi, Peyton!" Another cheery voice I don't recognize. I turn in the direction of the sound to find Liz on approach.

"Oh my gosh, Liz, it's so great to see you," I gush, closing the distance between us. "I'm so glad that I get to thank you for yoga in person. It's been a lifesaver!"

"It always is. I am so glad that you took me up on the offer. I've been thinking about you. You survived the funeral?"

"I did. It was tough, of course, but I'm leaving tomorrow, and I am sad about going back to L.A.—not something I expected. I am going to miss this place." I look around wistfully. We start to head down the hallway to class together.

"I'm glad you like yoga. I've been practicing for thirteen years and it's still hard for me to keep away the crazy. I've almost quit a few times because of these damn quotes." She laughs, pointing up to the wall.

"That's good to know. I was a little overwhelmed by the quotes, the people, and the poses, but my first class was with Alexandra and she convinced me I was good to go because all I had to do was breathe."

"Some days I am not even sure that I have the breathing part down, but I do love Alexandra. She makes me think I can conquer the world," she says, laughing again. "I need to buy her coffee or wine or something and soak in her wisdom. I wonder how she got so smart."

"No kidding. I hope when I grow up I can be just like her." It's my turn to laugh, recalling, "Once, a woman said to me 'one day after never'. That's pretty much what I think about my chances. But hey…" I stop at the Gandhi quote that reads "The future depends on what we do in the present". "I believe our next line was that a girl can dream." We laugh together.

On my mat, I contemplate the fact that though I have more questions than answers, I'll be leaving Detroit with new friends in Liz and Jack, and the dream of falling in love. My present is pretty damn good.

Returning from yoga I head immediately to the shower. Wrapping my wet waves into a towel, I flip back my head and proceed to cover myself with a second towel around my body, tucking the top over itself to hold it in place. Rounding the corner to my bedroom, I stop dead in my tracks, paralyzed by the vision before me. The bed is made for the first time since I've been sleeping in it. Neatly spread across the duvet cover is a quilt. A handmade, work-in-progress, quilt. I wait for my breath to catch as I feel the now-familiar formation of tears. A piece of paper lies upon the colored patchwork. Picking it up with trembling fingers, I read the message.

Peyton –

Meant to give this to you last night. Sorry for the sidetrack. Your mother loved working on this for you. I know the story for every shirt, just in case you can't recall. Hope you like it. Maybe you can finish it?

J –

I pick up the soft fabric in both hands, mesmerized by the purple and green chevron-patterned background, solid purple border, and the story of my life in t-shirts across the top. The first I see is a patch of yellow displaying a sheep. It's from a summer farm camp I attended at nine. The second is an even smaller shirt, probably size four! It says "Lake Michigan. No Salt! No Sharks!" with a white heart over the outlined state. I don't remember the trip, but it must have been significant for my mother to have saved this for twenty years. Those two are the only ones affixed to the quilt backing, but I pick up the perfectly sized patchwork of squares Jack has laid out that my mother hasn't lived long enough to attach. One by one, I live the memories that surface with each high school play shirt, the royal blue, pink and orange soccer team swatches of cotton, and my first Michigan State shirt. Worn more times than I could count, the green is a faded resemblance to the real MSU green of the original shirt color.

Peering into the rectangular wicker bin that held the supplies to complete the task my mother had begun, a patch of yellow and black catches my eye. I clear away what I assume is extra fabric. Quilting for Dummies stares up at me. Clutching the blanket tightly to my chest, realizing I am more sentimental than I once thought, I determine this is now my most prized possession.

Seven painstakingly long hours later, with only a few minutes for breaks, my fingers are sore and eyes crossing in the waning sunlight. Compelled to finish just one more square before packing my things, I drape my nearly finished project back over the bed where it laid incomplete earlier. My heart and soul did some pretty fine work with the help of You Tube and the Dummies book. My last connection to my mother and my childhood is splayed before my eyes. I climb under the cover, feeling a sense of peace and accomplishment I have not in a very long time.

NOVEMBER 13
CHAPTER 9 | Peyton

I settle into seat 24C to return to California on Thursday morning, my angst rising on par with the altitude. I might need the little puke bag. I am one thousand, nine hundred seventy-five miles from my California chaos. Days ago, I thought my lifestyle was glamorous. Minus the big break I still had faith would come, I thought I was living the dream. I hang with the rich and famous at the coolest bars, ride in fast cars and yachts and shop on Rodeo Drive. My life is the stuff rock songs sing of and tabloid magazine covers sell. What more could a girl from Detroit raised by a single mother really want?

Jack had been right on time this morning, as promised, and even brought me a coffee. He'd sent me off with a long, comfortable hug and an invitation to return at Thanksgiving, even offering to buy my plane ticket.

He sent me on my way with the hope that I could realize a dream I consider more elusive than Hollywood success. The chance to have a real family.

Fueled by the rage of my mother denying me the family experience, I birthed the dream to prove I didn't need her or anyone else. And for all intents and purposes, my L.A. friends serve the role, albeit we are a dysfunctional family. Jenna has held my hair on more than one occasion while puking before I rally. I'm good at that. Hayden is always good for retail therapy when I don't get a callback. Meredith can change any bleak situation into laughter with a ridiculous joke or one of her crazy good impersonations. And they all offer plenty of "motherly" advice such as wear the red shoes with that outfit and yes, your butt does look fat in that dress.

And in fourteen days J.T. returns home.

Damn you, Detroit, for turning my life upside down.

When the plane lands and my phone blinks back to life, I re-read the text Kyle sent just before I was getting out of bed. "Text me when you land." It felt bossy and demeaning, the hair on my neck bristling at his lack of emotion, excitement to have me home, reminder that he would pick me up, or any other word, phrase, or emoji that would have indicated he gives a shit about me. Maybe he had forgotten his offer to pick me up. He might not even crawl out of bed, like a vampire, until the sun is setting.

But, because I am back in California, and I do what Kyle tells me to do, I return his text. "Landed."

Surprisingly, my phone buzzes immediately. A single smile emoji? What does that mean? The passengers next to me are standing so I return the phone to my purse and file out behind them.

Stepping forward toward my rapidly approaching bag, I grab for the handle. "I got it." I know the voice. The bag smoothly lifts off the conveyor as I step left and it's placed at my feet as arms encircle my waist. Kyle pulls me close to his muscled warmth, lips pressed into my hair against my ear. "I missed you, baby." His hand reaches around my back, grabbing a handful of my ass. His lips crash into mine, a hard, wanting kiss. This is reentry.

I use my purse strap sliding down my shoulder as an excuse to break up the public display of affection, reaching down to heave it back up. From behind his back, Kyle produces a dozen long-stemmed white roses tipped with pink. Whoa, not what I was expecting! Isn't this exactly what I thought I wanted? Someone to meet me at the airport, to kiss me, with flowers? Once again, in a moment I have everything I thought I wanted, why am I not elated?

Kyle's eyes canvass my body from head to toe. "You look good, baby."

I can't return the compliment. He has dark circles and sunken cheeks. "Did you eat while I was gone?" My question should have been filled with more concern than annoyance, but I don't hide it well.

His eyes look right, avoiding mine. "Well, it's definitely better when you are looking out for me."

Even remembering to eat is hard when you spend all your time drunk or high. And sleep goes by the wayside when life is one long day-and-night party. He leans into my neck and bites me. I tuck my chin, pushing his face out of the way.

"Let's go," he says grabbing my suitcase in one hand and my hand in his other. "I parked illegally."

He leads me outside to a day much warmer than the one I left behind only five hours ago. It feels like a lifetime.

Kyle pulls into a lucky parking spot right in front of my building, opening the trunk to grab my suitcase. I am pulling my purse from the backseat when my door opens as well. Of course, he chooses chivalry now. He closes the door behind me as I look for my key in my purse.

"The girls are here; you don't need a key."

How does he know this? I press the elevator button and the doors slide closed. Kyle's body is instantly close, both hands on my breasts as he forces me against the wall. "Ow!" I exclaim as the motion catches me off guard and the metal rail around the middle of the elevator sides digs into the small of my back. His hands slide under my butt and he lifts me until my weight is resting on the metal railing and my arms are around his neck, holding myself up. I can't concentrate on kissing him back. The position is uncomfortable. And I know this is foreplay.

Saved by the bell. A chime indicates we have reached the third floor. The doors open, revealing an awaiting pair of women, Jenna and Hayden. "Pey!" Hayden squeals throwing her arms around me before I have even fully crossed into the hallway. "Don't hog her, Hayden!" Jenna leans in and gives her signature kiss to each cheek while holding my forearms. She pulls back to look at me but continues to hold on. "How was it? Are you okay?"

Not exactly okay. My lips form, "It was fine. I'm fine. Thanks." I can't exactly discuss J.T. or Jack for obvious reasons, and what else can I say? Luckily, I don't have to say anything else because Hayden and Jenna assume the places in the elevator we have just vacated. Hayden holds the button to keep the doors open. "We will see you later. We have plans tonight so rest up!"

"Thanks for hitting the road, girls."

"Like you gave us a choice, Kyle," Jenna jokingly scoffs. "But thanks for buying! Have fun, Pey—" Apparently, I am not the only one Kyle bankrolls to get what he wants.

We make our way down the hall to our apartment, and I step through the door then head to my bedroom to put my things away. Kyle follows with the luggage. My eyes dart to my bed where a black box is tied with a white ribbon bow. I know the box. Doors, roses, and lingerie. I know what this means.

Setting my suitcase in the corner, Kyle comes up behind me, and I can feel his hot breath on my neck. I close my eyes and brace myself. He reaches around my front, sliding both hands down my stomach inside my leggings until his middle fingers press firmly on my clit. Pulling his body more tightly into mine, I can already feel his desire mounting against my backside. I don't want this right now. Can I get away with claiming jet lag from Detroit to California?

He growls into my ear, voice raspy and desire-filled, "How about you open that present over there and show me just how much you missed me." Forcefully, he grabs my hand, limp alongside my right thigh and presses it hard into the bulge of his jeans. "Aren't you a lucky girl to have all this," he points to the box on the bed with his free hand then presses my hand into his erection again, "waiting for you?"

Lucky girl is not exactly what I am thinking.

I know acquiescing is the only possible outcome that won't end in disaster, so I comply and move toward the unopened gift. Untying the ribbon, I slowly lift the lid of the box and push back the red tissue paper. Not surprising, inside is black leather, skimpy and skanky. It's a harness of sorts, with a strappy ouvert and more straps around the waist and thighs connected front and back with a metal o-shape ring. This needs an instruction manual. Wrist cuffs are connected via leather strips to a neck cuff that looks to tie with a lace up in the front, perfect for choking. The leather bralette is studded, which will require concentration not to hurt another person who might be sliding skin upon skin. What if he wants me to hurt him for something he has done?

I turn to face him, noticing how dark his eyes are, large black pupils dominating the blue that had captivated me at one point. "How about I call you when I am ready to model for you?" A second later, he is gone.

Happy he took my bait, I take a moment to breathe. I need a little space to ease back into who and where I was when I found out I had lost my mother. Before I met seemingly kind and tender J.T., and before Jack entered my life.

Kyle's eager voice is impatient outside the door, "Does it fit? Come on, you're killing me! I picked it out myself."

"Ready," I call out and hear the doorknob turn. "As I'll ever be," I say in a hushed voice knowing in moments his tongue and teeth will be tearing me apart. Mind, body, and soul.

NOVEMBER 20
CHAPTER 10 | Peyton

One week post-Detroit visit and I've settled back into life as I knew it. Kyle starts filming a new television pilot tomorrow and I have thankfully gotten three extra shifts, one lunch and two dinner, at Conundrum. It's now the flavor-of-the-week restaurant because of star sightings post iCloud nude scandal, and Kim Kardashian's visit during her crazy internet-breaking antics.

I spent my three nights off at Kyle's house, no closer to cutting our ties than upon touchdown, but was happier sleeping in my own bed the three nights I worked. He seems like he would get along fine without me in his life. When I work he goes clubbing, and with me, he goes clubbing. Except on Monday night, when we'd gone together to a party with his new cast members. We'd stayed out way too late and I'd drank way too much. I didn't work until dinner, so we'd made our way into the sunlight—after three Advil—just after two o'clock.

Nothing seems to change day after day. Late nights and afternoon wakeups. I wonder if Kyle could ever be happy watching a movie or T.V. at home, and maybe even cook? Tonight, however, he'd have an 11:00 p.m. curfew for tomorrow's taping, and I'll probably get carry out with one, or all, of my roommates. I hope that no one wants to go out, but most likely, at somewhere around 11:00 p.m., I'll be strapping on my stereotypical too-high heels to go with my too-short skirt.

As expected, Jenna, Hayden, and Meredith are raring to go after our fine-dining experience. Fine dining in our house equals two split salads among four women, nothing but grilled chicken and low-carb veggies on top of the greens, and very little dressing, not surprisingly, ordered on the side.

Assuming party-girl primping position, we are two by two in each of our two bathrooms. All a similar shape and size, we share a revolving closet, minus the shoes. The girls' shoe sizes range from Meredith, at a mere size six, to Hayden, who clocks in at a size nine. Luckily, Jenna's and my feet are a perfect match, though she is tall and slender, with strawberry blond hair that she hates. She spends a small fortune, by others' standards, to blonde it up and hide the red every five weeks to the day.

I lean into the mirror, applying pink blush up my cheekbone with a makeup sponge. Black eyeliner swoops up to make my eyes more cat-like than they appear. I start the application process for fake eyelashes that are all the rage. Since everyone is doing it, I can't be perceived to have plain old normal lashes, but I would be happy to skip them.

Jenna returns to the bathroom with a shoe dangling from each index finger. "Which do you want tonight? I'm giving you first dibs. Your tits look great in that top, BTW."

"Why, thank you," I say and finish painting my lips red, smack them in the mirror, then lean back to check my outfit against the options she's offering. My lace skirt has three tiers, one cream, then black, then cream again. It curves tightly over my hips and butt, grazing the very top of my thigh. The tight-fitting black silk tank drapes over my breasts just so, and I found the perfect jewelry to match. A fake black and cream-colored intermingled pearl necklace and bracelet will appear demure and a tease to the slutty outfit. It will keep them wondering.

"Evening transformations complete, ladies? Come on! We've got a night to kill and I've got the lemon drops lined up! Let's goooo!" Meredith yells up from below.

Evening transformation. It's what I do here. Game face.

Uniform. I never wore either in Detroit. Which me am I?

"You can have the stilettos," I answer. "I'll take the wedges."

She tosses one shoe in my direction. "Good! That's what I wanted anyway. I'll grab you number two. Be right back." She leans her head back into the bathroom again. "Hey, where are your lashes? You look naked!"

"Skipping them tonight. Trying more of the real me."

She laughs. "Okay, whatever floats your boat. But why?"

She disappears, and I am grateful I don't have to answer her question.

An hour later, just after eleven, four decked-out women, five foot two and three-quarters to five foot six and one-half, more like undressed than dressed to the nines, breeze past a bouncer whose eyes stay affixed to each ass with a little nod of approval.

"Put your tongue back in your mouth!" Meredith says in a flirting tone, fake eyelashes batting as she looks back over her shoulder and wags her index finger back and forth scoldingly.

The music is nineties-themed tonight, if you can call it that since they jack it all up with the electronic stuff mixed in. It's before my time, 1990 birth and all, but I know most of the music from Kyle since he is nine years older and calls it the music he grew up with. One could argue that hasn't happened yet, but tonight, that is the last thing on my mind. What is, however, is getting a drink paid for by someone else.

Six minutes later, as I stand pretending to be waiting to order my own drink, anti-aggressively, my first suitor lingers at my elbow. Appearing to casually sip his drink, which is too full to be ordering another, he finally gets up the nerve to ask, "Hey there, you need a drink? I was just about to order. What can I get you?"

"Oh, thanks so much. That would be great. I'll have a vodka soda please."

"House vodka or something a little better?"

"House is fine."

He cringes and his demeanor changes. He'd been leaning toward me in a flirtatious way and now he eases himself away. Did I just get dissed because I saved him money not ordering overpriced Tito's? It isn't as if I don't appreciate the finer things, I just like the taste of the cheap stuff better. Since when did a man not appreciate low maintenance? I think of meeting Liz at Starbucks and our shared laugh over the audacious drink order. It makes me smile. Maybe I am not a true California girl after all. And maybe I should get my ass back to yoga.

Four drinks and two band sets later, the four of us have found four males who, for now, are willing to dance without sweaty-grinding and explorative hands. It's no small feat. Drinks come with expectations.

I need water and a break from the crowded dance floor. With a bob and weave through the swaying crowd, I am lucky enough to find an open bar stool to rest my aching feet. It sucks women can't look sexy dancing in anything besides high heels because they hurt like a bitch. I reach into my clutch to check my phone and am pleasantly surprised to find a text from J.T.:

hello from Lilongwe Malawi!!! selfishly hoping the complications are less complicated ☺

eight thousand miles hasn't stopped me from thinking about you...hoping to c u again

My heart skips a beat, while my stomach clenches. All THOSE feelings come tumbling back. I felt so alive when we met! The underlying energy that connected us when we touched! The lightness laughing again and again at dinner. How much I wanted him to kiss me on the porch. At the airport. The magnetic pull that drew me to him.

He is still texting me—from Africa, nonetheless. And I've done nothing with my complication. Kyle has been trying. He picked me up at the airport and made efforts this week to wine and dine me. And, if I am honest with myself, would I have any chance with J.T. if he knew what my life was really like? I'd sort of left out the part about ostracizing my mother for years. What would he think of me for doing that? He is flying around the world serving the poor, for heaven's sake! I am—more often than not—a scantily clad, drunken waitress with no dowry to bring to a relationship. I don't even have a family to offer him to join. The odds are not in my favor.

Except for the one sentence I've been clinging on to for hope. He fixes the broken.

I want to reply, but shame and fear hold me back. And, of course, there is my complication. Now that he knows I have a boyfriend I wouldn't want him to think I'd ever text another man behind his back.

I wander around until finding my friends in a high-backed, white leather, circular booth with multiple men nearly in their laps. I slide into the edge of the booth, next to a man I hear making promises of pleasure to Hayden. My eyes roll of their own accord.

Hayden leans forward, interrupting the conversation with said stranger. "Pey, I really have to go to the bathroom. Will you go with?" Universal bar language to say, "Get me the hell out of here". We both stand immediately, and I reach for Hayden's hand as she steps around the man and doesn't look back. Hayden mouths, "Thank you."

I lean against the sink inspecting my newly applied lips, waiting for Hayden. When she emerges from the stall she sways her way to the sink, gripping the edge of the counter for support. She turns to me, "Thanks for the rescue." Alcohol, or potentially worse, has induced a four-second version of the word rescue as it stretches in a slur.

"No problem," I return.

Hayden smacks the faucet as the automatic sensor isn't seeing her hands waving erratically to the right of where they need to be. I put my hands under the faucet until the water comes on, then move to get paper towel for both of us. "I'm sooooo glad you are back, Peyton."

"I'm glad to be back." Am I? Or is that one of those little white lies to myself?

"If you were gone any longer, I am not sure what would have happened to Kyle. Oh. My. God."

Oh shit. She has my attention now. "What are you talking about, Hayden?"

"He was like, an animal. He partied so hard we thought he might have been dead in your bed one night. We put a mirror to his face!" She laughs, pointing unsteadily to the big mirror above the sinks, then leans forward, opens her mouth to an "o" shape and exhales onto the glass, leaving the mark of her breath. Grabbing the sink again, she leans her head back laughing boisterously. Kyle had stayed in my bed? Without me? "OMG, he was seriously nutso without you, Pey. I think you keep him grounded."

She pushes her index finger into my chest. "Actually, Peyton Jennings, you should probably keep him the other kinda grounded. He is a bad boy."

No doubt, whatever follows this statement is something I don't want to hear. I suck in a breath and hold it.

Hayden is set on breaking my heart. "Do you know what that boy did?"

Clearly, a rhetorical question. Rip off the Band-Aid. "I'm thinking I don't," I say seriously. "Spill it, Hayden."

"Remember Kate?"

I don't need to hear more. Damn it. I'd been hanging onto hope that Kyle was different. His prior girlfriend cheated on him consistently, and when he spoke about it veins bulged, his jaw clenched, and his face turned beet red. His ferocity when speaking about her scared me. How could he do this? And while I was at my mother's funeral?

I pivot on the heel of my shoe, leave the bathroom, and beeline for the bar, pushing my way to the front. "I'll take a lemon drop and a vodka soda. Make it a double." I set the credit card for Kyle's account on the bar and turn to my left where a group of four women is waiting to order. "Put whatever they are having on my tab." To the women, I say, "Go big or go home, ladies. This one is on a cheating bastard." I say it loudly, drawing the attention of another group of women just approaching the bar. One yells out, "Hell, put ours on there too!"

"You got it! Bartender, you heard the woman!" The bartender grins broadly. "Hell hath no fury like a woman scorned. I like your style." He has no idea his tip is going to make him luckier than had he bagged the hottest blonde in this place.

The chivalrous actions—the door opening, the flowers, the lingerie—were all guilt-induced bullshit. How could I have been so stupid? All women are suckers when it comes to those acts, believing that is how men in love act. We all want the fairy tale and happily ever after.

Seventeen women order some variety of shot, and when they are lined up on the bar, I take a picture. Each woman grabs her shot, and I lift mine high. "To making complications a little less complicated!" A split second of curiosity crosses several faces before the high-pitched clink of glasses cuts through the booming bass and heads tilt back in unison. Unfamiliar voices echo thanks and good luck while several give me hugs and tell me they are sorry. I pull my phone from my purse again and text J.T. before the alcohol kicks in.

Handled. looking forward to seeing u soon…the sooner the better ☺

I feel a hand on my arm and whirl around to see Meredith, Hayden, and Jenna facing me, each with a varying look of concern. Meredith would have been pissed at the deep wrinkle in her forehead. "We didn't know where you went. We were worried about you." Apparently not worried enough to tell me sooner that my boyfriend has lived up to my deepest, darkest fears. Oh no, wait, he hasn't killed anybody with the guns on the boat or gotten his ass tossed in jail. That I know about anyway.

"I'm fine, just enjoying a toast with a few new friends." Hayden's right eyebrow shoots up quizzically. I am deeply satisfied they hadn't been present for the toast. I would have had to explain its meaning. I put my hands up and shake my hips, singing out the lyrics to the song playing. "I know what I want! Blah, blah, blah, blah, I'm Mr. Vain." If only they knew. I know what I want right now. To be free of my very own vain bastard who calls himself my boyfriend. "Let's dance, shall we?" I can't believe no one has yet to cast me in a leading role. Clearly, I am an Oscar-fucking-worthy actress.

NOVEMBER 22
CHAPTER 11 | Peyton

Two days have passed and not a word has been said among the women to substantiate Hayden's admission in the bar bathroom. It's doubtful she remembers bringing it up, drinking all night on nine whole bites of lettuce and chicken. None of them filling me in is disturbing. I want to make excuses. Maybe only Hayden knows? No way. If one knows, they all know. Perhaps they think they are protecting me from dealing with another loss on the heels of my mother's death. Still, how can I call them 'real' friends if they are letting me walk around like everything is just fine when they know damn well it's not?

Kyle has tried to contact me eighty-one times in the past two days. Twenty-two phone calls and fifty-nine texts. The little red numbers just keep rising. While I was working fourteen-hour days on Friday and Saturday it was easy to avoid him. I figured he'd show up Sunday morning, which is precisely why I have left the house at 7:30 a.m. for what I plan to be a very long run. I've made arrangements with my friend Lydia, who works at a gym around the corner, to let me sneak in a shower. I'll leave my laptop and clothes at the gym as well, so I can head to the coffee shop after and spend some time looking up Lilongwe, Malawi, to converse intelligently with J.T. when he returns. My roommates can deal with Kyle. They deserve the opportunity.

At 8:42 a.m. Empire State of Mind is interrupted by the incoming sound of a text. Jenna already:

please come get your boyfriend out of our house...woke us up at 8 and says not leaving til u talk.

I called it correctly. Sorry about your luck, ladies. You should have told me. My run continues with a full-fledged smile despite my legs and lungs yelling at me to stop. What he must have thought when he saw that text in the morning!

I enjoyed the revenge just a little bit. Revitalized, knowing I am making them all squirm there together, I tack on an extra mile before finally walking the last half-mile to the gym. When I step inside, I have a better idea than hitting the coffee shop right away. Why didn't I think of it earlier? I head to the yoga studio six blocks south, and buy the largest package I can, using Kyle's credit card.

Just after 12:00, I am wrung out. Physically, exercise endorphins have me void of emotional turmoil. More importantly, the yoga teacher said I could leave anything I wanted on my mat and start anew. I've got this. I text my people to get a status update on Kyle's whereabouts:

is he stttiillll there???

Jenna wins the reply contest:

Yep – moping around and won't leave – WTF?

Hayden's text immediately follows:

rescue us!!!!!! where the hell r u?

Time to handle my complication for good. I turn up the last block and mentally prepare to end my relationship with Kyle, and grab the chance to start anew. J.T. Walker, I hope you are up for this broken to fix.

I softly close the door behind me and lean against it, setting my purse and gym bag down on the floor beside me. I take a deep breath. Laughter floats over the loft balcony. One male and two females. Obviously, he isn't too torn up. Kyle is always a charmer, but I feel betrayed. They have taken his side.

I muster courage and step toward the balcony. Six eyes peer over. "Peyton." Kyle's voice is a breathy whisper. His eyes are red and puffy. Crying over me? Whatever he might be using to cope?

He takes the stairs down quickly. I back myself against the door. He puts both hands up like he is about to be arrested as he continues toward me. "Okay, I get it. You have to listen to me."

My stomach churns at the sight of him. An image of Kate's face fills my vision.

"Peyton, I told you I love you. I mean it. I've never said that to a woman before," he pauses for a moment, "and meant it. I had a bad night. I ran into someone I wish I wouldn't have."

Ran into her. With your penis. "She was in a bad place. She'd just lost her job. She was upset."

I can't help but react. "Are you fucking kidding me? She lost her job?" My voice was incredulous. "I lost my mother, Kyle! Not a job, my mo-ther." I emphasize the word, just in case the difference between job and mother was lost on the dumbass.

"It didn't matter, Peyton. It meant nothing."

He admits it that easily.

I keep myself composed, voice smooth and collected, "Well, it matters to me, Kyle. It damn well matters a whole hell of a lot. And it does mean something. It means that I am no longer your girlfriend." I turn my back to him and pull the door open, a clear indication it's time for him to leave. "And Kyle, make me feel a little better and admit the toast and the picture were well played, would you? It's the least you can do."

A muscle in his jaw jumps and his hands clench into fists at his sides. Through gritted teeth, he spits words in my direction. "I'll leave now, but this isn't over. This is far from over."

I say nothing else, close the door behind him, glower up at Jenna and Hayden watching from the loft, then head to my bedroom to let the tears come.

NOVEMBER 27
CHAPTER 12 | Peyton

I wake in my now-familiar-feeling childhood bed with the buzz of an incoming text. The sun is bright in the sky, so I guess it's not early, except to my body, still on Pacific Standard Time of three hours earlier. My phone sounds with another incoming text before I even open my eyes fully. I need five more minutes. What could be urgent this early on Thanksgiving? Now my brain jolts awake, like waking from a bad dream, when you aren't sure what is real.

Have I really agreed to spend today with Jack and his children? Since I had accepted Jack's offer I've been flirting with insanity. I've never done the family scene, and might as well have flown across the pond to the orient and not been told of any of the customs! I can only pray that Jack's easy-going nature has permeated his children as well and they had no issue with my mother. I'd been to yoga Sunday through Wednesday this week, and planned to go to class at Exhale this morning. Yoga has been very helpful for taking each of my crazy thoughts one at a time.

On the plane, I have formulated a Plan B as well. Just in case. It is to drink both the red and white bottles of wine I've been assigned to bring, lose my inhibitions, and not remember what I screw up. Then, I get back on a plane to California, never to be seen again. A girl has to have options.

I reach for the phone. I'm elated to see a text from J.T.:

second text on American soil – first was to mom! Happy Thanksgiving!

grateful to have met u…what r u up to this weekend?

A smile plasters itself from my left ear to my right. I read the other, from Jack:

Welcome back, Peyton! Happy Thanksgiving! Grateful you are here to join us today. Come over whenever you want. I know you like to cook, and this family, well, not so much. We could use your expertise! My kids know how important it is to me to have you here today. They look forward to meeting you.

Did two men just say they are grateful for me? I find myself equal parts surprised and grateful. I reply to Jack first while attempting to think of a witty retort for J.T.:

I am grateful for the invite, Jack! Going to yoga, grabbing wine, then will be there!

Careful to duplicate his style replying, I find his full sentences with punctuation endearing.

I open the text from J.T. again and type, then erase, and type again, laughing at myself for stressing over the perfect reply. I end up using real sentences to a man half Jack's age:

Thank you for the text and making me smile even if it's awfully early! I'm grateful you made it home! Did you have a good trip? Can't wait to hear! See any giraffes? Change the world? Fix the broken? Sure you did…

I follow it with not one, but three smile emojis. It's a lot of punctuation and a lot of questions. I want details. I want to know him. My phone is still in my hand when it rings. Casually, I answer, "Hey there," though the little stomach lurch says otherwise.

"Hey to you too! I'm sorry I texted too early. I don't even know what time zone my body is in. I do know I couldn't wait another second to hear your voice." He laughs.

My body flips around all over inside. He called. He apologized so easily. And he complimented me so genuinely. "You peppered me with questions but didn't answer the one I asked you. I thought it might be easier to call. But first, how has your couple of weeks been?"

I am not sure if this is a loaded question or if he is being courteous. In case it is the former, I won't make him beg for information. "To be honest, it was a little, um, roller coaster-ish."

"The kind where you get off and puke or the kind where you are scared to death but get off and can't wait to ride it again?"

It is my turn to laugh. I think about how to answer his question. The last few weeks had been filled with ups and downs, from the romance on my return to ruminating over what I should have done differently to avoid Kyle cheating on me. And now, talking to J.T. The high again. The hope and potential it holds. The persistent, deep-seated fear that he'd never get past my past.

"A little bit of both actually. But the good news is, the complication is handled," I answer. If he only knew Kyle was the one who ended it by cheating. Nobody wants someone's reject.

"Want to tell me more?"

"How about in person?" Defer and deflect. Easier than honesty.

"Now that sounds like a plan. A very good plan. What are you up to this weekend?"

"I'm in Detroit actually. I have plans today with—" I hesitate awkwardly. "Family." I can't very well tell him about my mother's secret lover. My life sounds like a freakin' tabloid. "That's it for the weekend." Then I throw in, "Nothing else." I hope he takes the hint.

"When you say nothing, do you mean nothing, or like a few commitments but nothing really worthy of mentioning?"

I laugh again. "I mean not a thing on the calendar or otherwise."

"Okay, I am just going to take a chance then. Since the complication is handled, would you like to come to Chicago?"

He has asked me if I would like to do something. I cringe thinking how Kyle always told me what I would do.

I push my lips into a thin line, trying to refrain from a smile he would be able to hear through the phone line. "Um, I've never been there, and I hear there are some great places to visit, so that sounds very tempting."

"You've never been? That's great. I'd love to show you around. And no pressure, my two roommates are not here this weekend so that leaves a couple of empty beds."

"You want me to sleep in one of your roommates' bed?"

"Well, not exactly. But I want you to know you have the option of sleeping alone in mine, so I'm sure the sheets are clean. I would sleep in the roommate's bed. Of course, with any luck, you'll exercise a different option. That, of course, would be the option to have me join you."

"In your roommate's bed?"

His amazing laugh makes me smile then break into a laugh myself.

"Well, he'll be none the wiser. We don't have to tell him."

"Clandestine. I like it. Count me in." I might be nuts, but I've taken chances that put me in worse positions.

"Okay, I will. Tomorrow then? What time can you be here?"

I'm going to need yoga for this. There is an 8:00 a.m. class. "I can be on the road around 10:00 and I get an hour so say be there around 1:00 p.m.?

"Okay then, sounds like a plan. A great plan. Anything in particular you do or don't do?"

My stomach lurches again, not in excitement this time. So many ways I could answer that, none of the answers good. Drugs? Illicit sex? Abusive relationships? With regard to what, J.T.?

"Nope, not fussy. Sports, dancing, movies, hanging out, food. Pretty much like it all."

"Well, since you're so fussy, it'll be tough, but I am sure I can come up with something for us to do!"

His sarcasm is clear, and I laugh again but feel an undercurrent of fear. I should have been fussier in so many ways.

"I'll text you our address. So, about those questions. Good trip? Yes. Very. I will fill you in in person. Giraffes? Yes. They are beautiful. Change the world? Fix the broken? I just hope to leave things a little better than I found them. They change and fix me more than I do them. Each and every time."

"Wow, that's great. I can't wait to hear more."

"And I can't wait to hear about your roller coaster. But I have to go. One more plane ride in my planes, trains, and automobiles. Then a train and a car and I'll be home sweet home. Twenty-eight-ish hours and counting. I'll be looking forward to tomorrow. I'll try to get a nap in today."

One more boisterous laugh tugs at my heartstrings, sucking me in. I am so screwed.

"Safe travels, J.T."

"Happy Thanksgiving, Peyton."

"You too. Bye." Holy shit, I am going to Chicago!

Several hours later, I am shakily climbing painted wood stairs to the beautiful covered porch of Jack's house. The house is old, just a little more modern than Victorian-looking, though I haven't paid enough attention in school to be sure which era. Detailed railings featuring multiple colors and the painted wooden slats under my feet scream pain in the ass to paint. As I wait for someone to answer the door, I picture my mother sitting with Jack on the turquoise-cushioned wicker seat for two next to the door. I imagine her head resting on his shoulder, enjoying a summer evening with a book. My throat constricts. Maybe this house holds more good memories than the one we shared. Her last ones of an angry teenager probably top those of a younger, sweeter me. I sigh and pull in a long deep breath. The cold is startling, and for a moment I miss California where it is probably, like most days, warm and sunny.

Moments later, footsteps and the voice of a little person growing nearer precede the old wooden door creaking in complaint as it opens. A woman who looks to be just a few years older than me leans into the doorway. "Hi, there! You must be Peyton. Come on in!" Before I barely step through the door, she is overwhelming me with kindness. "It's so nice to meet you. We're so glad that you could make it today." She leans in for a hug. Already? "I'm Dani."

"Thanks for having me," I answer so quietly I'm not even sure I used my outside voice.

Jack's voice booms from another room, "Come on in, Peyton. I'd come to greet you but I'm literally elbow-deep in turkey."

Dani now dons an accessory in the form of a little boy, who appears to be about two, peeking around from behind her legs. "Follow me." I follow two paces behind until I arrive face to face with Jack, whose arm fills the turkey's cavity in the sink. Quick math says the turkey not even in the oven means I'm here for a duration. I should have brought more wine.

Two other men peer over Jack's shoulders, backseat-cooking. "Got it!" Jack proudly exclaims, drawing his hand from the bird and tossing the contents into the other side of the sink. "Come on in, Peyton. Everyone, meet Peyton. Peyton, this is my son Griffin," he nods his head toward the man on his right, "And this is my son-in-law Evan." He finishes washing his hands and dries them on the towel tucked into the waistband of his khaki pants. "You met Danielle." He bends down and scoops up the little boy still attached to Danielle's leg. "And this is my main man, Tuck." He picks up his little hand and coerces a fake wave from the boy.

I had no idea that babies were in play for today, and not since I last babysat at sixteen have I spent any time around a toddler. I can practically hear Jack's voice inside my head warning that any less than stellar interaction with this family's center of the universe can and will be used against me in the Mannington family court of law. No pressure.

There are so many great reasons to be an actress. "He's sooo adorable," I coo, dragging out the word very purposefully for the right amount of emphasis. "How old is he?" I feel a little guilty feigning interest but do I have a choice?

"Twenty-two months. Two in January. Can't believe it! It goes by so quickly."

"So I've heard." I set the wine carrier on the counter out of the way, and Danielle's head turns toward the sound. "Dad, can we open one now?"

Jack looks in my direction. "Danielle has a very important role in cooking holiday dinners." Evan snickers. She grabs a small stuffed duck of Tuck's from the counter and hurls it in his direction. He shifts right, and it misses him by several feet. He laughs a full laugh.

"Hey now! Be nice! I have a very important supervisory role in this kitchen."

Griffin weighs in, "Oh, now you are creating fake jobs for yourself? Supervisory? Is that even a word? Is that an advisory supervisor?"

"Yes, I supervise all of you childish men while I advise on the status of the meal. And I have all the power, because I am in charge of the most coveted asset." She pulls a corkscrew from a drawer and outstretches it as a fake weapon. Stabbing the cork with a "Ha!", she fakes the opening requiring more power than it does. "There!" she exclaims after the pop. She holds the prize mid-air, pseudo-toasting toward the men. "I'm grateful for the opportunity to play such an important role in our holiday celebrations."

I have to chuckle, appreciating her flair for the dramatic. "She pours a sip then slurps loudly. "Really, I'm just grateful for the wine," she quips sarcastically, nose wrinkling. We all laugh, and I enjoy the feeling that this is what it's like to be a member of a family.

The memories of youth flood back. Memories I avoid. Not here. Not now. I can't let fear steal this chance at happiness. What do these people already know about me? Are they being kind because they feel sorry for me because of the past? Or because I'm an orphan? I don't want to be a pity guest.

"Where's the bathroom?" gushes out over the deafening pounding of my heart.

Evan points toward the back of the house, "Just around that corner."

"Thanks," I push through, the sound choked, and head in that direction. With the door safely closed behind me, I sit on the toilet with my head in my hands. Get it together! What had Alexandra said in yoga today about the challenges of the holidays? There is always something to be grateful for. Sometimes you just have to look a little deeper than other times. I close my eyes against the images that won't cease. I push my palms into my eyelids until lights dance where vivid hell is waiting. "I am grateful I get to see J.T. tomorrow. I am grateful."

I force my eyes open, take three more breaths, flush the toilet in case they are listening, and wash my hands. "I am grateful to be here," I say into the mirror. Wine time.

When I return, Jack invites me to jump into the cooking fray and we make easy conversation as I work alongside the three men. We chop, dice, and stir the usual Thanksgiving meal accouterments as delicious smells waft through the house.

Jack places seven spices on the counter in a line and proceeds to open each one. He catches me watching and gives a wink, then nods toward me, indicating I should come closer. I lean in and he whispers into my ear, "Your mother's stuffing secrets. She probably didn't get the chance to teach you her recipe, but I am happy to." He smiles broadly and tears well, matching my own. We blink in unison to hold them back and I return his smile. I walk to my purse and grab my phone to snap a picture of the line-up. As he sprinkles, pinches and spoons each one, I take notes.

Skillfully, all the dishes are ready at the same time, and Danielle and I have set a beautiful table. When we are seated, Jack raises his glass. It is apropos that he sits at the head of the table, while Griffin and I sit together on one side, and Evan and Danielle on the other. Tucker has the other end of the table. I imagine what it would have been like to have my mother here too. We could have made years of good memories to replace my first decade of horrendous holiday ones. Why had my mother denied me? What if it was Jack who had instead? I take a gulp of wine to suppress rising emotion, without regard to the pre-toast faux pas. I should make this my last glass. At least this hour.

Jack is struggling to hold it together. He is blinking back tears and his Adam's apple bobs as he repeatedly swallows. Noticing my pre-toast swig, with a quivering voice, he says, "I think we all need a drink before the drink." He puts his glass to his lips. The others do the same, though the depth of emotion isn't registering on their faces as much as it is on mine and Jack's. He blows out a breath. "Phew, this is harder than I was expecting." Pulling in another long breath, he clears his throat. "No words can express my gratitude to all of you for being here. I'd like to think of this as a toast to new beginnings and new memories, making up for lost time, and making the most of the time that we have together." He pushes his glass forward as we all lean into the center of the table. Our glasses pressing against one another leave that beautiful ringing sound in the air. There is a long moment of silence as we each take a drink.

Griffin finally breaks the tension. "Is it a requirement of growing old, to become a sap? If that's the case, it's yet another reason I'm not looking forward to the inevitable. That, along with the wrinkly ass part."

"Inappropriate." Danielle swats at him across the table, pretending to hit him upside the head. We all laugh and resume the casual conversation that had been taking place in the kitchen, vacillating compliments and criticisms, sarcasm and humor among siblings and parent. I've only ever been on the sidelines of this experience. This feels different, as they make me feel one of them. At twenty-nine and twenty-six, it seems in an instant I've picked up non-biological siblings in Danielle and Griffin. Who would have thought?

"Speaking of ass..." Griffin has a shit-eating grin on his face. He looks directly at Jack. "I'm just glad to know you were getting some. That's another one of those old things I don't want to have to face. You had me worried."

Danielle glares at him across the table, then promptly loads her fork with mashed potatoes and lets it rip straight in Griffin's direction. He turns his head and tries to duck right but they splat onto his temple. Evan turns to Danielle. "Nice shot, honey!" Then he puts his hand up to high-five her.

Danielle turns to the baby, who also has a handful of mashed potatoes. "Do as I say not as I do, Tucker Jack!" The baby happily stuffs his fist into his mouth. He isn't giving up his potatoes over childish nonsense.

I want to laugh but the thought of my mother and Jack together leaves me nauseous. I set my fork down on the plate. "Nice job, Griffin," Danielle says with a serious tone. "Now you've upset Peyton."

Griffin turns toward me, putting his hand on my arm. "I'm sorry. That really wasn't appropriate to say."

"It's fine, really. It was just the thought of—" I close my eyes and shake my head vigorously to remove the vision. I am smiling the whole time, however. Everyone relaxes.

Danielle speaks again, "In all seriousness, Dad, I'm glad you weren't lonely. I was always so worried about you! You should have told us you had a girlfriend even if we couldn't meet her, Dad!"

"I told you a million times not to worry about me. Did you think I was lying?" Jack responds.

"That's what all parents say! You aren't supposed to believe them! You are always supposed to worry about your parents!"

I'm reeling at the fact that Jack's kids didn't know about my mother either. I should have worried more about my mother, but I also thought kids should be able to trust their parents, and I wonder what Jack and my mother were hiding. What else don't I know?

Jack's tone is somewhat scolding when he replies to Danielle's proclamation, "Parents are wired to protect. They do, or don't, tell their children certain things for very good reasons. The best reason being we believe we know what's best, no matter how old you might get."

She is not fazed by his tone, probably quite the daddy's girl. "Well, thanks for proving my point, Dad. You just told me you are only going to tell me what you think I want to hear." She rolls her eyes and huffs, "You're infuriating!"

Griffin makes a face in mockery, serious, with eyebrows creasing, as he yells sternly, "You want the truth?" We all laugh knowing the famous movie line that follows. His comic relief lightens the mood.

Danielle lifts her white napkin and waves it in fake surrender, "Okay, fine, you win. You keep saying what you want and I'll keep worrying, end of story. We both win... if you call my being awake in the middle of the night, stressed about my father, a win."

"Sorry, babe, you're up anyway with the non-sleeper over there," Evan says, thumb pointing toward Tuck at the end of the table. "I got your back on that one, Jack. If you are going to be awake, you might as well be productive."

Danielle sticks her tongue out. "Thanks a lot, honey." Then she turns to me. "I'm glad I finally have another woman here who understands me!" I am not so sure that's true, based on how she has just enlightened me of the fact that parents lie and you are always supposed to worry about them, but I am glad to be the other woman anyway.

After dessert, when everyone is catching up on their phones, lounging over couches with bulging bellies, Jack makes his way to the kitchen. I follow. Looking at the stack of dessert plates on the counter and the running dishwasher, I carry them to the sink and start washing. Jack comes up beside me with a towel.

I've had a burning question since dinner. "Jack, I have a question for you."

He doesn't flinch. In fact, he looks as if he expects this. "Sure, Peyton."

"Obviously, my mother left out a lot of little details," I emphasize the word little sarcastically, "about her life. At dinner, you said parents don't tell their children certain things for good reasons. What was my mother's reason for not telling me about you?"

He hesitates none in his reply, as if this is an easy question to answer, "Love." He stops drying and stands facing me. "Everything parents do is because of love. I can't claim to understand all of Caroline's reasons, Peyton, and I am not saying I agreed either, but suffice it to say that she thought she was doing the right thing by you. You were always her first priority, and she just wanted to protect you."

My voice is small. "I didn't know that I was supposed to worry. Maybe if I had worried more then—"

"I know how that sentence ends, Peyton. I've said that same line in my own head a million times. It's no one's fault."

"But what if it is my fault? What if the stress I caused made her sick?"

"Pretty sure that teenagers aren't known to have caused much more than gray hair. Forgive yourself. You didn't have it easy growing up and Caroline did the best she could, but you were just a normal teenager finding your way."

Jack only knows a minute amount with regard to my transgressions. Those involving my mother don't equate to all my guilt and shame. I don't deserve his compassion. I could tell the truth and it could set me free. It could also set me free of my new-found pseudo-siblings I have enjoyed getting to know today and this man who is the closest thing I've had to a father figure. They might reject me, forever.

Returning home, I reflect on the day. Tuck's little babbles and attempts at putting sentences together like "me want" have me envious. If only it was so simple! Make sentences of the words you really needed to say and skip the stuff in between that gets you in trouble. I liked the jokes, even the inside ones I didn't understand, the easy camaraderie of Danielle and Griffin, and seeing that Evan has been welcomed into the family mix. I've enjoyed the day, and still have tomorrow! I don't have to look for things to be grateful for tonight.

I am waking up and going to Chicago! To see J.T.! I get nervous thinking about it. Am I crazy to have accepted his invitation?

I'm interrupted by the buzz of my phone on the nightstand. My stomach flip-flops. J.T? Not so lucky. A knot ties, instead. The text is from Kyle:

I had nothing to be grateful for today. Only plenty to be sorry for. I will make this up to you.

This is the last thing I need before bed and Chicago. Which part of this is hard for him to understand? There is no second chance. He has made his choice and I have made mine.

I don't reply, turn my phone to do not disturb, and fall asleep happy.

NOVEMBER 28
CHAPTER 13 | J.T.

I wake up confused as to where I am. I roll over and it's like a Mack truck has taken me down. Thirty-two hours of travel with only a couple of short naps will do that to a person. It resembles a hangover, though I haven't had one of those in a very long time. Thank God. Damn! Thank God is right. I am home in the USA, and with any luck, I won't wake up alone tomorrow.

Grabbing my phone, I catch a glimpse out the window. I'm awake now! Two days ago, I was in eighty plus degrees. Now there must be at least four inches of snow and a sky full of big white flakes coming down hard. This isn't part of my plan. It is romantic and all, but damn, what good is romance if she can't get here? No way Peyton is driving here in this.

I hop out of bed and grab my laptop off the desk across the room. I climb back into bed. It's cold!

Plan B is successful. I text Peyton:

pls let me know when u get this! if you look outside before you check your email then check your email! Don't panic – we got this!

I lie back against the pillows and wait. Not for long.

wow – who knew this was coming? #livingunderarock

I quickly reply:

email???

The minutes tick by as I assume she is checking. The screen lights up again.

Who knew trains still run in the snow?!?! u really do think of everything...don't forget the clean sheets

I breathe out a sigh of relief.

does that work? can you make it?

An immediate response:

Not if u don't stop texting me!!!! ☺☺☺ T-6...hours! will text from the train

Nice. She is good on the fly. No whining, no drama, she just rolled with it. Rare as the yellow M&M. The train station is only eight miles from her house, and I figure she can make that in the snow. I have gotten lucky. Hopefully not for the last time today.

As she'd said she would, Peyton texted when she made the train:

train virgin – this rocks!!! I'll have to thank you properly...later

I appreciate her witty and flirtatious comeback and the hint at what might come later. Hopefully, me.

My head hasn't been in this game for a long while. Disappearing to remote places on the globe for weeks at a time on a regular basis isn't something a lot of women want in a relationship. If they knew what my work entailed, they would realize I'm never off having flings. I'm usually finding spots for those sick from food to puke or use a bathroom, talking someone off the ledge about a random bug bite they think might be their death, or philosophizing on why someone was born in the privileged nation of the U.S. while those around us are suffering.

I won't sacrifice helping others for a relationship with a woman who doesn't understand why my work means so much to me, not that I share the reason often. It's far more challenging to a relationship than my work.

I didn't want to pursue Peyton, but when I met her, something was different. She is different. The connection that has been there since the first time I looked into her blue eyes, with situational dark circles. Her eyes seemed to pierce me, seeing deep inside. It was unexpected and eerie, yet somehow comforting.

Our date went too quickly, then stirred up emotional turmoil when she had dissed me at the end of the night. Thankfully, she explained herself. I'd thought about her during the trip more than I care to admit. Imagining her blond waves sliding through my fingers, the taste of her kiss, and soft skin. I might have to admit this one could change the game—and throw me off mine.

No. I can't let any woman have that power. I have honed focus and discipline over the last decade. If I could conquer what I have, a woman won't get the best of me.

I make my bed as always, then clean the apartment bathrooms and kitchen, and proceed to tackle my trip report. It's hard to admit, but I am jazzed up on nervous energy.

The number of times I look at my phone between our last communication and parking at the train station is painstaking. Country on the radio as I pull to a stop, lyrics about a love that breezes in, the torrid love affair that follows, and the ending everyone expects. What the hell am I doing?

Letting myself get carried away isn't my modus operandi and bringing a stranger to overnight here definitely constitutes carried away. It's a little late to change plans now so I switch to focus on gratitude, which is part of my program. The snow has been logistically challenging getting Peyton to Chicago, but since everyone acts like every snow storm is snowmageddon, I can be grateful for easy parking outside the train station.

Finally, after a long twenty-two minutes, I think I can see the approaching train. My phone agrees.

Here!!!

I can't help the corners of my mouth rising into a silly stupid grin.

I see u ☺ well ur train anyway ☺

She doesn't respond, assumingly gathering her things and making her way off the train. To me. I scan the crowd on the platform and see her before she sees me. I take her in from head to toe. The way her blond hair cascades over her shoulders, curls floating as she walks, takes my breath away.

She looks appropriately dressed despite being a California girl, with a long North Face puffy coat and ankle-high boots that will withstand the snow. I am pleased my plans will still fly, as they will take some walking.

Her pretty pink lips call to me. Literally. I see them form, "Hi, J.T." but I'm lost in wanting to feel them against mine and can't hear her words. Her smile takes over her entire face including her eyes, which glimmer the deepest shade of blue. It's beautiful, and I almost blush with the compliment of knowing it's for me.

The little race of my heart is because I picked up the pace to close the space between us, right? Stomach twist and turn is probably hunger? Must be. My palms aren't sweaty. Yet.

Not to worry about the palms; they are on the back of her coat as I embrace Peyton, lifting the weight of her body against mine, while her feet leave the ground. I feel the warmth of her in my arms, against my body, her hair tickling my hands as she throws her head back. My lips press her temple and I breathe in floral and feminine.

"Hey you," floats into my ear, lips brushing against it. I feel alive with a shiver down my spine. I feel a little weak in the knees and set her down but wanting to keep her as close as possible slide my palms up to cup her face. I hadn't intended to come at her quite so quickly or intensely, but I'm finally getting that first kiss. Right now.

I immediately feel guilty I've succumbed to desire so easily and soften my lips against hers, pulling back just a little. She leans in, equally passionate against my mouth, and I pull her tight and kiss her hard. Her lips are soft, smooth, and warm. Our breath is hot against the cold air, as one. I close my fingers around silky strands of hair. My hands cock her head slightly left, parting her lips so that my tongue has space to find hers. Her breath draws in before softly moaning on the exhale. This might be heaven.

Her hands move behind my head, fingers gripping my hair, pulling me closer as our lips part gently then more firmly, again and again. Her fingers slide down the sides of my neck, and I feel the light pressure of her fingertips everywhere. It is one of my favorite places to be touched, and she's found it in less than a minute. I groan instinctively into her mouth then push my tongue gently against hers. Her tongue runs along my bottom lip, then she bites it gently, and I know there is no turning back.

I feel her lips curve upward into a smile against mine. "You know we are in a public place, right?" My lips curl upward to match but I don't stop kissing her, tongue dancing against hers, in slow circles, and long strokes, perfectly intertwined. Nipping her bottom lip just a bit, she lets out a little squeal. I open my eyes but hers are still closed. If anyone is looking at us, I hope they don't glance below my belt.

I pull back, moving my hands to her hips. Her eyelids look unwilling to open. I don't want the moment to end either. "It is official. Not all first kisses are created equal. Damn, Jennings, where'd you learn to kiss like that?" If the answer is too much practice, I hope she doesn't come clean.

As if reading my mind, her eyes pop open. "I didn't know that I could, actually. And, um, well, I guess I wanted to make up for before."

I smile. "That was worth waiting for. It more than made up for it. Apparently, I should have raised my expectations for our first kiss."

She looks almost embarrassed by the compliment and tucks her chin, smiling. I put my index finger under her chin and lift her face until our eyes lock. I have that off-kilter feeling once again that she knows me like she shouldn't. I lean forward and place a soft kiss on her forehead.

I lean to pick up her bag, my eyes remaining locked in our gaze. The fingers of my left hand find hers and slide right into place.

Out of the cold, I need to make sure she is okay with what I've scheduled for us. "I have a plan for today, but promise me you will tell me if this doesn't work for you, okay?" Logistics in Chicago aren't easy. "I arranged to park at our friend's condo. Since he's out of town his garage spot is free. You can change or freshen up there if you like. Then, we will walk a couple of blocks to a bowling alley where a few friends are having an annual tourney for whoever happens to be in town. Then, we will walk several more blocks," I look at her to gauge any hesitancy but see none. I offer anyway, "Or we can cab if you want. To the train station. We'll take the train to the hockey game if that's cool?" I pause for her reaction.

"Okay, so, bowling then hockey game," she says looking down at her leggings and boots. "Okay, I'm good to go." Then she turns serious. "Wait. Actually, I don't think that plan is going to work out. There is one little detail. Well, more like kind of a major detail."

My eyes widen, fearful my calculated plan is about to be compromised. I should have asked if she liked hockey and bowling. What the hell had I been thinking? I guess I was hoping she'd just be happy because I planned something. But only if she likes the something! "What is it? You don't like hockey? I'm sorry, I just assumed, stupidly I might add," might as well throw myself under the bus, "everyone from Detroit loves hockey."

"I do, J.T. I do love hockey. But in fact, I might be violating my fan code of agreement attending a Blackhawks game as a Wings fan. I took the oath, and there are severe penalties and repercussions. I'm sorry, but do you think maybe we could do something else? I hear there is a great theater district here somewhere."

I look over, squinting her expression into focus. She looks serious as a heart attack, solid game face on, but I know she is playing me. Might as well have some fun with it. I match her sincerity. "Okay then, maybe I can scalp the tickets, though it's really too bad. Zach's family has had them for over twenty years. They are really, really good seats. I hear *Little Shop of Horrors* is in town. We can go see that instead."

She bites her lip, clearly trying not to laugh. "Hmm, maybe I could make an exception just this once? I think I'd rather eat liver for a week than subject myself to that particular musical."

"Or, maybe you could make an exception because the Red Wings are playing the Blackhawks?"

Now her surprised expression is spectacular. And beautiful. She turns her whole body towards me. "Get out! Really?"

I try to remain solemn. "I'm surprised the fan code of agreement wouldn't include a game schedule." I laugh out loud.

"Oh, yeah, about that. I made it up."

"Really? I wouldn't have guessed. Too bad though, I was kind of thinking I found the perfect woman if she'd trade hockey for a musical."

Her eyes widen as she blinks, summing up any reality I may have intended in that statement. Not many men would describe that as the perfect woman.

"Well, I'd really be fine with either, but since you already have the hockey tickets, how about we save the musical for next time?" Well played, Peyton Jennings. She wants me to know she likes both. I smile to myself, rethinking the perfect woman definition.

"Oh, and J.T.?"

I look toward her, indicating she has my attention.

"Can we see anything but *Little Shop of Horrors*?"

I laugh and nod. We've just made future plans.

As soon as I shift into park and turn the key in the ignition, Peyton turns to me. "That's my signal. That was a really long eleven blocks. I was counting to distract myself."

"From?" I ask quizzically.

"Thinking about how long it was going to be until kiss numero dos. I'm looking for a Union Station repeat," she replies sheepishly.

She has nothing to worry about because I am more than willing. I lean into her sweet smell and warmth and find her mouth. I grip the back of her head, lips tangling passionately, each movement intense, as we take each other in more fully.

When my tongue makes contact with hers, she moans into my mouth and the vibration against my lips causes the familiar stirring of arousal. I've never experienced a kiss this powerful. I'm not sure I like the loss of control. But self-control be damned, my hand, under duress from my brain, has somehow found her thigh. It's dark and private here, and my fingers can explore what they could not earlier. They curl into her flesh, massaging, then moving under her butt and up toward her hip. This wanting is going to make for a long day. In the best way, but still.

I'm managing to tame my hands, but holy hell if hers aren't misbehaving! I feel the pressure of her hand moving up the inside of my thigh. It doesn't come to rest until she is cupping me through my jeans. She squeezes and everything inside me clenches. Her hand finds its way under my shirt and her fingertips graze bare skin. Her touch is the perfect combination of tenderness and firm pressure. I want more.

Sweaters and coats are hindering this opportunity.

She starts to laugh, our lips still intertwined. "Are you as frustrated as I am?" She puts a minimal amount of space between us, just enough to speak. And breathe. Neither of us is doing either very easily. Our ragged breaths are coming in matching short bursts.

"How can you tell?" Words fit in between additional kisses.

"I am reading your mind. Way too many clothes."

Nailed it. Which is exactly what I want to do to her. "You got that right. If you thought eleven blocks was bad, how are we going to make it through the next five hours?"

She places both hands flat on my chest, over my clothes, of course.

"By anxiously," she says pushing the collar of my coat out of the way and moving her lips to my neck, delivering gentle kisses, "awaiting," more kisses, "your," chills run down my shoulders, "roommate's," chills down my arms as she tugs on my earlobe with her teeth, "bed."

"Well, I am glad we have that to look forward to. But if you don't stop that right now, I'm not going to be held responsible for what happens next."

"Promise?"

Could this get any better? "Uncle," I say moving my head away from her lips. "Uncle." I dodge left as she moves to keep her lips affixed to my neck, laughing all the while. "Uncle." The word flows, breathlessly, one more time from my lips as they find hers again and suck in her bottom lip slightly while pushing my tongue ever so slightly into the space it creates.

"Ugh, you're driving me—"

She pushes back off my chest and gives me a sexy grin.

"Wicked crazy, J.T. Walker."

She sits up straight and opens her own door, and her feet are on the ground before I can even think about getting around to her side. I am not even sure I can walk at this point, between the uncomfortable stiffness in my jeans and feeling like I've just done a full legs workout. Damn, what this girl does to me!

She doesn't have her bag. "You need to go inside for anything?"

She shrugs and looks down at her outfit. "Nope."

She can't possibly be this low maintenance, can she? I owe her an apology. I'd stereotyped her but she hasn't completely dismissed her roots. She is already making her way toward the elevator.

We walk the snowy blocks until the glowing arrow-shaped sign reading BOWL HERE is above our head. We share one more public-friendly kiss before we will need to rein in the affection.

Stepping out of the cold, we enter into a montage of music videos playing on screens all around us. It's a bowling alley placed in the middle of a night club. I take Peyton's hand and lead her toward a group of people, some standing around talking, some sitting on black leather couches at the end of the lanes. I introduce her to several on our way to the rack of balls stretching the length of the wall. I stop to face her and take inventory. "Everything good?"

She gives a sly smile. "Yep. I'm just getting ready to kick your ass in this good old-fashioned game of ten pin. Can we get a drink first, though?"

I try not to hesitate. Of course this was going to come up. It's the norm. Unless I was with my roommates, who I knew from group, drinking put the social in social life. Just how much of a woman's life is always the question. "Sure, you can, since I'm the designated driver tonight."

I know the look she gives me. I am used to it. "But you don't have to drive until after the hockey game, right? You've got time?"

"Really, I'm good, but let's get a ball then get you a drink." I try for nonchalant but inside say a little prayer this won't be a showstopper.

"Well, forget that! I can't take any chances on your beating me because you are sober, and I am not!"

I'm not used to awesome responses like she delivers. She spins on one heel and starts putting her thumb and two fingers into the myriad of balls to find one that she likes. Crisis averted for a little while longer.

I introduce Peyton to several people, hoping she isn't regretting her decision not to get a drink as she's required to make small talk. She is taking it all in stride, joking she hopes there won't be a name quiz. She hears the story of how the annual bowling bonanza came to be, and even proclaims everyone is "so cool".

We make our way to a lane with another couple, Helen and Dave. I set up the scoring for all of us. She looks to the scoreboard where I've put her name in as P.J. and mine as "The Dude". She laughs and it makes me laugh as well. "That's so not fair. I get a shortcut for pajamas and you get the dude? I want a cool nickname too!"

"Well, as soon as there is a cult movie favorite that involves a woman bowler, I'm happy to give you one."

"Fine then," she says, hoisting the ball and looking back over her shoulder. "Mine should be Asskicker." With that she lets the first ball roll, knocking down eight pins and turning back with a smug grin.

"Not bad, not bad." I nod in her direction as she waits for the next ball. I love her challenging me. Feisty and independent in a good way, I am looking forward to learning more about her. Was she born this way? Or has life shaped Peyton as it has me?

We keep it within three points through the first eight frames, and I'm enjoying both her competitive spirit and watching her ass each time she walks up to throw the ball. Her first ball of the ninth frame knocks down eight pins and leaves just the two on the right side. She is totally going to pick up this spare if I don't act fast.

While she's facing the alley, staring down the two remaining pins with her hands on her hips waiting for the second ball to come out of the chute, I capitalize. Sneaking up behind her, I put my arms through the crook of her elbows and embrace her from behind. As I go in for the kiss against her neck she jumps slightly, then pushes her hip to the right, breaking free and whirling around to face me. Her index finger finds the middle of my chest. "Oh, don't you even! I know exactly what you are trying to do, Mister!"

I retreat, laughing, as she picks up her ball and proceeds to knock down the two pins.

She spins toward me, clapping for herself.

"Grace under pressure, and don't you forget it!" She tosses her hair over her right shoulder and snarls while sipping her soda.

"Oh, so sassy, aren't you, Peyton? Well, I just might have another trick or two up my sleeve." I start to walk forward in the lane but turn back to her. "Don't you be looking at my butt while I am on approach, Jennings!"

"Takes one to know one, huh?"

The smile on my face would have me caught, so I turn away quickly, walk right up to the line, squat down, and wind up through my legs. I release the ball the way children do. We both watch as it rolls right down the middle of the lane. Turning back before the ball makes contact with the pins, I yell out, "I'm calling a strike!" She groans and throws her head back as the pins topple, leaving a hole where they once stood.

Peyton's head leaning back with a frustrated groan is too tempting. I kiss her exposed neck. It isn't too much PDA if it isn't on the lips, is it? I catch her off guard for the second time and her chin involuntarily tucks, shoulders hunching forward. Our lips end up only centimeters apart. It isn't too much PDA if I just kiss her briefly, is it? I can't resist. She can't resist kissing back. It's brief and leaves me wanting more.

"I can't believe you just got a strike with that ridiculous tactic!"

I am still inches from her face. "You are going down, Jennings."

One Day After Never

"Okay," she whispers. "As long as you aren't just talking about bowling." She drags her fingertips down the side of my face, then neck, shoulder and pulls me in again. Kisses me hard. With tongue. Definitely too much PDA. Damn. Maybe I should skip taking her down at bowling and just go down on her instead. There's an idea. Or, we could skip the hockey game and get on to another game of choice.

"Yo, love birds, get a room!" yells a voice from the distance.

"Zip it, Olson. You're just jealous!" I banter back.

"Damn right I am. I mean it. You should get a room. I would!"

They all laugh and Peyton blushes then throws a strike. And then, because her little plan had worked like a charm and I am a sucker who can't stop undressing her in my head, I do not. The game ends in a tie, and I decide to take that as a sign, even if ridiculous, that we are meant to be equal partners in a whole hell of a lot more than bowling.

When it's time to head out for the game, we say our goodbyes and make our way back onto the snowy Chicago street. The accumulation on the ground shimmers like diamonds, and new flakes are coming down in big, fluffy balls. Holding gloved hands, we stroll along the sidewalk toward the train station on the next block, streetlights casting a romantic glow. Few others are braving the weather and it seems we have our own winter white playground. We find two seats on the train and she snuggles up so closely that one additional inch would have constituted sitting in my lap. Not complaining. Her head rests on my chest as my arm drapes over her shoulders. She fits rather nicely in my arms.

I watch Peyton's face as she follows me, eyes growing wider with each step down toward the ice. Stopping at row four, and taking two of the expensive and exclusive seats, has her looking dumbfounded. Pleased to give her this experience, it's even better she hadn't expected it. I don't know her lifestyle expectations and I work for a non-profit.

Two periods in, and like our competitive bowling match, our respective teams are tied at two goals apiece. I am playing my own game called "try to keep my hands off her". I don't miss an opportunity to accidentally brush my skin against hers. Cheesily, I feed her a hot dog while trying not to consider the sexual implication of sliding myself into her mouth. Fail.

The Blackhawks score and I stand up to clap, with Peyton reluctantly following. She doesn't clap but uses one hand to pick at the cuticles of the other. I lean my shoulder into hers, pushing her slightly off balance kiddingly.

She looks up quickly. "Two minutes for roughing. You on me and number nine on that last play." She grabs me hard, below the waist. "Or maybe high sticking." Eyebrows raised, her head tilts to me, "We should have been on the power play."

All this hockey talk of high sticking, roughing, and power play is a lot for a man to take! "Do you want to get out of here?" I try to appear casual. "Should be a little less painful if you aren't here to watch your Wings go down."

Her eyes twinkle mischievously. She leans in closer, lifting onto her toes so we are eye to eye, and whispers, "Don't get me wrong, I'm enjoying the game, but I think I might enjoy something else a little more right now. I thought you'd never ask!" She takes my outstretched hand as I lead her to what comes next.

The first train car was crowded so I lead her to another, then another, until we are only accompanied by an elderly man sleeping. I sit and pull Peyton in next to me. Our lips meet in gentle chaos. A collision of soft flesh and tongue exploring, entwined, biting and releasing, learning the other. I run my hand the length of her inner thigh, teasingly, then over the outside of her thigh, down to her knee then back to her inner thigh again.

My body is on fire, and it isn't from the warmth inside the train, though the steam building on the window declares the temperature rising. It is effortless for my lips to fill the space that hers vacate, connecting and lingering. My fingertips trace her hairline from the crown of her head, behind her ear, then slide behind her neck. The train lurches to a stop and the familiar overhead crackle indicates we have arrived at our stop. In minutes we will be in the car, then arriving at my brownstone.

Once in the car Peyton suggests, "I guess we can pretend that we are still at the game if we listen on the radio?"

"Hit number four. It should be a sports station." We listen in silence, sexual tension mounting with the sensation of her touch against my leg. I try to focus on the game.

When we arrive, I reach behind the seat and grab her bag. I quickly exit the truck and head around the front to open the passenger door. She hops down from the seat and makes her way onto the porch beside me. Once our eyes lock, as if in some mesmerized state, neither of us can look away. I put the key into the lock and push the door open so she can slide past, still holding my intense gaze. I flip on the porch light and then an interior light. "Do you want a tour?"

"How about tomorrow?"

Her voice is lustful. "Do you want to watch the end of the game?" I ask, realizing my voice is equally licentious.

"How about we catch the highlights on ESPN later?"

I set down her bag and reach for the zipper of Peyton's black coat. Holding the collar with my free hand I slide the zipper down slowly until it breaks free. Lifting the coat over her shoulders, I wait while she shrugs her arms from the sleeves. My breath hitches. Whatever she is doing to me is collecting in one spot on my body. Right between the legs. I lay her coat over the couch on our right then unzip my own, tossing it in the direction of hers. Finally. Less clothes and less company.

Peyton's gaze is fierce and piercing, but I want to confirm we are on the same page. "Do you have something else in mind?"

Her eyebrows shoot up and she presses her lips together, an

unspoken answer in itself. "I might," she finally admits, sounding like it has broken free.

The words, the sultry tone of her voice, and the expression she wears give me permission and the confidence to cross another line. I pull her toward me and while our lips crash, my hands find her breasts. They have been screaming at me all day long to touch them. They are large and full, lifted high with the bra she is wearing. I use equal pressure to squeeze them both until she emits a gasp. I feel their fullness harden beneath my touch. The next breath forces the air from her lungs as she exhales strongly through gritted teeth, groaning out, "God, J.T."

Hearing my name in her sexual tone builds arousal and desire. My hands find her hips and I pull hers against mine, unsure if the intense pressure below my waist is our hips colliding or my stifled erection.

My hands move to her neck again where it is a little less dangerous. I kiss her slowly and deliberately, wanting this to build. We should start with a stable foundation, not some crazy passion impossible to sustain. Am I getting poetic? Instead of taking her as fast as possible when she's given the green light?

I pick up her bag and carry it up the stairs with her on my heels, fingers threaded. Once we reach the landing and the closed door of my bedroom, I drop the bag and push her against the door. Intertwining my hands in hers, I lift them above her head. Moans, groans, and animalistic pleas of yearning fill the hallway as our lips move rhythmically together, with only space for our shared breath. I bite her breast through her sweater, and her back arches instinctively, breasts pushing toward my face. Soon enough, I will enjoy taking them in my mouth and having my tongue firmly against the flesh of her nipple.

I set her hands free so mine can move back to her breasts. I cup them, massage and squeeze, and imagine what it will be like to feel them bare.

"For the love of God, J.T., please get rid of these clothes," she implores breathlessly.

Finding the hem of her sweater, I teasingly lift it to find the warm, smooth skin of her stomach. I caress the flesh with kisses, then drag my tongue up the center until I am stopped by her bra. I bite her nipple through lace. Closer. A pleasure-filled sound escapes.

Reaching around her back, unclasping her bra, I move to the front, scooping my fingers under the bottom to lift the cups over her breasts. They push free like I've done them a favor. I finally fill my hands with the full warmth of her. My fingertips graze her nipples and they come to life. I love how responsive she is to my touch. Her body writhes then my hands are separated from her body. The sweater hits the floor. Apparently, she has grown impatient.

Lacy straps of bra are between my fingers, and I slide them slowly down her arms. My hands immediately find the fully revealed flesh of her shoulders. I stroke the smooth curve down to the elbow then move to flatten my palms on the small of her back. Mouth envious of where my hands have explored, I lean down to kiss her left nipple. I take more of her breast in my mouth until it fills. My tongue circles the perimeter of her nipple then pushes against its swollenness. Her hands tangle in my hair until it hurts so good.

Peyton is pressed against the wooden door, probably uncomfortable as hell, so I slide one of my arms under her knees and lift her in one smooth motion into my arms. Her grip around my neck tightens so I can easily reach for the doorknob and carry her into the bedroom. I lay her gently on the bed then pull my shirt over my head. Socks and shoes are off in seconds. I position my body carefully over hers, my left knee on her right side with the other foot planted on the floor. I slide the dog tags I never remove around to my back. Her hands find my bare shoulders and I take in the feeling of feminine fingers with long enough nails traversing my skin. Goosebumps immediately appear under her touch and I remain still letting her trace up and down my spine.

Her hands move to my front and trace my chest and abs then find my shoulders again. Pushing them downward until my head is positioned over her breast, she whispers into the dark, "You left the right one hanging, out there in the hallway."

"Well, we wouldn't want that now, would we?" I resign myself happily into her right breast, exhaling a full breath. Her fingers curl into the skin of my back and I moan into the flesh beneath my lips. My tongue flicks a rock-hard aroused nipple.

Her hands move back to explore my chest, but I straighten my arms, pushing away. My heart is pounding too quickly and loudly inside of it. Not wanting to be exposed, I wonder its cause. Do I have performance anxiety? Is it excitement? Am I nervously anticipating what's to come?

No. None of these sound like intuition into my angst. The movement of her hands again distracts me. They are now below my navel, undoing my button-fly jeans. Nimble fingers are working their way down. I want to relieve the pressure of my erection against my pants. I would be a fool to stop this beautiful woman now. She reaches the last button and I finally take a real breath. It seems I have been holding it while she worked to set me free. Wriggling the jeans over my hips, she gives my throbbing erection the space it's craving. I let loose a guttural sound, growling from deep within. It rings out loudly in the quiet room.

"Feel better?" she whispers, tracing along the sides of my dick.

"So much better," I answer, but I'm not sure it comes out in an outside voice. I don't think she notices.

Peyton's hand points toward my feet, cupping me, massaging gently. Her fingers cradle everything hanging taut below. Each finger, one at a time, bends, curling up my shaft until her fingers surround me. Thumb rubbing back and forth over the tip, she procrastinates in my favorite spot. My breath is coming in ragged, uneven gasps and my voice and mind have escaped. We aren't even naked but the want is powerful! I'm grasping handfuls of hair on either side of her beautiful face. My core constricts and I long to have my whole body skin on skin. I want to be buried deep inside this woman. But not in a way I've felt before.

This is different.

I want to be with her, and in her, connected to a human being in a way I never have. I want to know her. Everything about her. I can't let myself be unraveled. If we do this now, it will be sex, and I no longer want sex. I want to make love.

I place my hands on either side of Peyton's body and straighten my arms, lifting away from her. She wraps her legs around my back in protest and tries to pull me back down on top of her. "Hey," I whisper, nuzzling into her neck, "Lie next to me." I move my body to run the length of the bed and pull her into the nook created by my outstretched arm. Reaching for the blanket I have folded at the bottom of the bed, I pull it up to cover us. I don't want her subjected to the cold. Her head rests on my shoulder and her right breast is pressing against my side. It feels amazing. She just fits.

I owe her an explanation. "I almost ditched the bed for a cold shower." She should know that was not rejection. "I've never wanted anyone so badly, Peyton." I breathe into her hair then lift her chin to brush my lips tenderly over hers. She is motionless and doesn't kiss back, probably waiting for me to add a "but," followed by something she doesn't want to hear. I run my thumb over her full, soft lips until it seems she realizes I meant what I said.

"Well, the feeling was mutual," she finally returns, leaning forward to meet my lips.

Her kiss lingers. I feel her body soften. She'd been tense. "Peyton, I want to know you better before we go there. I want to know about you. Your back story. We haven't talked about anything."

Any minute the man-card police are going to barge in demanding I hand mine over. I just put talking before sex. Where does this come from? First and foremost, if she shares her back story I have to share mine. My roommates, meeting mates, and mom are the few who know my past, and that's the way I like it. If I share, there is a good chance I'll never have the chance to make love to her. I remind myself of my promise to myself. Be authentic even when uncomfortable and surrender the outcome. Why can't I just have sex and keep it light?

"First time for everything, I guess. It's not every day that a guy stops a sure thing to, um, talk."

An unwelcome smirk happens from her sure-thing comment. I'm glad it's dark so she doesn't see it.

She doesn't hide her speculation, voice full of concern, "Was it something I did? Or didn't do?"

"No. No. Nothing like that," I reassure her. "It was all good. Incredible, Peyton. I don't know either. I just—" I really don't know how to finish the sentence. There is no explanation that makes sense to me so how can I explain it to her? "I just want to take this slower, okay?" I sense her hesitation.

"Okay. What do you want to know?"

What now? Ask her to start at the beginning? We spent the day together and kept it at surface conversation, talking to others, watching hockey, or were busy kissing. Anything but this is so much easier. I knew why I hadn't given up any information, but what about her? Is it the same? I decide to risk it and be vulnerable though it's damn scary. I extend the olive branch. "Okay, I'll go first. I was raised by a single mother."

"Oh. Me too," she returns.

Not uncommon, of course. "She is truly the best. Amazing. Beautiful. The best." She offers nothing so I ask, "How was your relationship with your mom?"

"Fine."

I feel her shrug against my arm. No expounding. Awkward silence follows until I break it.

"I don't know my dad. My mom was traveling for work in Paris and had a fling with a Parisian. Want to take a guess what he said his name was?" It isn't a laughing matter, but the tone is serious and I want to lighten it up. She finally finds her voice.

"Jacques?"

"But of course," I say in my best fake French accent.

"Seriously?" she chuckles.

Success. "She didn't know anything about him and didn't know, of course, that she was pregnant until she got back to the U.S."

"Wow."

I assume she will be unsure what to say in response, but instead, she starts to speak.

"Mine is kind of the same story. My mom was married to him but left him when I was a baby. I don't know why. She would never tell me. I found my birth certificate and called every Michael Jennings I could ever find a phone number for. Nine hundred and forty of them. There are over fifteen hundred in the United States. Can you believe it? None claimed me. I've thought about doing the DNA test someday, but wouldn't he have tried to find me if he wanted to know me?"

Her voice rises, emphatic, "And now, I just found out that my mother had a boyfriend for ten years that I never knew about! He just told me the same thing. Some BS about protecting their children and love being the excuse for not telling the whole truth."

Anger drips from the word love. I wonder how she found out about Jack. It is strange to mesh what I am hearing about Caroline Jennings with the woman that I knew as counselor and teacher. Mrs. Jennings had played a huge role in helping me pull my life back from the brink. How can it be that Peyton's mother is one of the only people in the world who knows everything about me, and soon enough, her daughter is going to be one of the only other? Is this coincidence? God's work? Fate? Whatever the answer, it's strange.

I press my lips to her temple and deposit a kiss. "I knew your mom well enough to say that she had a good reason. And I would bet that reason was you. I think parents do a lot of things, maybe right, maybe wrong, but for the right reasons. There isn't a better reason than love to do anything." I hope I don't piss her off. Perhaps this isn't a good time to start sharing what I learned earlier than most. Deflecting is more my style, but this time, like a boomerang, I pull my past to the forefront. Into this bed. Hoping she doesn't want to hightail her ass back to Detroit in the middle of the night.

I want her to know I understand, from experience, what she is telling me. "What my mom did, because she thought it was the right thing to do, was work seventy-hour weeks as an executive. She flew around the world and left me with a nanny. In her mind, she was doing the right thing because we had money and opportunity, and she was teaching me to be independent. Yeah, well, how'd that work out for her? I decided I was independent enough to live on my own at fifteen. She was in Europe, and coincidentally, we were living in L.A. She upgraded the house. I had to change schools. At no worse time. The year I started sophomore year of high school. Being the new kid when everyone had their groups from freshman year sucked. Rather than make friends, I ran away. I thought I would show her."

"Where did you go? What did you do?"

I feel her arm draped across my chest pull a little tighter. I shift, sliding my arm from behind her head. I need more space if I am going to confess my sins on our first day together. I interlace my fingers on top of my chest, protective armor over my heart. I should shut up, but instead, take a deep breath, "I did the usual stuff homeless people do. Found a crowd to hang within a bad area of town. Panhandled during the day. Used the money for things I shouldn't have to fill the hole in my heart and pass the time." My right hand moves to my left arm, rubbing up and down elbow to wrist. It's a reflex that happens in every group meeting I've ever shared my experience, as if it might erase the scars if I just keep it up.

Peyton's hand reaches for mine, stopping the movement. She tightly clasps it in hers. I roll toward her and our bodies face one another. She kisses my jawline tenderly. The sentiment eases the pain. The more I tell the story the less it hurts, but still, facing her potential rejection makes it more difficult this time. She's still here, but I haven't finished the story.

"There was a cop who patrolled our area, every night. One night when I was stoned out of my mind, he arrested me. I was too doped up to fight and he put me in the back of the cop car. When we were about a mile out, he took off the handcuffs and let me sleep in his back seat as he drove around his entire shift. In the morning, he dropped me off at the most affluent Starbucks in the area and I made just enough money to get my next fix before heading back to my dealer, then my crew that congregated under the viaduct.

"A couple of nights later he arrested me again, drove me away again, and undid the handcuffs again. I wouldn't speak to him. I didn't say thank you. I didn't say anything. I was just high, pissed off at the world. The next morning he told me the rowdies would get suspicious if he continued to arrest me. I had told them I was eighteen so they knew I wouldn't get set free with repeated offenses. He told me I'd need to keep myself together and walk to meet him. He promised me a hot meal and the backseat to sleep in. It was warm and it was safe, and I would have been a fool not to take him up on the offer. The nights were long. And scary. That's what we did for many nights. Sometimes I was too high to get there but when I got hungry enough or tired enough, I'd make my way to him and he was always waiting. I still have no idea what made him take pity on me but I wish I did."

"How long did that go on, J.T.?"

"About four months."

"Wasn't your mom looking for you? Didn't she go to the police?"

"Of course. But it's pretty easy to hide and, well," I am so ashamed of this part, "I told Tim, Officer Reilly, that I would just run away again if he turned me in. I think he knew it wasn't just a threat. He said that his wife told him to let it work itself out. He said she was the smartest woman in the world and he always listened to her. Sometimes he would tell me stories about their life. If I say anything that sounds smart, it's probably from Tim. The first time I understood my mother's hell was when I heard her tell her side of the story. She would work a fourteen-hour day and then drive around the streets of L.A. for hours, not sleeping for months." I blow out a long breath.

Peyton removes the space between our bodies completely by swinging her leg up over mine. "Hold me," she whispers into the darkness.

I wrap my arm around her, our bodies connected from head to toe. Her fingers traverse my sternum. This time I accept her closeness. I can't express what it means for her to be accepting me despite what I've revealed. "Thank you," I say sincerely.

"Okay, tell me more. I have to hear what happened, how you got home. Not to make light, but this is like a movie."

"Yes, I've thought about that. Spoiler alert. It gets more dramatic and the ending sucks. One night, when I didn't come to meet him, he came to look for me. An assholes I hung with was really jacked up and recognized Tim as the cop that had arrested me before. He had noticed my pattern of bailing and somehow put two and two together."

I close my eyes knowing it's futile to attempt to push the memory away. I will forever be indebted. Consciously, and in my nightmares.

"I hear Scout, as we called him, for the obvious reason, assessing Tim, circling and taunting with his raspy Freddy Krueger villain voice."

"Well, well, what do we have here? You been helping out our little friend? Let me guess, he's a rich kid from the burbs and his mommy sent you to keep him safe."

"I was frozen with fear. Scout's arm reached behind his back and I let out a bloodcurdling "No!" as he lunged. I can still hear my own scream in my ears and feel the vibration of the sound in my chest. I'd thrown myself forward to protect Tim, but it was too late. Scout had drawn a knife. Even in his compromised state he was too fast for us to stop him.

"The whole group had scattered, leaving me alone with no way to call 911. I'd kneeled beside his bleeding body for hours until another cop drove by and I ran for help."

"What happened, J.T?" She is tapping on my chest impatiently. I had been silent, watching the scene play out in my head.

"He was stabbed. It was my fault. I held him and he told me to go home and clean up my act. He told me to take care of his wife. Her name is Ellie. He told me to forgive myself. To make something of myself. To make a difference." My voice chokes, trying to suppress the suffocating emotion rising. "He said Trouble was my middle name. That's where J.T. came from. He said, "Happy Sixteenth Birthday," and pointed to his pocket. I reached in and pulled out his dog tags from the service. He said he'd brought them for me. His hope was to take me home for good that night. He told me he loved me and sometimes you didn't understand the rules but trust that love would always win out. Tim died in my arms. I was helpless. No phone or way to call anyone and I couldn't leave him. I saw a cop passing hours later and ran to flag him down.

"I was a minor, and it was clear I was too broken up about what happened to have killed him. Scout got away. No one spoke a word about him helping me for four months because my mom and Ellie were afraid they would say he got what he deserved. He was a hero and didn't get honored the way he should have dying in the line of duty. I have no doubt he saved my life. Needless to say, I don't celebrate birthdays anymore."

I tell her almost everything. My burden shouldn't be her burden, and I don't want to wreck special days for her too. I press my lips together tightly and blink hard to keep the tears at bay, thankful for the dark. Peyton snuggles in tightly. She doesn't appear to be going anywhere. I reach for her face to kiss her in gratitude, brush her cheek and feel wetness. Damn it. "I didn't mean to make you cry, Peyton."

"I know. I'm sorry. I just can't imagine."

Her words are shaky through the tears. When she processes this in the morning she may run away, but for now, she's still here. I've never told a woman this much of my past.

"So, did you go home, J.T.? What happened with Ellie after Tim died?"

"Obviously, I was crippled with grief and guilt. I went home and made amends with my mother. Classic prodigal son. I went to rehab for a month, and I am sorry for not telling you sooner, but I don't even drink. I can't. Ever. You were probably wondering about that. I totally understand if it's a deal breaker. I still attend AA and NA group meetings as often as I can. Do you know them?"

"Not really, but I probably should."

"Alcoholics and Narcotics Anonymous bring people together who follow a twelve-step process to staying sober. It's about admitting you are powerless over your vice but becoming powerful over yourself with your higher power's help."

"Do you ever still want to use? Is that why you still go to meetings?"

She is brave to ask. I am glad that I can be truthful with my answer. "Addiction is never cured, but I know I will never use again. I'll be ten years clean soon. It helps to help those who are new to the process. I want to show them that it can turn out okay. It's about offering experience, strength, and hope, and sharing what I've learned about gratitude and giving back."

"Oh wow." Her voice is filled with compassion, thankfully, not pity. "What happened with Ellie?"

"It was harder to make amends with Ellie. I wanted her to hate me. But you know what she said?" I pause. This part of the story is even harder for me to hold it together. I swallow. "She said it wasn't my fault. It was Tim's choice. He died doing what he loved, protecting someone he loved. For some reason, he thought of me as the son he never had though I gave him no reason and I told her so. She said it didn't matter, you didn't always understand. I still don't. I don't think I ever will. She was never mad or bitter, and wanted to stay close to my mom and me. When she moved to Detroit to be near their only daughter, my mom quit her job and we moved there too. She became our family and we celebrate holidays together. It's the strangest thing, yet it all seems normal now.

"It's been a long time, but I still have to work at forgiving myself every day when I look in the mirror. Forgiveness of others is hard. Forgiving yourself is nearly impossible. Forgive and forget? Longer than never."

This part she might like. "This is where your mom comes in. When we moved to Detroit, I met her, and Jack. I don't know where I'd be today if she didn't help me stay on track when I got there. She was my rock, Peyton. And obviously, my profession is the best thing to do to honor Tim and your mom. It's the least I can do."

She doesn't speak, but I feel her stiffen next to me. The mention of Jack? I'd seen him at the funeral making a hasty exit. Maybe that I had said her mother was my rock? Or maybe it is my story altogether. I've accepted this is mine to carry around forever. I don't expect anyone else to share the weight of my past. "If you want to leave this bed right now and this house in the morning, I won't blame you at all."

"I'm not leaving, J.T."

I'm grateful for her words.

"I just wish I could say I was an angel and couldn't relate."

Well, that hadn't made my list of reasons for her consternation. If she isn't an angel as she has confessed, perhaps she can accept me without judgment? Maybe she can see beyond the horrible things I've done to my mother and tearing Tim and Ellie apart. Beyond the things that could make someone unlovable. I can't fathom there is anything she can say that would surprise me or make me care for her any less.

"I think we need a little break from all this drama." I roll her onto her back and lovingly kiss her neck. Her hands find my shoulders and gently push me back.

"No, wait. Please. What if—" Her words are full of fear. "What if you don't want me after I tell you about me?"

"You are still lying here next to me after what I've just shared. I can't imagine anything you've done can measure up to my wrongdoings, Peyton." I hold her face between my hands. "I'm not here to be judge and jury. Sharing my story with you right now felt really freeing. I just want to give you the same chance." Then I kiss her for real, as tender as I possibly can. "Maybe we are uniquely qualified to accept each other."

"Wait! Stop. You mentioned Jack. How the hell did you know about Jack when I didn't?" She pulls away again, not acknowledging a word I've just said.

I prop my head on my hand, lying on my side facing her. "I caught them kissing once. In her office. It was a tough day and I didn't knock. We'd gotten pretty close so it wasn't unusual, but yeah, I saw them. She told me that she would get fired and her daughter would disown her if word got out. As she knew all my secrets, I assured her that hers was safe with me. At the funeral, I saw him and when he recognized me he gave me the 'don't say a word about me' look on this way out. I took the hint."

"What did she mean I would disown her if I found out? I have no idea what that means."

"I don't know. I'm sorry. It never came up again. How did you find out about him?"

"I met him at the funeral. He was hiding in the corner where I tried to escape. He ran away from me. I saw a Bible with his name on it in my mother's bedroom, and male clothes. I tried to track him down at the same time I was tracking you down. The address I got for him was my house. Well, my mother's house. When I went to the cemetery he was there. I invited him to dinner and that led to my being in Detroit for Thanksgiving. With him. And his kids. And grandson! It was my first real holiday with a family that didn't hate me. I don't usually do holidays."

I am selfishly distracted by our shared view of holidays. But no, I can't be, as this is important. "What do you mean? Your mom didn't hate you."

"Ugh, I know. It's complicated. I just meant the bigger family stuff that I always wanted. That didn't work out so well. I'll spare you the gory details."

"I want the gory details, Peyton." I try to kiss her again.

She kisses back briefly, but then tucks her head to speak. "My mom didn't hate me, J.T. I hated her. I blamed her for never having a father—or a family, for that matter. Her parents never forgave her for leaving my dad and neither did I. I was horrible to my mother. I left her emotionally as soon as I could, and then walked out the door as soon as I turned twenty-one. I never called or came home… and then she died. Already fearing I was a horrible person, now I am hearing I might be responsible for her keeping her boyfriend secret too. I've been blaming her all along for us not being a family when it really might have been my fault! I need to talk to Jack."

She starts to push herself up off the bed, but I catch her wrist gently. I pull her back carefully, with as little force as possible. She doesn't resist.

"It's an hour ahead in Michigan, so it's late. How about you call him in the morning. It won't change anything." She wriggles, but relaxes into me. I run my thumb across her cheek and she seems to calm in an instant.

"What kind of crazy magic did you just use on me to make my head spin back into place?"

I laugh. "I hope it's always that easy."

"Oh, I'm easy alright."

I sense there is more to the story. She is deflecting. "You are not getting off that easily."

"I could."

Her ability to create a sexual innuendo from the simplest of statements is at the least amusing, at the most, hotter than hell.

"Peyton, I want to know everything about you. What makes you tick, how you process, what might really piss you off, because I've hit a major nerve, and what your expectations are for this relationship. I want the good, bad, and ugly. I want all of it."

Shit. I realize I may have gone a little overboard throwing out the "r" word without knowing where her head is. Now it's my turn to deflect. And I know just the distraction.

CHAPTER 14 | Peyton

We finally come up for air after a kiss that says more than words ever could. I want you. I need you. Please don't run screaming from this bedroom when you find out who I really am. Thank God his kiss said that. I know it's my turn to share, and I am not ready. There is no special umbrella I can offer to protect him from my shame storm. I know he isn't going to let this slide so I might as well just get it over with.

"Thank you for that amazing kiss." I get down to business, taking a deep breath in and blowing it out audibly, cheeks puffing with air. "Okay, let me net this out. If I said 'don't do anything I wouldn't do' it doesn't take a lot of options off the table. Like you, I've put stuff in my body I regret. No needles though. I've seen things I wish could be unseen. And… I've done things with men that I wish I could take back."

A lot of things. A lot of men. He is probably wondering if there was money involved. "If it makes it any better, I've done a lot of what I've done with rich and famous people."

I try to read his expression but it's blank.

"So, that's it. Mother Theresa, I am not. I'm not serving the poor or fixing the broken. Hell—" my voice is weary and strained, "—I might be the broken. I heard someone say to you at the funeral that you fix the broken. That was the first thing that made me want to meet you. Because—" I hesitate, and his fingers fold around mine, pulling my hand into his heart. He flattens my palm against his chest and covers my hand with this own. "I felt so broken that day. And not just that day."

His thumb brushes across my lips as if he is wiping the words away. He kisses my forehead again, then strokes my cheek in the same manner that had worked to calm me before. Surprisingly, my defenses don't rise against his touch.

"We are all broken. That's how the light gets in. That's Hemingway. And I belicve every word."

I've just said I don't want a relationship, but I am lying to myself. Even I don't want to believe it, but I think I could fall in love with this man.

"I'm definitely learning all your good, but was that all of your bad and ugly? You got anything else to throw my way?"

I hear no angst, only desire. I'm leery it was too easy, but I feel lighter and willing to take a chance. "Now, where were we?"

"Both still here. You've had a lot of change. Mom, meeting Jack, handling your complication, taking a chance on me. I am, if nothing else, patient. I want to sweep you off your feet and treat you the way I learned from Ellie that Tim did her. She's told me stories of their courting and their married life. Being the best man I can be is what I have to do."

"J.T.?" I ask when he finally pauses. "That was all wonderful. Really," I say sincerely, "I do want you to be the best man you can be, but when I asked where we were I had something else in mind."

"Like being the best I can be with a beautiful woman between the sheets?"

I think I blush at the compliment. "Something like that."

"Oh, Peyton." I love the way he says it lustfully. He runs both hands through my hair on either side of my head, massaging my scalp, and I sigh. It feels so good. My hands slide down his arms over the curve of his biceps, then I use my nails on the way back up to his shoulders and around his back because a manicurist once told me how much men love a good back scratch. He seems to as he moans.

Then, our gentle touching of one another changes pace as his lips crash into mine. His intensity is unwavering, and I return his kiss with no hesitation. I want him, and I've been waiting longer than I would like. My hips rise into his involuntarily, making this clear. His fingers curl into the flesh of my hips. "Please get me naked already," I beg into our kiss. He stands up quickly from the bed and slides his open jeans down his thighs, stepping first one leg, then the other, out of the pant legs gracefully. Now, just one article of clothing remains. Hands reaching for the top of my pants, I push them away to instead find my way inside of his boxer briefs. I gasp as my fingers finally have the opportunity to explore him skin on skin, already ready for me. Curling my fingers around the length of him I feel flawless, soft skin that contradicts how hard he is.

J.T.'s fingertips skim over my thigh, tracing the curve of my hip and settling at my waistband. I roll flat on my back and lift my hips as he kneels over me to ease my leggings off. He sucks in a breath. He traces the lace of my underwear across my stomach from left to right.

I revel in the black-and-white silhouette of his body created by the light coming through the window. His neckline and the curve of his muscular, broad shoulders captivate me. Hands caress my neck, then cup my breasts. I reach up and run my hands across his chest.

"I am going to learn every inch of you, Peyton. Physically and emotionally."

I can get excited about half of that.

His palms flattening, moving down my sides, he leans back onto his heels, hands gliding down my thighs then calves. Arms stretching behind him, his right hand encircles my ankle. He bends my right leg up slightly, just enough to kiss the inside of my knee then move upwards one inch at a time. My hands grip his shoulders in anticipation.

He kisses my pubic bone then gently bites my inner thigh and begins kissing his way backward. I am a bit disappointed he has moved away from where he was just about to explore all of me. He is back soon enough like he can't wait either. He gently pushes my thong to the side and his fingers dance across my flesh. My hips rise wanting more.

J.T. hooks his thumbs on the lace sides of my underwear and I shift to make it easy to remove them. He takes his sweet time slowly moving them down the length of my lower extremities.

He hovers back over my body and I wrap my legs around his back and pull him down onto mine. I feel his wanting pushing into my thigh and I push myself toward it. My hands gently massage the muscles on either side of his spine as he finds my lips again.

I release my legs around him because there is no way for him to touch me unless I do. I need him to touch me. He seems to understand my unspoken request and finds me with his fingers. Finally! I want him inside of me, but I will be patient.

His thumb brushes lightly back and forth over my clit, touch divinely affectionate. His fingers massage the flesh of my labia before moving toward my wetness. One finger easily slides inside, and I revel in the feeling.

His head is moving downward, and I run my fingers through his hair applying gentle pressure to ensure he does not stop until he reaches me. Oh! Tongue taking over where his fingers used to be, I whisper his name into the dark. He traces the left side of me, pushes his tongue inside with a flutter, then up the right side back to my clit, sucking it into his mouth. I writhe in delight, hips lifting while my hands grip his hair.

His tongue moves up and down my skin, soft, then firm, flattening, then just with the tip. His thumb pulls my clit upward, continuing to massage it, and his finger inside me pulls downward. His tongue is buried in and out of me, lost everywhere in between. He draws long circles against the sides and pushes back inside. Both of his hands come to find my breasts. The stimulation of my nipples at the same time as everything else is so satisfying. I realize I've hit a new level of attention from a man. He cares about pleasing me.

My hips pulse into his mouth while my hands pull his head into me more tightly while fingers squeeze fistfuls of hair. I moan. Oh my God, this is divine. I shift my hips left and right in tiny movements against the ones his lips are making over mine. Intense pleasure begins to ripple from my core. I thrust into him and his movements become firm. My lifted legs begin to tremble, and I let the sensation wash over me. I feel my insides clench and pulse in response to him as his finger slides inside again and his tongue returns to my clit. My hips involuntarily push upward further. The pressure of his finger and tongue is everywhere from head to toe. "Oh my God," I gasp again. His lips and tongue swirl over me. "Oh my God." His finger moving inside of me. I meet his mouth again and again with each lift of my hips until the pleasure is all I feel and I still, riding it over the edge. OH. MY. GOD.

I suck in a breath and finally relax onto the bed, legs quivering, as his kisses return to my inner thigh. I need a few moments to recover and remember how to breathe. One finger draws images across my stomach, softly back and forth. I smile and ask, "Did you just write number one on me?" I had made out the number sign and number quite easily.

"Guilty," he says, not sounding embarrassed in the least.

"I assume you meant my first orgasm. Or were you having a moment of complete conceit calling yourself number one?" I'm messing with him, but my quick assessment of what has just happened is that both are true.

He laughs. "I'd like to think I am a little more humble than that. It should always be about you, not me."

I ponder for a moment the one hundred eighty-degree difference between his intention and what I know to be true about Kyle.

"I just want to make you happy, Peyton."

Wow. "Trust me, your mad skills just did." I hope mine return the favor adequately. Finally able to move beyond post-orgasmic bliss, I rise to my hands and knees and crawl in between his legs. Sitting back on my heels, I stroke the outside of his thighs to build tension. I run my flattened palms across his washboard stomach feeling each one of his muscles. Yoga can get me a matching six pack any day now. I'm thin but don't have definition as he does.

One hand still flat over his heart, I move the other downward slowly, taking my time and letting my fingertips linger. When I am below his belly button, I turn my flat hand sideways and rub side to side across his stomach. I feel his pubic hair against my palm and his erection brushing across the top of my hand. I spend a few moments getting lost discovering the area.

I can't wait much longer to feel how hard he is for me. Moving both hands beneath his shaft, I fondle his testicles, skin tightening under my touch. I massage gently with my fingers, then cup each ball in one hand, lifting them up and tickling his taint beneath. I hear and feel the vibration of his guttural moan, legs squeezing me in reflex.

His hips rise slightly off the bed. My hands can no longer be denied. His erection is just waiting for me. I wrap both around his shaft and my vagina twitches. I want him in me. But, first.

I wrap one hand around his shaft, sliding it up and down, feeling all of his length and girth. He will be perfect for my mouth and inside of me. Not too big, not too long. I want to be able to take him all in. I run my thumb over the top of him, back and forth, then switch hands to use my other index finger to trace around the head. I keep both moving up and down the shaft and over the head with light pressure, then firm, to keep him guessing at what might come.

When I've fondled every millimeter adequately with my fingertip tender touch, long, firm strokes, twists between my palms and rubbed up and down with encircled fingers, it's time to find him with my mouth. I lean forward, inch by inch, toward him, building suspense. His hands grip my thighs while his hips lift again to close the distance. I hover just above him.

I brush the tip with my lips, in a circular motion as I hold his penis firmly in one hand and his balls in the other. I nibble around the frenulum carefully, then lick the ridge of flesh at the base of the head. Finally, I close my lips and slide down his shaft until the fullness hits the back of my throat. Getting all of him inside of my mouth makes me happy. I moan. This makes him push deeper into me, and I move upwards to the top again. I twist my tongue while keeping my lips sealed and move my head side to side while he writhes beneath me.

Fingers find my scalp and tangle in my hair, pulling just slightly. He lifts my head and gently pushes it down around him. I constrict my lips and push him against the roof of my mouth until it gently pops when I've taken all of him in. His hips thrash upward.

"That feels so good. So good." He relaxes until I do it again and his hips thrust him deep into my throat once again. "Oh my God." His hands move from my head, smacking against the bed. I continue the motion and tighten my grip on his balls, gently pull away from his body then push upward slightly. He grips my shoulders and groans as his head turns side to side.

I still and lift my head. "I want you in me, J.T." I sound demanding. He stills. For too long. Something I said?

"I want to wait," he finally says.

What? For the second time of the evening I can't believe what I am hearing, so unlike anything I've known.

"I don't want our first time to be over. The anticipation will be amazing."

I sense his body about to move, and before I know it his legs swing off the bed and he is standing beside me, leaning in to kiss me.

"Where are you going?"

"Cold shower."

"Okay, not so fast. First, you deny me, then you leave me in bed alone?" I am surprised but proud. My conflict-avoiding self has just called him out. "I hate cold showers, or I would invite myself to join you. Quid pro quo. You took care of me, at least let me return the favor."

J.T. pushes my hip until I roll onto my stomach. He crosses one leg over me, straddling my body. His tongue finds the nape of my neck with a kiss. The kisses move to my left shoulder then back to the middle. Each time he kisses he exhales hot breath onto the spot as if keeping me warm from the wetness of the kiss. He finishes attending to the right shoulder and then his tongue slides the length of my spine.

Kisses again on the small of my back now. Teeth find my butt cheek and it clenches with his gentle bite. He moves to my right and his tongue circles my palm, face up on the bed. This is foreplay no one has been patient enough to give before. I feel cared for and wanted. I would have missed this if we skipped straight to sex. This makes my body feel revered, something I've never felt before. And something I will never forget.

He lies down again next to me and I roll onto my left hip. I pull his face to mine and thank him with a kiss. "That was wonderful."

"I told you I just want to make you happy."

"You know what would make me happy right now?" I rise up to straddle him this time, my hands immediately gripping his still hard dick. Thank God. There is no refuting he wants me, so I have to believe he is telling the truth about wanting to wait.

I don't give him a chance to answer or resist, and resume where I had left off a few minutes ago. I shake my head, lifting up and down on him, my tongue lashing about the entire time. I lick and caress, stroke and suck. I feel him grow and throb. His voice is urgent, "Yes. Yes. Yes." His hands return to my head, guiding my mouth on how to pleasure him. Faster, and a little more forcefully, the head hits the back of my throat as I squeeze the base of his shaft, hold his balls, and place pressure with my third finger on the spot just below them. His hands smack the bed again as his hips thrust and he holds himself still deeply in me. I feel his legs shake alongside my body as he pulses against my tongue, tasting his salty release. "God, Peyton, God." I don't belong in the same sentence as God, but I appreciate the sentiment. He blows out a long breath into the dark. Then quietly whispers, "Wow." Two for two on his and her orgasm wow factor.

"I'm happy now," I quip, snuggling into the nook again.

"Wow," he says again, sounding relaxed.

"Is it okay if I pass on sending you to your roommate's bed?" I whisper. My head is resting on his chest close to his heart. His arm encircles me, holding me close. I never want to move. I feel warm, safe, and content. The rise and fall of his breath slows, and deepens. His unspoken answer is the best answer. We are both exactly where we belong.

NOVEMBER 29
CHAPTER 15 | J.T.

Holy shit. I'm a spoon. Flesh on flesh, waking up holding Peyton Jennings in my arms. Apparently my subconscious already knew. Something is going on between my legs. I'm a man, and it comes with the morning territory. I back up my hips a little as not to disturb her.

We went to sleep without closing the deal. Call me crazy! I refused a ready and willing woman. I'm so glad that when she wakes we have the chance to see each other differently in the daylight. Despite all I shared, she's still here.

I smile against her shoulder, realizing I never answered her final question of the night. I smile even more broadly thinking about the killer blow job she had given me before I drifted off to sleep.

I want to feel her silken skin under my touch but the slow rise and fall of her chest against my body tells me she is sleeping deeply. Damn, she feels good in my arms. I am happy just to hold her. I wonder if she is a morning person.

"Hey you," I hear a faint feminine voice. Am I dreaming? Pressure on my shoulder moves down my bicep. A light tickle on the inside of my elbow. Warmth over my hand resting on my thigh. Something grazes over my chest.

It takes me a minute to put everything together. Peyton. I slowly open my eyes. I've fallen back to sleep after having awoken earlier. This time my body behaves itself upon waking, luckily. There is no better first sight for the day than her sparkling blue eyes. "Good morning, beautiful." I hope she likes my rugged morning voice. I reach my arm over her hip and pull her closer.

"I have to confess I am not a morning person, but if you say that every morning, I think I could become one."

I am happy she implies there will be other mornings. I can only be so lucky as to wake to her scratchy, sexy as hell, morning voice on many more occasions.

Her hand finds the stubble on my left jawline, fingertips tracing. It feels so good. "I loved waking up in your spoon," she says.

We gaze into each other's eyes seeing each other differently than the day before, no longer strangers. I never expected to find this feeling of acceptance for all of me. She is playing with the dog tags around my neck, rubbing the metal between her thumb and forefinger. I slide my fingers behind her neck and brush my thumb across her cheek. I pull her lips close to mine, morning breath be damned.

Her lips don't hesitate parting, and her tongue quickly finds my bottom lip, sliding from left to right, then back to the middle where she gently bites. I push my tongue past hers, feeling fully its perfect smoothness. I am ready to pick up where we left off last night. I am ready to make love to this beautiful woman.

As if my kiss speaks my thoughts, Peyton pushes her left leg in between my own to pull her hips into my groin. When she releases slightly, her hands find me, assessing my desire. It only takes a few strokes for me to be ready. But I will wait, and make sure that she has the time to fully want me before I slide inside of her for the first time.

I move to kiss her neck, making sure I give both sides and the middle adequate attention. Kissing my way down her chest, I subtly roll her onto her back in the process. Finally, I see her full breasts in the daylight. They are beautiful. Light pink nipples encircled by just a darker shade of pink. My mouth finds her right one, and it comes to life under the caress of my tongue. I hold her other breast, lifting it gently, then squeezing more firmly. Her hips rise into mine. Closer.

She makes a sudden motion to bring both of her hands to hold me. She is seeing me in the daylight for the first time too. Sliding her hands down the length, she reveals me inch by inch. I hope she likes what she sees.

Peyton spends time teasing the space between my navel and cock. Each little tug of pubic hair I feel in my shaft as a small twinge. Changing breasts, I pull her already hard nipple between my teeth, letting it fall back into place when I release it. I take two perfect handfuls of breast and massage them in a circular motion. Letting them go, I slide my chest over both mounds of flesh and move up and down, side to side. She moans, and I am glad that the pleasure is mutual.

I place my hand facing downward, against all of her. Her clit swollen and a slickness says it's time. I can't wait any longer to feel myself in her. Hopefully, she doesn't find it prudish that I want to be on top the first time, but I think it will feel the most like making love. I'm not sure I ever have. If I am lucky, there will be plenty of opportunity to experiment with other positions.

I reach right of her to my nightstand for a condom then rip it open with my teeth while still holding one breast. I search her face and piercing eyes for any sign of hesitance on her part but find none.

She must sense this. "I want you too, J.T." I like her assumption.

Her hands slide over my shoulders and behind my back to pull me directly over her. I anxiously await what will happen next. Filling all of her with all of me. "Oh, Peyton," I moan into her mouth as I kiss her again one more time. She moans in return, a vibration I feel in my lips and erection. I move closer to her, pushing into her clit. Her hands grip my ass and pull me in hard against her.

I pull back slowly and slide forward again, against more of her skin and wetness. So close! We lock eyes, and she bites her bottom lip. I lean in and gently bite the same spot, then continue to hold her gaze. She nods slowly, granting me permission. I am so hard. I am so ready.

I position the tip of me against the opening of her, feeling the warm wetness. I slowly enter her amazing body, ready, willing and wanting. We connect in this new way. I push my whole shaft inside, thankful she can accept all of me, until our hips collide. I hold still for a moment feeling the tightness cradle all of me.

Her legs lift, wrapping around my back, squeezing my hips. It becomes hard to distinguish where I end and she begins. I finally pull back and thrust inside of her again. A sound of desire crosses her lips. I am pleased with her enjoyment. I want to satisfy her, but she feels so good I am not sure I will be able to hold out. I will do my best.

She clenches more tightly around me. I pull out and push in against the additional friction, getting closer to my edge. No finishing yet. She deserves more. Her hips rise, grinding against me, and I lean forward to make smaller movements against her clit. She pulls her legs back and I can't resist looking away from her eyes to watch me move in and out of her. The pink flesh pulls forward then swallows me in.

I look up to find her looking down. She is also watching me. How hot! She doesn't look away so I hope I can safely assume she isn't turned off by what she sees. It's pretty unnerving revealing one's self especially after hearing women friends talking about the ugliness of the male organ.

We reconnect with our eyes. This is vulnerability, looking into someone's depths fully naked and exposed, beyond just the flesh-and-bones part. I allowed her to see me fully. Will she let me see her too?

My thinking has sidetracked me, allowing me to maintain composure a little longer. Thank God. Peyton is taking short gasps of breath, alternating with mmm's and ooh's. Her grip on my shoulders tightens. She straightens her legs, and it changes the angle and tightness. We breathe, "Oh God!" in unison. Moving her hips in a circular motion, she pulses them multiple times when she faces me straight on, then changes direction. I copy her motion, allowing just the tip to graze her lips and clit in the middle. She moans deeply and pulls against my hips to ask me to fill her fully again. I don't. I move my hips side to side with just the tip barely inside of her. I'm too close. She gasps then lets out a long moan of enjoyment. I push into the tightness. "J.T.!" she exclaims and my pride swells. Thank you for wanting me, Peyton.

She grabs around my back, pulling herself up off the pillow, breasts thrusting into my chest. Hard nipples draw lines I can feel as I move forward and backward across them. I lie down on top of her and slide my hands under her hips to raise them. The new angle offers more pressure against my base. She clenches more tightly. Her legs begin to tremble. Her gasps rise in intensity and intonation, becoming higher pitched as her orgasm overtakes her. Fingernails dig into my glutes, mixing pleasure and pain.

It feels so good to be inside of her. So damn good. She thrusts into me. I thrust into her. Our bodies feel like one.

We look into each other's eyes again. Never have I done this. Never have I cum together with a woman. Never with open eyes, watching every movement of her lips making the noises and words I'm bringing forth. Truth. Now I've made love. If I am reading her face correctly, it says the same.

An intense moan escapes from my gut. She returns it with one of her own. I pull all the way out and push hard into her again. Her sounds of satisfaction allow me to let go and find my own. The pressure. The throbbing. My dick pulses. Hard. It feels good to let go of control. I let out a final, loud groan.

We push into each other, me staying fully inside of her with short little movements, the involuntary tightening and releasing of her orgasm holding me captive. I'm lost in her. The feeling of her wriggling under me. Her touch holding me. Her wetness. Her body's warmth. I've emptied into her, but my heart is full.

I lie against her chest and stomach, spent, but careful to bear some of my weight. We are both working to catch our breath. "Holy shit," I say breathlessly, without thinking. Not very romantic. It was my first thought of the day and seems to have stuck.

"Holy shit," she says back.

I guess I am okay. I roll onto my back, still unable to get a full breath of air. I'm still twitching, and I want to grab myself but hold back. I blow out a long breath.

She finally has it together enough to speak, "You were right."

Everyone likes hearing those words. I roll on to my side and prop my head on my elbow and hand facing her.

"That was worth waiting for."

CHAPTER 16 | Peyton

I've just been taken apart. I looked in a man's eyes during sex and it became something different. Something more. Possibly, forever changed. I am scared of how I feel, so captivated by him. At the same time, I have never felt so safe with our sweaty, intertwined bodies melting into one.

I can still feel in my hands how his chest muscles flexed as he thrust forward into me. I can still see how his biceps grew into firm half-circles and his jaw clenched with exertion, unshaven sexy. The way he moved in and out of me was the same as he does everything, a mix of power and grace.

He reaches over and tucks a strand of blond behind my ear. My stomach tightens. I see his forearm telling the story of his past. Just below his elbow is a tattoo. I recognize it as a Celtic knot. The center of the knot is interrupted with a circle that looks like connected ropes. In the middle, the letters T.R. in emerald green, masculine script draw attention against the black of the rest of the design.

We make eye contact. "I loved seeing your tattoo when we were—" I almost slip and say making love. I hope it was that for him. I don't finish the sentence. "It's beautiful. T.R. Tim Reilly, I assume. What does the rest mean to you?"

"Yep. My dedication to Tim. The Celtic trinity can mean a few things. Past, present, future. Power, Intellect, Love. Creator, Destroyer, Sustainer. The circle is protection, and never-ending connection with the divine. I chose it for obvious reasons. It serves as my daily reminder."

I pull his arm to my lips. My lips skim across the tattoo in kisses and I feel raised flesh. I know where he got the scars the tattoo covers. I wish I could kiss them away.

He can't see my scars, neither can he kiss them away. I am not yet ready to share how they formed. How could he love someone who loved herself so little that she let a CEO tie her up and make her a sex slave? He hurt me so badly I couldn't walk for a week. I didn't like it but was too weak to tell him to stop. I wanted to believe so badly he would love me if I just gave him what he wanted.

It had seemed so promising with the music and candlelit dinner and penthouse condo featuring an incredible sunset view. He told me I was beautiful, smart, and funny. Everything I wanted to be. He said he had never felt about anyone else the way that he did about me. He knew how to seduce a woman for sure.

Would he care to know that I had friends who thought any old day ending in "Y" was just fine for cocaine, and maybe throw in a little something on top if Monday night football was involved?

"Thank you for kissing me there. Like that. I was hooked the first time I tried it. It filled the hole in my soul. I am one of the lucky ones that got away from it. I've known plenty who haven't. I am not proud of what I did."

Thankfully, he has interrupted my scratching the surface of my not so proud moments. I bury my head in his chest.

"What is it, Peyton?" he asks, his voice full of concern.

"You told me everything about you and I told you nothing."

"I'm counting on having plenty of time for that later."

Light kisses move over my temple, forehead, nose, mouth, and jawline. My secrets are safe. For now.

"I've never been with a woman like that."

Oh!

I find this difficult to believe but am elated to be special. I decide to take a chance on being vulnerable. "Do you mean, like, made love?" I cross my fingers on the hand behind his back. Please say yes.

"Yes, Peyton. Thank you for making love to me." He places a

very tender kiss on my forehead, then lips.

"I should be thanking you. It was my first time too." If only I could take away all the other times it was something entirely different. I feel disgusted with myself for letting my body be used the way I have. I can only move forward and be thankful this was a first for both of us.

He pulls back, looking at me like he is reading me. "I hope we share a lot of other firsts."

We lie there, lost in each other, for a few more minutes before J.T. startles, looking as if he remembers something. He stands, and I have my first chance to see the rest of him in the light of the day. Wow. He looks sculpted, like by the hands of one of Italy's finest. The width of his shoulders tapers to his hips, then strong, muscular thighs widen again. It's a bit breathtaking. I figure he is handling the condom, which he does, but then stands before me with outstretched hand containing my phone. I'm lying down. He's standing up. Eye level is the perfection that has just given me the best orgasm of my life.

"You wanted to call Jack in the morning."

"Thanks, J.T. I can't believe you remembered."

"It seemed kind of important."

He remembered and did something about it? "It is, but I can handle that later. It's not as important as you coming back to bed with me."

He lies down beside me, bodies facing toward one another. He takes my hand and presses his palm against mine, fingers straight, like two starfish.

"Tell me more about Africa. I think I might want to go someday," I say with genuine curiosity.

"You should. The people are amazing. They have no stuff, but they have more than we do in many ways."

I had done research. The pictures show people with no shoes, distended bellies, and open sores. The stories speak of women walking hours a day for clean water. They carry the water on their head, often with a baby on their back! I am pretty sure I wouldn't survive a day of that lifestyle.

"We think they are broken because they don't have what we have, but sometimes I think we are the broken ones."

I can relate to this.

"Anything beyond an ordinary day makes them wildly happy. Us just showing up with a smile is met with gifts of the highest honor. Not joking. They give us their chickens, their primary food, unselfishly. It's crazy. They have everything they need because they understand love. I think if you have that, you don't need much else. You've heard people say love is all you need, right? I almost believe it. It might be all you need to survive. And be happy."

I push through my constricting throat, voice small, "I don't know if I know how to love. I've never really let anyone in before. Not my mom, not my friends, not Kyle. So like you said, I guess I've never had much, because I've never had love."

"Hey, don't forget I learned this the hard way. You need someone to give you hope, and not judgement. If you want to call that fixing the broken, you can, but I just call it love. It's all we are really here to do. Love everyone, and everyone wins. And guess what? They don't even have to love you back for it to be okay. It's scary to put it all out there, but love is bigger. Bigger than fear. Bigger than broken. Bigger than everything. You know what else? I think you are already on your way to fixing your own broken Peyton Jennings. You are here, right? I still can't believe you just hopped on a train to visit someone you barely knew."

He leans in and kisses me deeply. I let his lips and words sink in. I do have hope. Hope for everything I want to offer to him. But also, what I hope in return, I can accept.

CHAPTER 17 | J.T.

Long eyelashes flutter awake and allow me to take in the brilliant blue hue. "You fell back to sleep. I was just admiring the view." She crosses her arms over her face. I probably shouldn't have been staring at her, but she looked so angelic as she slept. I plant kisses on her neck. "I don't know about you, but I could really use a shower."

"Is that an invitation?"

I guess I woke her up! I feel my eyes widen. "Yes." It wasn't, actually, but now that she mentions it, why not? I reach for her hand, pull her slowly to rise, and lead her to the bathroom.

I'm already downstairs making us coffee, but am surprised to hear feet on the wood floor coming closer so soon. I expected her to take much longer to get ready. I assess her from head to toe. The way her jeans cascade over curved hips and the hint of her navel teases. She wears a simple black turtleneck sweater. Her blond waves are swept into a high ponytail, and I can see the heart shape of her face more clearly. She requires no makeup to be stunning in my book, but she has applied just enough to look natural, yet accentuate her eyes that pierce me, and those lips I can't resist kissing every time they near. Like now.

I wrap my arm around her back and pull her close to smell her clean scent. "This is just a little bit of a problem," I say, pushing the fabric down her neck to move in for a kiss. I press the warm mug into her hand.

"Thank you. For the coffee, and the kiss. Not necessarily in that order."

I see her glance around the small, but tidy, kitchen, eyes stopping to rest on the kitchen table. "Yep, it's for you. Made a long trip."

She rushes forward, scooping up the six-inch-tall African teak wood giraffe statue and clutches it to her heart. "I love it! It's my new good-luck charm!"

"I thought maybe I was your new good-luck charm," I quip, because, why not?

"Trust me when I say I need both of you!"

She walks to where she has placed her bag on the floor and carefully tucks it in, zipping it so that the head is sticking out. Crossing the kitchen back to me, she sets her coffee on the counter and wraps her arms around my waist. "Thank you. I love it!"

I let her hold me, not wanting to let go. "Are you ready for another little adventure before I have to let you leave me?"

She groans. My sentiments exactly.

"Yep, ready. What are we going to do?"

"It's a surprise. If you are ready to go, we can just make the next train."

"I'm good to go."

I grab the truck keys from the counter. "Oh, you never got the tour."

"Oh, I got a tour alright," she says seductively.

I smirk. "This next tour should be fun, but it can't compete." I cup her ass and pull her in tightly, then surprise her with a loving spank.

"Oh, do not tease me with that spanking, J.T. Walker."

My eyebrows rise. "Feel free to misbehave." We circle each other around the kitchen like boxers in the ring, sexual tension building. I push her gently against the refrigerator, a deep kiss forcing my tongue into new depths of her mouth.

"Wow," she pants after we have groped each other adequately. "A girl could get really spoiled by this."

"I'm looking forward to spoiling you rotten. And I mean that literally," I growl into her neck. "There are plenty of spankings just waiting." I need to chill. Love-making to fantasy-making in too short a time.

Twenty-five minutes later, my dick still semi-hard from the kitchen flirtation, I am leading her up the last block to our destination. I stop, pointing upwards. "We're going there."

"Up there? Way up there?"

"Is one hundred three floors too high? Are you scared of heights?"

"I don't know actually!"

We head to the elevator, which we share with another couple. Peyton stands in front of me, and reaches behind her back to grab me. Damn her!

Her head swivels backward to me and hot breath is against my ear. "Going up?"

I suppress a laugh, but feel my body writhe with her touch.

Our one-thousand three-hundred fifty-three-foot ascent above Lake Michigan soon has Peyton ooh-ing and aah-ing. The view of the shoreline is breathtaking and the people dotting the scene below look hurried as a colony of ants with a purpose. I revel in each little noise she makes, happy to be the one providing her this first. She seems young and innocent, taking it all in with awe.

I lead her to the newest invention, which has us leaning out over the city with just glass beneath us. Her eyes are big and round, her mouth wide open in a silent scream.

"Do you like it?" I ask, and she nods then speaks, "It's terrifying and exhilarating at the same time!"

"Hmm, reminds me of something."

She cocks her head, raising one eyebrow as if to ask what I am referring to.

"Love?" It sounds like a question, though it shouldn't have. Does she agree?

"Definitely."

"Definitely," I confirm, glad we agree to the fact.

Exiting the tower formerly known as Sears, I am excited to introduce Peyton to another first. "I have something special in mind to do for lunch. I hope you are hungry."

"Something in mind to do? Perhaps you meant to say, someone?" She points to her chest with her thumb. "Are you propositioning me, J.T. Walker? Because I am not sure that I am in any position to refuse your chivalrous offer! And yes, I am hungry."

My head tilts back with laughter. "You have an uncanny ability to turn the simplest of statements into sexual banter of the best variety, Peyton Jennings! I love it!"

"Well, thank you, I think? You do seem to have that effect on me. So, was that a proposition or not?"

She looks like she is working to keep a straight face.

Not to leave her feeling rejected, I say, "I am anxiously awaiting our next time, but we may have already given the city enough of a show for one weekend yesterday."

"Well, okay then. Don't say that I didn't offer to take you up on your offer."

She is funny. I will give her that. "How about a consolation prize?" I ask, stopping at the street corner, though the white light of a man walking is illuminated in our direction. In a dramatic motion, I circle her waist and pick her feet up off the ground and twirl her around like no rush of a crowd is around to see. Holding her in the air, I find her lips with mine, warmth against the chill in the air. I love feeling her tongue in my mouth. I love the way our lips move against one another filling the space the others have just been occupying.

My head feels like the snowflakes being tossed about in the wind around us. I know our time together will end soon, and then what? I force myself to stay in the present. I don't want to miss a second of our time together.

"I thought lunch was going to be my consolation prize, but yeah, I guess that kiss will do too!" she concedes, nose wrinkling cutely, with a bright white-toothed smile.

Moments later, I am opening the door to a small storefront with stained wainscoting covering the perimeter of the lower walls while old-fashioned to modern pizza images decorate the walls above. Red-and-white checkered tablecloths are adorned by mason jars filled with parmesan cheese and hot peppers. Green glass bottles painted with little white flowers on a light green vine hold oil and vinegar alongside the other accoutrements.

Welcoming scents of garlic and tomato waft through the air. Accented voices float across the room as Italian servers carry small, medium and large circular trays to tables, announcing their delivery. It's classic Chicago.

We take seats, next to each other, in a red vinyl booth. "Can I safely presume our famous Chicago style 'za is another first?"

"Safe presumption. And I can't wait."

"Deep dish or thin?"

"Yes. You know I am going to eat it all and I shouldn't. Have you seen you naked? I can't compete as it is!"

"That's seriously funny. I've spent a lot of time taking in your body the last twenty-four hours and it's more than fine. It's damn fine. It's beautiful. Everything is beautiful. Your hair, your eyes, your smile. You on the inside. I should stop. I could keep going but I should stop before you think it's creepy." I laugh but see I've made her blush. Her eyes dart to the floor.

"The good stuff is pretty hard to believe," she mumbles, and I feel a twinge of guilt for surfacing this.

"What makes you say that, Peyton?" Please let me in. She gazes into the distance.

"I'm used to compliments as currency. I always wanted to believe so badly it was about more than getting to the bedroom, but they mostly were. When I would try to stop, the niceties became not so nice. I've been called a dick tease, blue-balling bitch and stupid c-word, to name a few."

"Oh my God, I want to go kick some ass. It's not like that. I'm not like that. You will learn that I mean what I say." I take her hand in mine and look her right in the eyes as I say this. "You can just let it sink in and say thank you. I'll show you it can be different."

I don't blame her. I've seen it firsthand, and I've heard the stories. But not all men abuse their power. If I do, it will be an honest mistake. I learned the true meaning of respect and dignity for a woman from Tim.

We are interrupted by the waiter, ready to take our drink order. "Miss, what can I get for you?"

"Diet Coke, please."

"May I please have the same?"

"Got it. Back to take your order shortly."

"You didn't have to do that, Peyton. Just guessing pizza usually goes with something else for you."

"Honestly, yes. Sometimes late night with more than alcohol." She looks uncomfortable. "But it seems like it would be flaunting it and rubbing it in. That seems hurtful, and the last thing I want to do is hurt you."

I lean over and kiss her forehead. "I know it's a lot to think about, going through life with someone sober twenty-four-seven by three-sixty-five until death do you part." I realize what I've just said. "Not that I am suggesting marriage after twenty-four hours!"

"I'll survive this meal just fine without, thanks. As for the rest of our lives, I think I'll have to take that as it comes." Her lips curl up and I know her brain has gone straight to the gutter again but I don't miss the insinuation of the future.

The waiter returns with our sodas and takes our order. We lift our glasses in a toast. "To many more firsts," I say as I push my glass into hers.

Her expression turns mischievous. "To seconds, and I don't mean of pizza."

This girl. I say a silent toast inside my head. To the potential of forever.

CHAPTER 18 | Peyton

What if I never see this man again after today?

I am undone for the second time of the day. Breathing heavily on my back, I can feel sweat roll over my breast, dripping onto the bed. J.T.'s labored breathing echoes mine next to me.

"Holy shit, Peyton. As much as I don't want you to leave, I am not sure I could take you one more time today. That orgasm was intense."

"I hope you can recover quickly, because one more time is sort of my plan. I need to leave you with something to remember me by."

"There is no chance I am forgetting anything about you."

He strokes my hair with the back of his fingers, then tousles my blond waves gently.

"I love getting tangled in this." He pulls a handful of my hair then releases it to fall against the pillow. "Let me tell you what is going to happen next." He kisses the left side of my collarbone inward, fluttering his lips over the center of my neck where they meet. Kisses caress the other half. Both hands forcefully find my breasts. My back arches.

"I am going to hold you until your fingers find me and tell me it's time again. You aren't leaving here without another orgasm."

"Or three," I drawl under the spell of his lips. They continue to explore my sternum and stomach, then the crease of my elbow. His fingertips trail behind his lips, double the sensation in the same exact spot, melding into one feeling of deliriousness. "That feels so good."

His fingers bend into gentle curls, slide down the sides of my ribcage, then hips, then the outside of my thighs. His nails scrape the flesh with just the right pressure of pleasure. Goosebumps ripple behind every inch.

"A man could get used to these curves," he nearly slurs, and I know the cause is a worthy one.

I reach to his shoulders and slide my palms over the top, then down over his biceps. "I know what you mean."

J.T. leans back into the pillow, my body missing his hands.

"I'm going to miss you."

My heart does a little happy dance. "I'll miss you too."

"What's next for us?" he asks, turning to his side to look me in the eye. His leg slides over mine and pulls me close.

I am happy to hear him announce there is an us. "Do you have something in mind?" Best to answer his question with a question.

"Well, I have another trip to make in a couple of weeks. Then I plan to be in Detroit somewhere around the 25th, with my mom, and Ellie."

He doesn't say for Christmas. Is it really too much to think he could share my disdain for trees, candy canes, and Santa?

"Do I dare ask if spending the New Year's together could be a possibility? In Detroit, or Chicago?"

Whoa!

"Oh. Wow. Well, I haven't thought about it yet, but that sounds great. I can't imagine kissing anyone else at midnight." I bat my eyelashes jokingly. "That seems like a long time away," I say wistfully, letting him lace his fingers through mine.

"Until then, I think someone might be spending too much time in my head."

"Well that's not very nice. Tell me who she is and I will kick her ass." I deliver the line without cracking any sort of a smile. He laughs.

"I love how you make me laugh, Jennings."

"I love how you call me Jennings."

"So, about that 'you filling my head' thing? You know how hard this is going to be?"

"Isn't this precisely why God made Skype?"

He laughs again. "I think we have Microsoft to thank, but yes, I guess so. Skype it is. Not exactly my first choice, but compared to the alternative, it will have to do."

He smirks, and for the first time I notice a slight dimple form. I'm learning more of him.

"If you ever want to share some skin, I won't object."

"I'll see what I can do." Skin makes me think of my wardrobe. Everybody sees my skin. Quick math says ninety percent of my closet wouldn't be J.T.-approved. What would he think of me if he knew? I wouldn't turn his head. He would assume I was a slut, or worse yet, a hooker. Those clothes are who I was but not who I want to be. I want to be better.

"I'm ready for you, Jennings. Ready to make love to you."

I reach down to him and feel the velvety flesh of his hard penis. I swirl my fingers around the head of him, feeling him twitch with my touch. "Not quite ready," I say nodding in the direction of the nightstand. He gracefully swings his legs over the bed and walks around to my side, opening the drawer for a condom. I lean over, wrap my arms around his thighs and pull him toward the bed. I wrap my lips around his cock, moaning as I do. This angle allows me to take him completely, and his long groan tells me he likes it. Impatiently, wait to feel him inside me again. I tickle under his balls and the skin constricts and shivers under my fingertips. He pulls himself back until just the tip brushes against my lips, and I move my head side to side, holding it against them.

He pushes my left shoulder to flatten my body against the mattress. Reaching behind my knees, he pulls my body to the edge of the bed. He is right there! His balls pushing against me cover my opening while his shaft covers my labia. He moves his hips, and every nerve below my waist comes to life. I grab behind his thighs and pull him forward. Taut balls move over my clit and he rotates his hips. I love the way it feels.

Then I panic as my past takes over the present.

The last time I was in this position was horrific. Yes, it started as consensual but how was I to know it would end up feeling like anything but making love? His heavy body leaned forward holding me down. My arms were bent like goalposts and his hands placed on top of mine forced them to remain in place. He thrust into me hard, relentlessly, painfully. I was raw from the lack of wetness. Can I do this? Should I stop him? What would I say the reason was?

Breathe. That was then. This is now.

J.T. lifts my left leg to rest on his shoulder. I wrap my right one around his back, feeling less vulnerable than when being scissored apart. He kisses my ankle, then knee. He reaches under my hips and lifts them to meet him.

"I am going to slowly and gently slide myself into you."

Just the words I need to hear. I relax enough to let him in. My eyes close and I feel him, just as he said, slowly and gently filling me. I am plenty wet. The pressure of his hands on my hips and him inside is wonderful. I grind my hips and the sensation against my clit intensifies, friction on the perfect spot in front.

He reaches for my leg around his back and guides it next to the other, against his chest. He deepens inside of me and my eyes open quickly.

"I got you, babe." J.T.'s voice is calm and soothing. His thumb finds my clit, tiny movements pushing against the fullness inside. Oh! My hips rock side to side, and side to side again, pushing myself over him more firmly. My hips rock up, and oh, down. No, I need him deeper. I push up again, hard. He is letting me control how I glide over him. I look down to see him sliding in and out so easily, wetness shining.

Oh! I like his thumb there. "Yes, there. There." He doesn't move his body, except for his chest jutting outward with a deep breath trying to control his ending coming too soon. I continue to thrust my hips upward, small, then larger, then small thrusts again. Oh God! Pulsing pressure in my head, I turn it side to side on the bed. I grab the edge of the bed tightly. He increases the speed. He presses my clit more firmly. I'm exploding. My fingers ache. My legs quiver. Yes!

I ride out my orgasm, hips writhing, vagina clenching and twitching. He groans. I hear him breathe in audibly again. He is holding on, waiting for me. "I want you to cum again, Peyton. I love hearing you. I love watching you. You look beautiful."

"Thank you." A fine time to put into practice what he said at lunch. It's all I've got.

"Right answer, babe. And the truth…" His voice is intense. "…I can't hold on much longer. You are so damn hot."

He leans forward. He is on top of me and it's my turn to suck a breath in. "Are you okay?" He's listening and he cares. I don't know the answer yet. He kisses me deeply. His hands tickle the nape of my neck while his palms cup my cheeks. His lips are exquisite. I feel the aftershocks below, and he moves more quickly. Then he stops, lifting a bit. "You didn't answer me. Is this okay? Does this feel good?" I want to cry. It does. But more importantly, he cared enough to ask.

"I'm more than okay," I whisper.

"Good. You always have to tell me if you aren't. Promise?"

I nod my head.

"I need to cum, Peyton. I don't want to yet but I need to."

He slows his thrusts into me and holds my hips firmly.

"You feel so—"

He seems at a loss for the right word. He lets out a long moan. Then he slides in and out with more force and speed. I am so pleased that I like it!

"You're so hot. And wet. And feel so—"

He tries again, but this time his sentence is finished with a long growl through clenched teeth. I'm right on the edge and want to finish, elated that I want him despite being completely at his mercy with my legs over my head. I pull on the back of my legs so his softening erection can penetrate me further. It's just enough to hit the deep spot inside. I lift my hips and clench down until forced to let go by more sensation of pleasure. I feel the powerful muscles of his glutes ripple under my grasp. Hold me tighter! He continues to try to satisfy me until my high pitch gasps tell him he has. My body involuntarily shakes from the intensity of the energy from my core to my toes. Amazing. Extraordinary. Remarkable. I can finish the sentence he couldn't with a million different words.

He slides out of me and lies on the bed next to me, holding my hand while we collect ourselves. I feel empty but couldn't protest because I am spent. I couldn't think of anything if I tried. It's nice to feel so quiet and peaceful inside.

"Well that was different," he pushes out through his gasps. "And felt so good."

I couldn't agree more.

"I think I finally just finished that sentence I left hanging."

"So good," I coo, echoing his reply.

He encircles my body, arm and leg, holding me close, and we lie wrapped limb in limb for a few more minutes before J.T. stirs. "It's time to trade the bed for the train. As much as it sucks."

"Nooo," I protest. "That's not trading up."

"What's just happened was trading up for me. Never expected that."

If he only knew.

He can never know.

CHAPTER 19 | J.T.

There is a void in my passenger seat. A pit in my stomach.
I miss her smile already. Her laugh. The feel of her hand in mine.
I'm screwed. For the third time today. The other two were so much better.
No matter what happens from here on out, this girl is going to leave a mark.

NOVEMBER 30
CHAPTER 20 | Peyton

I suck at the morning mad dash. I'm working the dinner shift at Conundrum, so I took the first flight out. Third-day hair messy ponytail on the top of my head and teeth brushed. All I got. I didn't pack last night but, well, I never really unpacked either.

Jack meets me in the doorway of the bedroom with a to-go cup of coffee. I muster a grateful smile. He takes my suitcase down the stairs and I follow behind. He loads my luggage into the car, closes my door, and even waits for me to have several sips of coffee under my belt before trying to start a conversation in the car to the airport.

"So, how was Chicago?"

Even not fully awake, a smile grows across my face.

"I'll take that smile as my answer," Jack chuckles.

"It was great, Jack, thanks for asking. We went bowling and to the hockey game, Blackhawks versus the Wings, no less, and that crazy sky-deck thing, and walked the Miracle Mile, and, yeah, it was great."

"Magnificent?"

I find his choice of adjectives for my trip interesting, but yes, I suppose it was. "Yes, magnificent." My voice sounds dreamy.

He is laughing at me. I am not sure why.

"Wow, you've got it bad. Do you always fall hard? Should I be expecting a phone call with tears soon? I don't mind, just want to be prepared."

He turns his head to smile in my direction, "To be clear, it's called the Magnificent Mile."

I startle to reality. "Oh, oops. Okay, yeah, that too. That mile. And you are right. I think I have it bad. And no, it's not typical."

He sits up a little straighter behind the steering wheel. "Well then, I am glad that you went. I might not have let you, had I not known you would be in good hands."

He is admitting he knows J.T. before I've had the chance to ask.

"It might have come up that you knew each other. I almost called you near midnight wanting answers."

He offers more information, "I recognized his face at the funeral home but couldn't place him. I haven't seen him in a long time, though I do remember him."

At least I wouldn't have to tell Jack about his past. "Okay. I have more questions. At the funeral home, why were you hiding and why did you leave the funeral home like that?"

"As upset as I was, there was no way that people, your family specifically, wouldn't have suspected I was more than a casual visitor."

I should ask why that would matter but I need a different answer first, "J.T. said my mom put the fear of God in him that I would disown her if I found out about you. Why would she say that?"

"Oh, Peyton. This is where it gets a little complicated. Nothing can change what has already happened, and I'd like to just go forward together from here."

"I need to know, Jack. Was the whole thing," dare I ask, "my fault?"

He closes his eyes and shakes his head. "You can't carry this burden. It was nobody's fault, Peyton. Everybody does what they think is right at the time. I have no regrets."

"But I do, that's the thing! I've been so angry that my mom denied me the chance to have a family, and now I think it was all my own doing, and I didn't just do this to myself, but to my mom!" I want to cry but am too angry for being selfish and having no chance to mend all of what I'd broken. "And to you, Jack. Did I do this to you?"

"Peyton, nothing will change with this conversation. And nothing will change the fact that I want you to be my family now."

No denial, but he isn't angry or blaming, offering the only chance I have to make amends. I think of J.T.'s story of Ellie's forgiveness. I fight the urge to question further and quietly accept his offer, resigned by my truth: "I want to be your family too."

"I need the truth, Jack. I ran away to chase a new dream because I never thought I would have a family. I had a chance to have a family with you, Jack? We could have been a family a long time ago. That was everything I wanted. Then I spent the last four years trying to find my father to get back at my mother. I'm so confused. I don't understand why she would keep you and my father from me. I need to know, Jack!"

I sound adamant. I am adamant. How can I face my future without understanding my past?

"I shouldn't be the one telling you this. Any of this. It should have been your mother. God, I miss her."

"Please, Jack!" I feel impatience rising. "You have to tell me. I have so many unanswered questions!"

I need to know but do I really want to know what he knows? What if in this case ignorance is bliss?

I can read Jack's anguish in his frown. "Okay. This is going to be hard for you to hear. But you should know, Peyton. You should know how much she sacrificed for you. She loved you more than anything."

Guilt. Saddle me. Overwhelm me. Drown me.

"Do you remember anything about your father?" He asks the question cautiously.

"No." I purposefully keep my answer short so he will keep talking.

"Caroline loved your father desperately. Maybe too desperately. He was rescuing her from her overbearing parents who had high expectations for the rest of her life. You were about eighteen months old when she had to leave him. Did you know that?"

"Yes."

He looks away, then back to me. "It was because he tried to do something. Something awful. To you, Peyton. She caught him nearly doing something horrible to you. She walked into your room and he—"

I can tell he doesn't want to continue. He is forcing the words over an invisible lump in his throat.

"He had his pants off. And he was over you, holding you down. She thanked God every day that she came home sick early that day. She threw him out. He was charismatic and convinced her parents that she'd gone off the deep end. She told her parents what had taken place and they didn't believe her. Isn't that un-fucking believable?"

I've never heard him swear. Fury pulses in the veins bulging up and down his neck.

"Your father was the shining star executive at their company. He had turned the company around and they needed him. They didn't want to let him go. Her parents thought she was exaggerating. She tried to go to the authorities but no one else would serve as a witness against his character. It's nearly impossible to prove in a he-said-she-said situation with no proof. She left him. He made her parents think she was nuts for leaving. He appeared devastated and heartbreak, though your mother thought it may have been an act. He convinced them he would need to move and start another business because she was pushing him away. They gave him $250,000 and told her that her money was gone and that if she ever had another relationship, they would take your inheritance away too. She wanted to make sure you were taken care of with the money to make up for what she thought she'd denied you by not having a real family, so she never introduced me to you. It was as simple as that. She never questioned for a minute it was the right thing to do.

"Everything was going to change when you were twenty-five. It's only a few months away. I'm sorry she wasn't able to tell you, Peyton, I really am."

I swallow hard, lightheaded, the landscape outside the window swirling into a blur as the details of my life stitch into a suffocating, perverse tapestry. Egregious acts by disgusting people and no amount of money can make my mother's sacrifice worthy. And to think of all the time, and emotions—anger and frustration among others—wasted pining for my father!

I had cyber-stalked the common name of Michael Jennings over the past four years and made calls to every phone number I could find. When a woman answered the phone, I couldn't bring myself to ask any questions. How could I potentially destroy someone else's life with news of a child she may or may know about?

"If only I had known, I would have told her to forget the money." I'm angry I didn't get to make the choice myself.

"That's easy to say now, Peyton. You have to make the best choice at the time and hope your best is good enough."

"What did you mean that everything was going to be different at twenty-five?"

"Your trust. I don't know much about it, but I know it's yours when you turn twenty-five. I know this is a lot to process. I'm here if you want to talk about it. I know we can't have the time or Caroline back, but we have each other now."

"You both sacrificed a lot for me, Jack. I haven't been worthy."

"That wasn't your choice to make. Just like we were doing our best, so were you."

He covers my hand on the console of the car. A conflicting cocktail of emotion mixes in my head and heart.

His voice is soft and comforting when he asks, "Is it too early to ask your plans for Christmas?"

Of course. Family to holiday is an easy leap. Unless you are me. He is undeterred by the absence of an answer.

"I'd love to celebrate together. I'm not sure if and when the crew will be in town, but you can definitely count on us."

"I think I would like that. Thank you. The only thing that could keep me from coming back is—" I can barely hold in the excitement as I squeal uninhibited, "I start a real acting job tomorrow!"

"Well, congratulations! I couldn't be more happy or proud of you!"

He seems genuinely excited. We ride the rest of the way in comfortable silence, my mind slipping to memories of being with J.T. the day before. Jack offers a long and warm embrace as I depart, and I know that everything that needed to be said between us, at least for the time being, has been said.

At the exit door of the airport stands a uniformed man with a sign. Handwritten, in black magic marker. I stop dead in my tracks. "That's my name on your sign. I'm Peyton Jennings. You are my driver?"

He tips his head toward me, then reaches for my suitcase. "Today, yes, I am." He opens the door and motions for me to step through. "Right this way, miss."

I follow him toward a row of cars, where he stops to open the door of an enormously long, especially for one, black limousine. Why am I sliding across a luscious leather seat looking at the expanse between me and the front of a vehicle?

I take in my surroundings, eyes landing on an envelope propped against a small shelf holding four crystal bar glasses. Nothing is written on the envelope, but I assume it is for me. I pick up the card and slide my finger under the edge of the glued corner to open it. On the cover is a large doghouse, with a very small, and very cute, yellow lab puppy. The inscription inside reads, *The doghouse is a lonely place without you.* Below it, with neat penmanship, the initials K.N. On the left inside page of the card he has written, 'I'm going to make this up to you. Life isn't life without you in it.'

My phone buzzes. J.T.! Sorry, Kyle Nixon, your initials can't compete with my favorite ones.

home safe & sound??? missing you....

A second message appears. The word 'already', followed by a sad emoji.

I reply:
right back at ya…but yes, back in L.A…...sigh
He returns:
Skype later, right?
Me:
will be counting the minutes… 7 pm!!!

This time his response is a line of emojis, varying faces of the happy variety. One more buzz and his text says to check Instagram. His updated bio says TAKEN. I update my profile and send a screenshot. ME TOO @jt4africa.

I smile out the window, watching the Hollywood hills pass by, each bold white letter dangling above the city, just a bit crooked, an imperfect but characteristic welcome. Skype and text a relationship will not make. I need to see him again. And soon.

DECEMBER 6th
CHAPTER 21 | Peyton

Saturday morning eye-opening marks my sixth day of happy wake-ups. It's easy to start a day happy when your head and heart are swooning over a boy and you have somewhere exciting to go. Today is extra happy because we aren't shooting and I have slept in until nearly 11:00 a.m. I didn't mind getting up at the crack of dawn all week, or spending sixty-five long hours on the set this week. I love pulling up to the Burbank gates and telling the guard on duty, "Peyton Jennings reporting to Studio 34B."

There is a lot of waiting around during filming, but the thrill of thinking I am "working in show business" overshadows any boredom. Star sightings, hair, makeup! I enjoy learning the secret language spoken between directors and cast for each scene to come to life.

Two people fell in love in front of my very eyes this week, chemistry and sexual tension building. I don't know how 'The Next Time I Go' will end, but if I have to guess, despair will be act two, with their love being ripped apart. I am hopeful they will overcome seemingly insurmountable odds and ride off into the sunset. Yep, I'm a hopeless romantic like that.

I hope my own romance skips act two.

My falling for J.T. this week isn't written into a script. It's very real. During our down time, we spent over three hours talking and probably near double that texting. One night we even fell asleep together on the phone. It was only 9:00 p.m. for me but I was getting up well before the sun.

I roll over to check my phone. He leaves for Africa this morning. There is a text from six hours ago:

Hope I don't wake you...had to say goodbye, will miss u more than u know! Zoo

We already have our own language. You must be ready to move when they call you to film. Once this week, as I hurried to my place, I had typed zoo instead of xo. It is our new inside joke.

I reply back just in case.

Miss you already! Please get back to me safely! Zoo

It's going to be a long nine days. But at least today yoga is on the schedule, and then, a red-carpet movie premiere I'd scored an invite to for me and three of my closest friends.

We are picture-worthy tonight. My dress is a Tory Burch toss-aside from Meredith, because she opted for short and sassy, as did the others. They called me Grandma upon leaving but I didn't care. The only outside opinion that would matter to me is J.T.'s, and he isn't here to judge. But dare I say that tonight I feel sophisticated? The dress drapes just right from my shoulders to the floor, in just a shade deeper, and more golden, than my flesh. Neckline plunging in a low "v" shape, it parts my uncovered breasts. I've Band-Aid-flowered the nipples, of course. The top is plain, as I like it, but interwoven silver threads from my hip to the floor shimmer as the skirt flows. Small groupings of black metal beads form six spiky-petaled flowers with stems and catch the light occasionally. Quick flashes of sparkle are like a firefly lighting up.

With the VIP tickets I'd scored—a little too easily, from one of the production assistants on the set—we are in the makeshift, yet fancy, bar area reserved for rubbing elbows with the rich and famous and red-carpet photo ops.

The champagne is never-ending. Servers with trays gracefully sway between people like a ballroom dance. The trays, and our glasses, always seem magically full. Hayden and Meredith are competing for the attention of a man across the room, dark-eyed, with more hair product than the four of us combined. There are plenty of well-groomed, well-off, tuxedo-clad suitors here, but my mind is preoccupied with the one who is somewhere halfway across the world.

I hold my champagne glass by the base between both hands as I rest my elbows on a high-top table. Hot breath scorches my neck. I sense a large presence. My body tenses. Kyle. Of course he is here. I should have thought of this and not been caught off guard. He tries to claim me with a kiss to the side of my exposed neck. I grimace and lean away. He is undeterred.

"Hey, baby."

He circles in front of me and takes me in.

"You look different tonight. Hot. But different."

Natural makeup will do that to a girl.

"You'd look even better without that old thing on."

"Hello, Kyle," I seethe through clenched teeth.

His hands reach for my waist, and I try to step backwards but Jenna, Hayden and Meredith are directly behind me. He succeeds at pulling me into him, and I shift to get out of his arms unsuccessfully as the girls crowd in.

"Hey stranger, we miss you!"

Speak for yourself, Jenna. Thankfully, his hands release me to hug her. I step left. Meredith grabs my hand. "Come on, we were just going to get our picture taken with the movie backdrop," she sing-songs, voice rising multiple octaves. She pulls me in close to her with both hands. "Maybe we can get a picture with Wes Bentley. OMG, I would die. He is beautiful. Full-on."

The four of us line up, legs appropriately positioned with a bend, shoulders back, chins up, elbows protruding, and stomachs sucked in, breath held, for maximum skinniness. The photographer lowers the camera, and Kyle has somehow replaced my three friends who've vanished into the crowd. I try to make my escape, but his hand catches my arm and holds it firm.

"Whoa, not so fast. Take a picture with me, babe."

"You really need to stop calling me that," I say through a plastered smile. I try not to stand too close, but his strong arm encircles my waist and removes every inch between us. I can't get away soon enough. I hear the click and abruptly step off the carpet before he can realize it. He takes one large stride and catches up.

"How's the gig going?"

How did he know I worked this week? "Great, thanks for asking."

"It's a good part, huh?" He nods, looking hopeful.

"It's just three scenes."

"But you've never had lines before, right?"

True, but he hardly needed to rub it in. "It's good. So, what about you? What are you up to?"

"Other than pining for you? Little else."

My eyes dart to the floor, then around the room, to avoid his penetrating gaze. I'm not going there with him. My heart is elsewhere. "You should move on, Kyle. Maybe call Kate."

"I've only ever loved you, Peyton. I only ever will."

My eyes roll of their own accord. I catch of glimpse of Hayden talking to the photographer out of the corner of my eye. In his hand is the little pad of paper where they capture people's names after they are photographed. I rush toward them. "Hi, um," I look at the pad and see four women's names then Kyle Nixon and Peyton Jennings beneath. "Yeah, could you scratch that one, please? I'd really appreciate it," I say pointing to where my name is associated with Kyle's. The photographer looks at me with one eyebrow raised, and instead of drawing a line through it, adds a star beside it. I lift my hands in a gesture to imply confusion, and he gives a half smile then turns away to take the next picture. What the hell? I hope that picture doesn't get out there for the world, but more specifically J.T., to see. I look back to Hayden, Jenna and Meredith. "I need you all to make Kyle go away. Pretty please."

"He's devastated about losing you, Peyton. He is begging us to help him."

Again, Meredith? "I know you were friends with him before me, but it's over. He screwed up. We're done."

"We kind of are all hoping maybe you will forgive him."

"We? As in all of you? You are taking his side?" I stare incredulously at three hopeful faces.

"You know we love you. We just think we know what's best for you."

The collective "we" hurts.

"And you think what's best for me is Kyle?" I debate telling them about the gentle and kind man who just happens to be hot and is off saving the world. I hadn't yet, because after the limousine I'd been worried about them telling Kyle. I don't want to give him any ammunition for digging his heels in deeper in his efforts to win me back.

Hayden shrugs. "We like you and Kyle together, Pey."

"It's never happening, Hayden."

Hayden appears to see someone across the crowd and begins to walk away, smugly throwing over her shoulder, "Never say never!"

I'm finally away from Kyle in a row of seats with just the girls. One more glance at my phone before the movie will begin. I decide to send J.T. one more text.

wish u were here....

I follow it with three sad faces. Three isn't enough but I don't want to be overly dramatic. I turn down the brightness on the screen, and keep my purse on my lap, just in case he replies during the movie. The opening scene is barely concluding when I feel the buzz against my leg. I quietly peek inside at the notification.

by here do u mean?

Huh? I try to process his question. Maybe an autocorrect screw-up? I open the message and see the picture he has included. A marquee reading *After the Fall*. My jaw drops. By here, he means here! As in L.A., outside the theater I am sitting in. I turn to

Meredith next to me. "I gotta go!" I nearly jump from my seat, whispering, "Excuse me, excuse me," and, "Sorry!" through the row of people.

My high heels on marble tile echo through the empty theater lobby. I push through the door as the warm night air surrounds my body. Goosebumps cover me from head to toe. Maybe the breeze, but more likely the sight of J.T. casually leaning against a cab, arms folded across his broad chest. The light of the marquee illuminates his features. I swallow him in, his longer, messy hair, jeans hanging just right, and a plaid, cotton button-up, sleeves rolled and tattoo peeking.

His looks define handsome, but even better is the way his whole body comes to attention when his eyes find me.

I hurry my pace as best as I can in heels, and he closes the distance between us. I can't believe he is standing before me! I want him to grab me and hold me in his arms, but he stops short. He reaches for both of my hands and takes me all in.

"You look too beautiful to touch. I don't want to mess you up."

"Mess me up, J.T."

His lips crash into mine, his hands on my hips holding me against him. My lips remember his. All week, imaginary kisses reminded me of his taste. Tongue against mine, tracing my lips, our mouths move as one, my fingers feel stubble to the touch. He's here!

His palms find the small of my back where the draping dress leaves bare skin for him to explore. He pauses our kiss, my lips still puckered. His hands return to my hips and he spins me slowly in front of him. "Wow," he whispers. "I had to see that dress in person. It's absurdly stunning."

"Thank you," I say with conviction.

He smiles at my reply knowingly.

"Pinch me! Is this real? How are you here?" My arms encircle his neck, fingers flirting with his hairline.

He reaches for his pocket, removes his phone and turns the screen toward me. The background of his display is the picture I posted earlier on Instagram in front of the theater. Its carousel-like marquee with a crown of lights and the letter "B" made it easy to know the Bruin theater location. "I showed this to the cab driver, and the rest, as they say, is history. This picture will get me through the next few weeks."

"But how are you in L.A.?"

"Usually a delay and mechanical trouble would be a total bummer, but not when you get to pick being re-routed through a place you really want to visit. It was a little out of the way, but seeing you like this," he leans forward and kisses me tantalizingly on the mouth, "Totally worth it."

"How long do we have?" My eyebrows rise.

"Not long enough for that. Though it might kill me. Especially after seeing you like this. Did I mention stunning? I need to be back at the airport in just over an hour. And I need to eat. I've only had peanuts and pretzels all day. I could really use a burger before I'm off the food grid for a few weeks."

"I could really use something else, but I suppose I can't be greedy. Thank you for finding your way to me. I am so glad that you are here."

"You and me both," he says with a kiss to my forehead. "That dress, Peyton—"

I interrupt, "Would look even better on your bedroom floor?"

He tilts his head back in laughter. "Your ability to turn any simple matter into something about sex is just one of the things that I love about you, Peyton Jennings."

He loves things—not just one, but multiple things—about me?

He opens the door of the cab. "In retrospect, this should be a limo, but it's what I've got at the moment. After you."

I slide across the seat and he climbs in beside me.

He whispers, "It's taking every ounce of will power not to grab your breasts." He leans forward to the small opening in the Plexiglas between the back and front seat. "Zane, she's killing me."

The cab driver, who I now know is named Zane, smiles in the

rearview mirror. "She is as you say, Mr. J.T., a beauty. And I think she like you too."

Even though it's delivered in broken English, I understand every word.

Because Zane and J.T. had made fast friends, he agreed instead of cab fare to let J.T. buy him breakfast for dinner, while we ate at a diner on the way to the airport. I can't imagine what I look like walking through the door in an evening gown, but we need quick. Apparently, it's a last supper of sorts, before fried potatoes will constitute his three meals a day. Where J.T. will be going, other than a lot of corn cooked to a soggy paste, not much else is a staple.

Zane, from the counter, turns on his bar stool to catch our attention. "Time to head out, Mr. J.T."

Dread fills me. Our time together is coming to an end much too soon.

In the cab, I rest in the crook of J.T.'s arm, back against his side, gazing out the window at passing lights. His fingers slide up and down my forearm. I'm mesmerized by his touch.

"I have a random question for you," he breaks our comfortable silence, kissing the top of my head.

"Okay. Good chance I have a random answer." I sit up and turn toward him, careful to keep my arm where he can still reach it.

"I need a new playlist for my next long flight. What songs would I pick if I was making the soundtrack of your life?"

"Oh, hmm. Let me think. *You Get What You Give*."

"New Radicals, okay. What else?"

"Natasha Bedingfield, *Unwritten*."

"Okay, like it. Anything else?"

"*Remember the Name* by Fort Minor and, of course, anything Kid Rock and Eminem, because I am, after all, from the D."

"But of course. Eminem *Guts Over Fear*. That's one of mine. And *The Fighter*. Gym Class Heroes. No country for you?"

"Oh, two of those. The *Broken Road* song and *Do It Anyway*. I guess those are kind of old and I have no idea who sings them. I don't really do country." I hesitate to see his response, then quickly add, "But I could. If you like it."

"That's sweet of you, Peyton. Since I only listen to country it would probably be a good idea if you did. It might be a deal breaker otherwise."

He feigns serious but I know him better now. "That's too bad. I hear I give a pretty good blow job."

"You kill me, Jennings. First tempting me with those barely covered breasts of yours, and now with that. I know you didn't believe music would get rid of me. You are stuck with me, baby."

He picks up my hand and kisses the top of it, in gentlemanly fashion.

"I'm happy to be stuck with you." I smile. "Add that song to the playlist."

"No, thanks. Hard pass on that one."

We both laugh. "I have a random question for you too. Right before I met you, you had just told a woman that you wanted to run away to Australia. Why Australia?"

He looks surprised, then hesitant. "Your mom, Peyton. We were both having a bad day. We both wanted to run away. As far as possible. At the time, it was the furthest geographical location I knew where they spoke English. It was kind of a running joke with us. I'm sorry."

"It's okay. I am glad it's something we all share. The reason it caught my attention is that I have contemplated the same on more than one occasion. I must have gotten it from her, or I guess from you." I consider the awesome factor of that detail. We seem fated to be together. "I had something from you before I knew you. How cool is that? I am happy to know."

"Let's go. Get on the plane with me."

"Sounds like a plan. Maybe stop in Bali too?"

He leans over, close to my lips. "I'm sure kissing you on a beach couldn't be better than this cab."

"I'd like to find out." I envision a beach kiss with waves lapping at my feet, him holding me in the ocean, and walking hand in hand on soft sand. I'm dreaming forward. A dangerous place for a girl.

I peek through our kiss to see the departure lanes are just yards away. The United sign at the curb. My heart is heavy.

"*One More Day.*"

"I couldn't agree more."

"Diamond Rio. My life's soundtrack. Please listen and think of me."

"I am sure it will be my new favorite song."

The car crawls to a stop and he leans into the open space to the front seat again. "Zane, apologies in advance for what I am about to ask. Any chance I could have just a minute of privacy?"

Zane laughs and covers his eyes with his palms jokingly. He gets out of the cab and leans his backside against the trunk.

"I can't leave without this, Peyton."

He pushes the low-cut v-shape fabric of the dress over my breasts. I quickly reach down and expose my nipples from beneath their cover. He cups each tenderly, thumbs drifting across my flesh, each nerve alive under his touch. Squeezing them together, and upwards, he places a kiss atop the left, then the right. I gasp. I run my hands up his thighs, from the knee to his hip, and find him with both hands. What I wouldn't give for more.

He releases the handfuls of flesh, and they retreat into place, already missing his touch. The fabric slides over my hard nipples leaving a visible memento of what he has done. His hands slide upward, holding my face in his hands and pressing his forehead to mine. "I do not want to leave you."

"Sorry-not sorry for your mechanical trouble. But don't you dare let that happen on the way home. Do not delay getting home to me one minute longer than necessary. And don't get malaria. Please."

"You make me laugh. And smile. And other things."

"You know I just went there in my head, right?"

"I was hoping you did."

He pulls away, then leans back in for one more worthy kiss. He opens the door. I need to hug him one more time. J.T. pays Zane, and they clasp hands while slapping each other on the back at the same time. Zane steps aside and J.T., seeing me there, scoops me into his arms. I lift my feet into the air as he leans back, the scene befitting a movie goodbye.

"Be safe, J.T. Think of me!"

"As if I have any other option," he says as our lips find one another's for the last time. He returns my feet to the pavement, though only physically. He backs away from me and blows a kiss. I want that to be his signature goodbye gesture. For a long, long time.

DECEMBER 8th
CHAPTER 22 | Peyton

It's been the longest forty-three hours of my life. Since J.T. and I parted I can't stop thinking of him. Feeling him ghostlike touching my back, holding my hips, caressing my bare breasts in the back of the cab.

A commotion outside my staging area distracts me, people parting as a cartoon character-meet rock-star assistant with large hair and even larger glasses moves through the crowd calling for Peyton Jennings.

"Hi, I'm Peyton." I stand to face him. We are eye to eye, but his hair takes me. He pushes the contents of his arms into mine. A long and large red box tied with a white ribbon of satin. How did J.T. pull this off? I haven't told him what set or building, or even the city I would be working in. Then again, he'd been clever enough to find me on Saturday night from my Instagram picture. I untie the ribbon and lift the lid of the box. Not one, but two dozen long-stemmed, red roses. Perfect. And perfectly expensive. He shouldn't have spent so much but I am thrilled to know I have made a flower-worthy impression on him.

A white envelope is held in place by a sticker on top of the decorative tissue cradling the flowers. I quickly open it. My stomach careens into my throat.

Peyton,
Seeing you this weekend only confirmed what I already knew.

All the reasons I need you by my side. I won't live without you.
You are my everything.
Kyle

Not at all what I had expected. How disappointing! I don't want flowers from him! A woman from behind comments over my shoulder, "Well, aren't you loved?" Another walks over to admire my goods. "Spoiled!" Chatter sweeps through the twenty plus people in the room, and I am suddenly the center of attention. Screw this. I set the box on a table in the corner, take each rose out and carefully hand one to each of the women in the room.

DECEMBER 9th
CHAPTER 23 | Peyton

I enjoyed a quiet day on the set, free of Kyle's antics, with plenty of time to wonder what J.T. might be doing in Africa. All day long I've been counting down the hours to wrapping. Tonight, we are hitting the Staples Center for the Jingle Ball with Taylor, Jessie J., Pharrell, Iggy, and Ariana among others. I arrived home late, which normally would have been tragic, but I am beginning to enjoy the extra time I don't spend primping.

Jenna bounds into the bathroom and assesses my white cropped jeans and long-sleeved, flowy black blouse that covers what it should. "Why aren't you dressed yet?"

"I am dressed."

"How long is this grandma phase going to last? I thought as a single girl you might want to doll it up a bit, in case. You never know who you might meet during a GNO!"

GNO. That reminds me of NGO. I lean toward the mirror and apply light pink, natural-looking lip gloss onto my very big smile. "I'm good, thanks." I feel a bit mischievous.

"Well, suit yourself then. Maybe you can pick up a Mormon or something looking like that." She waves her index finger up and down, pointing to my body, then shrugs.

"Maybe, if I'm lucky. They probably cheat less. And God knows I'd save the calories on the drinking." Oh! Something I had not thought about in dating J.T. Extra chocolate and ice cream calories. I think of his sculpted abs and ass. On second thought, hold the ice cream.

The cab is mercifully able to get close to the door—the fewer steps the better in our high heels. Not surprisingly, with the traffic, we are late, and Sam Smith is already crooning away. We each buy an overpriced cocktail and make our way to amazing seats. First row of grown-up seats, as close to the stage as you can get without being with the kids in the too-hot and crowded front standing-room-only section. I lean forward and look left, to Meredith on the aisle, and yell over the music, "These are great seats! Where'd you get the tickets?"

She leans forward but mouths something akin to not being able to hear while pointing to her ear. I notice Jenna and Hayden exchange glances before they look back to the stage. I decide not to ask.

Next up, OneRepublic is taking the stage, whirling lights and loudness. So many amazing artists are here tonight. Because everything makes me think of J.T., I can't help but wonder what he would be like at a concert. Does he dance? Well?

Hayden nudges me with her elbow. "Come with me!"

"Where?" I yell towards her while keeping my eyes fixed on Meghan Trainor, who has just started dancing in our direction.

"I've got friends in a suite!"

The invite appeals to me because I am hungry and don't want to spend money on food if I don't have to. "Okay," I yell back, standing up. "Is everyone coming?"

"No, just you. They can't get us all in."

Hayden leads, and I climb the stairs up from the floor behind her. Reaching the concourse, Hayden points to the sign directing us to the suites. She reaches for my hand and drags me forward, like a mom pulling her child. "Hey, I'm coming," I protest. "It's the damn shoes!"

We take the elevator to the fourth level, thank the elevator attendant, and head down the hall to suite 1416. Loud laughter and voices are floating into the hallway from the suite. I hear the familiar voice of Brad. If Brad is here, it means Kyle is too. Of course. The tickets. Damn it!

I turn on my heel and start to head back toward the elevator, but I am lifted off my feet, arms around my waist. "Not so fast!"

I kick my legs and wiggle in an attempt to set myself free. I feel like Naomi Watts in King Kong's grip. Kyle sets me just inside of the suite, where Hayden thrusts a drink into my hand with a charming smile I want to smack off her face, then disappears into the crowd. Brad steps over quickly, leaning in to kiss my cheek. "You don't look happy to be here," he whispers. Kyle knew when I crossed the threshold that I'd have to act civil. I plaster on a smile for several people who surround me and say they miss me. I resist rolling my eyes. It takes work.

Kyle has managed to besiege me with people like a caged bird, no room to fly. "Baby, we need to talk."

I can't even see around his hulk of a frame. I'm trapped, with no one to come to my rescue. "Don't call me baby, Kyle, and there is nothing to say." I could go rogue and make a scene with my words, but I know that won't end well for me.

"Listen, I'm sorry for getting to you like this, but I know we can work this out, Peyton. I know it. You know it. Your friends know it. We belong together, and I'm not letting you walk away from us."

"Oh my God, Kyle. Let's be clear here. Crystal fucking clear. I didn't walk away from us. You walked away from us. You chose to hook up with someone else, and that was the end of us. Do I need to spell it out for you? E-N-D."

"I promise you. It will never happen again, Peyton."

"I know it won't. Because I won't be with you to let it."

"I just wish you didn't seem so happy. I wish you seemed a little more bent about this."

"I've just found ways to make myself feel better, Kyle. You should try it sometime."

"Like what?" he demands. "Are you fucking someone else?"

"No, Kyle. That is your M.O., not mine." What J.T. and I had done was not in that category. "Yoga. It helps me let everything go. Specifically, you. It makes me happy." I see Brad watching me from across the room. I use the opportunity, waving across the space, then walking swiftly past Kyle in his direction.

"Everything okay?"

"Yeah, sure. Kyle is doing what he can to win me back. It's not going to happen."

"To be honest, I'm scared of what might happen if he doesn't have you, Peyton."

"How can I be responsible for Kyle, Brad? I can barely take care of myself."

"He loves you, Peyton, and you keep him grounded."

I can finally roll my eyes. "I'm tired of all of you saying that. If he loved me, he would have been consoling me for losing my mom and not consoling Kate for losing her job. And he is a grown man. I am not responsible for him. Brad, for all of our sakes, convince him. We're over."

"I don't know if I can do that, Pey, but I'll try."

"Try hard, Brad." I give him a quick hug. "I'm out of here."

"Okay, see you. And hey, I like the new look."

"Thanks, Brad."

I escape the claustrophobia of the suite to my seat, sans Hayden, who was deeply engrossed in a conversation with one of Kyle's friends, Jackson. I would have a chat with her later about that little plan of hers. In the meantime, I had to enjoy the view and the music. It was too good to pass up. Thanks for your generosity, Kyle Nixon.

DECEMBER 10th
CHAPTER 24 | Peyton

I need yoga. I miss J.T. and have fifteen more days until the chance to see him again. Kyle has sideswiped my friends and I am living on guard, wondering what his next move might be. I roll out my mat, excited for sixty minutes of focus on breathing and moving and listening to whatever message the teacher has for me today, though Alison doesn't hold a candle to Alexandra.

I ease onto my back, one vertebra at a time, and breathe deeply, relaxing into my own little world on the four corners of my mat.

"Pssst."

It's close to my ear. My eyes open. I startle to sitting, back to the unbelievability of the here and now. How dare he invade my sacred space! "What are you doing here, Kyle?" I hiss into the quiet of the studio.

"You said I needed to find a way to make myself happy, and you said that yoga made you happy." He is beaming proudly. "If A equals B and B equals C, then, you know, as they say, the rest is history."

"That's not exactly what they say, actually." I quickly assess the room for another spot to relocate my mat, but it's filled up, with class about to begin. I contemplate leaving, but damn it, I have been looking forward to this all day. I will have to use my infantile yoga skills and try to detach from the distraction of him. It may be fun, however, to see him in his first class. He is a large man, and athletic, having been a collegiate lacrosse player, but in my month on my mat, I've witnessed plenty of athletic men lacking grace and resting during class.

Struggling to breathe, my lungs under duress, I think Kyle is sucking the oxygen out of the whole damn studio. I can push through class, get beyond him, and on to J.T.! I know I can. Less than twenty feet away, on the wall just beyond the door is a quote that tells me so. "The future depends on what we do in the present." Yes! Kyle can't have my peace! I've got this. I close my eyes and slide more deeply into extended warrior. Stretching into the long line of the pose always makes me feel feminine and sexy. Eat it up, Kyle Nixon.

DECEMBER 11th
CHAPTER 25 | Peyton

Today's filming is wrapping early because tomorrow evening we are shooting until 6:00 p.m. to capture the sunset against the city's skyline view from one of the uber-expensive penthouses I'm thrilled just to step foot inside. This allows me to work a dinner shift at Conundrum, so I can purchase Christmas presents for Jack, his family, and J.T.

I'd heard from J.T., finally, as he was getting ready to wrap up his day, while I still had a seven-hour shift to work! He said that all was well, claimed to miss me like mad, and he was counting down the minutes until I was in his arms again. I couldn't have asked for a better pick-me-up after the Monday, Tuesday, and Wednesday I'd had with Kyle vying for forgiveness. Even if things didn't work out with J.T., I knew I would never be lonely enough to settle for Kyle.

Arriving at work, I am excited to be given the patio to work on a picture-perfect evening. I love working outside, the heat lamps flushing the chill out of the air, and being close to the passersby and activity of the street. Made up stories fill my head about the couples strolling hand in hand, or those rushing home from the office to waiting families.

My tables fill, nearly all at once, and I am ready to get my efficiency on! Hot sauce for table eight, extra ranch for table three, Chardonnay at nineteen dollars a glass for not one, but two ladies at table six. I peek up from my bar pick-up to see Kelly seat one older lady at my last two-top. She looks the part of L.A. matron. Her this-season Louis draping from her arm cost more than three months of my income. A long strand of pearls, no doubt real, decorate her tailored navy short-sleeve sweater. Slacks are the best word to describe her perfectly pleated and ironed white pants—no memorial and labor-day white rules for the rich. I can't make out her loafers, but they aren't Target knock-offs for certain. Kelly beelines toward me on her return to the hostess stand, whispering as she whisks by, "Take good care of that one."

I put on my best suck-up smile and greet her warmly, "Hello, I'm Peyton, and it's my pleasure to serve you this evening. May I start you with something to drink?" She orders a dirty martini, four olives, if we have blue cheese-stuffed, if not, only two, nothing near house vodka. No problem, Sally. The Meg Ryan pie order movie scene had helped shape who I didn't want to be when I grew up.

Her drink appears to be swallowed all in one gulp. Making eye contact, she lifts the glass indicating to bring her another. I am calculating the tip in my head. Hopefully, she isn't cheap. I take her equally high maintenance dinner order of grilled chicken breast and her own made-up greens and accouterments combining ingredients from the various salads on the menu. Admittedly, the combination does sound appealing, and I ask Eric to make two, one being for me to eat a bite at a time between taking orders and delivering drinks.

I return to Ms. Matron to check on the food that has been delivered via my runner, ready to compliment the guest on the concoction I've also been enjoying. She lays down her fork, clears her throat, and looks up at me. Looking down again, she folds her napkin tidily in her lap. "You said your name was Peyton, didn't you?

"Yes, ma'am."

"Peyton Jennings, you are?"

She asks the question backwards as if the common English version is beneath her, complete with old-money accent. She is the movie character I'd seen being filmed earlier. Overbearing rich mother disapproving of the slutty girlfriend her perfect son has fallen in love with. Everyone knows how it ends.

Of course, I am intrigued by her question. I don't recognize this woman in the slightest. "Yes, ma'am," I repeat, remembering my manners. "I am Peyton Jennings. I'm sorry, have I made your acquaintance prior?" I class it up as best I can.

"Peyyyttoonn."

It's the most drawn-out version of my name I've heard, and I swear I will die if she adds "dahling."

"I'm Patricia Nixon."

She pauses, probably to see if I will recognize the name. Which, of course, I do. Kyle has made this a family affair. I want to laugh at the irony, considering I was never introduced while dating him.

"It's nice to finally meet you, Mrs. Nixon," I lie, because it isn't nice at all.

"I'm glad to make contact with you this evening. Were you wondering if Kyle was an orphan?" A haughty, cigarette-induced, rough and raspy laugh follows. Clearly she finds herself humorous, though I don't at all.

I hate the word orphan.

"Why, pray tell, has he not introduced you to us? We don't mind," she clears her throat, "you're just a waitress." She pretends she hasn't just hurled an insult in my direction. "It's a lovely evening, isn't it, dear?"

It was before you arrived. "Yes, it is. May I help you, Mrs. Nixon? Is there anything else that I can bring you?" Patricia laughs again. This time, a long, loud, exaggerated one. I look around to see if she has turned any heads.

"You know what I was hoping you could bring me? A grandbaby."

I don't hide my surprise well. A little gasp of shock escapes. "Excuse me?" I ask with disbelief. I think she said baby.

"Oh, you heard me, Peyton. I know you are the object of Kyle's affection. The one that has him all tied up in knots, moping around like a broken-hearted schoolboy, so to speak." She rolls her eyes, waving her hand wildly. "For God's sake, just take him back already.

I've never seen him like this, so beside himself."

"Are you sure you are looking for me, Mrs. Nixon? I think you might be looking for a woman named Kate instead. Last I heard that was where he was getting his bread buttered, so to speak." I know it's wrong to throw him under the bus to his mother, but this has gone too far.

"It's you he wants, dear," she continues unfazed. "And frankly, I'm tired of hearing about perfect Peyton." She chokes on the word perfect, not hiding her disdain for Kyle's selection. "It's none of my business whom he desires. I know I'd never think anyone was good enough for my baby boy. The prenup would be a given regardless of my opinion, but I'm not unreasonable. I am willing to be flexible, and I am sure that it will be worth your while, even if you don't end up seeing eye to eye. And let me assure you, your children would always be, shall we say, taken care of."

My head spins as I attempt to process. Is she setting up an arranged marriage? A business agreement? Does she think I can be bought?

"Well, thank you for the kind offer, Mrs. Nixon. Unfortunately, I think I'm looking for a little bit more than Kyle can offer." Something like a real marriage. With love and admiration, trust and respect.

As if on cue, tears begin to stream down her face, leaving mascara-filled ruts in the foundation caked on her sagging skin. She dabs at her eyes with her napkin. "I'm going to die without a grandchild! I can't die without a grandchild. I'm not getting any younger. And you know," she leans in to whisper now, "I don't think Kyle will give up his little parties unless he becomes a father."

Does she actually believe Kyle will trade drugs for diapers? I'm certainly not going to be the one to test that theory.

"I knew I should never have let him become a child star. Those people just kept calling, with all of those opportunities. It's my fault."

As far as I know, those opportunities had only amounted to a handful of commercials as a child. At least now I know he comes by his narcissism honestly.

"Then, of course, there is his illness."

I freeze in place, unable to catch my breath. Does he have cancer? Am I his last dying wish?

"The doctor warned us it could happen again with too much stress, and things have been just fine for so long that we hadn't thought about it in quite a while. To see him so distraught, however, I don't know how much might be too much."

"What illness are you referring to, Mrs. Nixon?" Nothing seemed to be wrong with him in our time together.

She leans forward towards me, then looks around, blocking her mouth with the side of her hand. "The mental illness."

No. No. No. Not happening. Unhear. Rewind.

"We almost lost him, you know." She shakes her head, eyes closed as if trying to clear the memory. She catches a loud sob by covering her mouth with the back of her hand.

I can feel eyes burning into the back of me, people wondering what is taking place at this table. An inopportune time, but I have the predicament of needing to check on other tables. "Can you please excuse me for just a moment, Mrs. Nixon? I need to get someone to cover my other guests." I pat her hand softly and dash off for reinforcement.

My manager, Dickson, escorts me back to my section. My eyes dart from table to table garnering sympathetic looks from those who have full line of sight to our conversation. I return to my ungraceful squat alongside Mrs. Nixon.

"Peyton, you looked surprised just now. Is it safe to assume Kyle never mentioned his past? You didn't know that he spent significant time recovering from wounding himself?" Her voice is barely audible, "Depression and anxiety. He cut himself. He had the best care that money can buy, but they warned us it would be a lifelong battle for him to face."

Bewilderment, panic, fear and shock spin tornado-like between my head and heart. I may puke.

"It was after another relationship ended. And Peyton? He didn't care for her half as much as he appears to care about you. If you leave him now, God only knows what he might do to himself. I don't think you would want to carry around that burden for the rest of your life. Take that into consideration when you think about my offer."

She doesn't take a breath between sentences, releasing the final arrow in her quiver. She sets a one-hundred-dollar bill on the table and stands, brushing past where I am still half-kneeling, stunned into submission, on the restaurant floor.

Dickson is by my side, bracing me as I walk trancelike toward the ladies' room. He stops in front of the door to assess my current state. "Do you need to go home or just need a minute?"

"Min-minute," I stammer, retreating to a stall. I sit on the seat fully clothed, trembling, pressing into my temples with my fingertips. Do the girls know? They have known Kyle for a long time. Is this what they have been trying to tell me? Does Brad know? Are they all keeping his secret?

I know I am not obligated to be his savior, but still? Will I be faulted if something happens? Yes, I will. Someone always has to take the blame. As Mrs. Nixon said, I won't want to carry the burden for the rest of my life!

Breathe. Just one breath. Think of yoga. Just one more. And another. I run my hands under the water, first hot, then cold, then hot again. If only I could wash fear down this drain. I look at myself in the mirror, tuck a tendril of hair that has escaped back into my low pony, and tell my reflection, "You've got this."

DECEMBER 12th
CHAPTER 26 | Peyton

I'm panting. Something is dripping between my breasts. Blood. A knife is in my hand. I hear a man wailing. Screaming. More cuts. More blood. I drop the knife. I cover my ears.

I gasp awake, heart pounding.

It's going to be a long day.

I pull my completed quilt up to the head of my bed and fluff my pillows on top. I start to stumble to the shower and smell coffee when I open my door. With the tiniest slice of morning sun streaming through the living room window, I can see Meredith moving slowly in the kitchen. When I approach, she is leaning into the fridge and reaching for the cream. "Morning, Pey."

"Did you know about Kyle? The cutting?" I'm too tired and out of sorts to beat around the bush. Meredith doesn't answer. Damn it. Implied guilt. "Oh my God. Do all of you know?"

She tilts her head in a sympathetic gesture.

"This sucks, Meredith. That was a pretty big secret to keep. Now his mother is saying if I break up with him and he does anything to himself it's all my fault."

She still says nothing. Surely, she can't agree? How can his cheating not be enough for even one of them to take my side? "What the fuck, Meredith? He cheated on me! He's probably a drug addict and an alcoholic. Not exactly life-partner material. How can you not understand?"

"He said that he would quit if you took him back."

"What? The womanizing? Partying? He might. For a while. But it's who he is, Meredith. He isn't going to give any of that up for any woman. Only if he wants to change for himself. You of all people should know that." Shit. That was a low blow, referring to her own father's vicious cycle of choosing women and drinks over her mother, who has repeatedly kicked him out.

"I gotta get ready for work. Let's talk about this later," she says matter-of-factly. I don't even know what to say.

I have to set aside my angst. Quickly. This is a day I have waited for, and Kyle can't steal this moment. Usually, I am relegated to a bland room with chairs along the outside edge, a few couches and stuffed chairs no one vacates once they are lucky enough to get them, and mediocre food. Today, I am outside under a tent on a blocked-off street in L.A. right next to the real trailers of the stars, and I feel like one myself.

There is a row of makeup and hair stations with pop-up lighted mirrors, high-back chairs and hands flying as makeup brushes stroke and hair is straightened, teased and tousled. I share a station with only three others, our names printed on a cardstock sheet and affixed to the left side of the mirror.

Racks of clothes line another side of the tent, and names are being called regularly to report. I may delay when I hear my name, just to make them repeat it. "Peyton Jennings to costume! Peyton Jennings, costume, please."

I pace alongside the food table, deciding if it might calm my stomach or make the waves of nervousness worse. It's three sentences I've had more than enough time to practice on set the last few days, considering it takes all of fourteen seconds to repeat them to myself.

The spread is vast compared to the usual meat, cheese and vegetable trays for the extras. Today there are prime rib sandwiches with multiple dipping sauces, a full Middle Eastern buffet, and more-than-upscale finger sandwiches with trimmings of red and green something. Fresh, ripe fruit spills from cornucopia baskets, and a dessert tower of items chocolate brownie, lemon bar, and white cake-like is arranged into a mini-Jenga game. I want to grab a chocolate one near the midway point of the stack but am afraid the whole arrangement will topple over.

People move in every direction under the white tent, beautiful organized chaos, energy and excitement palpable. I am living my dream! Finally! If only I could send a selfie with this backdrop to my mom. I decide I will send one to J.T. instead, after hair and makeup.

I am nearly unrecognizable. In a good way. My blond waves have been straightened, with a blowout, gravity-defying lift at the roots. My makeup and costume are pink and proper. Lilly Pulitzer-preppy, but another designer, or vintage perhaps. It's like nothing I have worn in real life. The high scoop-neck eyelet dress has a wide darker pink, purple, blue and green floral grosgrain ribbon belt tied to a bow in the front. The A-line cut flatters my curvy figure. I feel pretty.

Just days from the winter solstice, sunset is looming near at 4:44 p.m. The time cop on set has been counting it down all day. "We've got a deadline here, people! Get your game on!" I have a fake party to attend. A surprise celebration for the bride-to-be.

I quickly raise my phone and snap a selfie with the full-on hustle and bustle behind me. I send off a message to J.T., hoping, because it would only be about 9:00 p.m. for him, I might have a response before being called up to the penthouse.

No such luck. The gopher calls Jennings, Blackstone, Kissinger and Markman, the other names listed on the mirror alongside my own. I stash my phone with my clothes and quickly make my way to Rachel, Avery, and Vanessa. We laugh when we see each other.

"Sandra Dee, much?" Avery says, fake-smoking a cigarette with her fingers.

"I prefer Grandma actually," I joke, the irony of my character not lost. Their previous office scene had the girls in normal workwear, but they now don short skirts, off-the-shoulder shirts and revealing tanks, with ridiculously high heels, depicting the promiscuous friends of the main character. I am the token, presumably prudish, white sheep of the bunch.

We are led across the sidewalk to the building entrance and the crew piles into the elevator. The headset worn by the gopher crackles. "Yes, on the way up with scene thirty-four." The elevator doors open to orchestrated madness. The energy of the street below was uplifting, but in the penthouse the sunset deadline imposes a tense buzz.

There isn't space to move, necessitating the tent below. Plenty of square feet of marble in normal circumstances, but not enough to accommodate the plethora of cameras and bodies. People are stacked wall to wall, and we are bumped along into place by others.

Standing on my toes, I can just catch a glimpse of the balcony where Kellen Bachman and Lexi Gallian, playing Nicholas Kaufmann and Victoria Madison respectively, are seated at a small white linen-covered table. Stoic waiters line the space behind them, with metal platters in their arms. The sky is breathtaking! Purple, pink and blue dance across the cotton-candy backdrop for falling in love.

Victoria's transformation is the point of the movie, evolving to classic beauty from lover of many. His life seemed perfect until of course, he found something he didn't know that he had wanted. A clichéd Cinderella tale told many times, many ways, because most women, including me, fall for it again and again. It never gets old.

The director's assistant calls for quiet then, "Let's roll!" The clapboard reads scene thirty-three and indicates take four. They'd better nail it, because the sun has no mercy. I can't hear what they are saying but can see Lexi's eyelashes fluttering while her lips are moving. Nick's hand slides behind her neck and pulls her face to his, planting a sweet kiss against her lips. Cameras move, then all is still. Everyone glances nervously around the room at one another. It's the look that says they nailed it. "Check the gate! And make it quick! The sun is not in our favor, people!"

I anxiously await the next scene—my scene!—as the production assistants stand poised to stage the next set of props. "And we are moving on!" Cameras and people move like a river flowing, with beautiful rhyme and reason, as new filming angles are arranged, and decorations are placed.

As always on set, I am awestruck!

I appreciate the small army of people who get to see their name in the long list of rolling credits on the big screen at movie's end. I am astounded at the sheer number of bodies involved, with their superpowers of never letting an errant sneeze or cough escape while the cameras are rolling.

Everything clears in front of me and my sidekicks. I am standing right next to the movie star main characters about to deliver my first lines. I am thrilled and terrified at the same time.

A woman with dark under-eye circles and a too-tight ballerina bun and a clipboard appears to be in charge of us. She lengthens her arm indicating we should move toward the right side of the set. We quietly shuffle behind until she holds up her hand abruptly in stop formation. "Watch Peter for your cue," she says curtly, pointing to a man across the room who doesn't look old enough to drink, with black John Lennon-round glasses, a vintage red corduroy vest, and black and white saddle shoes. Thankfully, he stands out from the crowd of people filling the space.

"Nick will open the two doors and he'll give you the cue to walk through." I know this, of course, as we have rehearsed it earlier in the day, but without the stars, the hair, the makeup, and the pressure of the sun falling in the sky. The woman guides us to stand behind tall, double-hung, faux-wood, intricately carved doors. The doors merely a frame, we can still see what is happening on the set around them.

"Quiet!" A random voice from the crowd. The makeup artist dusts powder across Lexi's forehead then disappears like someone has waved a magic wand. These people appear and make themselves invisible in a flash!

"First positions!" Both actors at the table assume the positions that they had just left, his lips almost brushing against hers. "Here we go!"

"Rolling!" A clapboard slams. Nick pushes his chair back, stands, and moves around the table.

"Cut!"

"Sorry." Kellen shakes his head. "My bad." He points left. He'd gone the wrong way around the table. The next take he moves left but Lexi stumbles when he pulls her to standing. A frustrated, more impatient, "Cut!"

The sunset hues deepen, morphing to orange and yellow striation against the blue, purple and pink. "Get it together, people. The sun ain't waiting for your fuck-ups!"

I exchange nervous glances with Avery, who whispers, "Third time's the charm?"

"Quiet on set!" A voice too near us. Avery mouths, "Oops!" with a grimace. This time things progress, with Nick's outstretched hands pulling a graceful Victoria to standing. Then, he immediately drops to one knee. An instinctually female gasp escapes my lips.

"Victoria, everyone thinks that I have it all. Since I met you what I've realized is that before you, I had nothing. I am not the man I want to be without you." He pauses for the first tear to well in the corner of Lexi's left eye. "You keep my feet on the ground. You make me smile. You make me want to be better." Lexi lifts her hand, fingertips covering her mouth. One tear smudges the perfect makeup of her cheek.

"I want to kiss you and hold you and comfort you. I want to show you the world. Today, tomorrow, and all the days of our lives. I want to stand in front of God, and our friends, and our families and say all of this again, at our wedding. That is, of course, if you'll just say yes. Love of my life and soulmate Victoria Madison, will you marry me?"

Both hands cover her nose and gaping mouth as his hand slips behind his back and pulls the ribbon draping from his back pocket.

Adept, practiced fingers smoothly move to cover the ribbon. The doorknob-sized diamond is held in front of the tearfully nodding Victoria, as they pause, letting the special effect lighting highlight maximum sparkle.

She lunges forward, throwing her arms around his neck. "Yes, I will marry you! Of course I will marry you! I'd be a fool otherwise!" As an entangled couple, they carefully turn one quarter so Nick can slide the ribbon into his sleeve, magician-like. Victoria feigns holding steady her convincingly trembling hand with her other. Nick slides the ring on her French-manicured ring finger. Victoria completes the scene with the signature move of outstretching her left arm with fingers spread, eyes wide and twinkling, matching the diamond.

Her right hand moves to her heart, smile widening. She twists and turns her hand ever so slightly, studying it from every angle, face glowing in the golden hour of sunset. After she's assessed and admired, she turns her fingers downward, of course, born for this engagement ritual of show off a ring. He, of course, takes her hand and brings it to his lips, kissing her knuckle below the diamond.

"You've made me the happiest man alive, Victoria. I have one more surprise for you. I was pretty sure that you'd want to run off and tell everyone the news of our engagement—" Nick slides behind Victoria, clasping his arms together in front at her waist, then kisses the back of her hair while turning her body toward the faux doors I stand behind. I hold back silly, happy tears of my own.

"And cut!"

I startle. I was caught up in the moment and nearly ran forward to congratulate a fake bride-to-be! It was surreal. And so real. It's doubtful Lexi needed any rehearsal. She's probably been dreaming about and imagining her own proposal for the last decade. Any single woman in the room could have acted her part. We love the love story whether written, played out on the big screen, or if lucky enough, lived.

"Great work, people! You scared the shit out of me but got it done. Check the gate. And damn it, it had better be clean, because we are done with the sun today."

Minutes tick by as the crew simmers with low chatter powered by nerves. It feels like we are awaiting a sentence being handed down at a hearing.

"Gate's clean!" An audible chorus of relief ripples through the crowd, complete with claps and high-fives.

"Moving on," the director declares, and Peter points right toward the door with his pointer and third finger. I stand, anxious, behind the closed door.

"Rolling!"

The clapboard smacks. "Thirty-four. One."

Footsteps move closer to the door. It's almost time to congratulate Victoria on her engagement. I will gush over the ring, which will hardly be acting. Even though I know it's a prop from a high-end jeweler that will receive promotional consideration buried in the credits, I can't wait to see it up close. I listen intently to the scene on the other side of the doors.

There is the obligatory post-engagement kiss. The director cuts the scene only a few seconds in. "Sorry, had to burp!" I hear Kellen confess, and everyone laughs. Maybe I will see that in an outtake at the end of the film and claim I saw it live.

Next, they cut after about a minute. Nick came to open the door and the fake doorknob came off in his hand. Kellen cutely peeks through the hole the doorknob vacated and says, "Looking fine, ladies!" to the group of us.

I shift from foot to foot, then shake out my shoulders, flopping my arms at my sides. The anticipation is excruciating. The scene starts again, and I hear Kellen deliver Nick's line, "There just might be one more surprise in order!" The door pulls open and I step over the faux threshold, no need to force my smile to stay in place just as it was. Game time!

An imaginary wall holds me in place as my jaw drops in shock. My hands move to cover my face, replicating the pose Lexi held just minutes before. I step forward with my left foot to meet the right, turning toward the crowd to the left, then slowly to the right, for dramatic effect and to rob time. I need it to compose myself.

In front of me is a tuxedo-clad actor striking the classic pose on one knee. This time, however, it is not Kellen Bachman portraying a character. Nothing about this looks fake. The man in front of me is Kyle.

I find myself staring into an unmistakable robin egg-blue box. The classic round Tiffany diamond would bring most women to their knees. I've dreamed of a sparkling diamond accompanied by words of devotion and dedication. In my wildest dreams, it would never look like this.

I look over my shoulder, briefly assessing the reactions of Avery, Rachel, and Vanessa. As expected, they are taking in the unfolding with awe. If I reject Kyle in front of these industry people, there is no telling what will happen. Cameras are everywhere, and I can see the tabloid headlines. Scandal comes to mind. I can't say no with this crowd watching.

I will just have to act.

I move my hands to my heart and step forward to Kyle and the big-ass diamond intended for me. I marvel at its size and sparkle. It is going to hurt a little to give it back.

Kyle pushes the box forward and upward, toward me. He clears his throat and I try to ignore the slight shake of the box. I'm not sure I've ever seen him so sober. Or sincere.

"Peyton, everything that Nick's just said is the way that I feel about you."

He is not going to use a proposal that was written for a movie and say ditto, is he? It will be humiliating if he is unable to conjure up a few original lines about what I mean to him. That enough is a reason to cry, but instead I have a horrible Christmas memory that makes tears spring to my eyes on demand. I feel a solitary one roll down my left cheek.

"You make me want to be the best man I can be."

My inside voice replies, "I'm sorry, Kyle, but your best is not good enough."

"I want to know that you are the one who will be by my side forever. In good times and bad, sickness and health. Just as Nick said, I want to say those vows with you in front of everyone we know. I want to declare my never-ending, over-the-top, can't-live-a-day-without-you love for you in front of the world."

He looks around, making eye contact with the crowd, privileged to see his pronouncement. This is for them, not me.

Then there is the question. I cringe from the multitude of bright flashes popping against the darkening sky. The crowd watches a stunned girl nod her head. I will not say yes out loud until I am accepting a proposal to marry my best friend. As I think of undoing this mess, more tears slide down my cheeks as the too-large ring slides down my finger. Like Victoria, I outstretch my arm and stare at my hand in disbelief.

Kyle stands, moving in for a kiss. The very last thing on earth I want to do is kiss him. You are an actress, Peyton Jennings. Act. His lips find mine. I count in my head, one one-thousand, two one-thousand, three one-thousand. Mercifully, it's over.

The crowd begins to clap and cheer. Kyle beelines to the director, who congratulates him with motions resembling a fraternity secret handshake. Kyle whispers in his ear and they laugh. I'm surrounded by a swarm of women enthusiastically congratulating and envying me, ogling my dead weight. A dozen times I hear the word lucky. Hardly the case.

"The real party is over, people. Let's get the fake one on. Pronto. Some of us have other things, and people, to do this evening," the director squawks crassly, cracking himself up at his joke. No wonder he and Kyle are friends.

Not one, but two makeup artists descend, scoffing at the disaster that is my face. One wipes at the mascara then tags out shaking his head. A woman steps in with a makeup sponge and aggressively applies a new layer of foundation. The director is huffing across the set, "Are we ready yet? First position, let's gooooo." He draws out the word and flops himself back into his tall chair.

The door in front of the four of us swings open, and we pass through with an entourage following, showering unscripted congratulations on Victoria, much as many others had done to me a moment before. I can feel Kyle's piercing eyes. Victoria gushes, recalling the beautiful words of love that Nick used to propose. My first spoken lines in a movie. "A girl certainly couldn't say no to that! I'm so jealous! We can't wait to help you plan the wedding, Victoria!" As I deliver the lines the irony makes me want to laugh out loud as I choke through the words.

Kyle is still waiting in the crowd lining the set as we wrap over an hour later. As I exit, he catches my hand, interlocking his fingers with mine. We walk hand in hand, fake-happy couple, to my car. He opens the door and I hurry inside to avoid kissing him again. "See you soon," he says, closing the door. I am grateful he lets me leave without much fuss.

Is he following me? I turn left, then right. He is still behind me. Hell no. Please no. I park and hurry to the elevator, where he casually leans against the wall, looking pleased, conquest complete.

"Please go home, Kyle. I am really tired."

"You should be," he says, reaching to pull me into his arms.

I push off his chest. "Seriously, Kyle, can we just talk about this tomorrow? Please?"

"Talk about what, babe? Your brilliant acting today?"

Yes, my acting had been brilliant.

"Aren't you so glad that I got you that part? You got to deliver your first lines! No way you won't make the final cut!"

I glare at him. "What did you say?"

"Which thing? You were brilliant?"

"About the part."

"That I got you the part? Of course I did. I owe you so much, Pey."

I am livid. Line crossed. Here I was, thinking all along I had earned my way, only to find out it is all a farce.

"It was clutch! How else was I going to have the perfect setting to propose to the woman I love?"

Finding no words to express my anger, I scowl and push open the door to my apartment. For the second time today, I am overwhelmed by a mob of women greeting me with congratulations. Multiple hands seize mine, twisting and pulling the ring in their direction for further inspection.

"Oh my God, it's beautiful!"

"It's sooooo big, Peyton!"

"I want my own Tiffany!"

How many minutes am I required to endure? Through the crowd I see there is a spread of food to feed twenty to thirty people to the left. Along the right wall, a long bar holds a plethora of glass bottles and mixers. A party? For our fake engagement? The doorbell rings. Let the hell continue.

A few hours and pain-dulling drinks later, I finally retreat to my bedroom. I wrap myself in my t-shirt quilt, wishing my mother could give me advice on getting out of this one.

I'm awakened by Kyle crawling into bed next to me. Hell no! I try to sit up, but he hovers over me, lips close to my face.

"Peyton," he slurs.

Drunk? High? Both? After I was coerced to smile through the obligatory toast, I managed to use the crowd to keep a distance. I have no idea what time it is or how much mayhem has ensued since I snuck away. I try to shift my body out from under him. "Please, Kyle, I'm so tired. Can we please just talk about this tomorrow? Can you please just leave me alone?"

"I'm never leaving you alone, Peyton. Don't you know that? We are getting married."

"Like hell, I am marrying you, Kyle."

Now I've done it. Why couldn't I just keep my damn mouth shut?

"What do you mean like hell you are marrying me? Did we not just get engaged tonight?"

I'm not stuck beneath him any longer because he's on his feet, hands firm on his hips.

"Just go, please!" I beg.

"You don't have any intention of marrying me, Peyton?"

"Did you really think I was going to marry you? You were just going to waltz in there with a diamond and I was going to forgive everything and spend the rest of my life with you?"

"When you said yes, yeah, Peyton, I kind of did. When I committed to you for the rest of my life? In front of all those people? That's how proposals work, Peyton. I asked and you said yes. You said yes to forever!"

"I said yes because hundreds of eyeballs were staring at me. What was I going to do? Humiliate you in front of all those people? If you knew anything about me or gave a shit, you would know that I would never want to be proposed to in front of a crowd of people."

"You lying bitch. You said yes!"

I feel his rage beginning to course.

"I won't live without you, Peyton."

The sliver of light from the open door illuminates the ring on my nightstand. He reaches for it, then for my hand. He tries to shove it back on my finger, but I move it into a fist and try to pull away.

"Let me go!"

He twists my wrist in his strong hand then pushes me back onto the bed. I grab my blanket and cover myself as if it will protect me, curling into a ball. I need a new plan. I say calmly, "You're a great catch, Kyle. I am sure someone will sweep you off your feet in no time."

"God damn it, Peyton. I don't want someone. I want you, and I get what I want. And if I don't, my mother does. No one says no to my mother."

He knew? A grown man relying on his mother to get a woman? I know better than to say another word about it. I change the plan. "It's not you, it's me. You don't want me. I am screwed up in a million ways. I wouldn't be a good wife. I wasn't even a good daughter. I've never had a normal relationship in my life." Including ours. Ours was definitely not normal. "Trust me. You can do better. You can even tell everyone that you broke up with me and I won't say a word."

I am hopeful this tactic will work. His silhouette is ominous. His shadow projects on the wall across from me looking like a bear ready to pounce. Play dead. I cover my head with my hands and squeeze my eyes closed as if not seeing him can make him not be here. He snatches the blanket and I hear the sound of fabric tearing. I scramble to my knees. "No! Please, Kyle, no!" I am on my feet and trying to pull the blanket from his hands. "Please, that's from my mother!"

"You've been nothing but a bitch since the day your mother died!" Another tearing sound. And again. Over and over. My fists pound his back in hysteria as he turns his body to keep it away from me. "It's better I shred this than your face!" His arm pulls the fabric taut and it gives way, breaking free. I am knocked backward onto the bed. My head hits the wall with an echoing thud. Ouch.

"Oh fuck, Peyton." He scoops me up like a baby, arm under bent knees and the other behind my back. I am crying. From the pain and because he has destroyed the last thing I had from my mother. As soon as I move past the pain in my head I kick hard, arching my back unexpectedly and throwing myself to standing.

"Get. Out. Now!" I don't recognize my roar, fierce and demanding. "Out! Now!"

"I'm so sorry, Peyton. Promise me we will talk about this. Promise me."

"Get. Out," I seethe through clenched teeth.

Hayden and Jenna appear in the doorway. "Everything okay? We heard a noise."

I remain staring straight at Kyle. "Don't worry about me, girls. It was just my head. Kyle was just leaving." Neither says a word as he brushes past, out of the room. Jenna starts toward me. "Leave me alone." Both back up and I slam the door, curl up in bed, and cry myself to sleep.

DECEMBER 22nd
CHAPTER 27 | Peyton

Something is ringing. Am I dreaming of Christmas bells? Is it my alarm? I'm definitely in a bed. It's a real ring somewhere. Phone. Yep, phone. I smack for the nightstand. Why did I leave the ringer on? Hoping for J.T. to call. Oh yes.

I half-open one eye and answer with a groggy, "Hello."

"Uh-oh. Maybe I should call back."

"Hi, Jack."

"I'd say good morning, but I think maybe I've just contributed to not so good." He laughs.

I smile. I am happy to be waking up in Detroit to Jack calling. Never could I have imagined feeling that. Then again, anywhere would have been better than California the last nine days, spent watching my phone blow up and avoiding my roommates.

The tense feeling inside our four walls was exacerbated when, on my way to work, I stumbled into their conversation about Kyle and an impending death march. I begged them to spend their time convincing him to get help for depression and addiction instead of spending time winning me back. I'm crushed they appear only to be worried about him and blaming me. I feel friendless and lonely. The very time a girl wishes she could call her mom.

At least I have a house and one friend in Detroit.

"It's all good, Jack. I just slept well is all."

"Sorry I didn't pick you up last night. You were kind to understand it was past my bedtime. Thanks for texting you had arrived. And Merry almost Christmas. I'm so glad you made it back. It means a lot to have you here. I miss your mom like crazy."

"Me too, Jack. There have been a few times I could have used some advice."

"Well, you got me, kid, if you ever need me."

My heart melts at his sentiment. I've finally got someone if I need someone. I don't know how this happened, but I am glad that it has.

"What are your plans today?" he asks.

"I've got some shopping to do."

"Well, if you are not too busy, I'd love an extra set of hands if you want to help me cook for Christmas Eve. No pressure though." He laughs again and I know he means it.

"I'd love to. I'll text you later."

"You plan to see that fine young man who had you smiling like the cat who ate the canary last I left you?"

"I hope so. He returns from Africa tomorrow."

"Well, he's welcome for dinner too. I'd love to see him again."

He seems genuine in his statement and I appreciate his offer. "Thanks, Jack. I'll let him know."

We hang up and I fall into my pillow, content. Never could I have imagined having hope of finding new meaning in Christmas. I spent yesterday's plane ride contemplating my future. I'll find out soon enough what my inheritance will bring. I feel forced to find a new place to live. Maybe it shouldn't be in California. Will I be able to keep my mother's house? Attend college in Michigan? Or perhaps, Chicago? Or maybe I should explore Africa and see if I have the potential to help others.

My phone dings again. A text from J.T.!

Counting down hours til home and u! back 23rd @ 11 cst...too late to call???

I quickly reply with,

please call...can't wait! Be safe! We have plans ☺

He returns:

wish I could talk, have to run but know I can't wait to see you...and a few other things 😉.

And yeah, I know your brain went there. ZOO

I reply,

Truth! ZOO 2U2!

I add a couple of lip emojis for good measure.

I flip through our Chicago selfies on my phone and laugh at our diner picture taken by Zane. I think about J.T. removing the dress after midnight on New Year's Eve.

I will see him soon! Will he spend Christmas Eve with me and Jack? I know he plans to spend Christmas with his mom and Ellie. Unfortunately for me, he'd made plans to continue an eight-year post-Christmas tradition of skiing in Northern Michigan. Two married friends have a hall pass to spend time with the guys, expecting babies to replace buddies next year. But we have couples kind of plans, kissing one another at midnight to bring in what will surely be my happiest new year.

Will J.T. introduce me to his mother? Buy me a Christmas present? Should I get him something?

Before my brain completely runs off the rails, I put my feet on the floor. I need yoga. The added bonus is doing it without having to look over my shoulder for Kyle.

The chill in the air is replaced by the warmth of the fire and the people in the yoga studio.

"Welcome back, Peyton!" greets me from across the room's reception.

"Hi, Lynn! It's good to be here!"

Alexandra strides toward me. "How's California this time of year? I sure miss that weather!"

"Hi, Alexandra. Yes, the weather is nice, but I sure missed you and this studio!"

"Are you here for the holiday?"

"Yep, as scary as it is. It's a new kind of celebration for me this year. I'm grateful to be here." I don't suppose I should share that I can't wait to see a guy I met at my mother's funeral.

"Gratitude rules the happy world. That's good. It's a tough time of year for a lot of people."

Her sincerity insinuates she might mean for herself as well. I hesitate, unsure what to say next, but I don't have to figure it out because she's distracted by other students. I watch as they interact then take in the others mingling in the lobby. So much goodness happens on the mat that can be taken into the real world. The welcoming fire, the quotes I know I can grow into, and the shared smiles in this studio make it feel like home.

We start class in child's pose because, as Alexandra's smooth voice cajoles us inside ourselves, we all need an extra moment to stop and settle down at the busiest time of the year.

"Take a deep breath in, feel your lungs expand against your legs, and blow out a long breath through your mouth. Let me hear you let it all go." The studio relaxes in a collective sigh, peace settling into the room.

"Everybody, allow yourself a seventy-three-minute break. The holidays can be a wonderful time, but they are always a stressful time. Most times people are just doing the best they can to get by, so proceed mindfully, keep breathing, and err on the side of love."

Forehead against the mat, and belly resting on my knees, with soft piano and string music playing, nearly lulls me to sleep. In just a minute I will move into poses that will force my limbs to California earthquake-tremble, but for this moment I am merely breathing, with nothing to break up the peaceful feeling I only experience here, with forty or so other people doing nothing but breathing together.

I'm almost an hour closer to talking to J.T. That's my gratitude in my exhaustion. Class has to be coming to an end. I hope his trip is easy and on time so we can talk before I fall asleep. Too bad he isn't coming straight to Michigan. He could be in my bed sooner. He'd needed his ski gear and said his shorts probably wouldn't cut the

Michigan winter weather. He should have shipped his stuff ahead. That would probably be expensive.

What did it feel like to come back to everything from a place that has nothing? Does he appreciate the basics so much more? Water coming from multiple faucets with just a turn? Toilets that flush with a touch? Electrical outlets every six feet by code?

Oh. My. God.

How long has my mind been off my mat? We are moving to Savasana and I missed a whole side of pigeon pose.

"If you've realized that your breath has taken a back seat to your thoughts, and you didn't even get sixty of the seventy-five-minute break that you were looking for, please come back and see us again tomorrow, because we call this practice for a reason."

Alexandra finishes class with her last bit of wisdom, many people chuckling at the comment. I take comfort in knowing we are all in this together, just trying to get through class, and life, one more breath at a time.

I head to Starbuck's after class, only to be greeted by a very long line. Luckily, I am still in a yoga Zen state. Turning to observe the crowd gathering behind me, I see Alexandra in line near the end. I motion for her to join me. Hopefully, those who notice her taking cuts are in the Christmas spirit. When it's our turn to order, I motion for Alexandra to go first so I can pick up the tab.

"Thank you for the offer, but it's not necessary."

"It's hardly a fair trade for what you give me. Since my peace is priceless, I can't return that favor!"

We both order and move to the pickup area.

"I'll let you in on a little secret, Peyton. I hate to admit it, but I think I might get more out of teaching than I give."

"What? Really?" I sound as incredulous as I feel. Maybe I should consider becoming a teacher.

"It's pretty powerful. Watching everyone grow stronger, and the energy that builds during class. I thrive on it."

"Is that why you became a teacher?"

She laughs quietly. "Oh, not at all. It's just a bonus. I became a teacher because I needed a new profession so I could be available for my son. A lot was going on in my life, and a way to cope and find some peace in the chaos topped my list. Serendipitously, I sat by a studio owner on the plane ride moving to Michigan. She happened to be coming to do teacher training. I had done yoga sporadically at best but liked it. I didn't have anything to do or anywhere to go once arriving in Michigan, so I showed up. And the rest, as they say, is history."

"Well, I guess that was being in the right place at the right time!"

"You could say that, or you could say when you're paying attention you never know what you might find right in front of you."

This makes me think of my mother. What had I missed that was right in front of me? "I haven't been paying attention for a long time."

"Well, all you can do is start now by living in the present. How about now, like the present?" She laughs at herself, and I have to laugh back, the mood lightened.

"You are young, Peyton. Give yourself a break. I've had a few decades to figure this out and I still have a lot to learn. I'm just the best student of life I can be. We figure out this life thing together, one day a time."

For once, I feel that with J.T., Jack, and Alexandra by my side, I might have a chance to do just that.

DECEMBER 24th
CHAPTER 28 | J.T.

Re-entry. There is always a place where I feel the calm pace of Africa contort to first-world freneticism. I should be used to it by now, but it always hits me like running head-first into an unexpected wall.

This morning, my own frantic pace is required, to get my ass to Detroit pronto. Considering my body's mid-afternoon time zone, pulling onto the highway at 5:10 a.m. isn't a stretch. Assuming I am still having dinner with Jack and his family, not falling asleep, head on my plate, might be, however. Coffee is always my companion in my commute around the world.

Dinner is no guarantee, keeping in line with my shitty holiday track record. I was so hopeful that I'd be holding Peyton in my arms within hours of being back in the United States, but my hopes were dashed by what I'd learned. My plane was ninety minutes late and my call upon landing had gone unanswered. The miles and days didn't deter my thinking about her, but there's a chance I'm walking into a full-fledged disaster.

I could blame an eighty-degree temperature swing in less than twenty-four hours, but it's more likely I am shivering on Peyton's front porch from nerves. Until that last hour of flight, I planned to kiss her then make love to her within minutes. Now, we need to talk. Outside of her bedroom.

She pulls the door open and takes my breath away. I thought I had etched the details of how the corners of her eyes rise when she smiles, but my memory hasn't done her face justice. Even with her blue eyes still coveting sleep, the way they smile at me hits me in the gut and groin at the same time. Damn this girl.

"Hi, you! Get in here out of the cold." She reaches for my hand to pull me in.

Curiosity before consternation. I let her take it.

I can feel her warmth to my core. I shrug out of my coat and hang it on the curved end of the wooden banister. She lunges forward and I wrap her in my embrace, breathing her in. Her cream-colored pajama top has the word love in black written in horizontal lines. Maybe the universe is telling me it will all be okay.

My hands slide over the silk down to the small of her back. They want to find more of her, but I resist. I'm sure she is expecting a kiss, but I can't go there yet. Too much unknown. I bury my face into her hair and smell the floral aroma of shampoo. She feels and smells so good.

"I missed you so much. I couldn't wait to hold you again, but I need to ask you something." I can barely squeeze the words out, my throat constricting in fear of what she may tell me. She releases her arms from our embrace and looks at me, eyes wide.

"Oh my God, what? I was expecting a different greeting than this, so please, ask me anything."

Her eyes close and she shakes her head. Her chin drops to her chest, before looking back into my eyes. "You know?"

Not exactly what I am hoping to hear.

"I'm so sorry, J.T." She holds up her left hand so I can see the absence of a ring. "I'll tell you everything. It's been a rough couple of weeks."

She steps backward away from me, and I want to pull her in again, not wanting her to feel rejected. I desperately want to believe there is a rational explanation. I take her hand and lead her to the couch, where we sit side by side.

"I was never in love with Kyle. I never even once told him that I loved him."

She seems adamant on this point.

"I broke it off before Thanksgiving, just like I told you. He went to all lengths to get me back. There were flowers, and concert tickets. The more I said no, the more he pushed. He even got his mom involved. I made it abundantly clear we had no future. I swear."

I notice her hand move to the side of her head. She rubs a spot without thinking. Did that bastard hurt her? I will protect her always. "I did think it was ironic that People magazine just happened to be left in my seat pocket on the airplane. I had a lot of time to kill and was flipping through. It's not something I would normally read, but it's hard to think maybe I wasn't meant to—"

Her hands start to wave as she interrupts, intent on getting something off her chest, "No. It's not at all what it seemed. When people started texting me Monday when the issue hit the stands, ugh! I would have told you if we talked. I should have texted you. The whole thing was infuriating. Thank God they barely showed my face! Sometimes it pays off to be no one. And, for the record, I deserve an Oscar for my performance."

"It sure looked like engagement photos. On bended knee, and after. I have to have a relationship based on trust, Peyton."

"I hated that kiss. It wasn't real. Kyle cheated on me. I know what it feels like and have no intention of inflicting that hurt on another human. It was awful. I had to say yes in front of all those people. I told him just a few hours later I was never marrying him. I haven't had contact with him since. I don't have the ring. I never wanted the ring."

"Okay, thank you."

"That's it? You didn't yell or accuse me or—"

"That's not my M.O., Peyton. I kind of give people the benefit of the doubt and err on the side of love." I run my finger from left to right along the words covering her nipples.

She looks at me quizzically. "I've just heard that same thing somewhere recently."

"I'm pretty sure I learned it from my mom."

"So you aren't mad?"

"I'm not mad. I was really hoping there was an explanation. Really, really hoping. I just needed to look into your eyes when you answered my question. I'm going to trust you until I think I have a reason not to. Screw me once, shame on you. Screw me twice, shame on me. I do real, regardless of whether it comes with a happy ending."

"I'm not used to someone who doesn't go stark raving mad on me. It's going to take some getting used to."

"Well, I think I can help with that." I'm unable to let another second pass without kissing her. I pull her face to my lips and let her blond waves fall over my hands. She covers my hands with her own, connecting us together in a new way. This is a different kiss, tender, with mutual understanding. Our tongues unhurriedly and affectionately tangle, her breath my exhalation, nothing separating us from one another. I want this moment in my memory forever.

"There are a few more inches I'd like to start exploring on your perfect body," I say sliding my hand up the outside of her black silk pajama pants, stopping at her waist and pulling her toward me. She surprises me by pushing on my chest and I am forced to lie back onto the couch with her on top of me.

My kiss shows her how much I missed her. I push my tongue deeper into her mouth and kiss her more forcefully. My hands find her ass and I pull her tightly against me, feeling an immediate arousal. Her covered breasts push into my chest and I anticipate feeling them with my hands and mouth before exploring the rest of her. I hope I am not thinking with my dick and overruling my brain, but I've thought of a million things I wanted to do to her over the last month and I can't fight nature.

Her legs on either side of my body, Peyton sits up, allowing me to unbutton her top. One. I see more of her chest and my dick flinches. Two. I can push the sides of her top around her breasts, remembering their shape and size peeking out from that beautiful dress. I know what is waiting for me below. My fingertips skim the sides and run along the u-shape curve of the underside. I watch her pink nipples swell. Her head falls backward.

Three. Her sitting on top of me gives me unabated access to two perfect mounds of flesh. I cover both breasts with my palms. She grinds her hips against my hard-on. I squeeze her nipples between my thumbs and forefingers. She grinds again. Oh, this girl. She drives me mad.

Four. Who needs to wait for the last button? My hands find the graceful curve of her shoulders as I slide the silk over them and down her arms, leaving her top half completely exposed. I'm looking up at her, and marvel at the view. Her long neck is feminine. Strands of blond flow gently over her shoulders, falling just short of her breasts. I run both thumbs from the base of her throat outward on each collarbone, then my hands down her arms again. She places her hands on my chest over my heart. I wonder if she can feel it pounding out of my chest with what she does to me.

She leans back onto her heels over my thighs. Finding the button of my jeans, I feel it release. She leans back just a little further to unzip me. I am free of the fabric holding me back. Sweet relief.

I lift my upper body just enough to put my arm behind my head and pull my sweater over it. I'm not wasting time, so I take off my gray t-shirt as well. I relax back into the leather, sliding my hands to her waist, thinking what it will be like to lift her up and down on me soon. Closing my eyes, her hands languish, flesh on flesh over my chest. Shoulders. Biceps. I enjoy her touch. Her thumbs sweep the sensitive skin of my elbow joint and I shudder as a jolt of energy runs the course of my spine.

She leans forward, whole body warm against mine. "I can't wait to have you in me, J.T. Walker." The whisper sends another wave of shivers head to toe, then her tongue explores my earlobe. She kisses downward along the side of my neck then each pectoral muscle, exhaling against my nipples. Shudder take two. My balls are rocks.

I reach to the hem of her top and pull it over her head, tossing it to the floor. I push the waistband of her pajama bottoms down and find nothing underneath. Just one more article of clothing separates me from her nakedness. I'll wait just a little longer.

My arms around her back pull her forward, flesh on flesh, together as one. She extends her legs slightly, my hard cock and her clit perfectly aligned. We move in unison, rhythmically rocking, her clit against me. Unexpectedly, her breath is becoming more hurried, mine matching its urgency.

"I love making you cum," I whisper into her exhale. She groans against my lips, then gasps. My hands on her hips, I guide her movements, feeling them quicken. A long, drawn-out, "Ooh," reverberates as she forcefully pushes into me and I back into her, holding her tightly.

"Oh God!" She trembles in my arms and I move to hold her, so she feels safe. I keep pushing my hips upward until she relaxes onto my body fully, hot breath coming in pants against my chest.

"I missed you, Peyton." I hope she doesn't think I just missed this. I missed her smile and her laugh and holding her talking as well. But I won't lie, the effortless turn-on is pretty remarkable too.

She wastes no time scrambling to her feet, standing on the side of the couch, breath still jagged and audible. I sit up with her between my legs, reach for the silk drawstring, untie the bow, and slide the pants over her shapely hips and legs. She takes both my hands and pulls me to standing, wiggling my jeans over my hips to the floor. I lean down to get rid of the socks quickly. When I return to standing, she slides both hands over my erection while moving up to my waist. She carefully maneuvers my boxer briefs around the protrusion. Finally, we are naked face to face.

I find her lips again and reach to lift her right leg to my hip. She locks it behind mine, and I find myself painfully close to her. My kiss says I can't wait to have her, lips intensely pushing against hers, demanding. Fingers tangle in the hair on the back of her head, but I am careful to avoid the area I saw her rub earlier. I won't hurt her.

Her hand closes around my shaft, gracefully gliding over its hardness. My right arm holds her hip in place while my left fondles velvety smooth skin between my fingers. Her grip on my shoulders tightens. I push my third finger inside of her. So wet.

I slowly move in and out until her palms pushing hard against my chest force me back to lying on the couch. She straddles me. I hold her hips, guiding her wetness to slide over me.

I can't wait any longer. Shit, I need a rubber. I reach my right arm down to the jeans on the floor and pull my wallet from the back pocket. She takes the package from my fingers and opens it, unrolling it over me, and returns to where we left off.

She lifts her hips slightly to position herself right over me, tip feathering against her opening. Finally! Letting me enter only about an inch, I move forward to where just the tip remains inside of her. She pushes back. Just a little deeper. Each inch feels like it's the first time. She pushes back again, just a little more, and releases me to the tip again. This build-up works. I've never wanted a woman this badly.

No longer able to be denied, I bury myself in her with a hard thrust. All of me. Heart included. Damn her, she'd better not break it.

Peyton's hot, wet pussy surrounds me to the base. She pulls forward and pushes hard into me again. A groan with animalistic undertones is forced outward from my gut. My hands around her back hold me deeply inside of her, feeling the constriction of smooth muscles.

I lift my hips, wanting to feel the friction again. With ease, I push in deeper yet and keep my hips raised. I feel her clench around me. Her breasts push into my chest and her hair tickles my shoulders and arms. I feel her everywhere.

"You feel so good," I groan into the base of her neck.

She slides her hands underneath my back, reaching over my shoulders from behind. Hands on the small of her back, I feel it arch, tuck under, arch again. Pressure in front. Pressure just above my balls. Pressure in the front. Tight pressure over my whole shaft.

Hips circling, grinding. Her hand gripping my balls, pushing them tighter into my body. Oh shit. Oh shit. Let go. I can't speak to tell her to let go or I will cum. It feels so good. So tight. So wet.

I find her hips again. I lift her hips up and slide myself out to the tip to hold off my impatient orgasm. She circles her hips and her labia move all around my head. Oh shit. I find her butt and pull her into me. We hold each other so tightly it's hard to breathe. Our hips and chest rock together in one forward, then backward, motion.

Peyton's body is trembling against mine from head to toe. She breathes fast and hard into my ear and I feel her heart beating against my own. I can barely catch a breath against the pressure in my balls, her body over mine, and her knees squeezing into my sides. Her hips thrust upward as her back arches deeply and I feel her pussy twitching into my release. I am so hard and so deep in her. I groan with the pressure and pulsing, squeezing the flesh of her hips. She is still trembling in my arms. I keep pushing inside of her, harmonious sounds of male and female pleasure, together. We hang on tightly.

Our moans retreat into silence. She is fully relaxing on my body. I feel goosebumps break out on her skin from the chill in the air. I move my arms around her back to cover as much as I can of her to keep her warm.

I never want to let go.

CHAPTER 29 | Peyton

"I'm all nerves on this porch," I say to J.T., shivering at the door of Jack's house.

"You should have seen me this morning on yours." He laughs. "I tried to blame the temperature swing from Malawi to Morganville but don't tell anyone. It was all you." He shoves his shoulder into me playfully with a wicked, crooked smirk. Oh, what that dimple does to me! His words and playfulness turn my crazy to calm in an instant.

Like the month before, Danielle opens the front door. "Pretty sure you should just be walking in by now! New rule, no more knocking for you." Now I am calm and happy. She leans back, still holding the door handle. "Incoming. And they have presents! Hopefully for me!" She laughs and holds back the wind by closing the door hurriedly behind us.

"It smells great in here," J.T. says with a wink, knowing I had helped the day prior. He follows me to the kitchen, where the informal receiving line is ready. J.T. goes down the line, shaking hands with Evan and Griffin. Jack pulls him in for a hug. By the time I have hugged to the end of the line, I stand in front of J.T., who has an armful of Tucker.

I hadn't thought about the possible parental preview but J.T.'s ease with the toddler in his arms causes the official line-crossing. My heart has gone where mere mortals dare to dwell. I am so screwed. J.T. lifts Tucker's hand to high-five me. My heart may melt right out of my chest.

Jack heads toward the refrigerator but says over his shoulder, "Great to see you again, J.T. I guess it's official that you have stolen the hearts of both of the important ladies I have had in my life."

"Hey, what about me?" Danielle says with a laugh, scooping up Tuck's dropped sippy cup.

Jack's thunderous laugh overwhelms her own. "Give it a few hours, Danielle, and he'll have yours too. J.T. is one of the good guys."

"Thanks, Jack. I have to give my mom and Mrs. Jennings the credit. And the school of hard knocks."

I watch Danielle's reaction to gauge what information Jack might have shared, but if she knows about his past, she doesn't give any indication. I change the subject anyway, lest Danielle decides to ask him about the comment. "Hey, fair warning that we are probably leaving here early."

"Well, of course," Griffin teases. "Hard to spend so much time out of bed."

I nearly choke as the heat of crimson blush creeps up my neck and fans across my cheeks.

"Griffin, you suck! Look what you did to her!" Danielle rescues me, putting down the potato she is peeling and throwing her arm around my shoulders. "Don't listen to him. Ever."

"It's fine. But wrong, Griffin." Partially, at least. "J.T.'s on another continent's time zone. He just got back from Africa and I think it's already the middle of the night for him."

J.T. slides to my side, assuming the position Danielle has vacated. "And I might have wanted to get up way too early to get to Detroit today." He smiles at me, eyes mischievous.

"Because you wanted to get laid," Griffin chides, relentless.

"Dude, it's obvious why you are the only one without a plus one here," Evan calls him out.

J.T. doesn't acknowledge his comment out loud but does flash a wickedly handsome smile in my direction. He mouths, "Guilty."

"I saw that! He mouthed 'guilty'."

Evan's arm finds Griffin's neck in a mock headlock. "You are just jealous, man."

"Guilty," says Evan, and laughter ensues all around.

Danielle sets the last potato on the counter. "Okay, I am out! Peyton, it's all you from here. Actual cooking is about to commence, therefore I acquiesce my duties to others more qualified. Where is the wine?"

I set the two bottles in front of her, and Danielle moves the white to the refrigerator. I watch her remove glasses from the cupboard. Four. Griffin has a beer, so I assume she hasn't counted him to partake, which means she knows. No glass for J.T. I catch her attention. She lifts a glass to me, and I carefully shake my head no. She returns it to the cupboard quietly. I am grateful. If J.T. has maneuvered the last ten years one situation at a time, surely I can learn as well.

While passing the salad, Jack suggests we save the toast for the New Year, and I am grateful once again. I don't want to cry in front of J.T., and I guess he feels the same. He does share how happy he is that we are all together, and I couldn't agree more.

After, we gather in the living room. I am astounded by the decorated tree. I've never realized how beautiful they can be with white lights twinkling brightly on each green bough. My favorite ornaments are red and white glass candy canes because of the cute way Tuck keeps pointing to them, saying in his baby voice, "Cahn-dee!" I also enjoy Jack giving me the tree tour of his and my mother's travels. A wooden palm tree with small fake lights with Key West in handwritten black font. A small purple metal Eiffel tower because they planned to go to Paris one day. A bunch of grapes and plastic champagne glass from northern Michigan.

Jack seems happy to stroll down memory lane with me, sharing his happy times with my mother. I am happy she had the chance to experience many places, but sad that I never asked her about their adventures together.

"Oh, I almost forgot!" Jack moves to huddle in the corner behind the tree, emerging with a gold rectangular box. He drops to his knees and makes a three-foot-wide gap in the semicircle of presents. He leaves toward the front door and returns with a small step stool, which he places in the space he has cleared.

He presents the box to me. "It was Caroline's tradition. Now, it's yours."

I lift the lid to see a beautiful angel wrapped in white tissue printed with swirls and snowflakes of gold and silver. I look up from the box and my teary eyes reflect Jack's.

"Thank you." I can barely push out the words as I take the two steps upward, stand on tippy toes, and place the hollow center above the top branch. I climb down and stand back to admire the tree that now looks complete.

I look to J.T. to share this special moment, but his easy-going nature seems to be waning. His hands are in his pockets and he looks a bit uncomfortable. Maybe he is getting tired. Or maybe it's something else? Is it possible he isn't all about this pomp and circumstance either? On the one hand, it might be nice to write this holiday off forever, on the other, it would be nice to make up for lost time.

Apparently, I am going to start tonight. A pile of gifts has started to amass at my feet. Danielle is under the tree looking childlike, handing each present to Tucker, who wears a Santa hat and toddles person to person, balancing the boxes. He sets each down with a squeal before running back to her.

When the presents are distributed, I gather mine in my lap where I sit cross-legged. I have three gifts stacked from Danielle, coordinating red and green printed paper tied up with a white and gold ribbon bow.

"I don't want to open it, Danielle! It's too pretty." I am giddy.

"Only you get an actual fabric bow instead of a stick-on. Only a woman appreciates the effort!"

"Hey, there's no bow from me but I wrapped it myself, and that should count for something, because I suck."

"It does count, Griffin, it really does." I mean it. It's poorly wrapped but I appreciate the effort. There is a gift from Jack in a big box next to me, because I can't fit it in my lap. I want to cherish all of them, so I insist the others open first.

Paper tears and bows fly. First, thrown by Tucker, but the grownups join in, each taking a turn being the center of attention with a chorus of oohs and aahs upon each item revealed.

Evan and Griffin seem to appreciate the iconic Detroit Shinola journals I give them. My gift to Danielle is met with equal fervor. She had texted after our Thanksgiving yoga conversation that she'd attended several classes. I give her a subscription to a popular yoga magazine and a trendy tank top. To Jack, I give an individual-sized Yeti cooler, because he had shared he likes to spend summer evenings with a beer and the elusive fish of a neighbor's pond up the road.

I slide my finger under each piece of tape and methodically open my gifts, savoring my turns. I am leaving with a new yoga mat from Jack, and a towel to match from Griffin. Danielle's shared gifts of her favorite things, stolen from Oprah. They are mine as well. Lush bath bombs, silver and gold wear-with-everything hoop earrings, a candle in a mouthwatering cinnamon apple scent, note cards with my initials engraved on the front in feminine font, and a large box of chocolate "for when all else fails." I am peaceful and content surrounded by my very own pile of gifts.

J.T. is gracious when opening his authentic Blackhawks jersey despite the ribbing he has to endure from us Red Wings fans about his fanship conversion after moving to Chicago. I notice his jaw clenching, and he is quieter than during dinner. He is game-facing.

After the present opening is complete and the mess cleaned, I fake a yawn. I make it a little louder than it needs to be, then quickly cover my mouth as if it were an accident. "Oh, oops!" Acting is my profession.

"Looks like Peyton needs us to wrap this evening up," Jack says jovially.

Danielle nods. "Santa has a LOT of work to do tonight."

Tucker's cute little voice rings out, "San-ta! San-ta!" They start the kids early on the Christmas magic.

I stand up, taking a leftover gift bag from Jack to put my presents in. He asks, "Are we on for tomorrow?"

"Sure thing," I reply.

"I'm gonna kick both of your asses," Griffin sing-songs.

I look to J.T. "We're going bowling tomorrow."

Danielle scoops Tucker into her arms. "I wish I could go bowling instead of to my in-laws!"

Evan chimes in, "Hey now!"

J.T. smiles, and points to me. "Look out for this one. She gets a little competitive."

"Yeah, yeah. I will own to that. And I will look forward to owning both of you tomorrow!" I say with a laugh.

Jack holds my coat while I slip my arms into the sleeves. He envelopes me in a goodnight hug. "Merry almost Christmas and see you tomorrow."

I complete my round of goodbyes and say thank you to the rest of the clan, then make my way into the cold, clutching my bag of goodies like a child with brand new toys. J.T.'s arm around my waist to keep me steady on the snow and ice completes the comfort I feel.

Safely in the car, J.T. remarks, "You and Jack held up well today."

"How about you? Did you hold up okay? That had to be a lot, to come with me. Thank you."

"Yeah, sure, of course. I'm just tired."

"I have an idea! Do you know where the Starbuck's is in Morganville?"

"Yes, I think so. But pretty sure they aren't open, Pey."

"Of course they aren't. Just go that direction." Then, realizing I sound bossy, I add, "Please."

As we approach the park that serves as the town square of Morganville, the life-size nativity scene is illuminated with spotlights as it nestles in the snow. "There," I say, pointing in the direction. I head to the plastic manger, climb over the rope designed to keep people out, and kneel on the hay between Mary and baby Jesus. I motion with my hand for him to come join me. I know my grin is ridiculous. "Let's take a selfie! I want to remember tonight with you!"

Secretly, I hope this might help get him out of his funk. He complies and holds the camera outstretched in front of us. I kiss his cheek in the photo.

"Let's take one with Joseph. My mom will love it. She went with Joseph because he already had the good name." He points to the baby Jesus figurine with his thumb.

He doesn't seem to be holding this little field trip against me, thankfully. We snap one more picture of me with the cow and the wise men. Then, as if on cue, white, cold flakes drift through the air all around us, like we are in a snow globe. We face the scene and hold each other for a silent moment. J.T. kisses the top of my head and I look up at him. Our lips meet in a delicate kiss, against the backdrop of love and grace.

I fall into bed, with J.T. right behind, and next to me. He finds my left hip with his right arm to pull my body parallel to his. "Hey," I say quietly. "This might surprise you, but I want to talk. I know you're tired, but I think there is more to your story." I reach forward and slide the dog tags around his neck between my fingers. "Please talk to me. I can tell something is bothering you." He is silent and I wonder if he is warring with himself. I am patient, waiting quietly until he rolls away from me onto his back as if needing space, but finally speaks.

"Tim. He was killed on Christmas."

"But you said it was on your birthday." The moment the words leave my lips I know, his apprehension no longer a mystery. My hand instinctively covers his heart. "Oh my God," I gasp. "Your birthday is Christmas Day. Joseph. Jesus. I get it now. Oh my God."

"Yeah. How's that for the worst day of my life? Every year. So I've got that going for me."

He tries to say it with a cavalier tone to make light, but I hear the pain he tries to disguise. I wish I could kiss and love his pain away. All I can do is hold him. I run my fingers through his hair and hold his head and heart at the same time I keep puckered lips against his cheek. I wrap my leg over his body. My reasons for hating Christmas just got a lot smaller.

"I'm so sorry," I whisper in his ear. "Everything is always better in the morning," I whisper again, my lips finding his earlobe and brushing against it.

His voice is solemn, "The last nine years, I've never slept on this night. I relive the images again and again."

"Tell me."

"Being torn away from Tim's lifeless body as it was covered with a white sheet. I was covered in blood, way beyond just my hands. I was so numb. I remember my mother hugging me for the first time again, not being able to feel her warmth. I didn't deserve to be warm when Tim's body was deathly cold."

My heart breaks a little more.

"I'm grateful for exhaustion right about now, and everything is better with you in my arms."

"I couldn't have said that better myself." I pull him even tighter into me.

"Don't worry about me, Peyton. I've got this."

I reach over his body to clasp his right hand with my left, then place our intertwined hands in the center of his chest. "No, J.T., we've got this. I know there isn't anything I can do to make it better, but this year, you don't have to do this alone."

DECEMBER 25th
CHAPTER 30 | Peyton

J.T.'s 5:00 a.m. shadow greets me in the morning. He tossed and turned all night, which meant I did the same. I tried to hold him but to no avail. It's early but the sun has risen such that I can take in his long eyelashes, angle of his jawline, and messy blond mop hanging over his forehead and eyes. His brow furrows. I reach to smooth it reflexively, and lovingly, with my thumb. If only I could smooth the pain away so he could enjoy today. His birthday! His twenty-sixth. And it's Christmas.

I hear a phone chime from the other side of the room. His phone. I move slowly and pull it from the back pocket of his jeans. I'm trying to be helpful, not spy, I convince myself. The notification still on the screen is from "Mom". It says: "I know you don't celebrate but Happy and Merry anyway. See you later." The full word "you", no abbreviating with the letter only, and no emojis. Grown-up texting.

J.T. stirs as I climb over him into the bed. He lifts his head and tries to open his eyes, then closes them again, returning his head to the pillow like it's too much work to face the day. He groans in protest. I cuddle up to his warm body and he puts his arm around me, pulling me close. I groan back, but out of contentment. He smiles, not opening his eyes. "What are you doing awake so early?"

"I'm sorry. I was making sure the world wasn't collapsing. Your phone made a noise. I'm a slave to the damn ding of a message." I stroke his cheek, loving the feel of the stubble against my palm.

"Did you handle it for me?"

"It was your mom."

"I could have told you that."

"I'm not sure what to say, J.T. I want to wish you a you-know-what and a you-know-what but I don't want to at the same time."

"Say it, Peyton."

"Are you sure?"

"Yes."

"Happy Birthday, J.T."

He pulls me on top of him with both arms in one swift movement and I laugh in surprise. "And Merry Christmas."

"Somehow, they sound so much better coming from you."

I smile. We've got this.

"Merry Christmas to you too, Peyton." He squeezes my flesh against his tightly.

"Did I not mention that I don't do Christmas either?" I casually let it slip, knowing I haven't shared the fact.

Wide blue eyes look into mine. Bewildered. "You could have fooled me. You looked like a little kid last night! You were glowing—beautifully, I might add—when you had those presents in your lap."

"It was the first time I've ever had that."

"What do you mean by that?"

"I've never really had a Christmas with a bunch of presents before. Not for me anyway."

He pushes himself up to both elbows. "I've been a selfish bastard. All wrapped up in myself, and here you are with a story of your own. God, I'm sorry. Why don't you like Christmas?"

How nice, but unnecessary, that he owned that. My reason seems unworthy. "It's really silly next to yours."

"I hope it is, but I doubt that. Silly is good, Peyton. I wouldn't want another soul to go through what I have. So, what gives?"

My fingers trace his tattoo. Past, present, future. "My Christmas memories, well, totally blow. My mom tried so hard, but she didn't have much money when I was little, and her family, well, they had plenty of money and not so much love."

"How could that be? You were just an innocent kid." His tone is filled with compassion and anger, together at the same time. His opposition to social injustice is palpable, and I understand his calling to fix the broken.

"My mom lost everything when she left my dad. Both his family and her own rejected her. How do you reject your own child? They thought she made a mistake and was choosing to live a life harder than it needed to be. I guess they decided she didn't deserve their help and she could figure out how to make it on her own. Something like she'd made her bed so she should lie in it. Maybe she made them look bad, embarrassed she was a single mother. I really don't know. I only had to see them once a year, at Christmas, because she said it was important to stay connected to family even if you had differences.

"There were five other cousins. My grandparents and aunts and uncles showered those kids with gifts. They always had a pile at their feet to open. They would rip through their boxes acting like nothing mattered. They left their toys scattered all over the floor and forgot them minutes after they were opened. I would wait and wait for them to open their boxes wishing I got what they did while I only ever got one present. I would hold that one like it was the Hope frickin' Diamond."

"Peyton, that sucks. I'm sorry."

"It sounds trivial when I say it now. I'm sorry for what you went through, but you've given me the gift of perspective. Seriously, I think I am over it. Last night, when people opened the presents I gave them, I think I learned my lesson. It is better to give than receive."

"I agree! And speaking of that—" He jumps up and starts toward the corner where his bag leans against the wall, then pauses, crouching down, next to my open suitcase. He looks back toward me. I move my eyes, unwillingly, from his ass to meet his gaze.

"What is this, Peyton?" He's picked up several shredded pieces of my quilt. I had brought it back to try to fix. I throw my head back into the pillow and close my eyes. "Let's talk about it later. It's too depressing."

"I'm going to respect that, because I don't want to spoil what's coming, but you do owe me some details."

I am still lying on my back when he returns to the bed, laying a small gift bag on my stomach. He got me a gift! It's my turn to jump up and grab the box I've carefully wrapped, and had hidden in my closet, in case I was the sole gift giver. I hand it to him and bounce on my knees on the bed.

"You are going first, Peyton. I insist. I'm invoking the ladies-first rule!"

I peek inside my bag. I can't believe what I see! The same robin egg-blue that days before made my stomach rise into my throat today makes me want to jump from the bed with joy.

It feels as if I can remove the contents of this three-by-three box, fill it with every horrible Christmas memory, and close the lid to banish them forever. Every Christmas wish I'd dreamed of is tied up in the perfect Tiffany bow of white ribbon. I am speechless. And grateful! I take my time untying the package, then lift the blue lid to reveal a silver bracelet. I know the collection. In cursive writing is the word "love".

I lift my new treasure from the box and hand it to him, then stretch my arm forward. He fastens the clasp and positions the word in the middle of my wrist. "I thought you'd like having love right there all the time. To remind you that it's all you need."

I smile. One that overtakes my whole face. "I can't even tell you how much this means to me." I throw my arms around his neck and kiss him deeply, pleasantly surprised he barely even has morning breath.

"How'd you pull off getting me a gift when you've been gone?"

"I might owe Zach. He said I cost him a small fortune buying for his own girlfriend since she was there."

"I'll be sure to thank him." I kneel and kiss him again then push a small box into his hands. "Now you!"

J.T. tears open the paper and lifts the lid on the box. It is a Shinola wallet on which I had J.J.W. imprinted. His thumb slides over the dents in the leather. "How did you know?"

"The monogram on your bag," I say pointing to his well-traveled canvas companion in the corner. I want him to have reminders he isn't Joseph Trouble.

"I love it, Peyton. Thank you. It's Jacob, by the way."

"I wondered. Thank you! We had the same idea. I wanted you to have something from me that would always be with you." I make a face at the end of the sentence. "On second thought, that sounds a little more selfish—"

"Stop. I love the thought. You know, had I known, I would have showered you with more gifts."

"This one was better than ten, J.T."

"I don't know about that, but maybe we could count what happens next as additional gifts." He leans over so I am forced onto my back as he continues to kiss me. When we finally come up for air, I know I wear a devilish expression. "I think I might know one exception to the rule about giving being better than receiving."

Three incredible orgasms later, my revered, cherished, and worn-out body can't move a muscle. His fingers, and tongue, and penis have wreaked havoc in the best way possible. We lie next to each other, both of our chests rising as our breath restores to normal.

"I don't deserve something this good," I gasp.

His head swivels quickly in my direction.

"Like hell. You've got make-up sex coming your way all day for twenty plus shitty Christmases. If I can deliver, that is. Holy hell. You wear me out."

"I'm not sure how much more I can take if you can dish it out." I can barely speak I'm so relaxed. I thought about the sex I've had prior with the perfect romantic backdrops. Here, I am just in my old double bed, but damn! I thought I had the fairy tale several times before but nothing has ever rocked my world like this. The English language doesn't contain adjectives to describe this.

"It's time to dish on your last few weeks, Peyton. God knows I can't do anything else but listen right now."

He's been patient, for sure. His healthy dose of satiation should help him to consume this information. "Okay, but don't say I didn't warn you. You don't want to know. Kyle went crazy trying to woo me back. First, he sent flowers to the movie set. I took apart the bouquet and shared them with all the single, and married, ladies. Then, he bought my friends and I floor-seat tickets to the hottest concert in town. They dragged me to a suite and trapped me so that I had to talk to him. He asked how I was so happy without him. I didn't share all my reasons." I reach out and touch my index finger to his lips. He puckers against it. "I told him it was yoga, which is also the truth. The next day, he showed up at my yoga class. Don't think for a second there I thought of going back with him. After I sent the picture, I was done."

"Picture?"

"Yep. Right when I got back from the funeral, my girlfriend let it slip that while I was gone, he helped console his ex-girlfriend through her job loss. He doesn't have a compassionate side, so I knew his idea of consolation. He wouldn't come with me for my mother's death, but apparently, job loss is fuck-worthy. Sorry about my French. After she told me, I gathered as many girls as I could around the bar, ordered them whatever shot they wanted, lined up the glasses along the bar and took a picture. Then, we toasted and the bartender took a picture of that. Then I took a picture of the receipt. I took the time to put the pictures in a collage. It said 'this one's on you, asshole.' That was it. Well that, and the $1,278 bar tab I put on his credit card. I tipped really well."

"Damn. Remind me not to mess with you, Jennings."

He laughs, but I wonder if he judges my actions as harsh or a minor transgression. Better not to know. He turns toward me, cupping my face, looking directly into my eyes. "In all seriousness, I won't do that. I don't want it done to me and I won't do it to you. I won't hurt you if it's in my control. It's not how I roll, and I hope you will extend me the same courtesy."

Well, that got deep quickly.

"Yes, I agree. I mean I will, or I do." Shit, that sounded like wedding vows.

"So, now that we've got that out of the way, you were saying?"

"I thought we were done, and I was glad because I'd told you I would deal with it and I had. I was shocked when the flowers came and, oh, the premier invite. That was him too. But you know how that worked out."

"That worked out very, very well. I got to see that dress."

"And I got the surprise of a lifetime. Well, that was before today and my amazing present. And a spoil-me-rotten amount of orgasms in twenty-four hours."

"Back to the story. How did you end up in People magazine?"

"Kyle got me an acting job that I was really excited about. In one of the scenes there was an engagement. He took the opportunity to say ditto to the fake proposal in the script. I had to say yes to him because I couldn't very well humiliate the hell out of him. Kyle does not do humiliation. He might have killed me."

"I hope you don't mean that literally. I don't know about you, but when I propose I would really prefer somewhere memorable."

He looks serious and I hang on his words hoping our wants match up.

"Somewhere like the mall."

I punch him in the stomach, just hard enough that he has to flex to avoid the blow. Bonus! It brings a new definition to the term ripple effect.

"Ha, ha, I am not falling for that! For the record, I want one-on-one and somewhere good. Like exotic or ski-hill good." Then I add a smile for good measure. "Just in case."

"Duly noted. And I couldn't have said it better myself." This is becoming my new favorite inside joke.

"So then, he followed me home from the movie set. There was an engagement party already in full swing, waiting for us. I finally escaped the party to my room and when he followed me, again, I told him I wasn't ever marrying him. That's when he shredded my blanket." I cringe at the memory. "It sucked, but then it was over and the rest, as they say, is history. I swear. And for the record, I was worried about you and the damn pictures the whole time they were snapping them. I would have told you as soon as you got here and asked how everything was while you were away. Quite frankly, it was terrible, and now you are here, and it's been incredible. More than incredible." I lean in and kiss him again. "Thank you. For everything."

"The pleasure, Peyton Jennings, is all mine."

"I suppose we should drag ourselves to the shower and separate?"

"I would take you with me today, but it will be a tough day for Ellie. It always is. I will break it to my mother that she is no longer the only woman in my life and then I will introduce you. Like, as soon as I get back from this ski trip I am now dreading more than my next dental appointment."

I snuggle up to him, basking in his kindness. "Go and have fun. Just miss me."

"You know I will."

"And we still have tonight, right?"

"Yes. I will be counting down the minutes until I am back in this bed with you. Finishing off the rest of your gifts."

"You know this was already my best Christmas ever, right?"

He nods. "*Daylight*. Maroon 5."

"What?"

"That's the song for today."

"I'm going to dread the daylight too. I'm just going to need to know that you are in one piece every day. Then we have New Year's Eve. I can't wait to kiss you at midnight."

"Me neither. And for that dress. I already can't wait to see you out of it. I mean, in it. Yeah, that's what I meant."

I laugh. He sighs. We are both happy.

"Just promise me I'll see you first thing on the 30th."

"You don't think that's the first thing I will do? That's an easy promise to make. I promise."

After returning from bowling, where I did indeed kick a little ass, I spend the rest of the afternoon primping for my last evening with J.T. When he texts he is counting down the minutes to seeing me, and there are only about twenty-five minutes left in the countdown, butterflies dance in flight in my stomach.

I am pacing the living room floor, hardwood cool under my bare feet, watching for headlights to come into view. I cinch the belt of my robe and shiver in the draft. Or maybe in anticipation of what is to come.

Everything is ready. Now I just need him.

He takes the turn into the driveway rather quickly. I hope it means he is equally as excited to be coming home to me as I am to have him here. I figure he will use the side door into the kitchen, and I figure correctly. He knocks twice then I hear the door open. "Peyton, you have to learn to lock the door. I hope you don't leave your door open in L.A.!" His voice is coming closer to the kitchen with each footstep.

He rounds the corner where I am waiting. He freezes in place. I've dimmed the lights but can see his eyebrows rise to reveal all of the beautiful blue that makes his eyes so special. One corner of his mouth crooks up, forming the sexiest smile I've ever seen on a man's face. He still doesn't move, a bit dazed at what's before him.

"Holy shit."

I am taking a chance. This could be unforgettable or end badly, but holy shit with a smile seems a good start.

He takes a step forward, mouth gaping, gaze carnal. "You are going to be my undoing." He stops abruptly, as if he has reached an invisible barrier. "I don't think I could stop looking at you if I tried."

He takes another step, narrowing his eyes into tiny slits as if to determine if they are deceiving him.

"Happy Birthday, J.T." I am sitting on the countertop, holding a small chocolate cake with three flickering candles in the white frosting. I lift it toward him. "I hope this is okay." He stands before me and the candlelight frames his finely featured face in silhouette.

"It's more than okay, Peyton."

He is standing between my legs, inches from my body. I can feel his heat, my whole body coming alive with the rush of sexual energy emanating. I lift the cake until the candle flames dance in front of his perfectly full lips. "Three candles. Past, present and future. Make a wish, J.T."

The sexy-dimple smile returns and his eyes blink, long eyelashes fluttering, then close in concentration. The flames extinguish with his breath and he reaches his index finger into the frosting on the cake. His finger finds my mouth and I suck the sweetness from it, swirling my tongue around the tip before he retracts it. He sucks in an inhale. "The most gorgeous woman I've ever seen is sitting on the counter decked out in the sexiest white lace I've ever seen. I'm not sure there's a wish I can make better than what's already come true."

My cheeks tinge hot with his compliment. I feel beautiful in this lingerie. It is wedding-night white, and I bought it when I wanted and needed to feel innocent, at a time my reality was neither. I'd only worn it once. Alone. It is a sheer nightgown with a flowy hide-any-imperfection bottom and a tight lace bodice with delicate ribbon straps. They tie halter-style, lifting my breasts into a perfect cleavage, full and voluptuous. Matching white panties have a g-string attached to a waistband of the same lace as the bodice. It is simple, feminine and pretty.

He takes the cake from my hands, sets it on the counter, and cups my face.

"You are so beautiful, Peyton. You look like an angel. A sight for sore eyes."

My brow furrows at the thought of his having sore eyes.

Hopefully, he hasn't been crying.

He leans into me, exhaling softly, then gently pinches the skin on the top of my bare thigh. "Making sure this is real."

It was a breathless whisper, just centimeters from my lips, and his closeness and warmth do crazy things to my insides. I lick my lips, ready for him to take me in a kiss. He moves the cake to the side, his eyes remaining steadfast, locked on mine.

"I can't, for the life of me, imagine what I've done to deserve this." He places his hands on either side of me on the countertop. He leans in. "I've never…"

I cross my ankles behind his back and pull him forward with my legs. His forehead is pressed against mine. "How can I ever thank you for today?"

Our lips are like magnets resisting the pull. I want him. "I can think of one way." My lips form the words brushing against his, then suddenly his hands are everywhere. Wrapped around my back, arms, breasts, shoulders, caressing and enveloping. His lips crash hard against mine, tongue an orchestrated assault against my mouth.

His hands pin my face in place as he ravishes my lips, his afternoon stubble scraping against my sensitive skin, but hurting in a good way. My fingers tousle and tangle in his hair as I grip it tighter and pull it harder. He sucks in breaths of air.

He pulls his sweater over his head and presses his naked torso into my lace-covered bodice. My arms wrap around his back and pull him into me. I want him closer! My breasts flatten against his chest and I scratch his back from his shoulders down to his waist. His hands slide up the outside of my thighs, his large hands gripping them tightly at the top.

J.T. surrenders the attack on my lips and moves to my left breast, taking it in his mouth over the lace. Slowly, he lets it slide through his teeth. I brace myself against the tantalizing sensation, hands gripping the edge of the counter.

One finger slides inside me.

"So wet. So hot."

The words float into my ear. Another finger joins. I moan as he twists them while sliding them outward. My head falls backward, and he kisses and nibbles both sides of my neck. "Come for me, baby."

It doesn't take long with his fingers moving in and out of me while his thumb brushes my clit. His other hand massages my breast and rolls my nipple between his thumb and finger. Chills run up and down my spine and I gasp loudly as the orgasm tears its way through me. My insides throb around his fingers. "Oh my God, Joe!"

I rest my head against his shoulder to catch my breath while my body settles back into itself. I realize he is standing stiff as a board, hands by his sides. His hands and lips are no longer anywhere on my body. "What is it?"

"You almost made me forget I don't do birthdays." His hand moves to his chest, rubbing the dog tags between his finger and thumb. It hits me. This is my fault. A one syllable mistake. I'd called him Joe.

I'd taken a chance with the cake, but I am going bigger now. My arms already around his back, I move them upward to the nape of his neck. I press our faces together, cheekbone to cheekbone, hard, to distract him. I take the chain in my fingers and move it up his neck slightly. "J.T.," I clearly articulate the two letters this time, "you've punished yourself enough." My tone is firm, not to be argued against. I feel every hard muscle in his torso tense but he isn't stopping me.

"No," he chokes out, agony in the word.

The chain is over his ears. "Yes. It's time to let go. Please. It's okay."

He shakes his head, mine moving in line with his. "I can't," his voice cracks.

"Yes. You can." My voice sounds strong against his resignation. I finish pulling the chain over his head and he gasps but remains in the embrace of my legs, not pulling away. I reach for his hand by his side and press the dog tags into his palm, then close his fingers around it. "You can keep it close enough to remember, but it doesn't have to own you," I whisper.

My lips move to his neck and I kiss all around the spot the necklace has just vacated. When I finish all the area I can reach, I cup his face between my hands and tenderly kiss his lips.

"I'll never forget."

It sounds agonizing.

"But it's been ten years. That's a long time. I can forgive myself enough to move forward."

It sounded a bit like he was asking me, but I know he must come to this on his own. I give him what I think is the truth, "I think so, J.T."

He closes his eyes looking like he is contemplating what comes next. "Will you make me forget about everything for a few minutes?"

He doesn't give me the chance to answer the question. The metal dog tags clank as they fall onto the granite countertop and his hands move from my shoulders down to my hips and back up again, clinging to me like I to him moments before. It is his turn now.

His lips never move from mine as my fingers find the button of his jeans and eagerly unfasten them. I feel the loss of his warm hands as he pushes his jeans and underwear down just enough to free himself. His hands find their way back to my thighs as I stroke him with both hands, feeling him become erect with my touch. He moans into my mouth then greedy hands cup my ass and pull me forward to the edge of the counter. I clasp my legs more tightly around his body until I am floating in the air, supported by his strength alone.

Sliding down his long body until my feet feel the cool tile floor beneath, I quickly spin toward the counter and arch my back. His moan is louder and more serious. I grip the counter with one hand and pass the conveniently placed, right next to the cake, condom, over my shoulder with the other. Pushing the string of my underwear aside, he slides into my wetness with one long, smooth motion.

His hands on my hips pull and push me into him and him into

me. Being fully clothed makes me feel less vulnerable and more playful. And, in this position, new and different sensations are controllable by arching my back more deeply and pushing into him. And oh, his hands! Wrapping around my front and cradling my breasts, caressing puckering nipples hidden beneath the lace. I love it! I like the strength of his legs alongside mine, bracing me as I weaken under his power. I also enjoy indulging J.T. with the sensual grinding of my hips, as evidenced by his carnal groans.

Then. He. Stops. He pulls out of me. Everything clenches. I feel empty. Surely this must not become a habit.

"Peyton, look at me."

I turn slowly in place to face him.

"That was too much like fucking. You deserve better. Not that I don't want to do you every which way to Sunday, because I do, but I want you to know how much I respect you first."

"Okay, thank you." I'm too stunned to say more.

"This is the kindest thing that anyone has ever done for me," he says reaching behind my back and picking up the knife next to the cake. He cuts a small piece and raises it to my lips. I take the bite, still being held around the waist with his free hand. I face the counter and cut him a bite as well. Lifting it to his mouth, I let him lick the frosting from my second and third fingers. I push my thumb into his mouth, then pull it out and trace his bottom lip.

"Delicious. Like you. Let me take you to bed and make love to you."

Um, okay. "Shall I bring the cake? I can think of a few places I'd like you to lick frosting from."

His smile looks wickedly sexy. "I'd be a fool to say no to that."

We race each other to the top of the stairs, stopping at the top for a sweet kiss full of vanilla essence. He holds my face between his hands. "Somehow, in your presence, the intolerable is a whole lot easier. My first birthday in ten years might be my new favorite day. Thank you, Peyton."

I lift the cake toward him, a toast-like gesture. "To new

beginnings." I mean this as much for us as for myself. I am changing, and this relationship will be different.

"To new beginnings," he repeats.

"Now, about that making-love thing? It's not nice to keep a lady waiting, you know!"

He takes the cake, sets it on the floor, and reaches for the hem of my nightgown. He pulls it over my head looking at my body from head to toe then back up again. "You are so beautiful." He kisses my forehead. "Here," then kisses my chest, near my heart, "and here." He presses his knees to the ground and kisses my pubic bone. "And here too." He picks up the cake and stands. "Lead the way."

Haunted pasts, zero. Love, one.

DECEMBER 27
CHAPTER 31 | Peyton

My grandmother had warned me this day would come. Ignorance and grief had me miss the foreshadowing from the funeral. She said we would be speaking more often. It is doubtful my inheritance will offer any comfort to the fact that these people abandoned their daughter, denied me a family, and treated me as the outcast while lavishing the inner circle of children.

I hope it will, however, afford me the opportunity to make different choices about my future.

The face of a man in a dark suit with a baby-blue tie and a book-lined wall backdrop flickers into view on the monitor perched atop the desk in front of me. Jack sits by my side. The lawyer who had contacted me to meet with my grandparents about my trust clumsily pivots the screen towards us.

He had introduced himself as James F. Greenburg. He told us the "F" stood for Franklin and it was a very presidential name considering that six past U.S. presidents were named James.

He seems as nervous as I feel but I think this might be his usual disposition. I fear he was probably chosen on purpose by my grandparents for their corporate lawyers to abuse his perceived weakness. I hope I am not the one who suffers.

I can make out the profile of my grandmother on the right side of the screen, and it eerily reminds me of Mrs. Nixon. I look to Jack for reassurance and he seems calm. I'll take him as my rock today.

"Are we ready to get started?" comes through a hidden speaker, voice of God like.

"I believe so," squeaks James.

"We are here today to discuss the disposition of a trust to Peyton C. Jennings on the date of her twenty-fifth birthday, on the date of March 24, 2015. Can both parties please acknowledge their understanding of the subject matter?"

What am I supposed to say? Inappropriately, my inside voice speaks loudly as I see the image in my head, "Show me the money!" I almost laugh out loud but contain it. Barely.

I hear both of my grandparents' voices in unison, "That is correct."

I jump to attention. "That is correct."

The voice of the other lawyer comes through the speaker again, "By the paperwork I have reviewed it appears we have a total sum of $500,000 to distribute to Miss Jennings over the course of ten years."

My spine straightens. I work to keep my jaw from dropping. My mouth wants to fall agape but I clench my jaw to avoid it. I force myself to breathe in. Jack's startled expression exposes he was not expecting this either.

The lawyer continues, "We are here today to discuss the viability of this disbursement or the potential need for amendment."

Is this as I fear? Is there a loophole for them to take it away?

"I understand that the Rhodes have something they would like to share."

The uncertainty of what will come next has my stomach flipping and palms sweating.

"Peyton, darling—"

My grandfather's use of the word darling makes me cringe inside. Could he have been protecting my father because of his own equally disgusting acts? I think of my uncle Gus and how he whistled at me during the funeral, appalling and repulsive. I always suspected him of despicable behavior. What if they were kindred spirits of the vilest nature?

"We aren't unreasonable people, but rather, clearly generous. We understand that you may fall on hard times without your mother, and if you need us to provide you with more of your trust now versus later, we want to take that into advisement.

"We may not have agreed with your mother's choice to forsake the opportunities we provided to partake in our company, but you are not your mother. You shouldn't be punished for her mistakes."

Now Jack loses control, his jaw dropping to his chest. He quickly realizes and corrects but doesn't make eye contact with me.

My grandmother jumps in, "We want you to be a part of our lives, Peyton. Please let us know how we can help you."

I knew she resembled Mrs. Nixon! She wants to buy me also. Why do these people think money can buy my love?

"You don't have to decide immediately, but please know the offer is there," my grandfather says, sounding as if this concludes the meeting. The lawyer is probably charging by the minute.

"Okay, thank you. That's very generous," I offer in return.

We are escorted out of the room by James. Jack and I move swiftly to the car in silence. The moment we are behind closed doors he turns to me, "Congratulations. I'm not sure that's the right sentiment, but I don't know what else to say. That's a hefty sum of money you can use. I already knew you had a bright future, but it gives you an awful lot of options. I had no idea. What do you think?"

"I think I want to come home." When I say home it just feels right. "I'd like to keep the house, and you can stay any time. It's your home too. I think I will take classes. I'm not sure where. Dare I say see where things go with J.T. and maybe go from there? I'd also like to go to Africa!"

"That all sounds great," he says with a broad, genuine smile.

"I couldn't help but notice your reaction when my grandfather mentioned the company. Help me understand," I inquire, my curiosity palpable.

"All this time we believed it was about her leaving your father. Now I wonder if it wasn't more about his pride. Your grandfather wanted her to be his successor. He raised Caroline with the intention of her being the next CEO. I remember she said he told her he chose her name to start with the letter "C" because it sounded good with CEO. After the incident with Michael, she left the business. She felt her father took Michael's side and she couldn't work beside him any longer. He lost Caroline and Michael. If you were stuck with only Gus, you'd be pretty pissed off too."

He laughs a hearty laugh. "I shouldn't laugh; it's unkind. That's how your mother ended up a teacher. She lost a lot too. Her marriage and her job. But she knew something. You can't feel sorry for yourself when you are helping others. Every bird with a broken wing she came across, and every person who needed a little extra something, she fixed, and she gave."

Every person like J.T. How was this for coming full circle? Because of my scumbag father and the disownment of her own, my mother had helped save J.T. from himself.

"So yes, Peyton, I think the house and college are a great idea. And Africa? That's even better. Like mother—"

I interrupt him to finish his sentence with a smile, feeling deeply grateful to say, "Like daughter."

DECEMBER 29
CHAPTER 32 | Peyton

This California girl is going to learn to ski. Oh, brother. I decided to take Jack up on his offer to teach me since it's something J.T. loves to do. It goes along with my testing country music since he'd mentioned his affinity for it. I am not trying to morph into someone I am not, just expand myself to new possibilities.

We are leaving at 9:00 a.m. so I am dragging myself to 6:00 a.m. yoga. I need to be New Year's Eve body-best so a two-workout day it is. The local "mountain" won't be much exercise, because it's a small, old garbage dump, but still a movie star in its own right, making an appearance in Aspen Extreme. I've been on a high since Christmas anyway, so who needs sleep?

I enter Exhale still half asleep, but see Liz talking to Alexandra, giving me a good reason to wake up quickly. I hurry toward her and squeeze her in a tight embrace. "Liz! It's so great to see you! Thank you, thank you, thank you! Yoga has been amazing."

I reach for Alexandra's hand then grab Liz's as well, holding them up, grace at dinner or Our Father at church-style. "Meeting the two of you was the best present ever. I had such a wonderful holiday, and I know this will be the best New Year—probably even year—I've ever had. Seriously, I can't thank either of you enough!"

Alexandra laughs. "I see someone is happy. A year's a long time, but I wish you many happy moments!"

I throw my head back. "Ugh! Of course, I am getting ahead of myself. Well, hope and love will do that to a girl. Good thing I am here so you can bring me back to reality."

Liz doesn't laugh with the two of us but says sincerely, "You are very welcome, Peyton."

Maybe the holiday took its toll on her, and here I am, blabbering and blubbering with happiness. Hopefully, the class will give her what she needs to deal with whatever is on her plate.

I settle right into quiet breath, content inside the four corners of my mat. The studio is still and hushed despite the large post-holiday crowd. It's dark and warm, inviting peace and quiet.

Alexandra enters the studio, closing the door softly behind her. "The holidays are a difficult time to be mindful. Busy begets breathing, and the next thing you know you are wrapped up in knots."

Her soothing voice lulls me to a new state of relaxed. I feel such gratitude. My eyes well with tears as it washes over me. Tears of joy. I finally have the family I've always dreamed of having, and dare I say, a new boyfriend. If only my mother was still with me, life would be perfect!

Alexandra continues, "When all else fails, find one little thing to be grateful for."

I have gotten to grateful before Alexandra has told me to. Maybe I am getting the hang of yoga, and life!

"Find one thing, and then another, because there is always something. Build upon it, and it gets better from there. You can't be in a state of gratitude and anger. You can't be in a state of gratitude and fear. Let gratitude claim its space as the only space."

Yes, live in the space of gratitude. I can do this.

"Now, rise up from child's pose, slowly and mindfully, to table pose. And keep breathing. Your breath doesn't have to be loud, but it does have to be louder than your thoughts."

Light laughter from the thinkers, present company included. I push myself up into the pose. The line of the song Alexandra is playing is about remembering a kiss. It makes me think of J.T. and the way he kisses me, sometimes tenderly, sometimes passionately, always awesomely. He tastes and feels so good.

The songs says he will still be loving her at seventy. I can picture it. Us together, on a swing like on Jack's porch, holding hands and resting my head on his shoulder. Us, walking on a beach hand in hand. Dare I let my mind wander to the edge of he could be the one? I'm lost in happiness and hope.

My head spins toward an unwelcome sound that pulls me from my peace. The wooden door to the studio has been forcefully pushed into the wall.

My heart stops beating.

The oxygen is sucked from the room, my lungs leaden.

I am frozen in place, filled with anger. Rage. Terror. It permeates the studio, infiltrating the space that was silently sacred one second before.

A large form has imposed himself among us, his eerie and familiar shadow dancing on the wall. It reminds me of the last time I saw him.

"Peyton, where the hell are you?"

He slurs my name into two long and horrible-to-hear syllables. This is bad. So bad. How can he be here? I forget for a moment where I am. I'm in Detroit, right? Is Kyle really here? Is this my worst nightmare, or reality? I want to wake up. Wake up!

Bodies move abruptly in sharp angles, scrambling to their feet and scattering left and right. I am swallowed up in the middle of the crowd of thirty-some people moving hurriedly in a protective pack from the room into the hallway amidst a chorus of screams.

"Everyone out!" rings in the air. I think it's Alexandra's roar. It's large and loud from someone so little.

"Peyton!"

Kyle. I'm outside the studio but the sound inside is fiercely hostile.

"Peyton!"

Is anyone still inside, unsafe? I don't know. Or what to do next. I lean against the wall, chest heaving, finally taking a breath away from his toxic presence. Someone yells, "Call 911!" The reality of the situation bears down on me. What will make him stop? If he doesn't find me here, will he leave and look for me elsewhere? Does he know for certain I am here? Was he stalking me? Had he seen me enter then filled his body with who the hell knew what?

A million unanswerable questions flood me. How can I know the answer? What should I do? Will he hurt anyone? How can I know what will save the lives of these innocent people if he is out of his mind? He's proven this won't end until he gets what he wants, but what does he want? Me? Alive? Or dead? Me to take him back?

I close my eyes, which heightens my sense of hearing. Large boot-clad feet staggering overtly.

"Where the fuck are you, Peyton? You think you can leave me? I don't think so." His voice is shriller and more anxious.

A hoard of screams fills the lobby and my ears, but they are dissipating as people exit through the front door. Cold air envelopes the studio, shoving against the heat of the crackling fire. The draft surrounds me and I shiver from its effect. Or from fear. Others are freeing themselves from Kyle. Free of the fear of dying here at the hands of a jilted lover. My ex-boyfriend. Wreaking havoc in a place of peace in a small town where things like this DO NOT HAPPEN.

I want to be one of those people who has escaped. A voice inside me screams to run, at war with what I know is right. There are still people inside. There must be or he would have emerged. I can't leave while others' lives hang in the balance. I lean forward and put my face in my hands, catching the silent scream I need to release.

My ears ring! Gunfire! My stomach rolls over and contorts, knowing. Oh God! I have to go back in there. It should be me and no one else. No one else should be a victim here! I force my feet to move. One. Then the other. Forward. Move, Peyton! I can see into the studio, barely, through the front door left open, but can remain hidden from sight. I clamp both hands over my mouth to catch the gasp. Alexandra's lifeless body is sprawled across the floor in a pool of blood. Kyle is moving towards the side wall I can't see, towards his next victim, I have to assume. A sound I can't interpret. A woman's blood-curdling howl of pain. A dull thud like a body crumpling to the ground. What has he done to her? Is Alexandra dead? Has another woman just been murdered?

I'm weary by what is happening inside these four hallowed walls. I steady myself, palms pressing into the wall. I may pass out. I know how to breathe. We practice in class. What had Alexandra just said? Your breath has to be louder than your thoughts. I need to replace the short bursts of panic compressing my airway. I am so dizzy. My head is a whirl of images and sounds unfolding before my eyes. I need useful legs to go in there. They are shaking uncontrollably.

GO! I push myself off the wall with new strength. I'm going in there. I have to move.

"Don't you DARE hurt him!" From the ground, I hear Alexandra growl.

She's alive! Thank God she's alive! Now I know there are others in the studio. Damn it!

Another awful sound echoes off the walls of the studio. Another body hitting the floor. A man's voice full of pain and fear. "NO!" The noise of something hitting the wooden floor then the rubber of a mat. Please, God, let it be the gun!

I step into the doorway, observing the destruction left in Kyle's wake. The circle of red around Alexandra has grown larger, and her body is draped protectively over another woman's body in a rag-doll heap, on the floor next to Alexandra. Another woman is slumped against the wall writhing in pain, so she is alive. Oh God, no! No, no, no, no, no. It is Liz!

"Kyle, I am right here. I'm not leaving you. Come with me. Let's talk about this." I don't recognize the voice as my own.

He is going for the gun but stops. I walk towards the back of the studio to distract him and allow the other man to get the gun. Kyle turns to the sound of my voice, swaggering towards me. He is so fucked up! He doesn't look like the Kyle I know. His eyes are piercing, more menacing and dark than I've ever looked into. He reaches me then drops to his knees. On a yoga mat. In table pose just as I had been before he changed the world I know.

Kyle melts into a sea of tears, in opposition to his strength and stature. One moment he was dauntingly huge, towering over us, wielding the power of a gun, and the next, a shell of that man, seemingly under my control.

"Peyton, oh God, Pey. When I thought you left me in California… I can't live without you. I won't live without you."

I can barely make out the words through his tears and drug-induced state.

I put my hands on his head and pull his face into my body. Now that he can't see the room I mouth "Get Out!" and point feverishly toward the door.

I'm on the floor and can't breathe. What the hell's just happened? Kyle is on top of me, so heavy. I can't breathe. "Kyle!" I gasp with forced air. I try to push him off me, but he is limp. I realize he has passed out and pulled me under his nearly two-hundred pounds of dead weight, burying my small frame. Thankfully I have landed on a mat, but everything hurts from the impact of the fall. "Kyle!"

He doesn't move. I wiggle my body until my legs are out from under his, then push off the floor with my feet to roll out from underneath him. Is he breathing?

I look around at the bodies sprawled before me, the enormity of the situation crashing down. There is blood on my hands. This is all my fault! I start to cry uncontrollably. I pull my knees into my chest and form a ball, body shaking and rocking. Sobs of pain, fear, relief, confusion, and anger play a haunting melody echoing off the walls, yet I can't stop the explosion of tears. Too much emotion, not enough courage.

I am vaguely aware of another woman in the room coming toward me. She is covered in blood. It's the woman Alexandra has been protecting. She is alive and moving.

"Freeze. Police!"

Voices close enough to be just outside the door of the studio. Thank God! Thank God! The woman moving towards me puts her hands in the air signifying she isn't the perpetrator. She yells, "Hurry! In here!" When they are inside the studio, she points to Kyle still in the same face-down position on the floor. The officer stands over him, gun drawn. His free hand reaches for his radio as he calls for paramedics through the crackle and static.

Everything goes eerily silent. Until I scream. The woman bending down with outstretched arms to hug me has, like Kyle, fallen to the floor next to me. Damn it! Her head has missed the mat and bounced off the wood floor with a gut-wrenching thud. Another sound takes up residence to haunt me later.

Sirens scream in the distance, then moments later the room is overtaken with police, fire, and paramedics. Stretchers pop up, commands are yelled and more chaos than in the gunfire seems to ensue. Someone is in my face, yelling at me, trying to pull me from my fog. I can't focus. Everything is a hazy blur through tears.

"Ma'am! Ma'am! Are you injured?"

Is my body responding? Do I shake my head?

"Are you okay?" He retreats so I am sure I have nodded but my internal voice is relentless. I AM NOT OKAY. I try to assess the situation around the room. People. Blood. Liz. My fault. Too overwhelming.

I put my ears between my knees and squeeze tightly as I learned in elementary school to take cover. I'm not safe. Not safe from the sounds ringing in my ears. Nor the images flashing movie scene-like on the screen of my tightly closed eyelids. I just want one moment of peace to try to compose myself.

I find the strength to open my eyes, only to see three paramedics surrounding Kyle and the other woman's lifeless body. Two men are on Kyle's left side and a woman is on the right. The two male paramedics are twisting between Kyle and the other woman, pulling gear from the large bag situated on the floor next to them. The woman is shoving something down Kyle's throat and one man is poised with a plastic apparatus, floating in mid-air waiting for a cue.

The other male paramedic fits a collar around the lifeless woman's neck.

"I'm in. Bag him!" The man turns back to Kyle and covers his face with the plastic device and squeezes the bag. I know what this means. He is alive, but not breathing. I can't look away. I'm helpless.

A policeman squats in front of me, obstructing my view of the unfolding madness. "Ma'am," he quietly tries to get my attention. My throat is clutching too tightly to respond with words. I try to reply with desperate eyes. Telepathically, I tell him to get me the hell out of here. Thank God he understands! He moves his arm around my back and positions himself by my side, then gently lifts me to standing. My legs ache and head throbs from crying. I am selfish for thinking these ailments matter considering the damage that surrounds me. Short of carrying me like a baby from the room, the officer bears all my physical weight as I'm unable to make my limbs comply with the motion of movement. If only he could bear my emotional pain as well.

I stop short of the exit to survey the scene one final time. The river of blood where Alexandra lay minutes ago is smeared and darkening. It makes me queasy with the sight. Alexandra is on a stretcher with the other two paramedics moving swiftly around her body.

Liz is braced upright against the wall, but I can't tell if she is conscious. Her head is tilted sideways, eyes closed, hands affixed to her mid-section, hugging herself. The unresponsive eyes of the only other man in the room speak volumes. Though he is conscious, he is as damaged as the rest of us. He stares in the direction of the woman I didn't know, playing the staring game I knew as a child with no blinking and unwavering focus. He wears a stoic expression of defeat and is covered in blood. I don't even know whose. Kyle has already been taken from the studio. The bastard who has done all of this. I'm filled with rage.

The police officer moves me swiftly to his car, opening the door and carefully guiding me into the back seat. He opens the door again and offers me a blanket he has procured from his trunk. I am barely dressed in cropped leggings and a tank top, and I shiver, both from the cold and the adrenaline.

"What's your name, miss?" he asks, voice kind.

"Peyton. Peyton Jennings."

"Okay, Peyton, I'm Officer Fitzpatrick."

His lips keep moving but I don't hear another word. Fitzpatrick makes me think of O'Reilly, which makes me think of J.T. I need him by my side.

He closes the door leaving me all alone, each sob seeming to fill the car with despair. I stare out the window, a sickening feeling growing in my stomach, as the first, second, and finally, third stretcher emerges. Another officer is covering the window of the studio with yellow crime scene tape. I start to bang on the window. The car has suddenly become a coffin, unbearably hot, and suffocating. I am going to get sick.

The officer opens the door and I spring forward, barefoot, into the cold air, hot liquid rising in my throat. The contraction of my stomach sends me forward at the waist as vomit pours from my mouth. I watch as the snow turns dark against the pure white. It turns to blood in front of my eyes, as I remember the pool of red surrounding Alexandra's body. I hold in a scream with the next gag. Crossing my arms around my body, I spit the remaining bile into the snow.

The kind officer has turned his back to offer me privacy but approaches when I stand up. "Let's get you back in the car. Do you want me to leave the door open or do you need to warm up?"

"Open, please," I tell him in a hoarse whisper. "Thank you."

The ambulances pull away with the haunting melody that tricks your ears into thinking they are farther away than they are. No such luck. They were right here, with my people, because of me. Apologies and prayer are all I have now.

The officer finally slides into the front seat and speeds off, red and blue lights reflecting on the windows of the once-serene small-town street. The others are going to be treated, but I am going to relive this story because someone has to tell them what happened in that studio. That someone is me.

The police car pulls into the same semicircle entrance as the four ambulances. The officer opens the door for me. What am I stepping out of this car into? Two other police cars pull in behind us.

Four other officers, three male and one female, walk towards me in an imposing line. Their guns and billy clubs around their waists bump up and down, menacing-looking against the pristine white snow backdrop.

I need some clothes. And shoes. My teeth are chattering like the old windup toy my dentist let me pick from the kids' treasure chest in his office.

The officers flank me, and we are in an elevator. It dings, indicating we have arrived at the fifth floor. Muffled voices accompany a whirlwind of activity taking place in an area that looks like one of the hospital movie sets I worked on once. Strangely, the makeshift triage is nestled amongst construction on the floor. It isn't the standard emergency room.

I count nine scrub-clad doctors and nurses, twisting between the equipment and spinning in between three beds. I can make out Alexandra's gray hair, Liz's dark, and I know the other is the woman I don't know.

The officer who has driven me here makes eye contact with an African American doctor, who from the looks of things is the doctor leading the show. The doctor nods as if they know each other. He motions for the officer to approach. Their conversation takes place in hushed tones, with the officer nodding in conclusion.

He returns to me and I know my eyes are questioning.

"Come with me. We'll get you some scrubs."

I follow him into the elevator again. Once the door quietly closes, he informs me of what he has learned, "Three stable and don't appear to have life-threatening injuries. That's first glance, so no one is out of the woods."

Relief floods over me. For the first time since the studio, I take a real breath. "What about Kyle?"

"He doesn't know. We are headed there next."

The elevator doors slide open and a woman with an armful of scrubs is waiting. Arms outstretched, she says with a sympathetic smile, "Size small is on top. Here's a bag for your clothes, with some booties. Sorry, I don't have any shoes I can spare. There's a bathroom around the corner to the right."

"Thank you."

When I emerge from the bathroom scrub-clad, the officer is leaning over the nurses' station desk. She types quickly then relays a message to him. Anxiety creeps into my chest.

The officer's radio crackles. He walks down the hallway away from the patients' rooms. I can only hear, "Copy that," as he moves swiftly back toward us.

"Thanks, Marcy."

He leads me back to the elevator. "Where are we going? What is happening?"

"Keeping you out of the news, Miss Jennings."

J.T.! I think of J.T. again. The news. I wish I could contact him. He shouldn't hear about this in the news.

"There are reporters outside. We just need to buy some time for security to get things handled. We'll keep you out of harm's way, don't you worry."

"Okay. Thank you. I need to know about Kyle. Did the nurse tell you anything?"

"She didn't have any details, but no codes were called the last hour in the hospital."

I don't know if he was alive when he got here, but if he was, he still is. I can't be responsible for his death! I just can't!

We stop on the first floor and are met by the other three officers. Officer Fitzpatrick offers introductions, "Peyton, this is Officer Braun, Officer Stosman, and Officer Klem. Peyton Jennings."

I force a smile because saying "it's nice to meet you" just doesn't work.

Our group winds our way through corridor after corridor, clearly not the first time they have done this. We arrive at an Administration sign and enter what looks to be the business offices of the hospital.

"Morning, Sarah." Officer Fitzpatrick tips his hat.

"Morning, Tim."

Tim. It reminds me of Officer Reilly. My gut clenches.

She stands, leading us down a hallway where she stops in the doorway of a conference room. "All yours. You know I've got your back. I'll be back with coffee and water."

A chorus of thank yous send her on her way.

We enter single-file and take seats around the table. I do not enjoy being surrounded by four police officers. Officer Fitzpatrick wastes no time. "I know this isn't an easy time, Miss Jennings, but we need to get more information on what took place in the studio today. We are just going to ask you some questions."

Horrific scenes flash through my mind. The sound of the studio door smacking open. Kyle's ominous presence. The screams of fear of the other people running out of the studio. Gunfire. Liz's screaming in pain. The thud of the woman's body crumpling to the floor. The image of Alexandra lying in a pool of her own blood. Liz slumped against the wall. The weight of Kyle's lifeless body suffocating me. Sirens. Bag him! Bile rises again against the back of my teeth.

Mercifully, the door opens to interrupt. Sarah sets a carafe of coffee on the edge of the table. A cup holds little cream and sugar packets. "Be right back with the water."

Officer Braun produces a bag I hadn't noticed and removes papers from it onto the table. He holds a pen poised to begin. "Do you know the perpetrator, Miss Jennings?"

"Yes."

"What is his name?"

"Kyle Nixon."

"And your affiliation?"

"He was my boyfriend."

"For what duration?"

"Just about a year."

"Does he have a history of drug use?"

"Yes."

"Violence?"

"Some."

"Mental illness?"

"I've just recently learned that to be the case, yes."

"Do you know any reason why he would have committed this crime today?"

Me. It's my fault. If he dies it will be my fault. If he lives and goes to jail it will be my fault too. How did I end up here?

What seems like hundreds of questions later, I am drained and exhausted. I need J.T. or Jack. I need someone who can tell me that somehow this will all be okay. I wish I had my phone and wallet. Are they still at the studio, evidence in a crime? How long will I be in this room safely out of the way of news-stalking reporters?

The female officer with the nametag reading Klem seems to read my mind. "Peyton, do you need to call anyone?"

Yes. Yes, I do.

"That would be great, thank you."

"Come with me."

"Thanks, Officer Klem."

"You can call me Desi."

She opens the door and just outside is the man from the yoga studio. He too is scrub-clad, free of the blood covering him earlier. Looking at his face, I know from where the blood had spilled. "I'm so sorry about today," I gush with sincerity.

"You should be."

I'm stunned. Tears well, then spill. Desi grabs both of my shoulders, turns my body away from him and escorts me across the hall into a small office. She hands me a tissue from a box on the desk. "Ignore him. It's okay. Everyone responds to trauma a little differently. This isn't your fault, Peyton. It's the perpetrator's. He committed the crime, not you. I'm going to give you some privacy. Make your phone calls."

I slump into the desk chair, tears still streaming. I sniff and dial Jack's number. No answer. I can't very well leave the details on voicemail and have no number for him to call me back. I try J.T. but it goes straight to voicemail.

Through the office window, I can see the man in the conference room across the hall being put through the same faux trial. I am the reason. He was right to say I should be sorry!

A fresh set of tears spills forth. I crumple forward, head in my hands, feeling so alone.

I don't know how long I am in that little office by myself with just my tears before there is a knock on the door. I grab another tissue and open the door.

"We have an update that Alexandra will be out of surgery soon. Want to go wait in the lobby to be there when there are more details?"

Gratitude washes over me, for Alexandra and for anywhere else to be. "Yes, thank you. Thank you, Desi."

As we are leaving the office, another officer appears in the lobby. He is carrying a large box. "This has been cleared," he says, offering it to Desi.

"Great, thanks." She sets the box down on the seat of the black leather lobby chair. It's our things from the studio! I nearly dive into the box as Desi steps aside.

I procure my wallet and phone from the box of many. If only they had my clothes and shoes, I could have felt a bit of return to my former self, but I'm still grateful.

"Can I make two quick calls to leave messages?"

Desi nods and walks over to speak with Sarah and offer me some space.

Two voicemails. Again. I ask them to call me back without

leaving any details. I hope it's soon.

In the privacy of the elevator Desi provides me an update, though she isn't technically allowed to do so. She says it's a cruel practice and she knows how she would feel so she will break the rule. Liz has minor injuries and isn't staying overnight. Cassandra, the other woman, has a severe concussion but nothing life-threatening. Kyle's life hangs in the balance. I feel evil when I wonder what outcome would be best for all involved. He's going to jail if he lives. What if he has permanent physical damage, not to mention the potential mental issues he may face?

I think Desi may understand without anything spoken when she says, "Grace is the best gift you can give him." I reply with tears but no words.

We are in the surgical waiting room to check on Alexandra. My phone rings. Jack! Several signs dictate no phone usage here. I text him that I will call him right back. Desi escorts me around the corner to the nurses' station where she has a telepathic conversation with the woman behind the desk. "Twenty-two zero four." Desi gives a wave of thanks.

I follow her to an empty room and she outstretches her arm for me to pass through the door then closes it behind me. Jack answers on the first ring and starts right in, "I got your message. Car is loaded up and I took a quick trip to Target for provisions. Plenty of junk food!"

He is so enthusiastic I hate to burst his bubble. "I'm not on my way, Jack. I am at the hospital."

"What? Oh my God, Peyton. Are you okay?"

"I am fine. Unfortunately, several others aren't, and it's because of me." Fresh tears find their way down my cheeks.

"Car accident?"

"No, Jack. It was Kyle. My ex-boyfriend from California. He overdosed on something and came to the yoga studio. He shot my yoga teacher, and a few others were injured in the process."

"Oh my God, Peyton. Where are you? I'll be right there."

I appreciate his willingness to come because right now I have no one else. If only J.T. was in town, I might be in his arms right now, getting through this together. I tell him to text me when he arrives.

We make our way back to the waiting area, and since we may have missed them coming out to provide an update, approach the reception desk. I'm counting on the badge to get information that is only provided to family members. Considering I don't know Alexandra's last name I can't exactly pretend I am that.

The elderly woman wearing a round green and white 'I'm A Volunteer' pin on her blazer consults her clipboard, a raggedy finger scrolling to the bottom where a name is written in ink beneath those typed. The woman picks up the circa 1990 phone—with a cord!—and dials four numbers. After a brief pause, she asks, "Is there any update on Alexandra Walker?"

The room spins under my feet. My knees buckle as the earth seems to drop from underneath. Sounds and faces blur together in a kaleidoscope of images. Voices sound like they are underwater, incomprehensible over the dialogue in my head. Alexandra Walker. It's a common name, right? There has been no mention of a yoga teacher in any conversation. Alexandra Walker cannot be related to J.T. Walker, can she? No. No. No. Err on the side of love. What had she said about the plane ride meeting the yoga teacher? She was moving to take care of her son. She had struggles. She had insinuated she might not like Christmas. I know a reason that might be. This cannot be happening. God's joke was cruel enough without this for a punchline. Someone is sitting me into a chair. I am far, far, away. I may avoid coming back to reality forever.

"Peyton! Peyton!"

It sounds faint and distant but it's right in my ears. My shoulders are shaking. They have been all day with the rhythm of my crying. This is different. More urgent.

"Miss Jennings!"

I close my eyes, then reopen them, with the intention to focus on what is in front of me. Desi. Yes, Desi. Strong hands. Holding me by the shoulders. I blink rapidly to bring her into focus.

"Phew, I thought I lost you there. Are you okay, Miss Jennings?"

Definitely not. I force a nod.

"Good news. They said Alexandra is out of surgery and in recovery. She made it through the surgery just fine. I have a good feeling." She smiles, her compassion-filled eyes twinkling. I am glad someone has a good feeling about something. On the contrary, I have a very bad feeling.

DECEMBER 30th
CHAPTER 33 | J.T.

I am finally within ten miles of the hospital just after midnight. It's been a hell of a five-hour turned six-and-a-half-hour drive with blowing snow squalls. Doing it after a long ski day doesn't add to its ease. I'd returned to the condo and into the car in record time after I got the call, but I'm still too late. I berated myself for four hours for being out of town but finally flipped the script. I could have been in Africa, continents, not counties, away.

It makes me shudder to think how my head, heart, and gut each responded to the words, "Your mother has been shot." And damn it, I sent Peyton skiing because she wanted to be able to do it with me. I haven't been able to get hold of her, and she is the one I need to talk to. I know it won't seem so bad if I can process what is happening with her. I need her by my side at the hospital. I can get used to not handling tough shit alone.

We had a great day on the ski hill, behaving like kids again, making up games to compete with one another, like longest distance on one ski, best crash and best trick. The adult reality check happened as I'd just sat down in the log cabin-themed restaurant for an après-ski snack. I'd been bummed I couldn't have a drink. Not indulging in a cold beer with the guys after a long ski day is one of my recovering addict triggers. It had made me think about midnight on New Year's Eve, another tough one. How would Peyton handle my lame non-alcoholic juice toast? It all seems so irrelevant now.

What was worse, I'd ordered nachos and a soda. I had taken my time in the production of helmet, goggle, gloves-removal and hit the head before ever checking my phone. The cold kills the battery so I'd had it off. We'd taken a lunch break and I'd checked it but with little signal on the hill I didn't have any call notifications, just texts, and none from Peyton. No one calls, so it didn't cross my mind to worry about calls. I could kick myself now. The nine calls from numbers I didn't know set off my worry radar, and it only took the word "officer" to have panic permeate my every cell from head to toe. The message was cryptic, only saying please call back regarding an accident involving a family member. I only had one. My short-term memory failed me three times when trying to remember the number to dial, the number different to the one I could just hit "call back" on.

My stomach drew into a tighter knot with each ring until Officer Fitzpatrick had answered. I couldn't even get lucky enough to get any other of the thousands of nationalities besides Irish. I replay the conversation in my head as I white-knuckle the steering wheel the last mile.

I said I was calling regarding a message about an accident. They called Tim's death the same. Like hell, it was an accident, and most likely this isn't either. He'd said it was good that he hadn't gotten hold of me until some time had passed because he had good news. My mother had been shot but was out of surgery. She didn't appear to have life-threatening injuries.

Not exactly good news in my book, but I'd sighed in relief that she was alive. I won't breathe again until I see her with my own eyes and can be sure. He explained there had been an incident at the yoga studio. I am unsure that incident is the right word, but what the hell else do you call it?

I'd processed the information. Shot. Surgery. She had survived. Who had done this? How had this happened? Who shot people up in a yoga studio? I'd asked what happened and how but knew the answers were irrelevant. He said he would share the details when I arrived. I said I was on my way.

I have a new appreciation for how my mother felt the night she got the call. The punch in the gut. I will never be able to make up for what I put her through, but I can spend the rest of my life trying.

I finally arrive at the hospital still in my ski gear, with caffeine jitters and a full bladder from the coffee I'd consumed to stay awake on the drive. I'm met with the cold gaze of an uninterested woman at the information desk. It doesn't look as if she has any intention of making this easy. I pull the most charming smile I can amid the exhaustion and fear. I show my license and she types then lifts her eyes. "First name of the patient?"

"Alexandra."

"Nine-thirty-four, north tower. But you can't—"

I've already started walking and let her words fade into the distance.

As I'm taking a deep breath, the elevator doors open to bring the nurses' station into view. No one is there. I can't feel my feet as I move forward across the gray-tiled hallway, managing to sidestep any nurses or another medical professional before I stand outside room nine-thirty-four. Anyone could sneak in here! What if whoever has done this is still on the loose? Surely she would have police protection if it was needed? I anxiously bite my nails while worrying about what could happen and what I will find on the other side of the door. I taste blood. I've been doing it for hours, though I hadn't done it since I was ten. Courage can't find me soon enough.

I crack the door to get a glimpse and ease myself in. I need to prepare myself before she sees me. I hope she will be sleeping, but just in case, I wouldn't want her to read any expression of horror at her appearance I might be unable to hide.

As luck would have it, her eyes are closed, and she doesn't look nearly as bad off as I had made out in my head. Her hair splays a rainbow of soft gray across the pillow, and only one shoulder is covered with a gown. The right one is covered in a large white bandage and held in place against her body with a sling. I rush to her side but remain silent, gripping the bed rail with both hands until my knuckles turn white. So much for giving that up, having finished driving. This is a whole new level. Who the hell had done this? And why? It's probably good I don't know because if I did there is no telling what I might do.

She must have sensed my presence because she stirs, and without even opening her eyes says my name, "Joe." Her voice is hoarse but still retains the cheerfulness she is so well known for. Somehow, I know deep down she will be fine. I blow out a breath and relax.

"Mom. I came as fast as I could. I'm sorry. I didn't know."

"You would have just sat around biting your nails." She manages a light chuckle as she opens her eyes, directly looking at my hands on the rail. "I hope you got your full day of skiing in. I was in good hands. Really good hands."

"Are you in pain?"

"Not more than I can handle."

Of course not. I'd already put her through the most insufferable pain. Nothing could compete.

"Is there anything I can do for you?"

"Can you get me out of here?" She hushes her voice, "You know I don't do doctors! This is torture!"

"I know, Mom, but in this case, I think you are going to have to suck it up."

"In that case, then you should go home and get some sleep. I am sure you are tired."

It is so like her to be thinking of me instead of herself. "Sure. I will. Right after you tell me what happened."

Her eyes have closed again, groggy from pain meds. Damn it. I need to know. My laptop is in the car and my phone is now dead, having left my charger in the condo wall in my rush to be getting out of there. Too daunting to get back to the car and back in here sight unseen. And no one had been there to stop me, so I need to be here just in case.

I do need a shower badly too, and can only do so many more things before sleep takes over. The rose leather recliner looks very inviting. I guess I will have to wait a few more hours for details.

Time passes, and sleep evades me with the onslaught of pokes and prods from nurses. I wake each time to make sure everything is okay. Just after 7:30 a.m. I figure I should just coffee up. On the way back from the cafeteria and coffee area, I pass the hotel gift shop open at the ungodly hour, and pick the nicest bouquet on display, and thankfully a phone charger. I need to text Peyton.

Stubborn as she is, my mother has refused the pain meds she can control herself so I figure nine o'clock will be the next visit. I have time and my laptop. I don't want to wake her with a video so I read the articles written. A picture of the studio covered in yellow tape turns my stomach. The caption reads 'small town shocked by studio shooting' and the writer explains that a deranged ex-lover of one of the yoga students shot one person. One person. And it had to be my mother? I know she put herself in harm's way protecting someone else. Damn her kindness! It's not enough to be my hero, she has to be one to others as well. Of course, I love her and hate her for it in the same breath.

The news report also explains that three others had been wounded. They said the suspect was also being treated for an unknown condition and is in police custody. Is the bastard in this very hospital? I feel the blood rushing to my head, face hot, veins in my neck throbbing.

"Hey, relax over there."

My mother's voice is scolding. Even in her compromised state I can't get a thing by her. "Mom." I shut the laptop and move quickly to the side of her bed. "I hope I didn't wake you."

"Nope. The smell of flowers did actually. They are beautiful. Thank you. Stop watching that trash and I will fill you in on the details. Everything is fine, Joe. Life happens. It's my fault for not locking the door."

"Mom, this is not normal life stuff."

She lifts her good arm up to my face, wincing as she shifts to reach it. I lean forward to make it easier for her to lay her palm on the side of my cheek. "It never is, and it always is."

I want to tell her that her stupid metaphors and mantras annoy the shit out of me. She isn't Yoda, or Buddha, or Jesus, but I know exactly what she means. Everything we have gone through together might not be normal, but yet, it is our normal.

"The man was on drugs, Joe."

She pauses and I know it is on purpose. She wants me to have some compassion, considering.

"He was out of his mind because of drugs and love. Unrequited. He was looking for one of the students in the studio, distraught over their breakup. I am worried about the woman he was coming for. I don't know what ended up happening to her."

Her eyes look away from me and to the doorway upon hearing a knock. "Well, speak of the devil. Come in. I was just telling my son I was concerned about you."

I turn to face the woman who has just entered the room and feel the blood drain from my face. "Peyton?"

Clearly, I've pissed off God.

I watch almond shape eyes form circles with a much wider diameter though they are swollen and puffy. Definitely not the angelic image I'd been expecting to return to this morning. I see her deflate with the realization that we will never be the same. Everything inside me relates. How the fuck did we end up here?

"You two know each other?"

My mother looks up at me. I face her, eyes locking. A look of understanding washes over her face, then her lips curl up into a big smile, "Well, I feel much better about sharing my Joe now." She looks back to Peyton. "I hate it when he calls himself J.T. I never understood why he'd want to think about trouble all the time."

She looks back to me. Through clenched teeth, I share the truth, "Because it does seem to follow me." I couldn't make this up as my worst nightmare. She was too good to be true.

"Give the girl a hug or kiss or something," Mom says, waving her good hand in Peyton's direction. "God knows she needs one."

I can't even think of touching her. She is the only reason my mother lies in this hospital bed and the reason I might have lost her. I just stare across the room, knowing my eyes radiate hatred and bitterness. I want to push it away but 'deranged ex-lover' takes all the space in my head. I can't swallow the building fury.

"Joe!"

I look away from Peyton and back to her. "I can't do that, Mom."

"Joe, please. It's not her fault. You two should go talk."

I shift my eyes to avoid seeing the disappointment in hers. She won't understand my need to choose her over Peyton.

"No way I am leaving you. If she is here, you aren't safe. Peyton, I think you should go." My voice sounds so cold I almost ache on Peyton's behalf. I avoid her eyes, not wanting to take the risk they will suck me in.

"I understand. I'll go." Her voice is quiet.

"Joe! I am perfectly safe. No, Peyton, please. Don't."

She cringes with the painful effort to talk loudly enough for Peyton to hear, because she's disappeared from the doorway.

"Mom, relax." I try to settle her back into the pillows. Her resistance is fierce.

"How could you just let her walk away? You were so happy at Christmas talking about her! I saw the adoration in your eyes and heard it in your voice. Don't be ridiculous. She has enough going on without losing you. Go after her!"

The disdain in her voice hurts. "Mom, there was a chance I could have lost you yesterday, and it was her fault!"

"You didn't. And it wasn't. She is the reason we all survived. Her courage was admirable, Joe."

I am not in the habit of letting her down. "I'm sorry, Mom. I don't think I will ever be able to be with the woman whose crazy ex tried to kill my mother."

I swallow hard, not liking the permanency of my words. She sighs, "Oh Joe," and her eyes take me back to another place in time.

A place I had hoped to never be again.

CHAPTER 34 | Peyton

How. Can. This. Be. Happening?

A cold cinderblock wall is holding me up as I lean my back against it. I can't believe what's just happened. How could his eyes be so cold? Just days ago, those eyes smiled at me and for me.

My heart was just ripped from my chest.

A quick assessment of my life in the last sixty days says the universe is cruel. How else can you look at my mother dying and my boyfriend's mother—whom I didn't know until I didn't want to know—almost dying at the hands of my ex-boyfriend? But the joy in between! How can life be such an eddying mix of happy and hell?

There is no doubt I am presently in hell. Maybe this is the true definition, and heaven means we don't have to do people problems anymore? I can't imagine a place worse than where I am against this wall, rejection stinging my soul.

The silver lining is that no tears come. I may not have any left after yesterday, or maybe I've just surrendered to hell. I don't know where to go or what to do next.

I just stand against the wall and will myself to keep breathing.

I have no idea how much time passes as groups of students and doctors on morning rounds file past me down the hallway in focused conversation. Not one person stops to ask what I am doing standing there. I don't know what I would say so I don't mind seeming invisible.

My phone rings in my purse clutched tightly against my stomach, startling me. I need a distraction from my misery so I answer the unknown number.

It is never a good idea. I have the sinking feeling everything is about to get worse. How is it even possible?

I am back in the same conference room I was in yesterday. I hated it then. I hate it more now. It is stifling and this is insufferable. Only one thing could make it tolerable. Being wrapped in J.T.'s arms. And it will never happen again. Once again, I feel completely alone.

Now the tears come. I want to scream at God, the world, or anyone who will listen. Instead, I straighten my bracelet. I remember what J.T. had said. Love is all you need. I had hope for love with him. Now, all I have is a metal written word on my wrist.

"Are you Peyton?"

A beautiful blond woman with sympathetic eyes and a kind voice enters the room, filling it with compassion.

I wish I wasn't right now. "Yes, I am."

"As I said on the phone, my name is Amy, with Gift of Life. I'm here with regard to Kyle Nixon. First, let me say I share your heartbreak. This isn't an easy situation. I know it's difficult to face losing someone you care about."

I am ashamed. My heart is broken, but it isn't about Kyle potentially losing his life. It's about losing my potential for true love. I would worry about going to hell for my evil thought but have already established it's too late. It's found me.

For. The. Love. Of. God.

We are interrupted. Officer Fitzpatrick's frame fills the doorway, but I can see behind him two people he is escorting as he had me to this very room yesterday.

It's the Nixons.

I can't do this.

"Peyton, how are you holding up?" he asks.

My heart is pounding. I feel sick to my stomach with the sight of Kyle's parents. I'm afraid if I open my mouth to answer vomit may spill out. I close my swollen eyes and shake my head. He pats my shoulder in kindness. I slump into my chair as my shaky legs no longer want to keep me upright.

The Nixons shake hands with Amy and take seats across the table from me. Neither makes eye contact. Why am I here?

"Let me reiterate how sorry I am for your situation," Amy starts again. "I realize what a difficult time this is, and these are difficult decisions to make. I am here to help, and my team of counselors is here to help. We find it best to bring all interested parties together to keep you informed. So just to be certain, Mr. and Mrs. Nixon, is there anyone other than Peyton, who I understand is Kyle's girlfriend, who should also be here?"

Amy turns to me when she says girlfriend. I look toward Mrs. Nixon and see her conceal a grimace with a handkerchief she pulls from her purse. She dabs at her eye, but I don't see tears welling, nor is her makeup the least bit marred. There were plenty of tears when it was all about her at the restaurant.

"Oh, I am not his girlfriend any longer. I probably shouldn't be here," I say, maybe with too much enthusiasm.

Mrs. Nixon jumps in quickly, lowering her handkerchief and turning to Amy. "Oh, she should definitely be here."

Because I clearly wanted to leave, she will make me pay. Why would she want me here?

"Kyle made the choice to be an organ donor, as evident by his driver's license in police evidence. It is an admirable choice."

"If only we all made admirable choices, perhaps we wouldn't be having this conversation. We all have to suffer the consequences of others' poor choices. Kyle's never hurt anyone before."

Now I know why she wanted me here. What other opportunity would she have to place the blame squarely on my shoulders? Her eyes are daggers from across the table directed at me. Yes, he made one admirable choice but let's pretend his choices to board a plane to Detroit, abuse drugs, and shoot a woman don't have consequences beyond measure? I press my lips together tightly to form a straight line. I might bite my tongue off preventing words from escaping.

Amy carries on, mediating as necessitated, "Again, we are all here to understand the good that can come from this through the gift of organ donation. We have a short window to make some decisions about how to proceed should his condition remain unchanged. It's what Kyle wanted."

What Kyle wanted was me. They may have been Kyle's choices, but I am the reason for everyone's suffering.

DECEMBER 31st
CHAPTER 35 | J.T.

Today I wake up praying yesterday was only a nightmare. Since I haven't slept in two nights, I know it wasn't. I am sweating, probably leaving a bodily imprint in the leather where many others have kept vigil before me.

I've had shitty days. I've skipped a decade of my birthdays and the Christmas holidays. Why not add New Year's Eve to the list?

Such a short while ago I was counting down the days to spending the evening, and all night long, with Peyton. I'd envisioned the moment I'd see that dress again first on her, then on my bedroom floor. I had the playlist ready to make love post-midnight.

Weeks of anticipation dashed in one second. The second I realized her crazy ex-boyfriend had nearly killed my mother.

I've had time to process this fact. And the fact that he is still alive, though barely, in the ICU just seven floors below us. If he wasn't already in a hospital bed, I would have put him there myself.

How did I spend the last—longest—one thousand, four hundred and forty minutes of my life? Pacing and praying in this room. I feel claustrophobic, like the walls are closing in. It could also be my heart, closing down. Trying to clot itself to close a gaping wound. There are no sutures, tubes, bandages, IVs, medications to treat the problem I have. A whole hospital of paraphernalia and people who save. Of course, there isn't a damn thing anyone can do for me.

I am so grateful my mother is alive. I am so grateful I can be by her side. I am grateful Ellie is here as well. But I have another fourteen hours to kill in a hospital. I won't see midnight nor toast to a happy new year. Sometimes, gratitude just isn't enough.

JANUARY 1st
CHAPTER 36 | Peyton

Gratitude. I have to stay there or I will not make it through another hour. I can't be grateful and angry. I can't be grateful and heartbroken at the same time. I can't be hopeless and grateful at the same damn time. Alexandra had given me that wisdom. It's so damn hard.

Kyle is still alive and seems to be slowly returning to the living world but isn't out of the woods, and the permanent damage is still to be determined. Alexandra is healing but due to a complication isn't going home as expected today. We've arranged to get together in her hospital room, Cassandra and Liz included, to pretend that noon on the first of January has the same significance as its twelve-hour earlier counterpart. A New Year's midnight makeup toast. None are placing blame on my shoulders. Liz had called me yesterday to tell me this. For a complicated reason, she said the incident had done her a favor. And she said that Cassandra had learned about forgiveness the hard way. For this, I am grateful.

The tiny hospital room is crowded, with all of us gathered around Alexandra's bedside. Liz has snuck in the contraband in a large purse, while Cassandra holds four champagne flutes. She sets them gently on the food tray that has been swiveled in front of Alexandra, while Liz and I unwrap the protective white tissue paper.

"Please just let me unwrap my own glass."

It's the closest thing to a whine I have heard from Alexandra. "I've still got five good fingers, and no one will let me lift one of them. I feel useless. It's making me crazy."

By no one, I know she is referring to J.T.

"Well, I can't do anything. Moving is excruciating." Liz has been attempting to open the bottle but is cringing with each turn of the little metal basket that holds the cork in place.

"Can I help?" I ask, and she relinquishes the task.

"I can't decide if I love it or hate it. I might have an excuse not to vacuum or load a dishwasher for months. There are silver linings in everything."

"Hey you two, this too shall pass!" Cassandra offers.

"Thanks, Cassandra," Liz says, laying her hand along her forearm. "I appreciate you trying to cheer us both up."

I notice Liz and Alexandra share a look.

I use a washcloth from a moveable cart near Alexandra to keep the cork from exploding across the room. The loud pop echoes. I fill the four glasses.

"I shouldn't drink this on pain meds," Alexandra laughs, "but I am going to."

"I shouldn't either," Liz adds, "but I am as well."

"Well, that makes three of us," Cassandra says raising her glass.

I am the only one without physical pain needing medication. If only they knew my heart was broken like their bodies. There is no pill for my pain, however.

Liz lifts her glass to meet Cassandra's already raised one. "Let's get to it, ladies. Happy New Year. Auld Lang Syne."

"To A Happy New Year," we all say together with varying intonation. The chime of crystal sings out loudly in the sparsely decorated room.

"I just toasted to Auld Lang Syne and have no idea what it means," Liz says. "I probably shouldn't admit to not knowing, but I have no clue."

Soft laughter breaks out amongst us, minus Cassandra, I notice. Maybe she could only muster one round of cheeriness.

"We should Google it." I pull out my phone and read aloud, "The song, traditionally sung to celebrate the New Year, poses the rhetorical question whether it is right that old times be forgotten, and is generally interpreted as a call to remember long-standing friendships."

Alexandra raises her glass again. "I know it's not exactly what they mean, but to long-standing friendship among us. We need each other for this one."

Never would I have imagined. I meet her glass first, repeating the phrase. I need these women. None seem angry with me the way I fear the L.A. girls will react with whatever happens to Kyle. I may be a decade younger than Cassandra, and Liz and Alexandra are old enough to be my mother. There is something to learn from the experiences of these women. The others raise their glasses to meet ours.

"Shall we drink to forgetting the old times?" Cassandra proposes. An odd toast, but the meaning is implied in her swollen, red-rimmed eyes.

"I'm not sure I want to forget all the old times," Liz chimes in, with a bit of a mischievous look, "but I'll drink to forgetting some."

We clink our glasses again. Our eyes lock. Silence falls. The shared experience is fresh and raw. We all want to forget what happened in that studio.

Alexandra is the first to smile, like she has moved past the past. She raises her glass again, the sun reflecting in a rainbow that envelopes us. "We've got this, girls. To do-overs. Together."

"To do-overs, together," we echo in perfect unison, hopeful smiles spreading across our faces.

Quiet conversation and a few more laughs follow, but not for long, as everyone's ailments call for rest. The others begin to file out. I linger, hoping for just a little time with Alexandra.

"Peyton, can you stay?"

I am so grateful she has asked. "Yes, of course," I reply, giving Liz a gentle, hurried hug and moving to her bedside. Alexandra covers my hand with hers, over the cold metal rail. "Peyton, I want to apologize for Joe."

"There is nothing to apologize for, Alexandra. I understand. I just… well, I hoped that maybe with what he'd been through he would be able to forgive me."

Alexandra looks taken aback. "He told you? About Tim?"

I nod.

"Well, I guess I shouldn't be surprised based on the way he talked about you at Christmas. I already knew there was something special about you from class, I just didn't know that my son and I shared the same fondness."

She smiles. It's weary; she is clearly growing more tired. "It's going to be hard for him. It seems like he should be able to understand. Time often has a way of working things out. I'm hopeful. Please try to be patient. Have faith."

She's in pain and tired, but still sharing her wisdom. I admire her grace.

"Forgiveness takes time, Peyton, but love wins. Somehow, love always wins."

"Thank you, Alexandra," I say with a careful hug to her good side, knowing I've just heard her quoting Ellie.

The doorway fills.

J.T.!

I don't know if I am thrilled to have my breath taken away with the sight of him, or devastated I didn't make a quick enough escape.

Freshly showered, his messy blond hair is still damp and tussled in its painfully sexy way. I ache with longing to run my fingers through it. He wears a just tight enough long-sleeve black t-shirt that leaves me remembering what it feels like to touch him. Lay my head on this chest. Entangle my limbs in his. I can feel him. Taste him. Smell him. I now know why someone would sell their soul to the devil in the name of love. There isn't a thing I wouldn't do for him to walk in here and sweep me into his arms.

It doesn't happen, of course. His eyes narrow to angry slits when he takes me in.

"It's time for you to go."

His tone is cruel.

"Joe!" Alexandra reprimands but he seems unfazed. Resolute. He steps backward out of the doorway to make room for me to pass by. Our bodies are inches apart as I slide past him. Just grab me and hold me, J.T.! I have to will my hands to remain at my sides. I need to feel him under my fingers. I need to feel him against my lips! But no, I avoid looking him in the eyes. Still, his burning hot glare pierces me. I blink hard to hold back welling tears.

I feel fragile to my core. This take-two is too much. I am in the same hall as yesterday, against the same wall, with shallow breath and quivering legs I can't trust. Find gratitude. Cinderblock to hold me up.

I hear Alexandra's voice through the open door. I am adding eavesdropping to my list of transgressions.

"Joe, I'm asking you, for everyone involved, to try to let this go. I've just told Peyton to have patience with you, hoping you would come around. Don't push her away. Have I taught you nothing about love and forgiveness, Joseph Jacob?

His retort is insidious. "I'm Joseph Trouble, remember? I know what you have taught me, but love doesn't always win, Mom. This isn't some romance novel. It's real life."

My heart shatters into irreparable shards.

"You are wrong, J.T.," she says definitively.

I close my eyes and imagine their matching steely eyes in a staredown.

"Come here." Alexandra transforms to complete compassion.

There is silence in the room, and I picture the man I thought I was falling in love with being held against Alexandra's slight frame with one good arm.

All I have left is faith. I say a silent prayer. Please, God, let love win. And get me the hell out of here.

Unsure how it took me so long to conclude that God is my last hope, I'm carried to the car by an unknown force. I think of one of the little plastic cards my mother has on her bedroom mirror. Something about footprints in the sand. A picture shows two sets dwindle to one. I remember it quoting Jesus as saying, "It was then I carried you." I feel the tiniest sense of peace.

My phone rings in the car console. A picture of my roommates covers the screen. It's Jenna calling. Might as well know where I stand.

"Can you Facetime?"

"Sure." I'm not yet moving, and it won't kill my data to do one call. I am wasting gas, however.

The girls fill the frame, each taking turns saying hello. They still have the remains of last night's makeup and hairdo. I smile wistfully. They probably haven't been to bed yet.

"Pey! We missed you last night. I'd say it was epic, but that wouldn't be nice to rub in. Plus, well, it wasn't the same without you. We called you at midnight!"

"I know. Thank you." My phone had been off for hours by 3:00 a.m.

"I think I am still drunk. Peyton, are you drunk?" Hayden giggles a high-pitched squeal.

We are living in different universes at the moment. Meredith smacks her, and the screen image goes gray and bounces as the phone falls from her hand. Meredith fills the picture and in an unlikely moment of mothering says, "Peyton, sorry. My God. Obnoxious much? Happy New Year. I'm sorry they are babbling on about parties and drunken stupors."

She pauses, probably trying to decide what to say to the pathetic girl she knows has nothing to celebrate. "I'm guessing it's not so happy over there? You know we have been trying to get hold of you, right?"

An eager Jenna jumps in, "Brad told us what he knew. It wasn't much. His dad—" She realizes she should not finish the sentence. I know where this is going. Brad's father is a very successful attorney in L.A. One of those on retainer for many a superstar who are in need of connections to absolve misdemeanors and felonies alike. Of course the Nixons have hired him.

"Please, Peyton, talk to us. We need the deets."

True concern the motive? Or unadulterated gossip? I fear any one of these girls would sell me out to the tabloids in a New York minute for the right price.

I go with the truth, not having much to share anyway. "I'm not sure what's going on with Kyle. I haven't had any contact with him or his family in a couple of days. He's alive is all that I know. It was close. They made me talk to organ-donation people." I leave out the details of the blame placed squarely on me by his unaccountable parents.

"No one else has life-threatening injuries." Not physical ones anyway. The emotional ones still feel lethal, mortal, and fatal.

"Talk to me. Are you okay?"

"I'm fine."

"You do not sound fine. When are you coming back? We'll take care of you. We're here for you, sweetie."

I want to believe that. "Thank you. I'll be back the day after tomorrow." Anywhere would be better than here right now. An echoing chorus of goodbyes are said, and I hang up, grateful they seem to finally be on my side.

JANUARY 8th
CHAPTER 37 | J.T.

Damn it. I pasted Column F into Column K, not Column P. Undo. If only there was a button so easy to press for my life. I slam the Control-V. My keyboard will never be the same. Nothing will ever be the same. I let hope run away from my past. An impossibility I should choose to accept. Never should I think there will be a day that trouble won't haunt me.

Distance from the past won't ease the pain, nor would being in Africa be far enough away from Peyton not to miss her. The high to low of the past weeks shrouds me in darkness from morning until night. Neither miles nor time will replace missing everything about her.

What's worse is the pummeling of memories every year post-Christmas. The two weeks of hell following Tim's death. The police investigation. Meeting Ellie and the daughter who would never have a father walk her down the aisle. Ellie's face in her hands at the funeral. Walking back into a school where I knew no one. A whole new life in Michigan where I knew no one. Rehab. Facing myself in the mirror every day. Learning twelve steps that would ultimately dig me out of the hell hole I'd dug for myself. I thought maybe I would have Peyton to help me through this year. I should have known I would never have the chance to have her shoulder the burden with me. I'll never duck karma.

Then I fast-forward to an image of Peyton's face as I rejected her, not just once, but twice. Her expression of horror as the dots connected that J.T. to her was Joe to Alexandra and her son. I push it aside and successfully convert kwacha to dollar in my spreadsheet. Numbers I can make fit neatly in rows and columns of a cost model for our next project. Numbers I can control when there is seemingly not another damn thing I can.

My phone skids across the desk with the vibration of an incoming call. And there it is again. The ghost I'd just ridden myself of seeing. A broadly grinning Peyton in a selfie of us. My arms are wrapped around her waist and I am kissing the side of her neck sideways but looking forward. Only my eyes show in the picture, wide and alive. I stare at the phone and her name across the screen. My hand instinctively moves to my heart, as if it can somehow mask the pang of loss I feel right there in the center of my chest.

I hover my finger over the screen. My fingers curl into a fist. The screen fades with the missed call. My fist pounds the desk.

I can't force my eyes to move, desperate to see a voicemail symbol appear. Nothing. Damn it. A Snapchat notification. I have to look. There is a picture of her holding the repaired quilt across her chest. I had secretly snagged it from her room and Ellie had repaired it. I might not be able to be with her, but I am not an asshole. It was just the right thing to do. The caption says, "Means the world…u have no idea. Thx….x a million." I feel a little relief to hear from her, but it's a Band-Aid on a gaping wound.

Reply.

Do not reply.

Don't lead her on.

You should say something.

You should not say a thing.

Not saying anything wins the internal debate sparked by her contact. I notice the ache in my chest is even more painful than before.

My phone buzzes again and I want to throw it across the room. It's only from Owen:

nice getting me a HOT new volunteer for africa

What? I have no idea what he is referring to and respond with *WTH*.

His response is immediate:

Peyton??? figured all u

WTH? Of course she would do this! I knew she was a special woman. My emotions swing around. I am furious she would sign up to spend weeks with my friend, jealous it isn't me who would be showing her the continent, and thrilled she will have the experience. I have to respond now.

I text, short and sweet, promising myself, like the addict I am, just one more.

u r welcome. Thank Ellie for quilt. Heard about Africa – know u will love it as much as I do

The phone vibrates again:

Thank u for Africa too…zoo

Zoo. My heart wrenches. I had what I never thought I would in Peyton. Inside jokes. Passion. And most importantly, complete acceptance of all of my scars. My fingers find my forearm, remembering.

I move to a small conference room in our shared space, leaving the phone behind to avoid the temptation of replying again. I'm practiced in removing temptation. I've heard falling in love causes the brain to think it is on drugs. No argument from me. Coming off the high of having Peyton Jennings in my life is one hell of a withdrawal.

I grab my keys and wallet, knowing exactly where to go. Fuck ten years of sober suffering. I know something that will ease this pain.

JANUARY 17th
CHAPTER 38 | Peyton

"Shit. Shit. Ouch. Shit."

I hop on one foot, trying to grab the aching toe I've just smashed into the doorjamb while racing across the apartment to my ringing phone on the kitchen table. Wishful.

I've purposely turned off his special ring tone just to torture myself with the potential it could maybe, possibly, be him if it is ringing. Then, I always keep the phone as far away from me as I can, otherwise I will waste more hours of my life willing a call, text, email, Snapchat, Facebook, or Instagram message from J.T. It's not far from the truth that I've lost my mind along with love.

Days of the last weeks have been wasted under my reconstructed quilt, with a laptop, in the dark. I've cried through *Fault in Our Stars* four times, *The Notebook* three times, and laughed, cried, and lived vicariously through hope, heartbreak, and happily ever after of Charlotte, Miranda, Samantha, and of course, Carrie. I'm not sure how long I can subsist on the stereotypical post-breakup diet of ice cream and television binging, but I have no goals to end my streak. I am content to be crying over fake lives and people because maybe it means I've hit my lifetime quota on tears spilled at my pity-party for one.

My lunacy is curbed when I am close enough to see Cassandra Lewis flashing across the top of my phone screen. Should I answer? Why would she be calling me? Is she going to berate me for ending her relationship? Is she calling because misery loves company and she just needs to talk? I owe her, in any case, so I answer hesitantly, "Hi, Cassandra."

"Hi, Peyton, it's Cassandra. How are you?"

I let my guard down just a bit, her tone showing no evidence of angst yet. "To be honest, I've been better." I try to laugh at myself but I just don't find me funny.

"I wish I could say I didn't know what you mean," she says, trying to force the same laugh. "But that's why I am calling. This is going to sound crazy, but I know you do yoga and I'm hoping maybe you can come with me to a yoga retreat. It's in five days, and for a week."

I do quick math. I have to give up four shifts working, but soon enough I will have an inheritance coming, and I saved all the money from my last movie shoot. I can do this.

"My boyfriend gave it to me for Christmas. It's for two, and… well—"

She doesn't finish the sentence.

"It's in San Diego, so I thought of you. I know it's last-minute so I understand if you can't, but it's yoga, spa, and beach. I think it's going to be incredible, but I can't go alone."

"It sounds great, Cassandra, if you are sure that you want me—"

She interrupts, "I probably shouldn't throw myself under the bus like this, but hell, it's not like you aren't going to know everything about me soon enough."

Now she does manage to laugh. Nervously. "I haven't exactly invested much time in making friends, Peyton. I feel a little extra-bonded with you, and Liz and Alexandra, if you know what I mean."

I do. The incident. And broken hearts. A rough start to a friendship, but nonetheless, a start.

"Well, then, definitely a yes."

"Thank you, Peyton. And everything is my treat. I insist."

She sounds grateful I've accepted, but I am pretty sure I should be the thankful one. "My flight to San Diego gets in around ten o'clock in the morning on the 22nd."

"Okay, that's easy. I can drive down and pick you up." My other line rings. When it rains it pours. Who calls anymore? It's an unknown number, and I feel compelled to answer on the slim chance it is J.T.! I interrupt and ask Cassandra to hold on for a moment, then flip to the other call.

"Hello."

"Peyton."

I freeze, paralyzed by the throaty yet unmistakable voice.

"Peyton, please don't hang up. I need to talk to you."

I lean against the table to steady myself, heart racing. My palms instantly sweat, the hair on the back of my neck rises and my scalp prickles. I pull out a chair. This is a sit-down conversation. My phone tries to jump from my trembling hand. "Kyle." His name comes out in a shallow breath.

"Peyton. I need to talk to you. To apologize. You are the one and only phone call I am allowed, and I picked you."

Should I feel even more guilt for this fact? Haven't I had a lifetime's worth already, between him and his mother?

Because of Brad's affinity for me, he's been making sure to eavesdrop. I know his father is using temporary insanity as his defense, calling what had happened "tweaking". Prolonged days of no sleep and meth use. Aggression, violent outbursts, and psychotic behavior are just part of the program.

Brad heard words but not details. Medically induced coma. Cardiac collapse. Mini-stroke. Dialysis. Permanent damage. I knew he was being moved to a rehab facility then was supposed to attend a court-ordered full-time rehab program after discharge. It will probably be a cushy one at that, and Brad's father has managed to delay his sentencing. No doubt by the time he plea-bargains, Kyle will get off as if he only put a scratch on all of us he has harmed.

"You don't know how sorry I am. I am going to spend the rest of my life making it up to you."

My eyes widen. Make it up to me? As in, be a part of my life? I think not!

"Like hell, you will, Kyle! Do you know what you have done? The lives you have devastated? The people you have hurt?"

"I never meant to hurt anyone else, Peyton. I was only going to hurt myself. It was an accident. It wasn't me. It was the drugs. Haven't you heard? It happens after no sleep. But now we have a second chance. I'll be sober forever. You are still the only reason I have to live, Peyton. The only reason to get better. To be better."

No more can I be this man's muse! "No, Kyle. I am sorry but you will stay the fuck away from me, my family, and my friends." My voice is firm and in control. I choose my words carefully and consciously.

My phone pulls me away from the agony with a buzz. Cassandra had been on the other line. I had forgotten! Now she is texting:

hung up after while - hope all ok????

Not okay. The reason you need me to accompany you on your vacation is still delusional about our future. I text her:

So sorry! Will call you back!

"I'll never be the same, Peyton. Physically, I mean. That's penance. But losing you is the biggest punishment."

He doesn't think he is going to jail.

"I'm sorry, Kyle. I hope you get better. I hope you find a way to move on." What I want to say is heal quickly so you can serve your time, but I hear Alexandra. Her words flood over me, "Forgiveness always takes time but love wins. Somehow, love always wins." Kyle's delusional love for me cannot win.

"That means a lot to me, Peyton. Thank you. I have to go. I have to earn my five minutes of phone time every week. Pretty harsh, huh?"

What is harsh is all the damage you caused, Kyle. "Goodbye. And good luck."

I'm still shaking in the chair several minutes after I hang up. I was clinging to the hope that if Kyle was in jail, J.T. might acquiesce his need to protect Alexandra. Kyle doesn't think he will go to jail. His parents can buy the best defense. He still wants me. Will I one day have peace?

Peace. That's what I want. What I need. And I know how to make it for myself. I have forgotten and been fearful since the incident, but Cassandra has reminded me.

Rolling out my mat, I feel edgy. My eyes keep darting toward the door. I tried to keep it in full view, but the class is crowded so I am stuck with the proverbial looking over the shoulder.

Class begins and the hush of slow and steady breathing falls over the room. I hear and flinch at each little sound. Gretchen is the teacher today, and she speaks to challenges faced in life. You have to move through, not around them, she says.

I think of my first fender-bender in the high school parking lot and driving after that loud sound I knew left a big dent in my bumper without even looking. I thought of my first back handspring in gymnastics after the cast came off my broken wrist. My mother's lifetime of suffering under her evil parents.

Gretchen says lightning never strikes twice unless you tempt it to do so. Her words resonate. Right here and now, in this studio, I feel in the eye of the storm, hoping to get spit out still standing on the other side. I remind myself I am safe because Kyle is tucked away safely at the moment.

I rock the side planks, warriors, and even try a backbend with the strong energy built in the room. We don't have to go through anything alone as long as we are willing to let others help. When Gretchen had said to set an intention for class, mine was to gather up peace enough for both Cassandra and I for the weekend. My body complied fully, my brain, almost. I only got anxious and took child's pose one time. Normally I would consider resorting to child's pose a failure, but under the circumstances, I was able to offer myself some compassion. I am learning, as Alexandra had said, to be a student. Of life.

Class flies by, and I feel ready to take on the big, bad world again. Gretchen's calm voice revealing her displaced tinge of southern accent tucks us into Savasana, "Once you get through the challenges you face, be in the present moment, moment after moment, and keep moving forward. Stay ahead of the past. Leave it where it is. Be grateful it's behind you and can't hurt you anymore."

I have my breath and gratitude in the present. I have found the peace of being in the four corners of a yoga mat. Alexandra and Liz will be able to practice in a few more weeks, and we will share yoga together again. Kyle didn't die, so I can live with myself. I have, mostly, forgiven myself for all of this. My mother's courage and sacrifice protecting me. Having Jack in my life as the family I always wanted. Amazing sex! An upcoming yoga retreat. New friendships! And Africa. I have everything I never even knew I wanted.

That is, except J.T.

We move through fetal pose and I leave behind on my mat the fear of what comes next. Gretchen says to push ourselves up into our do-over leaving behind what we don't want to take. I'm happy to relinquish some of the baggage I started yoga with, even though Louis Vuitton is hard to give up.

Sitting up into a cross-legged pose, my hands move into prayer at my heart. I feel my bracelet slide down my wrist, settling into place. I may only have this metal word but I'm happy to have learned that love is all we need. J.T. has helped open my heart to what I'd never known. I may never have his love, so for now, loving myself will have to be enough. But I know. With a little more time and a little more life, I will know love in a way I never thought I would. One day.

"The love and light in me salute the love and light in you," Gretchen closes class. We are all in this together and reply in unison, "Namaste."

JANUARY 31st
CHAPTER 39 | J.T.

Ellie's embrace lifts my spirits. Everything about her is grandmotherly. She is warm, fleshy, and smells like she has been in the kitchen. Cinnamon and cloves is my best guess. Her hug feels like unconditional love, given to me in spite of the conditions under which we were brought together.

"Happy birthday, Ellie," I say with a final squeeze, moving past the doorway where she has greeted me.

"Thanks for coming, J.T. It wouldn't be a birthday without you reminding me I am getting better with age, not just old."

She laughs heartily, and it makes me smile. She always seems to be wearing a smile. "I wouldn't miss it for the world," I say, but I would prefer to be anywhere but Detroit.

Her lips purse into a fine line stretching cheek to cheek. She isn't smiling anymore. We are only a few minutes in, and I have the sneaking suspicion I am about to be ambushed. I should have known. My mother's work, no doubt. I know John hasn't shared my secret.

I try to escape. "I'm sure you have other guests to chat with. Is my mom here yet?" I try to avoid eye contact and look around. I've come right from the airport, and she was desperate to get back to teaching, so she couldn't pick me up today.

"Not yet, and there is no one else I'd rather spend my time with than you. Let's go put your coat away."

I know better than to argue. I am going to lose. She had a

temperamental Irishman wrapped around her little finger, and I am no match for Eleanor O'Reilly.

"Everything for the party looks beautiful," I say, shrugging out of the sleeves of my coat as we reach the closet in the back hallway.

"It's all Grace. Amazing she pulled it off with that Julia tugging at her all day."

"How are the girls?"

"Grace is toddler-raising tired, and Julia is growing like a weed and getting to be quite the whippersnapper. She reminds me of her grandfather and her mother. I'm sure they didn't get that stubborn streak from me."

I smile, knowing she is plenty stubborn, but it isn't my place to point it out. My smile fades quickly, however, because each time I think of the little three-year-old never knowing her grandfather the hole in my heart formed by Tim's death gets a little deeper. Someday she will know I am the reason why.

"What about you? How are feeling? Mom said you had to see a doctor about some chest pains."

"I did but I checked out just fine. Can you relate?" One eyebrow rises.

I bite my lip outwardly, and my tongue inside my mouth. She is relentless.

"I didn't see a doctor recently, except with my mom for her injury."

"She says she is doing just fine. I am not missing anything, am I? She just wants to get back to her yoga."

Truthfully, she is well on her way to recovery. "She is definitely a terrible patient, pushing the envelope on everything. She does a great job of keeping her Type-A at bay with all her yoga, but without it I can see how she used be one hell of an executive. I think she has pulled the data from every study she could find on the internet about getting back to exercise after injury sooner than later. I'd hate to be the doctor that has to listen to her business case and turn her down. I actually saw her practicing her pitch in front of the mirror. She might have even used PowerPoint."

"In all seriousness, J.T.— " Ellie says in a scolding but loving tone.

Here we go.

"You know what I meant about the chest pains. I heard you talk awfully fondly of that girl at Christmas. I saw the way your eyes sparkled when you said her name. I felt your feelings for her."

I've heard more than enough. "Tim said it best, Ellie. Trouble has a way of finding me. My mother could have died. I've already done more death than I can bear." I pause to swallow the lump in my throat. She seems unfazed. I continue, "Peyton's ex-boyfriend is still alive. How do I know that he won't come after me? Or Peyton? I can't do it. Love isn't worth the chance. Too much potential for pain."

"How bad are those chest pains of yours?"

I feel claustrophobic in this hallway. She sees through me. I try to talk a good game, but I know my words just now were strained. It does pain me to think about a world without Peyton in it. The world seems a little more dull without her laughter and kisses. I miss her more than I will ever admit. "I'm fine, Ellie, I've got this."

"Do you now?"

That damn eyebrow again. No way has John broken my trust. Can she know? "I don't know what you are referring to."

"Pain is hard to manage without help."

She lets the words linger.

My head falls in shame. It's doubtful she knows, but it's not an illogical conclusion.

"How bad is it, J.T.? Is it bad enough?"

I suck in a breath, eyes still facing the floor. I can't look into hers. Damn it.

"Almost."

She puts one hand on her heart, and one on mine. "Thank God. Oh, thank God." I hear her breathe a sigh of relief.

I look up. "I almost lost the ten-year war. Almost. But I didn't. I won just one more battle. I can only do this one at a time. John saved me. Again."

"Oh, thank God," she repeats and takes my face in her hands. "Alexandra said it was bad." Her hands fall to clasped in front of her chest, prayer-like.

"If I hadn't called John, if he wasn't such a willing and able sponsor, and if he hadn't answered my call, I'm not sure where I would be right now but I am sure it wouldn't be pretty."

"You can't let the bad guys win. We can't give up on love. We can't let violence or drugs beat out love. I know you know this, and I know it's harder to live and love when you are scared of what might happen. There will always be fighting somewhere, but we can't give up the fight for love. Love has to win, it's as simple as that."

"I love my mom. I have to put her first. I have to protect her. What if something happens to her?"

"What if it does? There is never any guarantee. That's something none of us ever have. Would I have loved to have more time with Tim? Of course. First, he was in the service, then a police officer. I knew what I was getting into and so do you. It's better to know. You make the best of what you have. I may not have had forever, but what if I chose to have nothing because I was scared? I would have missed out on knowing true love. And I believe true love is exactly what is happening here."

I'm saved by the bell. There is another guest at the door. I want to believe her words, and I hate the thought of losing Peyton forever, but I just can't imagine taking this chance. Tim is in my arms, his life draining from his body with every drop of blood pooling on the ground beside us. When his heart stopped beating a part of me died as well. I can't give away what I no longer have.

I make my way toward the kitchen and Grace and Julia. Julia darts behind her mother's legs as I approach. She peeks around and I squat down to her level. I put my hand up and, knowing just what to do, she slaps her small palm against my large one in a high-five.

Damn it. I'm reminded of the last time I interacted with a toddler. Tucker. At Jack's house. With Peyton. I watched her interact with the little boy and could picture her as a mother, something I'd never done with a woman prior. Damn it.

I am not sure if my mother is purposefully gracious, or if I have been strategic enough to never be alone with her, but we avoid the topic of Peyton through lunch and gift opening. We were full after the spread of Ellie's favorite, bangers and mash, so we postponed cake in favor of gifts. Now, I just have to make it through cake and then can kindly tell my mother we can discuss anything besides my current situation. It's going to be a long night.

Clearing the last of the plates from the table, I follow Grace into the kitchen. I place the stack into the sink, turn on the water to rinse, and open the dishwasher. Grace is retreating to the dining room for the serving dishes, but turns and over her shoulder says, "Hey, leave those. Let's have cake. Mind grabbing it from over there?" She nods towards the butler's pantry.

"No problem," I answer, turning the faucet to the off position.

I make my way to the cake. And realize it is, actually, a problem. My heart seems to ache harder and more than I've ever felt before. I was wrong. It's still there. Whatever I thought had died, I was wrong. If it had it wouldn't hurt like this.

My hand moves to my pocket and slips inside. I stare at the white frosting of the small circular cake with the three candles perched atop. I close my eyes and rub my fingers across the smooth metal of the dog tags in my pocket. I feel his name beneath my fingers. I owe my life to Tim. I owe everything to my mother.

I think of Peyton and my birthday. We toasted to new beginnings and I was so filled with hope. I thought my haunted past had lost that day and love was going to conquer all. I thought we had a fighting chance. Sadly, I was wrong.

Grace appears by my side. "You've got this?"

I can't answer and just nod. I pick up the cake and she the lighter for the candles.

I set the cake in front of Ellie. Grace, Julia on her hip, hands me the lighter. "Do the honors. I've got baby on board."

I light the first candle. Past. I've got plenty of that. The second. Present. My present is painful. I know what will help, and it isn't what used to soothe my pain. The last candle takes its time finding the light. I understand. The future takes its time to come to life. Maybe Ellie is right and we have to fight for love because it's the light in a world of darkness. Can I really believe we have a fighting chance?

We sing—off key, of course, because the song isn't an easy one, but Ellie beams, nonetheless. Ellie sucks in a breath and puckers her lips. The three flickering flames extinguish. She looks directly into my eyes. "There is nothing I believe in more strongly than the power of the birthday candle wish!"

In spite of myself, I find myself hoping she might have made a wish for me.

FEBRUARY 18th
CHAPTER 40 | Peyton

The sky, the animals, and the people express themselves more freely in Malawi.

I thought I had seen sunsets. The sun falling into the California ocean is pretty spectacular. But it's hard to determine in Africa whether the sunsets of the deepest orange and brightest yellow, or the people of all shades of happy are more beautiful.

Solitary, expansive trees dot the landscape of the harshest conditions. Perhaps they rise just to show off the magnificent backdrop of bright golden seams that gate the heavens. As the honey circle of sun drifts downward through amber shades, burnt orange spreads like wildfire across the sky. Breathtaking.

We had one day to explore on a safari when we arrived. The sound of the wild elephant's trumpet, trunk raised in defiance, is oxymoronic, a mix of beautiful yet alarming. We watched two of the largest in the herd hook tusks in ire while mothers herded their young, shielding their eyes from the fight.

Giraffes ran across the plain looking as if floating on the clouds of dust that follow in their wake. Without seeing it firsthand, it's hard to imagine the gracefulness of their swift gallop. And the hippos, plentiful in small calves and oversized adults alike, move with the air of knowing they have nothing to fear. Eyeballs protruding like submarine periscopes, it's hard to imagine they belong to the sizeable creatures lurking beneath the water with their day and night cacophony of grumpy old men bellows.

But it was the singing of the people that moved my earth. Hair-raising, spine-tingling voices that held nothing back putting forward melodies that inspired tears to stream down my cheeks. I didn't need to understand the words because I understood the emotion. Happiness was embodied in the high pitches of song and bodies moving, interwoven with one another in dance. Their song and dance emulate life. Unconstrained, no chorus or planned steps, just an innate, uninhibited rhythm to glide through feast or famine, celebration or tragedy.

I crawl into my twin bed, our last evening, next to my roommate Arianna, to process our day as we have now done for the last nine nights. I remember how I felt more trepidation than thrill when we pulled up to the small lodge after twenty-nine long hours of travel. I didn't know what to expect. Could I find water? Would there be enough food? Will I be able to sleep in whatever arrangements are provided? What if I get sick?

Turns out, those were the same questions the people of Malawi ask themselves daily.

Our hotel room is modest, with wooden log bed frames and just a small nightstand between the two beds. The floor is covered in deep green ceramic tile and there is a toilet. Hot and cold water is available with just a turn of a faucet on a sink and in the shower.

It's easy to appreciate when your day has been spent with those who sleep on a flat mat on dirt, use a hole in the ground for a bathroom, and water and light aren't part of the life equation.

"How about those legs?" Arianna asks, propping herself up on her elbow to face me, with just her head poking through the mosquito netting. Another luxury where we are.

"They hurt."

"Can you believe we only walked half the distance they do every single day?" She sounds incredulous because she is referring to our six-mile walk earlier in the day alongside twelve mothers, nine of whom carried babies on their backs and a heavy load of water on their heads.

"No, I can't. And we had shoes."

"And that water from the muddy stream. Yuck. I felt so guilty getting back in the truck and slugging down two clean bottles."

"Me too," I reply. "I've felt guilty more than once here. I think I just need to make sure that I appreciate everything we have so much more than before I knew."

"Completely agree. I so sucked at carrying the water on my head." Arianna flops back into the pillows. "It was so heavy."

"I know, right! Their poor necks! That is a skill that takes practice. At least we gave the women a good laugh with our trying. I've never felt less elegant."

Arianna giggles. "It was definitely a vain attempt to impress. It's okay though, because we had all those shoes to give. I've loved giving away all the shirts and shoes we have on this trip!"

"I can't believe how much time I've spent worrying about having the right clothes and shoes at home."

"Well, I share your first-world problems. I am happy to be going home a changed woman. I think forevermore I will just be happy that I have shoes."

"I hope I never forget to appreciate. I'd like to think that I won't take what I have for granted anymore."

"Damn. Me too. I didn't know what I didn't know. But I can't unknow."

"You know what I think has been equally cool to give?"

"No, what?"

I think of our first day here, when I was scared and unsure. I'd never spent time with people that didn't look and act like me, for all intents and purposes. The second day we visited an orphanage, and eight thousand miles away from home the children were singing and clapping their hands to the 'If You Are Happy and You Know It' song we all knew and joined along in English. It was the moment I realized we are so much more alike than different.

"The hugs." I'm ending the trip having learned to give them freely.

"Definitely. Especially today."

"Yes, definitely," I say recalling the emotional experience.

"My heart is still aching for that mother. How do you pick up the pieces?"

Her voice breaks, and I know she is holding back tears because I am doing the same. "Together. You pick up the pieces together."

We were in the center of a small circling of clay huts with thatched roofs. The women were huddled over a pot hanging in a fire. They spoke in hushed, somber tones and passed babies to one another, and to us, as they took turns stirring their corn mixture. We didn't know what they were saying but we sensed the heaviness in their hearts.

From one of the small buildings a woman came running. She fell to her knees with an ear-piercing wail of pain. The lifeless body of a male toddler was lifted toward the sky with both hands. She screamed in native tongue through tears streaming down her face, falling to dot the red, dusty dirt beneath her. She pulled the small child to her chest and bent over him. Other women came from the same hut, too many to have fit comfortably inside. They formed a circle around the distraught mother, holding her, and one another.

One by one, each woman joined the circle, layer upon layer, surrounding her. We joined the coalition of love. Our tears were her tears. Her heartbreak was our heartbreak. We shared an immeasurable anguish, but together we were impenetrable.

Arianna and I lie in a moment of silence for the young mother. And the other mothers that were losing their children day in and day out. Our hosts told us of disease, AIDS primarily, but also many dying of diarrhea alone. I vow this won't be my last trip, and I will do more.

She interrupts the silence, "I wasn't sure what to do. I think I learned an important lesson when I went into that circle. You don't have to know exactly what to do or say, you just have to show up."

"You just have to show up," I repeat, feeling and understanding the meaning of her words. Like carrying the water, it's going to take some practice, but it's a lesson I am happy to learn.

"I think I'm leaving a little piece of myself here," Arianna shares.

"Me too." The piece of my heart that broke today will be left behind on that dirt, and with the other women. My heart broke hard today, but like J.T. had said, I believe it's how the light gets in. Because of J.T., and the people in Africa, I understand how love is the light. I want to share what I have felt, and learned, during this experience with him. I want to tell him I understand what he said in a different way, and how he was right. Now, I know too. You only need love to survive. And how I wish I had the chance for his!

FEBRUARY 19th
CHAPTER 41 | Peyton

ome!!!!! I'll text you which door I come out! Missed u!!!
The captain welcomes us to Detroit. I've just texted Jack that I am home. I never expected to be calling Detroit home.

My life the past four months has been a series of takeoffs and touchdowns, beginnings and endings. My life as a daughter had ended but I finally had a father figure in Jack. Because of him, my life as an L.A. want-to-be actress is going to soon come to an end. I'll begin as a student again. In just weeks I will begin my next year as a twenty-five-year-old and a trust-fund recipient. It will allow me to work, for now, with little pay in an industry I love as a production assistant starting next week.

The ending of my relationship with Kyle sparked the hopeful possibility of a new romance with a happy ending. Eight thousand two hundred miles didn't ease the persistent, hollow ache in the center of my chest. But I do have the beginning of a friendship with Liz, Cassandra, and Alexandra, all of us trying to Namaste through the world the best yogis we can be. Cassandra and I had enjoyed an amazing time together bonding through heartbreak, and we all came together to support Liz as she hosted a charity event that gave us all perspective. Alexandra's hard-earned wisdom guides us all through our messy, but beautiful, lives. We have gotten through the hardship caused by Kyle together. We have shown up for one another.

What a journey it's been! Both literally and figuratively. I'm returning from a four-bus, six-plane, and hundreds-of-people-amazing trip to Malawi. It seems much longer than ten days ago that Jack packed long skirts from my mother's closet over Facetime before he and the girls accompanied me to the airport for my sendoff to another continent.

Jack replies:

Missed u too! See u soon!

I smile, knowing I influenced his texting with just the letter "U" in place of the word. I can't wait to share the details of my trip with Jack, though it will be painful not to share them with J.T.

I noticed how things looked different when we changed planes in Amsterdam. Somehow, the lens of my world is more crisp and colorful. I looked into the eyes of people in a new, and deeper, way. Like J.T. looked at me. I get it now. You see and feel things differently after getting away from first-world problems for the gift of perspective. As J.T. had taught me, but I couldn't know without living it, God and love are everything.

I'm forced to stand up as the plane door is open. The people seem harried and I am bumped and jostled as I'm still in the slow pace of people who can't live their lives by the clocks they don't have. It may be chaos here on the outside, but I won't let it disturb the peace and calm of my inside.

I clear customs easily with nothing to declare and head down the long escalator to baggage claim, hoping my luggage has also made the trip across multiple airplanes and time zones. Appreciating the beauty in the diversity for the first time, my eyes hesitate on blond, messy and sexy distinguishable, just-the-right-length-for-someone-I-haven't-seen-in-two-months hair. My eyes narrow, disbelief in what they perceive they know. The man is holding a sheet of paper. I must be creating a mirage in my mind and he's a man with a sign indicating the name of an incoming passenger.

I'm too far away to see clearly. Plus, Jack is picking me up. And J.T. had made it clear long ago we were finished. He'd never replied to my last thank-you Snapchat for the quilt so it seems unfathomable and improbable that he is in the waiting crowd. But I am coming closer and am still finding familiarity that makes my heart skip a beat and stomach flip-flop in that way that only J.T. Walker's presence can arouse. Then there is everything else that he arouses as well. Oh. My. God. Is it too good to be true?

My brain reacts to make sense of what I see. Finally. Has something happened to Jack? Is J.T. here with bad news? No. It can't be. He texted me just minutes ago.

"Excuse me." I turn sideways and take the next step down the escalator. I need to get closer more quickly. "Excuse me," I say again with more urgency. I need to make eye contact. My heartbeat quickens, then stutters. The logo on the black down vest is easy to make out. SFS, with my now-favorite continent embroidered behind it. It's him! It's a good thing I've just been in Africa and learned about inner beauty because my messy bun and no-makeup traveling look wouldn't be the intended reunion look!

His head finally turns toward me. Those eyes. They take me in, see my soul, perfect sunny-day sky-blue meet mine. Lips creep upward and don't stop until the smile overtakes his eyes, embodying happy. Mine do the same. Broad, childlike, uninhibited.

He gently and smoothly twists and turns through the crowd. I can see his lips moving, "Pardon me. Pardon me. Pardon me."

I have carefully navigated the people of the escalator, and my feet float towards him. He has picked up his pace to close the distance between us. What happens next?

I'm held in familiar arms I've missed beyond measure, my feet no longer feeling the earth beneath me. My embrace is tight, filled with longing for lost time. His breath is warm in my ear, against my hair. Lips find my temple, and he whispers, "Do you hate me?"

I answer him with my lips, not words. Our mouths collide. I waste no time wanting to feel his tongue against mine. I grip around his back and hold his shoulders, desperate for the closeness I'd been denied for so long. We've been denied. Our lips entangle and entwine. I breathe into him and him into me. We make up for lost time, tasting him again like it's the first time. But I remember the feel of my tongue brushing across his bottom lip. I remember the pressure of his lips against mine. It fades, and I push forward into him, harder, my tongue more deeply in his mouth, then his lips everywhere on mine. Intense. Craving. He holds my head. He owns my heart. His lips relent but still brush against mine. Shallow gasps of breath whisper into my mouth, "I think we've just put the train-station kiss to shame."

"I think we did. We had some lost time to make up."

"Yes, we did."

He pulls away, despite the resistance of my hands dragging along his arms. I'm never letting go again.

The sign is behind my back, and he holds it in front of his chest.

I read it aloud, in my newly learned Chichewa, "Ndine wachisoni. I don't know what it means."

"It's the closest translation I could get to 'I am so sorry'."

"You are so forgiven. Good thing you taught me a little something about that. But you do owe me a New Year's and Valentine's Day."

"Done. When I saw you just now my heart had a tremor. I think it skipped a beat. Or twenty. I don't know what I would do if I could never have you again."

"You've got me. And I love the sign."

"I stole the idea. I'll fill you in later. Or Cassandra can."

I'm curious how Cassandra fits into the story and how he ended up here, but there will be time for that. I need to touch him again. I reach my hand up, pressing my palm against his cheek. He circles my wrist with his fingers mid-movement, turning it upward. His eyebrows rise at the black ink.

"This is new."

"Yep. The Om sign. Thank yoga. It's my past, present and future reminder. Connection to the divine. Connection to Alexandra, Liz, and Cassandra." I look down, a little embarrassed. "Connection to you," I say softly.

"Sounds a little familiar."

His lips press against the black ink. I remember when he bared himself to me, literally and figuratively, what seems like a lifetime ago. "You were right, you know. I get it now. Everything you said about not needing anything but love to survive."

"I was right about that, all right. So right that I have a confession to make. I told you I need a relationship based on truth. I'm ashamed of this but I have to tell you."

Damn it. I don't know where this is going but from the sound of it, I am not going to like it.

"The last time I heard from you in the office that day, I left and went to a bar. I needed something to dull the pain. I hadn't felt pain like that in a long time. I knew what would make it stop because, if nothing else, I wouldn't remember for at least a little while."

"Oh no. Oh, J.T. Oh my God, I am so sorry."

I know I didn't make him drink any more than I pulled the trigger on the gun Kyle shot, but the thought I am the reason for compromising ten years of his sobriety makes me weary.

"I sat on a bar stool and held the glass."

He looks away; too hard to admit while looking in my eyes and finding disappointment or judgment.

"I got lucky. My sponsor answered the phone, and before I lost ten years of pride, his hand was on my shoulder. God had my back on that one. I almost blew it. I didn't think anything had that power over me any longer, but I wasn't sure I wanted to survive without you. What I believed then, I know with certainty now. I never knew if I'd have the chance to love someone. I want the chance. With you. You are what I need. I missed you so much, Jennings."

"I couldn't have said that better myself."

He smiles, recognizing our inside joke.

"I missed you too, Joe Walker. J and T are my two favorite letters, but I'd like to keep trouble away for a while."

He laughs. It's so good to hear. Deep and guttural, yet innocent and playful, holding nothing back.

"It sounds better when you say it. I can work with that."

He leans in again to kiss me. Like he means it. I always wanted to be met like this. Wanted like this. Loved like this. Where I am. For who I am. I never expected to have it, but hoped for all of it. One day.

My one day has come.

Hi, it's Peyton.

I know I wasn't exactly the star of the show, but the movie where I delivered my first real lines (regardless of how I got the job) has finally been released. Fingers crossed for good reviews! And just like in the movies, everyone knows that with books, reviews make or break you. If you thought my performance worthy, I am hoping you will head on over to Amazon and tell the world you enjoyed One Day After Never. Thank you!

Afterword

Addiction's impact is felt throughout families and the numbers affected in the United States is astounding. In 2017, 19.7 million people over the age of 12 battled a substance use disorder according to the National Survey on Drug Use and Health. Throughout the book I referenced several programs, and if someone in your life is battling addiction please get help to keep hope: Alcoholics Anonymous and Al Anon – for family members. Because of my personal experience with addiction and these organizations, a portion of proceeds from this book will be donated to organizations supporting this cause